DATE DUE	
SEP 0 6 2008	NOV 2 1 2008	
OCT 0 7 2008		
NOV 2 0 2008		
JAN 1 9 2010		

Brian Lumley

Bob Eggleton

HAGGOPIAN
AND OTHER
STORIES

HAGGOPIAN
AND OTHER
STORIES

Best Mythos Tales, Volume Two

BRIAN LUMLEY

Subterranean Press 2008

First Edition

ISBN 978-1-59606-165-1

Subterranean Press
PO Box 190106
Burton, MI 48519

"The Caller of The Black," from the collection of the same name, Arkham House, 1971.
"Haggopian," from *F&SF No. 265*, 1973.
"Cement Surroundings," from *Tales of the Cthulhu Mythos*, Arkham House, 1969.
"The House of Cthulhu," from *Whispers No. 1*, 1973.
"The Night Sea-Maid Went Down," from *The Caller of The Black*, Arkham House, 1971.
"Name and Number," from *Kadath, Vol. 2 No. 1*, July 1982.
"Recognition," from *Weirdbook No. 15*, 1981.
"Curse of the Golden Guardians," from *The Compleat Khash, Vol. 1*, Weirdbook Press, 1991. "Aunt Hester," from *The Satyr's Head*, Corgi, 1975.
"The Kiss of Bugg-Shash," from *Cthulhu 3*, Spectre Press, 1978.
"De Marigny's Clock," from *The Caller of The Black*, Arkham House, 1971.
"Mylakhrion the Immortal," from *Fantasy Tales, Vol. 1 No. 1*, 1977.
"The Sister City," from *Tales of the Cthulhu Mythos*, Arkham House, 1969.
"What Dark God?" from *Nameless Places*, Arkham House, 1975.
"The Statement of Henry Worthy," from *The Horror at Oakdeene*, Arkham House, 1977.
"Dagon's Bell," from *Weirdbook 23/24*, 1988.
"The Thing from the Blasted Heath," from *The Caller of The Black*, Arkham House, 1971.
"Dylath-Leen," from *The Caller of The Black*, 1971.
"The Mirror of Nitocris," from *The Caller of The Black*, 1971.
"The Second Wish," from *New Tales of the Cthulhu Mythos*, Arkham House, 1980.
"The Hymn," from *HPL's Magazine of Horror No. 3*, 2006.
"Synchronicity or Something," from the chapbook of the same name, Dagon Press, 1989.
"The Black Recalled," from the *World Fantasy Convention Book*, 1983.
"The Sorcerer's Dream," from *Whispers 13/14*, 1979.

CONTENTS

Dedication:
To the Memory of August Derleth

FOREWORD:

Notes on the Cthulhu Mythos, August Derleth, and Arkham House

This book of short stories is presented as a companion volume to my Subterranean Press collection of Cthulhu Mythos novellas, and to repeat what I said in the introduction to *that* book, it isn't my intention to offer any kind of in-depth definition of the Mythos here. That has already been done by too many others. Also, because it seems you've opted to read this book, I think I can be reasonably sure that you are already familiar with H. P. Lovecraft's most enduring, most fascinating creation. (Well, at least he created its roots, since when the vast bulk of the Mythos—much like the gradually expanding acreage of diseased earth and vegetation around HPL's "Blasted Heath"—just keeps on growing, though by no means as slowly!)

When they talk about the Mythos, most people automatically associate it with HPL. And rightly so, *to a degree*, insofar as Cthulhu was his creation...but the Mythos itself was not. It came into being when HPL's friends—fellow authors with whom he regularly corresponded, certain revision clients, and others that he himself invited to build upon his literary foundations—when they began to contribute their own stories fashioned in the same vein. But it was not until August Derleth established Arkham House to immortalize Lovecraft, and set about publishing his own Lovecraftian pastiches and so-called "collaborations," along with the Lovecraft-inspired works of other authors, that the more solid foundations of the Mythos were laid. Indeed, it was with Derleth's remarkable landmark anthology, *Tales of the Cthulhu Mythos*—the Arkham House volume that finally tied the ungainly thing together—that the first real cornerstone was set in place. For Derleth had collected together such an appropriate list of titles—some of which, because of their vague yet tantalizing similarities, themes and allusions, had puzzled and obsessed me when first I had read them as individual tales in this, that or the other magazine or anthology—that now in their entirety they loaned a semblance of order to the Mythos, making a generally acceptable sort of sense of everything.

The book was full of the stories of former correspondents and friends of HPL—such people as Derleth himself, Robert E. Howard, Clark Ashton Smith, Frank Belknap Long, Robert Bloch, J. Vernon Shea and one or two others—along with more recent or relative newcomers to the Mythos, such as Ramsey Campbell, Colin Wilson, and myself. I found *Tales of the Cthulhu Mythos* an excellent read and Derleth's choice of material first class…but then I would say that, wouldn't I? For after all, this was the very first hardcover book in which a story of mine—two of them, in fact—had seen print.

Anyway, from an entirely personal point of view I believe that second only to *Necroscope*, my breakthrough book, *Tales of the Cthulhu Mythos*, was (probably) more important to me than any other volume; my reading copy has long since been thumbed close to death!

But where Derleth and Arkham House were concerned I wasn't the first (or last) writer who would have his initial forays in fiction preserved in shining Holliston Black Novelex; no, not a bit of it! For Derleth had published Robert Bloch's first collection, *The Opener of the Way*; and A. E. van Vogt's first hardcover, *Slan*; even Ray Bradbury's first book, *Dark Carnival*. And there were many others, and several still to come even after I, a relative latecomer, had made it onto the list.

So then, surely we should thank August Derleth for all of this, especially for the preservation of Lovecraft's works, including five vast volumes of his letters, but in particular for turning Arkham's spotlight on the Cthulhu Mythos. We should…but has he in fact received such thanks?

No, not really. Instead Derleth has been much criticized in certain quarters with regard to his treatment of the Mythos: which is to say that mainly, in a somewhat cursory "definition" of the Mythos, he grafted onto it elements of a religious background that parallel the Christian mythology and appear not to sit well with HPL's original intentions. This and certain other minor "crimes" perpetrated in his editorial capacity, during a short lifetime of publishing among others a long list of otherwise neglected authors, have seen Derleth castigated for being (of all things) "a heretic"; this, paradoxically, by the self-same people who insist upon Lovecraft's (religiously) destitute Mythos-ideology! Indeed, it has sometimes seemed to me that the most fanatical of HPL's readers have made a god—or at least fashioned an idol—out of Lovecraft himself!

Such has been the outcry against "the heretic" that even the title of Derleth's anthology, *Tales of the Cthulhu Mythos*, and of the Mythos itself, have been criticised; mainly because another member of the Great Old Ones, one Yog-Sothoth, is seen as being rather more central to the pantheon. But, as I pointed out elsewhere, could we really expect Derleth to have published a book called *Tales of the Yog-Sothoth Cycle of Myth*? Too long, complicated, and even—dare I say it?—too risible. Whereas *Tales of the Cthulhu Mythos* fits the bill precisely, not only in its length but in that it "sounds" so very right.

Myself: I believe that where H. P. Lovecraft is concerned, August Derleth's efforts were heroic. Because of him the Mythos lives on. And also because of him—again on a personal level—I am what I have since become: the moderately successful author of this, the book you now hold in your hands, and of many other books.

All of which to explain why, and not for the first time, I have dedicated a volume—this volume—to the memory of August Derleth…

Brian Lumley.

THE CALLER OF THE BLACK

One of my first stories, written in 1967 before any of my work had been published, "Caller" is derivative not only of H.P. Lovecraft's work but also the work of others, more especially of August Derleth. Looking back I think this was probably a deliberate ploy; it was the sort of story that Derleth published, the sort I was reading in his collections and anthologies, and it was a Cthulhu Mythos story. In short I had been "studying the markets," but the only market I had going for my work was Arkham House! Anyway, Derleth liked the story and it eventually saw print in 1971, in my first book from Arkham House, which was published under the same title: "The Caller of The Black". Incidentally, the capitalized definite article in the tale's title is also deliberate, because as you will discover, "The" Black is pretty much a one-of-a-kind sort of thing…thank goodness!

On monoliths did ancients carve their
*   warning*
To those who use night's forces lest they bring
A doom upon themselves that when, in
*   mourning,*
They be the mourned…
—Justin Geoffrey

One night, not so long ago, I was disturbed, during the study of some of the ancient books it is my pleasure to own, by a knock at the solid doors of my abode, Blowne House. Perhaps it would convey a more correct impression to say that the assault upon my door was more a frenzied hammering than a knock. I knew instinctively from that moment that something out of the ordinary was to come—nor did this premonition let me down.

It was blowing strongly that night and when I opened the door to admit the gaunt stranger on my threshold the night wind gusted in with him a handful of autumn leaves which, with quick, jerky motions, he nervously brushed from his coat and combed from his hair. There was a perceptible aura of fear about this man and I wondered what it could be that inspired such fear. I was soon to learn. Somewhat shakily he introduced himself as being Cabot Chambers.

Calmed a little, under the influence of a good brandy, Chambers sat himself down in front of my blazing fire and told a story which even I, and I have heard many strange things, found barely credible. I knew of certain legends which tell that such things once were, long ago in Earth's pre-dawn youth, but was of the belief that most of this Dark Wisdom had died at the onset of the present reign of civilized man—or, at the very latest, with the Biblical *Burning of the Books*. My own ample library of occult and forbidden things contains such works as Feery's *Original Notes on The Necronomicon*, the abhorrent *Cthaat Aquadingen*, Sir Amery Wendy-Smith's translation of the *G'harne Fragments* (incomplete and much abridged)—a tattered and torn copy of the *Pnakotic Manuscripts* (possibly faked)—a literally priceless *Cultes des Goules* and many others, including such anthropological source books as the *Golden Bough* and Miss Murray's *Witch Cult*, yet my knowledge of the thing of which Chambers spoke was only very vague and fragmentary.

But I digress. Chambers, as I have said, was a badly frightened man and this is the story he told me:

"Mr. Titus Crow," he said, when he was sufficiently induced and when the night chill had left his bones, "I honestly don't know why I've come to you for try as I might I can't see what you can do for me. I'm doomed. Doomed by Black Magic, and though I've brought it on myself and though I know I haven't led what could be called a very *refined* life, I certainly don't want things to end for me the way they did for poor Symonds!" Hearing that name, I was startled, for Symonds was a name which had featured very recently in the press and which had certain unpleasant connections. His alleged heart failure or brain seizure had been as unexpected as it was unexplained but now, to some extent, Chambers was able to explain it for me.

"It was that fiend Gedney," Chambers said. "He destroyed Symonds and now he's after me. Symonds and I, both quite well-to-do men you could say, joined Gedney's Devil-Cult. We did it out of boredom. We were both single and our lives had become an endless parade of night-clubs, sporting-clubs, men's-clubs and yet more clubs. Not a very boring life, you may think, but believe me, after a while even the greatest luxuries and the most splendid pleasures lose their flavours and the palate becomes insensitive to all but the most delicious—or perverse—sensations. So it was with Symonds and I when we were introduced to Gedney at a club, and when he offered to supply those sensations, we were eager to become initiates of his cult.

"Oh, it's laughable! D'you know he's thought of by many as just another crank? We never guessed what would be expected of us and having gone through with the first of the initiation processes at Gedney s country house, not far out of London, processes which covered the better part of two weeks, we suddenly found ourselves face to face with the truth. Gedney is a devil—and of the very worst sort. The *things* that man does would make the Marquis de Sade in his prime appear an anaemic cretin. By God, if you've read Commodus you have a basic idea of Gedney but you must look to the works of Caracalla to really appreciate the depths of his blasphemous soul. Man, *look at the missing persons columns sometime*!

"Of course we tried to back out of it all and would have managed it too if Symonds, the poor fool, hadn't gone and blabbed about it. The trouble with Symonds was drink. He took a few too many one night and openly down-graded Gedney and his whole box of tricks. He wasn't to know it but the people we were with at the time were Gedney's crew—and fully-fledged members at that! Possibly the fiend had put them on to us just to check us out. Anyway, that started it. Next thing we knew Gedney sent us an invitation to dinner at a club he uses, and out of curiosity we went. I don't suppose it would have made much difference if we hadn't gone. Things would have happened a bit sooner, that's all. Naturally Gedney had already hit us for quite a bit of money and we thought he was probably after more. We were wrong! Over drinks, in his best 'rest assured' manner, he threatened us with the foulest imaginable things if we ever dared to 'slander' him again. Well, at that, true to his nature, Symonds got his back up and mentioned the police. If looks could kill Gedney would have had us there and then. Instead, he just upped and left but before he went he said something about a 'visit from The Black'. I still don't know what he meant."

During the telling of his tale, Chambers' voice had hysterically gathered volume and impetus but then, as I filled his glass, he seemed to take a firmer grip on himself and continued in a more normal tone.

"Three nights ago I received a telephone-call from Symonds—yes, on the very night of his death. Since then I've been at the end of my rope. Then

I remembered hearing about you and how you know a lot about this sort of thing, so I came round. When Symonds called me that night, he said he had found a blank envelope in his letter-box and that he didn't like the design on the card inside it. He said the thing reminded him of something indescribably evil and he was sure Gedney had sent it. He asked me to go round to his place. I had driven to within half a mile of his flat in town when my damned car broke down. Looking back, it's probably just as well that it did. I set out on foot and I only had another block to walk when I saw Gedney. He's an evil-looking type and once you see him you can never forget how he looks. His hair is black as night and swept back from a point low in the centre of his forehead. His eyebrows are bushy above hypnotic eyes of the type you often find in people with very strong characters. If you've ever seen any of those Bela Lugosi horror films you'll know what I mean. He's exactly like that, though thinner in the face, cadaverous in fact.

"There he was, in a telephone kiosk, and he hadn't seen me. I ducked back quickly and got out of sight in a recessed doorway from where I could watch him. I was lucky he hadn't seen me, but he seemed solely interested in what he was doing. He was using the telephone, crouched over the thing like a human vulture astride a corpse. God! But the *look* on his face when he came out of the kiosk! It's a miracle he didn't see me for he walked right past my doorway. I had got myself as far back into a shadowy corner as I could—and while, as I say, he failed to see me, I could see him all right. And he was *laughing*; that is, if I dare use that word to describe what he was doing with his face. Evil? I tell you I've never seen anyone looking so hideous. And, do you know, in answer to his awful laugh there came a distant scream?

"It was barely audible at first but as I listened it suddenly rose in pitch until, at its peak, it was cut off short and only a far-off echo remained. It came from the direction of Symonds' flat.

"By the time I got there someone had already called the police. I was one of the first to see him. It was horrible. He was in his dressing-gown, stretched out on the floor, dead as a doornail. And the *expression* on his face! I tell you, Crow, something monstrous happened that night.

"But—taking into account what I had seen before, what Gedney had been up to in the telephone kiosk—the thing that really caught my eye in that terrible flat, the thing that scared me worst, *was the telephone.* Whatever had happened must have taken place while Symonds was answering the 'phone—*for it was off the hook, dangling at the end of the flex…*"

Well, that was just about all there was to Chambers' story. I passed him the bottle and a new glass, and while he was thus engaged I took the opportunity to get down from my shelves an old book I once had the good fortune to pick up in Cairo. Its title would convey little to you, learned though I know you to be, and it is sufficient to say that its contents consist of numerous notes purporting to relate to certain supernatural invocations. Its wording, in parts, puts the volume in that category 'not for the squeamish'. In it, I knew, was a reference to *The Black*, the thing Gedney had mentioned to Chambers and Symonds, and I quickly looked it up. Unfortunately the book is in a very poor condition, even though I have taken steps to stop further disintegration, and the only reference I could find was in these words:

> *Thief of Light, Thief of Air…*
> *Thou The Black—drown me mine enemies…*

One very salient fact stood out. Regardless of what actually caused Symonds' death, the newspapers recorded the fact *that his body showed all the symptoms of suffocation…*

I was profoundly interested. Obviously Chambers could not tell his story to the police, for what action could they take? Even if they were to find something inexplicably unpleasant about the tale, and perhaps would like to carry out investigations, Chambers himself was witness to the fact that Gedney was in a telephone kiosk at least a hundred yards away from the deceased at the time of his death. No, he could hardly go to the police. To speak to the law of Gedney's *other* activities would be to involve himself— in respect of his "initiation"—and he did not want that known. Yet he felt he must do something. He feared that a similar fate to that which had claimed Symonds had been ordained for him—nor was he mistaken.

Before Chambers left me to my ponderings that night, I gave him the following instructions. I told him that if, in some manner, he received a card or paper like the one Symonds had mentioned, with a peculiar design upon it, he was to contact me immediately. Then, until he had seen me, he was to lock himself in his house admitting no one. Also, after calling me, he was to disconnect his telephone.

After he had gone, checking back on his story, I got out my file of unusual newspaper cuttings and looked up Symonds' case. The case being recent, I did not have far to search. I had kept the Symonds cuttings because I had been unhappy about the coroner's verdict. I had had a suspicion about the case, a sort of sixth sense, telling me it was unusual. My memory had served me well. I reread that which had made me uneasy in the first place. The police had discovered, clenched in one of Symonds' fists, the crushed fragments of what was thought to have been some type of card of very brittle paper. Upon it were strange, inked characters, but the pieces had proved impossible to reconstruct. The fragments had been passed over as being irrelevant.

I knew that certain witch-doctors of some of this world's less civilised peoples are known for their habit of serving an intended victim with a warning of his impending doom. The trick is usually accomplished by handing the unfortunate one an evil symbol and—having let him worry himself half to death—the sorcerer then invokes, in the victim's presence or *within his hearing*, whichever devil is to do the dirty work. Whether or not any devil actually appears is a different kettle of fish. But one thing is sure—*the victim nearly always dies…* Naturally, being superstitious and a savage to boot, he dies of fright… Or does he?

At first I believed something of the sort was the case with Symonds and Chambers. One of them, perhaps helped along in some manner, had already worried himself to death and the other was going the same way. Certainly Chambers had been in a bad way regards his nerves when I had seen him. However, my theory was wrong and I soon had to radically revise it. Within a few hours of leaving Blowne House Chambers 'phoned me and he was hysterical.

"I've got one, by God! The devil's sent me one. Listen, Crow. You must come at once. I went for a drink from your place and I've just got in. Guess what I found in the hall? An envelope, that's what, *and there's a damned funny looking card inside it*! It's frightening the daylights out of me. He's after me! The swine's after me! Crow, I've sent my man home and locked the doors like you said. I can open the front door electronically from my room to let you in when you arrive. You drive a Merc', don't you? Yes, thought so. As soon as you say you'll come I'll put down the 'phone and disconnect it. Now, will you come?"

I told him I would only be a few minutes and hung up. I dressed quickly and drove straight round to his house. The drive took about fifteen minutes for his place lay on the outskirts of town, near the old Purdy Watermill. The house is completely detached and as I pulled into the driveway I was surprised to note that every light in the house was on—*and the main door was swinging open*! Then as I slowed to a halt, I was partly blinded by the lights of a second Mercedes which revved up and roared past me out onto the road. I leapt out of my car to try to get the other vehicle's number but was distracted from this task by the screams which were just starting.

Within seconds, screams of utter horror were pouring from upstairs and, looking up, I saw a dark shadow cast upon a latticed window. The shadow must have been strangely distorted for it had the general outline of a man, yet it was *bulky* beyond human dimensions—more like the shadow of a gorilla. I watched, hypnotized, as this black caricature clawed frantically at itself—*in a manner which I suddenly recognised*! The shadow was using the same brushing motions which I had seen Chambers use earlier to brush those leaves from himself in my hallway.

But surely this could not be Chambers? This shadow was that of a far heavier person, someone obese, even allowing for inexplicable distortion! Horrified, I watched, incapable of movement, as the screams rose to an unbearable pitch and the tottering, clawing shadow grew yet larger. Then, abruptly, the screams gurgled into silence, the shadow's diseased scrabbling at itself became a convulsive *heaving* and the bloated arms lifted jerkily, as if in supplication. Larger still the monstrous silhouette grew as its owner stumbled, seemingly unseeing, towards the window. And then, briefly as it fell against the thinly latticed panes, I saw it. A great, black imitation of a human, it crashed through the window, shattering the very frame outwards in a tinkling of broken glass and a snapping of fractured lats. Tumbling into the night it came, to fall with a sickening, bone-breaking crunch at my feet.

The broken thing which lay before me on the gravel of the drive was the quite ordinary, quite lifeless body of Cabot Chambers!

When I was able to bring my shrieking nerves under a semblance of control, I dared to prise open the tightly clenched right hand of the corpse and found that which I had guessed would be there. Those stiffening fingers held crushed, brittle shards which I knew had once had the outlines of a card of some sort. On some of the larger pieces I could make out characters which, so far as I know, can only be likened to certain cuneiform inscriptions on the Broken Columns of Geph.

I 'phoned the police anonymously and quickly left the place, for the smell of weird, unnatural death now hung heavily over the entire house. Poor Chambers, I thought as I drove away—seeing that second Mercedes he must have thought his other visitor was I. I tried not to think about the shadow or what it meant.

I did not sleep too well that night. The first thing I did when I awoke the next morning was to discreetly check up on the activities of a certain Mr. James D. Gedney. I have many friends in positions which, to say the least, make them extremely useful to me when a bit of detective work is necessary. These friends helped me now and through their exertions my task was made considerably easier. I checked Gedney's telephone number, which was not in the book, and made notes of his personal likes and dislikes. I memorized the names of his friends and the clubs and places he frequented and generally built up my picture of the man. What I discovered only confirmed Chambers' opinion.

Gedney's *contacts* were the worst sort of people and his favourite haunts were, in the main, very doubtful establishments. He had no visible means of support yet appeared to be most affluent—owning, among his many effects, a large country house and, most interesting yet, a brand-new Mercedes. All the other things I discovered about Gedney paled beside that one fact.

My next logical step, having completed my "file" on Gedney, was to find out as much as I could about that mystical identity "The Black," and towards this end I spent almost a week in the pursuit of certain singular volumes in dim and equally singular archives at the British Museum and in the perusal of my own unusual books. At the museum, with the permission of the Curator of the Special Books Department, another friend, I was allowed to study at my leisure all but the most secret and hideous of volumes. I was out of luck. The only reference I found—a thing which, in the light of what I later learned, I find of special significance—was, as was that other reference I have mentioned, in one of my own books. Justin Geoffrey supplied this second fragment in his raving *People of the Monolith*; but apart from these four inexplicable lines of poetry I found nothing more:

> *On monoliths did ancients carve their warning*
> *To those who use night's forces lest they bring*
> *A doom upon themselves that when, in mourning,*
> *They be the mourned...*

Then I remembered an American friend of mine; a man wonderfully erudite in his knowledge of folklore and things of dread and darkness. He had studied in bygone years under that acknowledged genius of Earth's elderlore, Wilmarth of Miskatonic University. We exchanged one or two interesting telegrams and it was this New Englander who first told me of the Ptetholites—a prehistoric, sub-human race who allegedly were in the habit of calling up devils to send against their enemies. At the very beginning of recorded time, if one can believe the legends of Hyperborea, the Ptetholites sent such devils against Edril Ghambiz and his Hell-Hordes, ensconced on the pre-neolithic isle of Esipish in what was then the North Sea. Unfortunately for the Ptetholites they had seemingly forgotten their own warnings, for it had been elders of their own tribe, in even older days, who had inscribed on the Broken Columns of Geph:

> *Let him who calls The Black*
> *Be aware of the danger*

His victim may be protected
By the spell of running water
And turn the called-up darkness
Against the very caller...

Hence, I believe, Geoffrey's remarkable lines. Exactly what happened to the Ptetholites has gone unrecorded, or such records have been destroyed, except for the vaguest of hints in the most obscure tomes. There are, I now know, certain monks of a peculiar order in Tibet who know and understand many of these things. If history did pass down anything but the most sketchy details of the destruction of the Ptetholites such records were probably burned in the time of the witch hunts of the 16th and 17th centuries; certainly, except in those few cases I have mentioned, such knowledge is non-existent today.

Apart from this information from Arkham the remaining results of my research were disappointing. One thing was positive though; I had now definitely given up my theory of self-induced death through fear. Both Symonds and Chambers had been far too intelligent ever to have succumbed to the suggestions of any witch-doctor and besides—there was that disturbing thing about Chambers' shadow. Moreover, Gedney was certainly no quack witch-doctor and somehow I felt sure that he had access to a very real and destructive magical device. The final telegram I received from America convinced me.

I have great faith in Abdul Alhazred, whom many have called the "mad" Arab, and while my copy of Feery's *Notes on the Necronomicon* is hardly what one could call a reliable guide, Alhazred's actual book, or a translation of it, at Miskatonic University, is something else again. My learned friend had found a dream-reference in the *Necronomicon* in which *The Black* was mentioned. The said reference read thus:

> ...from the space which is not space, into any time when the Words are spoken, can the holder of the Knowledge summon The Black, blood of Yibb-Tstll, that which liveth apart from *him* and eateth souls, that which smothers and is called Drowner. Only in water can one escape the drowning; that which is in water drowneth not...

This was the foundation I needed upon which to build my plan. A hazardous plan, but—taking into account how touchy Gedney appeared to be about people threatening him—one which was sure to produce results.

Soon I began to put my plan into operation. First, in the guise of a drunk, I frequented the places Gedney used when pursuing his jaded pleasures. Eventually, in a dingy night-club, I had him pointed out to me for future reference. This was hardly necessary, for Chambers' description fitted him perfectly and from it alone I would have recognized the man had the place not been so crowded and dimly lighted.

Next I made it known, in conversation with people I knew to be directly connected with Gedney, that I was a former friend of both the dead men and that from what they had told me of Gedney he was an abominable creature whom, if the opportunity presented itself, I would gladly expose. I put it about, drunkenly, that I was collecting a dossier on him which I intended eventually to present to the appropriate authorities. But though I play-acted the part of a regular inebriate the truth is that I have never been more sober in my entire life. Dealing such antagonistic cards to Gedney, I was sure, would produce results which only a very sober person could hope to turn to his advantage.

Yet it was over a week before my assault took effect. I was in the dimly lit Demon Club, slumped in a typically alcoholic attitude against the bar. Perhaps I was overacting, for before I realised Gedney was even in the place I found him at my elbow. I had been forewarned of his overpowering character but even so I was unprepared for the meeting. The man radiated power. He was so tall that I, myself six feet tall, had to look up at him. Typically dressed in a cloak with a flaring collar and with his dark, hypnotic eyes, he gave an impression of amused tolerance—which I knew was forced.

"Mr. Titus Crow, I believe? Need I introduce myself? No, I thought not; you already know me, or *think* you do. Let me tell you something, Mr. Crow. You are following a very dangerous trail. I am sure you get my meaning. Take my advice, Mr. Crow, and let sleeping dogs lie. I've heard of you. An occultist of sorts; a mere dabbler, one I would not normally bother with. Unfortunately you're blessed with an unpleasant turn of mind and a slanderous tongue. My advice is this; stop poking your nose into matters which do not concern you before I am forced to take reprisals. How about it, Mr. Crow?"

"Gedney," I said, "if I am correct you are the very foulest kind of evil and you have access to knowledge the like of which, in *your* hands, is an abomination and a threat to the sanity of the entire world. But you don't frighten me. I shall do my level best to prove you are responsible for the deaths of at least two men and will play whatever part I can in bringing you to justice."

It was important to let Gedney know I was onto something without making him feel that I had any tricks up my sleeve. Having said my piece and without waiting for an answer, I brushed past the man and staggered out into the late evening. Quickly I lost myself amidst the pleasure seekers and made my way to my car. Then I drove to Blowne House and set up my defences.

I live alone and the next night, as I was making the rounds of Blowne House before retiring, I found that a blank envelope had been dropped through my letter-box. I had expected it. I knew exactly what I would find inside the thing; not that I intended to open it. I was not *entirely* convinced that Gedney's powers were magical and there was always the chance that the card within the envelope was heavily impregnated with some deadly and obscure poison; a poison which, of necessity, would have to have the power of almost instant dispersal.

I fully anticipated the next occurrence, but even so I still froze solid for an instant when my telephone rang. I lifted the receiver an inch from the cradle and let it fall, breaking the connection. I was obliged to repeat this action three times in the course of the next half-hour; for while I have been guilty of *certain* follies in the past, one of them was never indiscretion—or lunacy, as it would have been to answer that 'phone.

Symonds had *died* answering his 'phone, and whether it was a case of hearing a trigger-word in connection with some post-hypnotic suggestion or other which Gedney had previously supplied—or the more fanciful one of hearing an invocation—I was not sure; and I was certainly not eager to learn.

Then, though I waited a further twenty minutes, the telephone remained silent. It was time for the action to begin.

Gedney, I reasoned, must now have a damned good idea that I knew just a bit too much for his good. The fact that I would not answer my 'phone showed that I obviously knew *something*. If I had merely disconnected the 'phone on receipt of the envelope there was the possibility that Gedney, on getting no dialling-tone, might have thought I was not at home. But he had heard the receiver lifted and dropped. He *knew* I was at home and if he had taken the trouble to check up on me he must know I lived alone. I hoped my refusal to answer his call had not frightened him off.

I did something then which I know must seem the ultimate madness. I unlocked the main door of Blowne House! I was satisfied Gedney would come.

After about thirty minutes I heard the sound of a car driving by outside. By this time I was in my bedroom, seated in an easy-chair with my back to the wall, facing the door to the hall. Close to my right hand was that abhorrent envelope. I was wearing my dressing-gown and at my immediate left hung ceiling-to-floor plastic curtains. Directly in front of me stood a small table on which lay the envelope and a book of poems. It was my intention, on Gedney's arrival, to *appear* to be reading.

Now, Blowne House is a sprawling bungalow, and one particularly suited to my own singular tastes. I had utilised the unique design of the place in my plan and was satisfied that my present position offered the maximum of safety from the assault which I was reasonably sure was about to commence.

Presently I heard the car again and this time it stopped right outside the house. Before the sound of the motor died away I heard the distinct crunch of gravel which told me the car had entered my driveway. After a few seconds a knock sounded upon the outside door. Again came the knock, following a short silence, but I remained quiet, not moving a fraction from my chair. As my hair stood slowly on end, a few more seconds crawled by and then I heard the outer door groan open. With a shock I realised that the sudden constriction I felt in my chest was caused by lack of air. Such was my concentration I had momentarily stopped breathing.

My nerves had started to silently scream and though every light in the house was on, the place may as well have been as dark as the pit the way I felt. Slow footsteps sounded in the hall, approached past my study and halted just beyond the door facing me. My nerves stretched to breaking point and then, with startling abruptness, the door flew open to admit Gedney.

As he strode in I rose from my seat and put down the book of poems. I was still acting but this time, though I tried to appear just a trifle drunk, my main role was one of utter astonishment. As I got to my feet I burst out:

"Gedney! What on Earth...?" I leaned forward aggressively over the table. "What the devil's the meaning of this? Who invited you here?" My heart was in my mouth but I played my part as best I could.

"Good evening, Mr. Crow." Gedney smiled evilly. "Who invited me? Why! You did; by your refusal to accept my warning and by your unwillingness to use your telephone. Whatever it is you know about me is matterless, Crow, and doomed to die with you tonight. At least you have the satisfaction of knowing that you were correct. I do have access to strange knowledge; knowledge which I intend to use right now. So I repeat: Good evening, Mr. Crow—*and goodbye!*"

Gedney was standing between the table and the door, and as he finished speaking he threw up his hands and commenced bellowing, in a cracked, droning tone, an invocation of such evil inference that merely hearing it would have been sufficient to mortify souls only slightly more timid than mine. I had never heard this particular chant before, though I have heard others, but as the crescendo died away, its purpose became immediately apparent. During the invocation I had been frozen, literally *paralysed* by the sound of the thing, and I could fully understand how it was that Symonds had been forced to listen to it over his 'phone. From the first word Symonds would have stood like a statue with the receiver pressed to his ear, unable to move as his death-certificate was signed over the wire.

As the echoes of that hideous droning died away Gedney lowered his hands and smiled. He had seen the envelope at my fingertips—and as his awful laugh began to fill the room I discovered the meaning of "The Black"...

No witch-doctor's curse this but an aeon-old fragment of sorcery handed down through nameless centuries. *This* came from a time in Earth's abysmal past when unthinkable creatures from an alien and unknown universe spawned weird things in the primeval slime. The horror of it...

A black snowflake landed on me! That is what the thing looked like. A cold, black snowflake which spread like a stain on my left wrist. But before I had time to examine that abnormality another fell onto my forehead. And then, rapidly, from all directions they came, ever faster, settling on me from out of the nether-regions. Horror-flakes that blinded and choked me.

Blinded?...Choked?

Before my mind's eye, in shrieking letters, flashed those passages from Geoffrey, the *Necronomicon* and the *Ibigib*. "Thief of Light—Thief of Air..." The inscriptions at Geph, "...The spell of running water..." Alhazred—"That which is in water drowneth not..."

The bait was taken; all that remained was to spring the trap. And if I were mistaken?

Quickly, while I was still able, I drew the curtains at my left to one side and flicked the still-unopened envelope towards Gedney's feet. Shedding my dressing-gown I stepped naked onto the tiles behind the curtains, tiles which were now partly visible to the fiend before me. Frantic, for a gibbering terror now held me in its icy grip, I clawed at the tap. The second or so the water took to circulate through the plumbing seemed an eternity, in which thousands more of those blasphemous flakes flew at me, forming a dull, black layer on any body.

And then, mercifully, as the water poured over me, "The Black" was gone! The stuff did not *wash* from me—it simply vanished. No, that is not quite true—*for it instantly reappeared elsewhere!*

Gedney had been laughing, baying like some great hound, but as I stepped into the shower and as the water started to run, he stopped. His mouth fell open and his eyes bugged horribly. He gurgled something unrecognisable and made ghastly, protesting gestures with his hands. He could not take in what had happened, for it had all been too fast for him. His victim was snatched from the snare and he could not believe his eyes. But believe he had to as the first black flakes began to fall upon him! The shadows darkened under his suddenly comprehending eyes and his aspect turned an awful grey as I spoke these words from the safety of the shower:

> "Let him who calls The Black,
> Be aware of the danger
> His victim may be protected
> by the spell of running water
> And turn the called-up darkness
> Against the very caller…"

Nor did this alone satisfy me. I wanted Gedney to remember me in whichever hell he was bound for; and so, after repeating that warning of the elder Ptetholites, I said:

"Good evening, Mr. Gedney—*and goodbye…*"

Cruel? Ah! You may call me cruel—but had not Gedney planned the same fate for me? And how many others, along with Symonds and Chambers, had died from the incredible sorceries of this fiend?

He had started to scream. Taken by surprise, he was almost completely covered by the stuff before he could move but now, as the horrible truth sank in, he tried to make it across the room to the shower. It was his only possible means of salvation and he stumbled clumsily round the table towards me. But if Gedney was a fiend so, in my own right, was I—and I had taken precautions. In the shower recess I had previously placed a windowpole, and snatching it up I now put it to use fending off the shrilly shrieking object before me.

As more of "The Black," the evil blood of Yibb-Tstll, settled on him, Gedney began the frantic brushing motions which I remembered so well, all the while babbling and striving to fight his way past my windowpole. By now the stuff was thick on him, inches deep, a dull, black mantle which covered him from head to toe. Only one eye and his screaming mouth remained visible and his outline was rapidly becoming the bloated duplicate of that hideous shadow I had seen on the night of Chambers' death.

It was now literally *snowing* black death in my room and the end had to follow quickly. Gedney's bulging eye and screaming, frothing mouth seemed to sink into the ever thickening blackness and the *noises* he was making were instantly shut off. For a few seconds he did a monstrous, shuffling dance of agony, and unable to bear the sight any longer I used the pole to push him off his feet. My prayer that this action would put a quick end to it was answered. *He pulsed!* Yes, that is the only way I can describe the motion of his smothered body: he pulsed for a moment on the carpet—and then was still. Briefly then, the lights seemed to dim and a rushing wind filled the house. I must have momentarily fainted for I awoke to find myself stretched out full length on the carpet with the shower still hissing behind me. As mysteriously as it had come, "The Black" had departed, back to that other-dimensional body which housed it, taking Gedney's soul and leaving his lifeless shell behind…

Later, after a stiff drink, I opened the envelope and found the flaking, brittle shards I had expected. Later still, with the rapidly stiffening, lolling corpse beside me, I drove out towards Gedney's country home. I parked his car in a clump of trees, off the road, and in the small hours made my way back on foot to Blowne House. The brightening air was strangely sweet.

HAGGOPIAN

This one was written in mid-1970, by which time it seems I had improved somewhat! Still in the Army, I was a recruiting Sergeant in Leicester. When business was slow you would find me scribbling away at my desk. I did send a copy of "Haggopian" to Derleth at Arkham House, but he was ill and in 1971 died tragically young, leaving a gaping hole in the publishing of weird fiction which no one else seemed capable of plugging. The story was accepted by Jerry Page, for his magazine Coven 13 *(later* Witchcraft & Sorcery)—*which almost immediately ceased publication! Finally, via my agent, Kirby McCauley, it found a home in the prestigious* Magazine of Fantasy & Science Fiction, *and appeared in the issue for June 1973.* Haggopian *was, and still is, one of my personal favourites.*

I

Richard Haggopian, perhaps the world's greatest authority on ichthyology and oceanography, to say nothing of the many allied sciences and subjects, was at last willing to permit himself to be interviewed. I was jubilant, elated—I could not believe my luck! At least a dozen journalists before me, some of them so high up in literary circles as to be actually offended by so mundane an occupational description, had made the futile journey to Kletnos in the Aegean to seek Haggopian the Armenian out; but only my application had been accepted. Three months earlier, in early June, Hartog of *Time* had been refused, and before him Mannhausen of *Weltzukunft*, and therefore my own superiors had seen little hope for me. And yet the name of Jeremy Belton was not unknown in journalism; I had been lucky on a number of so-called "hopeless" cases before. Now, it seemed, this luck of mine was holding. Richard Haggopian was away on yet another ocean trip, but I had been asked to wait for him.

It is not hard to say why Haggopian excited such interest among the ranks of the world's foremost journalists; any man with his scientific and literary talents, with a beautiful young wife, with an island-in-the-sun, and (perhaps most important of all), with a blatantly negative attitude toward even the most beneficial publicity, would certainly have attracted the same interest. And to top all this Haggopian was a millionaire!

Myself, I had recently finished a job in the desert—the latest Arab-Israeli confrontation—to find myself with time and a little money to spare, and so my superiors had asked me to have a bash at Haggopian. That had been a fortnight ago and since then I had done my best towards procuring an interview. Where others had failed miserably I had been successful.

For eight days I had waited on the Armenian's return to Haggopiana—his tiny island hideaway two miles east of Kletnos and midway between Athens and Iraklion, purchased by and named after himself in the early 40s—and just when it seemed that my strictly limited funds must surely run out, then Haggopian's great silver hydrofoil, the *Echinoidea*, cut a thin scar on the incredible blue of the sea to the south-west as it sped in to a mid-morning mooring. With binoculars from the flat white roof of my Kletnos—hotel?—I watched the hydrofoil circle the island until, in a blinding flash of reflected sunlight, it disappeared beyond Haggopiana's wedge of white rock. Two hours later the Armenian's man came across in a sleek motorboat to bring me (I hoped) news of my appointment. My luck was indeed holding! I was to attend Haggopian at three in the afternoon; a boat would be sent for me.

At three I was ready, dressed in sandals, cool grey slacks and a white T-shirt—the recommended civilised attire for a sunny afternoon in the Aegean—and when the sleek motorboat came back for me I was waiting for it at the natural rock wharf. On the way out to Haggopiana, as I gazed over the prow of the craft down through the crystal-clear water at the gliding, shadowy groupers and the clusters of black sea-urchins (the Armenian had named his hydrofoil after the latter), I did a mental check-up on what I knew of the elusive owner of the island ahead:

Richard Hemeral Angelos Haggopian, born in 1919 of an illicit union between his penniless but beautiful half-breed Polynesian mother and millionaire Armenian-Cypriot father—author of three of the most fascinating books I had ever read, books for the layman, telling of the world's seas and all their multiform denizens in simple, uncomplicated language—discoverer of the Taumotu Trench, a previously unsuspected hole in the bed of the South Pacific almost seven thousand fathoms deep; into which, with the celebrated Hans Geisler, he descended in 1955 to a depth of twenty-four thousand feet—benefactor of the world's greatest aquariums and museums in that he had presented at least two hundred and forty rare, often freshly discovered specimens to such authorities in the last fifteen years, etc., etc....

Haggopian the much married—three times, in fact, and all since the age of thirty—apparently an unfortunate man where brides were concerned. His first wife (British) died at sea after nine years' wedded life, mysteriously disappearing overboard from her husband's yacht in calm seas on the shark-ridden Barrier Reef in 1958; number two (Greek-Cypriot) died in 1964 of some exotic wasting disease and was buried at sea; and number three—one Cleanthis Leonides, an Athenian model of note, wed on her eighteenth birthday—had apparently turned recluse in that she had not been seen publicly since her union with Haggopian two years previously.

Cleanthis Haggopian—yes! Expecting to meet her, should I ever be lucky enough to get to see her husband, I had checked through dozens of old fashion magazines for photographs of her. That had been a few days ago in Athens, and now I recalled her face as I had seen it in those pictures—young, naturally, and beautiful in the Classic Greek tradition. She had been a "honey"; would, of course, still be; and again, despite rumours that she was no longer living with her husband, I found myself anticipating our meeting.

In no time at all the flat white rocky ramparts of the island loomed to some thirty feet out of the sea, and my navigator swung his fast craft over to the left, passing between two jagged points of salt-incrusted rock standing twenty yards or so out from Haggopiana's most northern point. As we rounded the point I saw that the east face of the island looked far less inhospitable; there was a white sand beach, with a pier at which the *Echinoidea* was moored, and, set back from the beach in a cluster of pomegranate, almond, locust and olive trees, an immensely vast and sprawling flat-roofed bungalow.

So this was Haggopiana! Hardly, I thought, the "island paradise" of Weber's article in *Neu Welt*! It looked as though Weber's story, seven years old now, had been written no closer to Haggopiana than Kletnos; I had always been dubious about the German's exotic superlatives.

At the dry end of the pier my quarry waited. I saw him as, with the slightest of bumps, the motorboat pulled in to mooring. He wore grey flannels and a white shirt with the sleeves rolled down. His thin nose supported heavy, opaquely-lensed sunglasses. This was Haggopian—tall, bald, extremely intelligent and very, very rich—his hand already outstretched in greeting.

Haggopian was a shock. I had seen photographs of him of course, quite a few, and had often wondered at the odd sheen such pictures had seemed to give his features. In fact the only decent pictures I had seen of him had been pre-1958 and I had taken later shots as being simply the result of poor photography; his rare appearances in public had always been very short ones and unannounced, so that by the time cameras were clicking he was usually making an exit. Now, however, I could see that I had short-changed the photographers. He did have a sheen to his skin—a peculiar phosphorescence almost—that highlighted his features and even partially reflected something of the glare of the sun. There must, too, be something wrong with the man's eyes. Tears glistened on his cheeks, rolling thinly down from behind the dark lenses. He carried in his left hand a square of silk with which, every now and then, he would dab at this telltale dampness; all this I saw as I approached him along the pier, and right from the start I found him strangely—yes, repulsive.

"How do you do, Mr. Belton?" his voice was a thick, heavily accented rasp that jarred with his polite inquiry and manner of expression. "I am sorry you have had to wait so long. I got your message in Famagusta, right at the start of my trip, but I am afraid I could not put my work off."

"Not at all, sir, I'm sure that this meeting will more than amply repay my patience."

His handshake was no less a shock, though I tried my best to keep him from seeing it, and after he turned to lead me up to the house I unobtrusively wiped my hand on the side of my T-shirt. It was not that Haggopian's hand had been damp with sweat, which might be expected—rather, or so it seemed to me, I felt as though I had taken hold of a handful of garden snails!

I had noticed from the boat a complex of pipes and valves between the sea and the house, and now, approaching that sprawling yellow building in Haggopian's wake (his stride was clumsy, lolling), I could hear the muffled throb of pumps and the gush of water. Once inside the huge, refreshingly cool bungalow, it became apparent just what the sounds meant. I might have known that this man, so in love with the sea, would surround himself with his life's work. The place was nothing less than a gigantic aquarium!

Massive glass tanks, in some cases room length and ceiling high, made up the walls, so that the sunlight filtering through from exterior, porthole-like windows entered the room in greenish shades that dappled the marble floor and gave the place an eerie, submarine aspect.

There were no printed cards or boards to describe the finny dwellers in the huge tanks, and as he led me from room to room it became clear why such labels were unnecessary. Haggopian knew each specimen intimately, his rasplike voice making a running commentary as we visited in turn the bungalow's many wings:

"An unusual coelenterate, this one, from three thousand feet. Difficult to keep alive—pressure and all that. I call it *Physalia haggopia*—quite deadly. If one of those tentacles should even brush you...*phttt*! Makes a water-baby of the Portuguese Man-o'-War" (this of a great purplish mass with trailing, wispy-green tentacles, undulating horribly through the water of a tank of huge proportions). Haggopian, as he spoke, deftly plucked a small fish from an open tank on a nearby table, throwing it up over the lip of the greater tank to his "unusual coelenterate". The fish hit the water with a splash, swam down and straight into one of the green wisps—and instantly stiffened! In a matter of seconds the hideous jelly-fish had settled on its prey to commence a languid ingestion.

"Given time," Haggopian gratingly commented, "it would do the same to you!"

In the largest room of all—more a hall than a room proper—I paused, literally astonished at the size of the tanks and the expertise which had obviously gone into their construction. Here, where sharks swam through brain and other coral formations, the glass of these miniature oceans must have been tremendously thick, and backdrops had been arranged to give the impression of vast distances and sprawling submarine vistas.

In one of these tanks hammerheads of over two metres in length were cruising slowly from side to side, ugly as hell and looking twice as dangerous. Metal steps led up to this tank's rim, down the other side and into the water itself. Haggopian must have seen the puzzled expression on my face for he said: "This is where I used to feed my lampreys—they had to be handled carefully. I have none now; I returned the last of my specimens to the sea three years ago."

Three years ago? I peered closer into the tank as one of the hammerheads slid his belly along the glass. There on the white and silver underside of the fish, between the gill-slits and down the belly, numerous patches of raw red showed, many of them forming clearly defined circles where the close-packed scales had been removed and the suckerlike mouths of the lampreys had been at work. No, Haggopian's "three years" had no doubt been a slip of the tongue—three days, more like it! Many of the wounds were clearly of recent origin, and before the Armenian ushered me on I was able to see that at least another two of the hammerheads were similarly marked.

I stopped pondering mine host's mistake when we passed into yet another room whose specimens must surely have caused any conchologist to cry out in delight. Again tanks lined the walls, smaller than many of the others I had so far seen, but marvellously laid out to duplicate perfectly the natural environs of their inhabitants. These inhabitants were the living gems of almost every ocean on earth; great conches and clams from the South Pacific; the small, beautiful *Haliotis excavata* and *Murex monodon* from the Great Barrier Reef; the amphora-like *Delphinula formosa* from China, and weird uni- and bivalves of every shape and size in their hundreds. Even the windows were of shell—great, translucent, pinkly glowing fan-shells, porcelain thin yet immensely strong, from very deep waters—suffusing the room in blood tints as weird as the submarine dappling of the previous rooms. The aisles, too, were crammed with trays and showcases full of dry shells, none of them indexed in any way; and again Haggopian showed off his expertise by casually naming any specimens I paused to study and by briefly describing their habits and the foreign deeps in which they were indigenous.

My tour was interrupted here when Costas, the Greek who had brought me from Kletnos, entered this fascinating room of shells to murmur something of obvious importance to his employer. Haggopian nodded his head in agreement and Costas left, returning a few moments later with half-a-dozen other Greeks who each, in their turn, had a few words with Haggopian before departing. Eventually we were alone again.

"They were my men," he told me, "some of them for almost twenty years, but now I have no further need of them. I have paid them their last wages, they have said their farewells, and now they are going away. Costas will take them to Kletnos and return later for you. By then I should have finished my story."

"I don't quite follow you, Mr. Haggopian. You mean you're going into seclusion here? What you said just then sounded ominously final."

"Seclusion? Here? No, Mr. Belton—but final, yes! I have learned as much of the sea as I can from here, and in any case only one phase in my education remains. For that phase I need no...*tuition*! You will see."

He saw the puzzled look on my face and smiled a wry smile. "You find difficulty in understanding me, and that is hardly surprising. Few men, if any, have known my circumstances before, of that I am reasonably certain; and that is why I have chosen to speak now. You are fortunate in that you caught me at the right time; I would never have taken it upon myself to tell my story had I not been so persistently pursued—there are horrors best unknown—but perhaps the telling will serve as a warning. It gives me pause, the number of students devoted to the lore of the sea that would emulate my works and discoveries. But in any case, what you no doubt believed would be a simple interview will in fact be my swan song. Tomorrow, when the island is deserted, Costas will return and set all the living specimens loose. There are means here by which even the largest fishes might be returned to the sea. Then Haggopiana will be truly empty."

"But why? To what end—and where do you intend to go?" I asked. "Surely this island is your base, your home and stronghold? It was here that you wrote your wonderful books, and—"

"My base and stronghold, as you put it, yes!" he harshly cut me off. "The island has been these things to me, Mr. Belton, but my home? No more! That—is my home!" He shot a slightly trembling hand abruptly out in the general direction of the Cretean Sea and the Mediterranean beyond. "When your interview is over, I shall walk to the top of the rocks and look once more at Kletnos, the closest landmass of any reasonable size. Then I will take my *Echinoidea* and guide her out through the Kasos Straits on a direct and deliberate course until her fuel runs out. There can be no turning back. There is a place unsuspected in the Mediterranean—where the sea is so deep and cool, and where—"

He broke off and turned his strangely shining face to me: "But there—at this rate the tale will never be told. Suffice to say, that the last trip of the *Echanoidea* will be to the bottom—and that I shall be with her!"

"Suicide?" I gasped, barely able to keep up with Haggopian's rapid revelations. "You intend to—drown yourself?"

At that Haggopian laughed, a rasping cough of a laugh that somehow reminded me of a seal's bark. "Drown myself? Can you drown these?" he opened his arms to encompass a miniature ocean of strange conches; "or these?" he waved through a door at a crystal tank of exotic fish.

For a few moments I stared at him in dumb amazement and concern, uncertain as to whether I stood in the presence of a sane man or—?

He gazed at me intently through the dark lenses of his glasses, and under the scrutiny of those unseen eyes I slowly shook my head, backing off a step.

"I'm sorry, Mr. Haggopian—I just…"

"Unpardonable," he rasped as I struggled for words, "my behaviour is unpardonable! Come, Mr. Belton, perhaps we can be comfortable out here." He led me through a doorway and out onto a patio surrounded by lemon and pomegranate trees. A white garden table and two cane chairs stood in the shade. Haggopian clapped his hands together once, sharply, then offered me a chair before clumsily seating himself opposite. Once again I noticed how all the man's movements seemed oddly awkward.

An old woman, wrapped around Indian-fashion in white silk and with the lower half of her face veiled in a shawl that fell back over her shoulders, answered the Armenian's summons. He spoke a few guttural yet remarkably *gentle* words to her in Greek. She went, stumbling a little with her years, to return a short while later with a tray, two glasses, and (amazingly) an English beer with the chill still on the bottle.

I saw that Haggopian's glass was already filled, but with no drink I could readily recognize. The liquid was greenly cloudy—sediment literally swam in his glass—and yet the Armenian did not seem to notice. He touched glasses with me before lifting the stuff to his lips and drinking deeply. I too took a deep draught for I was very dry; but, when I had placed my glass back on the table, I saw that Haggopian was still drinking! He completely drained off the murky, unknown liquid, put down the glass and again clapped his hands in summons.

At this point I found myself wondering why the man did not remove his sunglasses. After all, we were in the shade, had been even more so during my tour of his wonderful aquarium. Glancing at the Armenian's face I was reminded of his eye trouble as I again saw those thin trickles of liquid flowing down from behind the enigmatic lenses. And with the reappearance of this symptom of Haggopian's optical affliction, the peculiar shiny film on his face also returned. For some time that—diffusion?—had seemed to be clearing; I had thought it was simply that I was becoming used to his looks. Now I saw that I had been wrong, his appearance was as odd as ever. Against my will I found myself thinking back on the man's repulsive handshake…

"These interruptions may be frequent," his rasp cut into my thoughts. "I am afraid that in my present phase I require a very generous intake of liquids!"

I was about to ask just what "phase" he referred to when the old woman came back with a further glass of murky fluid for her master. He spoke a few more words to her before she once more left us. I could not help but notice, though, as she bent over the table, how very dehydrated the woman's face looked; with pinched nostrils, deeply wrinkled skin, and dull eyes sunk deep beneath the bony ridges of her eyebrows. An island peasant woman, obviously—and yet, in other circumstances, the fine bone structure of that face might almost have seemed aristocratic. She seemed, too, to find a peculiar magnetism in Haggopian; leaning forward towards him noticeably, visibly fighting to control an apparent desire to touch him whenever she came near him.

"She will leave with you when you go. Costas will take care of her."

"Was I staring?" I guiltily started, freshly aware of an odd feeling of un-reality and discontinuity. "I'm sorry, I didn't intend to be rude!"

"No matter—what I have to tell you makes a nonsense of all matters of sensibility. You strike me as a man not easily...*frightened*, Mr. Belton?"

"I can be surprised, Mr. Haggopian, and shocked—but frightened? Well, among other things I have been a war correspondent for some time, and—"

"Of course, I understand—but there are worse things than the man-made horrors of war!"

"That may be, but I'm a journalist. It's my job. I'll take a chance on being—frightened."

"Good! And please put aside any doubts you may by now have con-ceived regarding my sanity, or any you may yet conceive during the telling of my story. The proofs, at the end, will be ample."

I started to protest but he quickly cut me off: "No, no, Mr. Belton! You would have to be totally insensible not to have perceived the—strangeness here."

He fell silent as for the third time the old woman appeared, placing a pitcher before him on the table. This time she almost fawned on him and he jerked away from her, nearly upsetting his chair. He rasped a few harsh words in Greek and I heard the strange, shrivelled creature sob as she turned to stumble away.

"What on earth is *wrong* with the woman?"

"In good time, Mr. Belton," he held up his hand, "all in good time." Again he drained his glass, refilling it from the pitcher before commencing his tale proper; a tale through which I sat for the most part silent, later hypnotised, and eventually horrified to the end.

II

"My first ten years of life were spent in the Cook Islands, and the next five in Cyprus," Haggopian began, "always within shouting distance of the sea. My father died when I was sixteen, and though he had never acknowl-edged me in his lifetime he willed to me the equivalent of two-and-one-half millions of pounds sterling! When I was twenty-one I came into this money and found that I could now devote myself utterly to the ocean—my one real love in life. By that I mean all oceans. I love the warm Mediterranean and the South Pacific, but no less the chill Arctic Ocean and the teeming North Sea. Even now I love them—even now!

"At the end of the war I bought Haggopiana and began to build my collection here. I wrote about my work and was twenty-nine years old when I finished *The Cradle Sea*. Of course it was a labour of love. I paid for the publication of the first edition myself, and though money did not really matter, subsequent reprints repaid me more than adequately. It was my success with that book—I used to enjoy success—and with *The Sea: A New Frontier*, which prompted me to commence work upon *Denizens of the Deep*. I had been married to my first wife for five years by the time I had the first rough manuscript of my work ready, and I could have had the book published there and then but for the fact that I had become something of a perfectionist both in my writing and my studies. In short there were passages in the manuscript, whole chapters on certain species, with which I was not satisfied.

"One of these chapters was devoted to the sirenians. The dugong and the manatee, particularly the latter, had fascinated me for a long time in respect of their undeniable connections with the mermaid and siren legends of old renown; from which, of course, their order takes its name. However, it was more than merely this initially that took me off on my 'Manatee Survey', as I called those voyages, though at that time I could never have guessed at the importance of my quest. As it happened, my inquiries were to lead me to the first real pointer to my future—a frightful hint of my ultimate destination, though of course I never recognized it as such." He paused.

"Destination?" I felt obliged to fill the silence. "Literary or scientific?"

"My *ultimate* destination!"

"Oh!"

I sat and waited, not quite knowing what to say, an odd position for a journalist! In a moment or two Haggopian continued, and as he spoke I could feel his eyes staring at me intently through the opaque lenses of his spectacles:

"You are aware perhaps of the theories of continental drift—those concepts outlined initially by Wegener and Lintz, modified by Vine, Matthews and others—which have it that the continents are gradually 'floating' apart and that they were once much closer to one another? Such theories are sound, I assure you; primal Pangaea did exist, and was trodden by feet other than those of men. Indeed, that first great continent knew life before man first swung down from the trees and up from the apes!

"But at any rate, it was partly to further the work of Wegener and the others that I decided upon my 'Manatee Survey'—a comparison of the manatees of Liberia, Senegal and the Gulf of Guinea with those of the Caribbean and the Gulf of Mexico. You see, Mr. Belton, of all the shores of Earth these two are the only coastal stretches within which manatees occur in their natural state. Surely you would agree that this is excellent zoological evidence for continental drift?

"Well, with these scientific interests of mine very much at heart, I eventually found myself in Jacksonville on the East Coast of North America; which is just as far north as the manatee may be found in any numbers. In Jacksonville, by chance, I heard of certain strange stones taken out of the sea—stones bearing weathered hieroglyphs of fantastic antiquity, presumably washed ashore by the back-currents of the Gulf Stream. Such was my interest in these stones and their possible source—you may recall that Mu, Atlantis and other mythical sunken lands and cities have long been favourite themes of mine—that I quickly concluded my 'Manatee Survey' to sail to Boston, Massachusetts, where I had heard that a collector of such oddities kept a private museum. He, too, it turned out, was a lover of oceans, and his collection was full of the lore of the sea; particularly the North Atlantic which was, as it were, on his doorstep. I found him most erudite in all aspects of the East Coast, and he told me many fantastic tales of the shores of New England. It was the same New England coastline, he assured me, whence hailed those ancient stones bearing evidence of primal intelligence—*an intelligence I had seen traces of in places as far apart as the Ivory Coast and the Islands of Polynesia!*"

For some time Haggopian had been showing a strange and increasing agitation, and now he sat wringing his hands and moving restlessly in his chair. "Ah, yes, Mr. Belton—was it not a discovery? For as soon as I saw the American's basalt fragments I recognised them! They were small, those pieces, yes, but the inscriptions upon them were the same as I had seen cut in great black pillars in the coastal jungles of Liberia—pillars long cast up by the sea and about which, on moonlit nights, the natives cavorted and chanted ancient liturgies! I had known those liturgies, too, Belton, from my childhood in the Cook Island—*Iä R'lyeh! Cthulhu fhtagn!*"

With this last thoroughly alien gibberish fluting weirdly from his lips the Armenian had risen suddenly to his feet, his head aggressively forward, and his knuckles white as they pressed down on the table. Then, seeing the look on my face as I quickly leaned backwards away from him, he slowly relaxed and finally fell back into his seat as though exhausted. He let his hands hang limp and turned his face to one side.

For at least three minutes Haggopian sat like this before turning to me with the merest half-apologetic shrug of his shoulders. "You—you must excuse me, sir. I find myself very easily given these days to over-excitement."

He took up his glass and drank, then dabbed again at the rivulets of liquid from his eyes before continuing: "But I digress; mainly I wished to point out that once, long ago, the Americas and Africa were Siamese twins, joined at their middle by a lowland strip which sank as the continental drift began. There were cities in those lowlands, do you see? And evidence of those prehistoric places still exists at the points where once the two masses co-joined. As for Polynesia, well, suffice to say that the beings who built the ancient cities—beings who seeped down from the stars over inchoate aeons—once held dominion over all the world. But they left other traces, those beings, queer gods and cults and even stranger—minions!

"However, quite apart from these vastly interesting geological discoveries, I had, too, something of a genealogical interest in New England. My mother was Polynesian, you know, but she had old New England blood in her too; my great-great-grandmother was taken from the islands to New England by a deck hand on one of the old East India sailing ships in the late 1820s, and two generations later my grandmother returned to Polynesia when her American husband died in a fire. Until then the line had lived in Innsmouth, a decaying New England seaport of ill repute, where Polynesian women were anything but rare. My grandmother was pregnant when she arrived in the islands, and the American blood came out strongly in my mother, accounting for her looks; but even now I recall that there was something not quite right with her face—something about the eyes.

"I mention all this because…because I cannot help but wonder if something in my genealogical background has to do with my present—*phase*."

Again that word, this time with plain emphasis, and again I felt inclined to inquire which *phase* Haggopian meant—but too late, for already he had resumed his narrative:

"You see, I heard many strange tales in Polynesia as a child, and I was told equally weird tales by my Boston collector friend—of *things* that come up out of the sea to mate with men, and of their terrible progeny!"

For the second time a feverish excitement made itself apparent in Haggopian's voice and attitude; and again his agitation showed as his whole body trembled, seemingly in the grip of massive, barely repressed emotions.

"Did you know," he suddenly burst out, "that in 1928 Innsmouth was purged by Federal agents? Purged of *what*, I ask you? And why were depth-charges dropped off Devil's Reef? It was after this blasting and following the storms of 1930 that many oddly fashioned articles of golden jewellery were washed up on the New England beaches; and at the same time those black, broken, horribly hieroglyphed stones began to be noticed and picked up by beachcombers!

"*Iä-R'lyeh!* What monstrous things lurk even now in the ocean depths, Belton, and what other things *return* to that cradle of Earthly life?"

Abruptly he stood up to begin pacing the patio in his swaying, clumsy lope, mumbling gutturally and incoherently to himself and casting occasional glances in my direction where I sat, very disturbed now by his obviously aberrant mental condition, at the table.

At that distinct moment of time, had there been any easy means of escape, I believe I might quite happily have given up all to be off Haggopiana. I could see no such avenue of egress, however, and so I nervously waited until the Armenian had calmed himself sufficiently to resume his seat. Again moisture was seeping in a slow trickle from beneath the dark lenses, and once more he drank of the unknown liquid in his glass before continuing:

"Once more I ask you to accept my apologies, Mr. Belton, and I crave your pardon for straying so wildly from the principal facts. I was speaking before of my book, *Denizens of the Deep*, and of my dissatisfaction with certain chapters. Well, when finally my interest in New England's shores and mysteries waned, I returned to that book, and especially to a chapter concerning ocean parasites. I wanted to compare this specific branch of the sea's creatures with its land-going counterpart, and to introduce, as I had in my other chapters, oceanic myths and legends that I might attempt to explain them away.

"Of course, I was limited by the fact that the sea cannot boast so large a number of parasitic creatures as the land. Why, almost every land-going animal—bird and insect included—has its own little familiar living in its hair or feathers or feeding upon it in some parasitic fashion or other.

"Nonetheless I dealt with the hagfish and lamprey, with certain species of fish-leech and whale-lice, and I compared them with fresh-water leeches, types of tapeworm, fungi and so on. Now, you might be tempted to believe that there is too great a difference between sea- and land-dwellers, and of course in a way there is—but when one considers that all life as we know it sprang originally from the sea…?"

"When I think now, Mr. Belton, of the vampire in legend, occult belief and supernatural fiction—how the monster brings about hideous changes and deteriorations in his victim until that victim dies and then returns as a vampire himself—then I wonder what mad fates drove me on. And yet how was I to know, how could any man foresee…?

"But there—I anticipate, and that will not do. My revelation must come in its own time, you must be prepared, despite your assurances that you are not easily frightened.

"In 1956 I was exploring the seas of the Solomon Islands in a yacht with a crew of seven. We had moored for the night on a beautiful uninhabited little island off San Cristobal, and the next morning, as my men were de-camping and preparing the yacht for sea, I walked along the beach looking for conches. Stranded in a pool by the tide I saw a great shark, its gills barely in the water and its rough back and dorsal actually breaking the surface. I was sorry for the creature, of course, and even more so when I saw that it had fastened to its belly one of those very bloodsuckers with which I was still concerned. Not only that, but the hagfish was a beauty! Four feet long if it was an inch and definitely of a type I had never seen before. By that time *Denizens of the Deep* was almost ready, and but for that chapter I have already mentioned the book would have been at the printer's long since.

"Well, I could not waste the time it would take to tow the shark to deeper waters, but none the less I felt sorry for the great fish. I had one of my men put it out of its misery with a rifle. Goodness knows how long the parasite had fed on its juices, gradually weakening it until it had become merely a toy of the tides.

"As for the hagfish, he was to come with us! Aboard my yacht I had plenty of tanks to take bigger fish than him, and of course I wanted to study him and include a mention of him in my book.

"My men managed to net the strange fish without too much trouble and took it aboard, but they seemed to be having some difficulty getting it back out of the net and into the tank. You must understand, Mr. Belton, that these tanks were sunk into the decks, with their tops level with the planking. I went over to give a hand before the fish expired, and just as it seemed we were sorting the tangle out the creature began thrashing about! It came out of the net with one great flexing of its body—and took me with it into the tank!

"My men laughed at first, of course, and I would have laughed with them—*if that awful fish had not in an instant fastened itself on my body, its suction-pad mouth grinding high on my chest and its eyes boring horribly into mine!*"

III

After a short pause, during which pregnant interval his shining face worked horribly, the Armenian continued:

"I was delirious for three weeks after they dragged me out of the tank. Shock?—poison?—I did not know at the time. *Now* I know, but it is too late; possibly it was too late even then.

"My wife was with us as cook, and during my delirium, as I had fever-ishly tossed and turned in my cabin bed, she had tended me. Meanwhile my men had kept the hagfish—a previously unknown species of *Myxinoidea*—well supplied with small sharks and other fish. They never allowed the cyclostome to completely drain any of its hosts, you understand, but they knew enough to keep the creature healthy for me no matter its loathsome manner of taking nourishment.

"My recovery, I remember, was plagued by recurrent dreams of mono-lithic submarine cities, cyclopean structures of basaltic stone peopled by strange, hybrid beings part human, part fish and part batrachian; the am-phibious Deep Ones, minions of Dagon and worshippers of sleeping Cthulhu. In those dreams, too, eerie voices called out to me and whispered things of my forebears—things which made me scream through my fever at the hearing!

"After I recovered the times were many I went below decks to study the hagfish through the glass sides of its tank. Have you ever seen a hagfish or lamprey close up, Mr. Belton? No? Then consider yourself lucky. They are ugly creatures, with looks to match their natures, eel-like and primitive—and their mouths, Belton—their horrible, rasp-like, sucking mouths!

"Two months later, toward the end of the voyage, the horror really began. By then my wounds, the raw places on my chest where the thing had had me, were healed completely; but the memory of that first encounter was still terribly fresh in my mind, and—

"I see the question written on your face, Mr. Belton, but indeed you heard me correctly—I did say my *first* encounter! Oh, yes! There were more encounters to come, plenty of them!"

At this point in his remarkable narrative Haggopian paused once more to dab at the rivulets of moisture seeping from behind his sun-glasses, and to drink yet again from the cloudy liquid in his glass. It gave me a chance to look about me; possibly I still sought an immediate escape route should such be-come necessary.

The Armenian was seated with his back to the great bungalow, and as I glanced nervously in that direction I saw a face move quickly out of sight in one of the smaller, porthole windows. Later, as mine host's story progressed, I was able to see that the face in the windows belonged to the old servant woman, and that her eyes were fixed firmly upon him in a kind of hungry fascination. Whenever she caught me looking at her she withdrew.

"No," Haggopian finally went on, "the hagfish was far from finished with me—far from it. For as the weeks went by my interest in the creature grew into a sort of obsession, so that every spare moment found me staring into its tank or examining the curious marks and scars it left on the bodies of its unwilling hosts. And so it was that I discovered how those hosts were *not* unwilling! A peculiar fact, and yet—

"Yes, I found that, having once played host to the cyclostome, the fishes it fed upon were ever eager to resume such liaisons, even unto death! When I first discovered this odd circumstance I experimented, of course, and I was later able to establish quite definitely that following the initial violation the hosts of the hagfish submitted to subsequent attacks with a kind of soporific pleasure!

"Apparently, Mr. Belton, I had found in the sea the perfect parallel of the vampire of land-based legend. Just what this meant, the utter horror of my discovery, did not dawn on me until—until—

"We were moored off Limassol in Cyprus prior to starting on the very last leg of our trip, the voyage back to Haggopiana. I had allowed the crew— all but one man, Costas, who had no desire to leave the yacht—ashore for a night out. They had all worked very hard for a long time. My wife, too, had gone to visit friends in Limassol. I was happy enough to stay aboard; my wife's friends bored me; and besides, I had been feeling tired, a sort of lethargy, for a number of days.

"I went to bed early. From my cabin I could see the lights of the town and hear the gentle lap of water about the legs of the pier at which we were moored. Costas was drowsing aft with a fishing-line dangling in the water. Before I dropped off to sleep I called out to him. He answered, in a sleepy sort of way, to say that there was hardly a ripple on the sea and that already he had pulled in two fine mullets.

"When I regained consciousness it was three weeks later and I was back here on Haggopiana. The hagfish had had me again! They told me how Costas had heard the splash and found me in the cyclostome's tank. He had managed to get me out of the water before I drowned, but had needed to fight like the very devil to get the monster off me—or rather, *to get me off the monster*!

"Do the implications begin to show, Mr. Belton?

"You see this?" He unbuttoned his shirt to show me the marks on his chest—circular scars of about three inches in diameter, like those I had seen on the hammerheads in their tank—and I stiffened in my chair, my mouth falling open in shock as I saw their great number! Down to a silken cummer-bund just below his rib-cage he unbuttoned his shirt, and barely an inch of his skin remained unblemished; some of the scars even overlapped!

"Good God!" I finally gasped.

"Which God?" Haggopian instantly rasped across the table, his fingers trembling again in that strange passion. "Which God, Mr. Belton? Jehovah or Oannes—the Man-Christ or the Toad-Thing—god of Earth or Water? *Iä-R'lyeh, Cthulhu fhtagn; Yibb-Tstll; Yot-Sothothl!* I know many gods, sir!"

Again, jerkily, he filled his glass from the pitcher, literally gulping at the sediment-loaded stuff until I thought he must choke. When finally he put down his empty glass I could see that he had himself once more under a semblance of control.

"That second time," he continued, "everyone believed I had fallen into the tank in my sleep, and this was by no means a wild stretch of the imagination; as a boy I had been something of a somnambulist. At first even I believed it was so, for at that time I was still blind to the creature's power over me. They say that the hagfish is blind, too, Mr. Belton, and members of the better-known species certainly are—but *my* hag was not blind. Indeed, primitive or not, I believed that after the first three or four times he was actually able to recognize me! I used to keep the creature in the tank where you saw the hammerheads, forbidding anyone else entry to that room. I would pay my visits at night, whenever the—*mood*—came on me; and he would be there, waiting for me, with his ugly mouth groping at the glass and his queer eyes peering out in awful anticipation. He would go straight to the steps as soon as I began to climb them, waiting for me restlessly in the water until I joined him there. I would wear a snorkel, so as to be able to breathe while he—while it…"

Haggopian was trembling all over now and dabbing angrily at his face with his silk handkerchief. Glad of the chance to take my eyes off the man's oddly glistening features, I finished off my drink and refilled my glass with the remainder of the beer in the bottle. The chill was long off the beer by then—the beer itself was almost stale—but in any case, understandably I believe, the edge had quite gone from my thirst for anything of Haggopian's. I drank solely to relieve my mouth of its clammy dryness.

"The worst of it was," he went on after a while, "that what was happening to me was not against my will. As with the sharks and other host-fish, so with me. I *enjoyed* each hideous liaison as the alcoholic enjoys the euphoria of his whisky; as the drug addict delights in his delusions; and the results of my addiction were no less destructive! I experienced no more periods of delirium, such as I had known following my first two 'sessions' with the creature, but I could feel that my strength was slowly but surely being sapped. My assistants knew that I was ill, naturally—they would have had to be stupid not to notice the way my health was deteriorating or the rapidity with which I appeared to be ageing—but it was my wife who suffered the most.

"I could have little to do with her, do you see? If we had led any sort of normal life then she must surely have seen the marks on my body. That would have required an explanation, one I was not willing—indeed, unable—to give! Oh, but I waxed cunning in my addiction, and no one guessed the truth behind the strange disease which was slowly killing me, draining me of my life's blood.

"A little over a year later, in 1958, when I knew I was on death's very doorstep, I allowed myself to be talked into undertaking another voyage. My wife loved me deeply still and believed a prolonged trip might do me good. I think that Costas had begun to suspect the truth by then; I even caught him one day in the forbidden room staring curiously at the cyclostome in its tank. His suspicion became even more aroused when I told him that the creature was to go with us. He was against the idea from the start. I argued however that my studies were incomplete; that I was not finished with the hag and that eventually I intended to release the fish at sea. I intended no such thing. In fact, I did not believe I would last the voyage out. From sixteen stone in weight I was down to nine!

"We were anchored off the Great Barrier Reef the night my wife found me with the hagfish. The others were asleep after a birthday party aboard. I had insisted that they all drink and make merry so that I could be sure I would not be disturbed, but my wife had taken very little to drink and I had not noticed. The first thing I knew of it was when I saw her standing at the side of the tank, looking down at me and the…thing! I will always remember her face, the horror and awful *knowledge* written upon it, and her scream, the way it split the night!

"By the time I got out of the tank she was gone. She had fallen or thrown herself overboard. Her scream had roused the crew and Costas was the first to be up and about. He saw me before I could cover myself. I took three of the men and went out in a little boat to look for my wife. When we got back Costas had finished off the hagfish. He had taken a great hook and gaffed the thing to death. Its head was little more than a bloody pulp, but even in death its suctorial mouth continued to rasp away—at nothing!

"After that, for a whole month, I would have Costas nowhere near me. I do not think he *wanted* to be near me—I believe he knew that my grief was not solely for my wife!

"Well, that was the end of the first phase, Mr. Belton. I rapidly regained my weight and health, the years fell off my face and body, until I was almost the same man I had been. I say 'almost', for of course I could not be exactly the same. For one thing I had lost all my hair—as I have said, the creature had depleted me so thoroughly that I had been on death's very doorstep—and also, to remind me of the horror, there were the scars on my body and the greater scar on my mind which hurt me still whenever I thought of the look on my wife's face when last I had seen her.

"During the next year I finished my book, but mentioned nothing of my discoveries during the course of my 'Manatee Survey', and nothing of my experiences with the awful fish. I dedicated the book, as you no doubt know, to the memory of my poor wife; but yet another year was to pass before I could get the episode with the hagfish completely out of my system. From then on I could not bear to think back on my terrible obsession.

"It was shortly after I married for the second time that phase two began…

"For some time I had been experiencing a strange pain in my abdomen, between my navel and the bottom of my rib-cage, but had not troubled myself to report it to a doctor. I have an abhorrence of doctors. Within six months of the wedding the pain had disappeared—to be replaced by something far worse!

"Knowing my terror of medical men, my new wife kept my secret, and though we neither of us knew it, that was the worst thing we could have done. Perhaps if I had seen about the thing sooner—

"You see, Mr. Belton, I had developed—yes, an organ! An *appendage*, a snout-like thing had grown out of my stomach, with a tiny hole at its end like a second navel! Eventually, of course, I was obliged to see a doctor, and after he examined me and told me the worst I swore him—or rather, I *paid* him—to secrecy. The organ could not be removed, he said, it was part of me. It had its own blood vessels, a major artery and connections with my lungs and stomach. It was not malignant in the sense of a morbid tumour. Other than this he was unable to explain the snout-like thing away. After an exhaustive series of tests, though, he was further able to say that my blood, too, had undergone a change. There seemed to be far too much salt in my system. The doctor told me then that by all rights I ought not to be alive!

Nor did it stop there, Mr. Belton, for soon other changes started to take place—this time in the snout-like organ itself when that tiny navel at its tip began to open up!

"And then…and then…my poor wife…*and my eyes!*"

Once more Haggopian had to stop. He sat there gulping like—*like a fish out of water!*—with his whole body trembling violently and the thin streams of moisture trickling down his face: Again he filled his glass and drank deeply of the filthy liquid, and yet again he wiped at his ghastly face with the square of silk. My own mouth had gone very dry, and even if I had had anything to say I do not believe I could have managed it. I reached for my glass, simply to give myself something to do while the Armenian fought to control himself, but of course the glass was empty.

"I—it seems—you—" mine host half gulped, half rasped, then gave a weird, harshly choking bark before finally settling himself to finishing his unholy narrative. Now his voice was less human than any voice I had ever heard before:

"You—have—more nerve than I thought, Mr. Belton, and—you were right; you are not easily shocked or frightened. In the end it is I who am the coward, for I cannot tell the rest of the tale. I can only—*show* you, and then you must leave. You can wait for Costas at the pier…"

With that Haggopian slowly stood up and peeled off his open shirt. Hypnotized I watched as he began to unwind the silken cummerbund at his waist, watched as his—*organ*—came into view, as it blindly groped in the light like the snout of a rooting pig! But the thing was not a snout!

Its end was an open, gasping mouth—red and loathsome, with rows of rasplike teeth—and in its sides breathing gill-slits showed, moving in and out as the thing sucked at thin air!

Even then the horror was not at an end, for as I lurched reelingly to my feet the Armenian took off those hellish sunglasses! For the first time I saw his eyes; *his bulging fish-eyes—without whites, like jet marbles, oozing painful tears in the constant ache of an alien environment—eyes adapted for the murk of the deeps*!

I remember how, as I fled blindly down the beach to the pier, Haggopian's last words rang in my ears; the words he rasped as he threw down the cummerbund and removed the dark-lensed sunglasses from his face: "Do not pity me, Mr. Belton," he had said. "The sea was ever my first love, and there is much I do not know of her even now—but I will, I will. And I shall not be alone of my kind among the Deep Ones. There is one I know who awaits me even now, and one other yet to come!"

On the short trip back to Kletnos, numb though my mind ought to have been, the journalist in me took over and I thought back on Haggopian's hellish story and its equally hellish implications. I thought of his great love of the ocean, of the strangely cloudy liquid with which he so obviously sustained himself, and of the thin film of protective slime which glistened on his face and presumably covered the rest of his body. I thought of his weird fore-bears and of the exotic gods they had worshipped; of *things* that came up out of the sea to mate with men! I thought of the fresh marks I had seen on the undersides of the hammerhead sharks in the great tank, marks made by no parasite for Haggopian had returned his lampreys to the sea all of three years earlier; and I thought of that second wife the Armenian had mentioned who, rumour had it, had died of some "exotic wasting disease"! Finally, I thought of those other rumours I had heard of his *third* wife: how she was no longer living with him—but of the latter it was not until we docked at Kletnos proper that I learned how those rumours, understandable though the mistake was, were in fact mistaken.

For it was then, as the faithful Costas helped the old woman from the boat, that she stepped on her trailing shawl. That shawl and her veil were one and the same garment, so that her clumsiness caused a momentary expo-sure of her face, neck and one shoulder to a point just above her left breast. In that same instant of inadvertent unveiling, I saw the woman's full face for the first time—and also the livid scars where they began just beneath her collar bone!

At last I understood the strange magnetism Haggopian had held for her, that magnetism not unlike the unholy attraction between the morbid hag-fish of his story and its all too willing hosts! I understood, too, my previous interest in her classic, almost aristocratic features—*for now I could see that they were those of a certain Athenian model lately of note! Haggopian's third wife, wed to him on her eighteenth birthday! And then, as my whirling thoughts flashed back yet again to that second wife, "buried at sea", I knew finally, cata-clysmically, what the Armenian had meant when he said: "There is one who awaits even now, and one other yet to come!"*

CEMENT SURROUNDINGS

Two months before writing "The Caller of The Black", in June 1967 I had finished "Cement Surroundings", which August Derleth had immediately accepted for Tales of the Cthulhu Mythos, *an anthology he was then preparing for publication. I took my payment (seventy-five dollars—wow!—for which I was most grateful) in Arkham House books. This was a wise move; those books would be worth a fortune now, if I still owned them! But while I might shed a tear now and then I can't complain, because they've saved my skin (financially speaking) on several occasions. Anyway, in due time "Cement Surroundings" did indeed appear in TOTCM along with one other Lumley tale, plus stories by a good many literary heroes of mine and various contemporaries. "Cement Surroundings" didn't rest there, however, for I then used it as a chapter in my first Mythos novel—*The Burrowers Beneath.

I

It will never fail to amaze me how certain allegedly Christian people take a perverse delight in the misfortunes of others. Just how true this is was brought forcibly home to me by the totally unnecessary whispers and rumours which were put about following the disastrous decline of my closest living relative.

There were those who concluded that just as the moon is responsible for the tides, and in part the slow movement of the Earth's upper crust, so was it also responsible for Sir Amery Wendy-Smith's *behaviour* on his return from Africa. As proof they pointed out my uncle's sudden fascination for seismography—the study of earthquakes—a subject which so took his fancy that he built his own instrument, a model which does not incorporate the conventional concrete base, to such an exactitude that it measures even the most minute of the deep tremors which are constantly shaking this world. It is that same instrument which sits before me now, rescued from the ruins of the cottage, at which I am given to casting, with increasing frequency, sharp and fearful glances. Before his disappearance my uncle spent hours, seemingly without purpose, studying the fractional movements of the stylus over the graph.

For my own part I found it more than odd the way in which, while Sir Amery was staying in London after his return, he shunned the underground and would pay abortive taxi fares rather than go down into what he termed "those black tunnels". Odd, certainly—but I never considered it a sign of insanity.

Yet even his few really close friends seemed convinced of his madness, blaming it upon his living too close to those dead and nigh-forgotten civilizations which so fascinated him. But how could it have been otherwise? My uncle was both antiquarian and archaeologist. His strange wanderings to foreign lands were not the result of any longing for personal gain or acclaim. Rather were they undertaken out of a love of the life, for any fame which resulted—as frequently occurred—was more often than not shrugged off onto the ever-willing personages of his colleagues. They envied him, those so-called contemporaries of his, and would have emulated his successes had they possessed the foresight and inquisitiveness with which he was so singularly gifted—or, as I have now come to believe, with which he was cursed. My bitterness towards them is directed by the way in which they cut him after the dreadful culmination of that last, fatal expedition. In earlier years many of them had been "made" by his discoveries but on that last trip those "hangers-on" had been the uninvited, the ones out of favour, to whom he would not offer the opportunity of fresh, stolen glory. I believe that for the greater part their assurances of his insanity were nothing more than a spiteful means of belittling his genius.

Certainly that last safari was his *physical* end. He who before had been straight and strong, for a man his age, with jet hair and a constant smile, was seen to walk with a pronounced stoop and had lost a lot of weight. His hair had greyed and his smile had become rare and nervous while a distinct tic jerked the flesh at the corner of his mouth.

Before these awful deteriorations made it possible for his erstwhile "friends" to ridicule him, before the expedition, Sir Amery had deciphered or translated—I know little of these things—a handful of decaying, centuried shards known in archaeological circles as the *G'harne Fragments*. Though he would never fully discuss his findings I know it was that which he learned which sent him, ill-fated, into Africa. He and a handful of personal friends, all equally learned gentlemen, ventured into the interior seeking a legendary city which Sir Amery believed had existed centuries before the foundations were cut for the pyramids. Indeed, according to his calculations, Man's primal ancestors were not yet conceived when G'harne's towering ramparts first reared their monolithic sculptings to pre-dawn skies. Nor with regard to the age of the place, if it existed at all, could my uncle's claims be disproved. New scientific tests on the *G'harne Fragments* had shown them to be pre-triassic and their very existence, in any form other than centuried dust, was impossible to explain.

It was Sir Amery, alone and in a terrible condition, who staggered upon an encampment of savages five weeks after setting out from the native village where the expedition had last had contact with civilization. No doubt the ferocious men who found him would have done away with him there and then but for their superstitions. His wild appearance and the strange tongue in which he screamed, plus the fact that he had emerged from an area which was "taboo" in their tribal legends, stayed their hands. Eventually they nursed him back to a semblance of health and conveyed him to a more civilized region from where he was slowly able to make his way back to the outside world. Of the expedition's other members nothing has since been seen or heard and only I know the story, having read it in the letter my uncle left me. But more of that later.

Following his lone return to England, Sir Amery developed those eccentricities already mentioned and the merest hint or speculation on the part of outsiders with reference to the disappearance of his colleagues was sufficient to start him raving horribly of such inexplicable things as "a buried land where Shudde-M'ell broods and bubbles, plotting the destruction of the human race and the release from his watery prison of Great Cthulhu..." When he was asked *officially* to account for his missing companions he said that they had died in an earthquake and though, reputedly, he was asked to clarify his answer, he would say no more...

Thus, being uncertain as to how he would *react* to questions about his expedition, I was loath to ask him of it. However, on those rare occasions when he saw fit to talk of it without prompting I listened avidly for I, as much as if not more so than others, was eager to have the mystery cleared up.

He had been back only a few months when he suddenly left London and invited me up to his cottage, isolated here on the Yorkshire moors, to keep him company. This invitation was a thing strange in itself as he was one who had spent months in absolute solitude in various far-flung desolate places and liked to think of himself as something of a hermit. I accepted, for I saw the perfect chance to get a little of that solitude which I find particularly helpful to my writing.

II

One day, shortly after I had settled in, Sir Amery showed me a pair of strangely beautiful pearly spheres. They measured about four inches in diameter and though he had been unable to positively identify the material from which they were made, he was able to tell me that it appeared to be some unknown combination of calcium, chrysolite and diamond-dust. *How* the things had been made was, as he put it, "anybody's guess." The spheres, he told me, had been found at the site of dead G'harne—the first intimation he had offered that he had actually *found* the place—buried beneath the earth in a lidless, stone box which had borne upon its queerly angled sides certain utterly alien engravings. Sir Amery was anything but explicit with regard to those *designs*, merely stating that they were so loathsome in what they suggested that it would not do to describe them too closely. Finally, in answer to my probing questions, he told me they depicted monstrous sacrifices to some unnameable, cthonian deity. More he refused to say but directed me, as I seemed so "damnably eager," to the works of Commodus and the hagridden Caracalla. He mentioned that also upon the box, along with the pictures, were many lines of sharply cut characters much similar to the cuneiform etchings of the *G'harne Fragments* and, in certain aspects, having a disturbing likeness to the almost unfathomable *Pnakotic Manuscripts*. Quite possibly, he went on, the container had been a toy-box of sorts and the spheres, in all probability, were once the baubles of a child of the ancient city; certainly children—or young ones—were mentioned in what he had managed to decipher of the odd writing on the box.

It was during this stage of his narrative that I noticed Sir Amery's eyes were beginning to glaze over and his speech was starting to falter—almost as though some strange, psychic block were affecting his memory. Without warning, like a man suddenly gone into a hypnotic trance, he began muttering of Shudde-M'ell and Cthulhu, Yog-Sothoth and Yibb-Tstll— "alien *Gods* defying description" and of mythological places with equally fantastic names; Sarnath and Hyperborea, R'lyeh and Ephiroth and many more...

Eager though I was to learn more of that tragic expedition I fear it was I who stopped Sir Amery from saying on. Try as I might, on hearing him babbling so, I could not keep a look of pity and concern from showing on my face which, when he saw it, caused him to hurriedly excuse himself and flee to the privacy of his room. Later, when I looked in at his door, he was engrossed with his seismograph and appeared to be relating the markings on its graph to an atlas of the world which he had taken from his library. I was concerned to note that he was quietly arguing with himself.

Naturally, being what he was and having such a great interest in peculiar, anthropoligical problems, my uncle had always possessed—along with his historical and archaeological source books—a smattering of works concerning elder-lore and primitive and doubtful religions. I mean such works as the *Golden Bough* and Miss Murray's *Witch Cult*. But what was I to make of those *other* books which I found in his library within a few days of my arrival? On his shelves were at least nine works which I know are so outrageous in what they suggest that they have been mentioned by widely differing authorities over a period of many years as being damnable, blasphemous, abhorrent, unspeakable and literary lunacy. These included the *Cthaat Aquadingen* by an unknown author, Feery's *Notes on the Necronomicon*, the *Liber Miraculorem*, Eliphas Lévi's *History of Magic* and a faded, leather-bound copy of the hideous *Cultes des Goules*. Perhaps the worst thing I saw was a slim volume by Commodus which that "Blood Maniac" had written in AD 183 and which was protected from further fragmentation by lamination.

And moreover, as if these books were not puzzling enough, there was that *other* thing!! What of the indescribable, droning *chant* which I often heard issuing from Sir Amery's room in the dead of night? This first occurred on the sixth night I spent with him and I was roused from my own uneasy slumbers by the morbid accents of a language it seemed impossible for the vocal chords of Man to emulate. Yet my uncle was weirdly fluent with it and I scribbled down an oft-repeated sentence-sequence in what I considered the nearest written approximation of the spoken words I could find. These words—*or sounds*—were:

> *Ce'haiie ep-ngh fl'hur G'harne fhtagn,*
> *Ce'haiie fhtagn ngh Shudde-M'ell.*
> *Hai G'harne orr'e ep fl'hur,*
> *Shudde-M'ell ican-icanicas fl'hur orr'e G'harne...*

Though at the time I found the thing impossible to pronounce as I heard it, I have since found that with each passing day, oddly, the pronunciation of those lines comes easier—as if with the approach of some obscene horror I grow more capable of expressing myself in that horror's terms. Perhaps it is just that lately in my dreams, I have found occasion to speak those very words and, as all things are far simpler in dreams, my fluency has passed over into my waking hours. But that does not explain the tremors—the same inexplicable tremors which so terrorized my uncle. Are the shocks which cause the ever-present quiverings of the seismograph stylus merely the traces of some vast, subterrene cataclysm a thousand miles deep and five thousand miles away—*or are they caused by something else?* Something so outré and fearsome that my mind freezes when I am tempted to study the problem too closely…

III

There came a time, after I had been with him for a number of weeks, when it seemed plain that Sir Amery was rapidly recovering. True, he still retained his stoop,—though to me it seemed no longer so pronounced—, and his so-called eccentricities, but he was more his old self in other ways. The nervous tic had left his face completely and his cheeks had regained something of their former colour. His improvement, I conjectured, had much to do with his never-ending studies of the seismograph: for I had established. by that time that there was a definite connection between the measurements of that machine and my uncle's illness. Nevertheless, I was at a loss to understand why the internal movements of the Earth should so determine the state of his nerves. It was after a trip to his room, to look at that instrument, that he told me more of dead G'harne. It was a subject I should have attempted to steer him away from…

"The fragments," he said, "told the location of a city the name of which, G'harne, is only known in legend and which has in the past been spoken of on a par with Atlantis, Mu and R'lyeh. A myth and nothing more. But if you give a legend a location you strengthen it somewhat—and if that location yields up relics of the past, of a civilization lost for aeons, then the legend becomes history. You'd be surprised how much of the world's history has in fact been built up that way.

"It was my hope, a hunch you might call it, that G'harne had been real— and with the deciphering of the fragments I found it within my power to *prove*, one way or the other, G'harne's elder existence. I have been in some strange places, Paul, and have listened to even stranger stories. I once lived with an African tribe who declared they knew the secrets of the lost city and their story-tellers told me of a land where the sun never shines; where

Shudde-M'ell, hiding deep in the honeycombed ground, plots the dissemination of evil and madness throughout the world and plans the resurrection of other, even worse abominations!

"He hides there in the earth and awaits the time when the stars will be *right*, when his horrible hordes will be *sufficient* in number, and when he can infest the entire world with his loathsomeness and cause the *return* of others more loathsome yet! I was told stories of fabulous star-born creatures who inhabited the Earth millions of years before Man appeared and who were still here, in certain dark places, when he eventually evolved. I tell you, Paul," his voice rose, "*that they are here even now—in places undreamed of!* I was told of sacrifices to Yog-Sothoth and Yibb-Tstll that would make your blood run cold and of weird rites practiced beneath prehistoric skies before old Egypt was born. These things I've heard make the works of Albertus Magnus and Grobert seem tame and De Sade himself would have paled at the hearing."

My uncle's voice had been speeding up progressively with each sentence, but now he paused for breath and in a more normal tone and at a reduced rate he continued:

"My first thought on deciphering the fragments was of an expedition. I may tell you I had learned of certain things I could have dug for here in England—you'd be surprised what lurks beneath the surface of some of those peaceful Cotswold hills—but that would have alerted a host of so called 'experts' and amateurs alike so I decided on G'harne. When I first mentioned an expedition to Kyle and Gordon and the others I must have produced quite a convincing argument for they all insisted on coming along. Some of them though, I'm sure, must have considered themselves upon a wild goose chase for, as I've explained, G'harne lies in the same realm as Mu or Ephiroth—or at least it did—and they must have seen themselves as questing after a veritable lamp of Aladdin; but despite all that they came. They could hardly afford not to come, for if G'harne *was* real…why! Think of the lost glory… They would never have forgiven themselves. And that's why I can't forgive *myself*; but for my meddling with the fragments they'd all be here now, God help them…"

Again, Sir Amery's voice had become full of some dread excitement and feverishly he continued.

"Heavens, but this place sickens me! I can't stand it much longer. It's all this grass and soil. Makes me shudder! Cement surroundings are what I need—and the thicker the cement the better… Yet even the cities have their drawbacks… Undergrounds and things… Did you ever see Pickman's

Subway Accident, Paul? By God, what a picture… And that night… That *night*! If you could have *seen* them—coming up out of the diggings? If you could have felt the tremors… Why! The very ground rocked and danced as they rose… We'd disturbed them, d'you see? They may have even thought they were under *attack* and up they came… My God! What could have been the reason for such *ferocity*? Only a few hours before I had been congratulating myself on finding the spheres, and then… And then…"

Now he was panting and his eyes, as before, had partly glazed over. His voice had undergone a strange change of *timbre* and his accents were slurred and alien.

"Ce'haiie, Ce'haiie… The city may be buried but whoever named the place *dead* G'harne didn't know the half of it. *They were alive!* They've been alive for millions of years; perhaps they *can't* die… And why shouldn't that be? They're Gods aren't they, of a sort?… Up they come in the night…"

"Uncle, please!" I said.

"You needn't look at me so, Paul, or think what you're thinking either… There's stranger things happened, believe me. Wilmarth of Miskatonic could crack a few yarns, I'll be bound! You haven't read what Johansen wrote! Dear Lord, *read the Johansen narrative! Hai ep fl'hur*… Wilmarth… The old babbler… What is it he knows which he won't tell? Why was that which was found at those Mountains of Madness so hushed up, eh? What did Pabodie's equipment draw up out of the earth? *Tell me those things, if you can?* Ha, ha, ha! Ce'haiie, Ce'haiie—G'harne icanica…"

Shrieking now, and glassy-eyed he stood, with his hands gesticulating wildly in the air. I do not think he saw me at all, or anything, except—in his mind's eye—a horrible recurrence of what he imagined had been. I took hold of his arm to calm him but he brushed my hand away, seemingly without knowing what he was doing.

"Up they come, the rubbery things… Goodbye Gordon… Don't scream so—the shrieking turns my mind… Thank heavens it's only a dream!… A nightmare just like all the others I've been having lately… It *is* a dream, isn't it? Goodbye Scott, Kyle, Leslie…"

Suddenly, eyes bugging, he spun wildly round.

"*The ground is breaking up! So many of them…I'm falling…*it's not a dream! *Dear God!* IT'S NOT A DREAM! No! Keep off, d'you hear! Aghhh! *The slime*… Got to run!… Run! Away from those—voices?—away from the sucking sounds and the chanting…"

Without warning he broke into a chant himself and the awful *sound* of it, no longer distorted by distance or the thickness of a stout door, would have sent a more timid listener into a faint. It was similar to what I had heard before in the night and the words do not seem so evil on paper, almost ludicrous in fact, but to hear them issuing from the mouth of my own flesh and blood—and with such unnatural *fluency*...

> *"Ep ep fl'hur G'harne,*
> *G'harne fhtagn Shudde-M'ell hyas Negg'h.*

While chanting these incredible mouthings Sir Amery's feet had started to pump up and down in a grotesque parody of running. Suddenly he screamed anew and with startling abruptness leapt past me and ran full tilt into the wall. The shock knocked him off his feet and he collapsed in a heap on the floor.

I was worried that my meagre ministrations might not be adequate, but to my immense relief he regained consciousness a few minutes later. Shakily he assured me that he was "all right, just shook up a bit!" and, supported by my arm, he retired to his room.

That night I found it impossible to close my eyes so I wrapped myself in a blanket and sat outside my uncle's room to be on hand if he were disturbed in his sleep. He passed a quiet night, however, and paradoxically enough, in the morning, he seemed to have got the thing out of his system and was positively improved.

Modern doctors have known for a long time that in certain mental conditions a cure may be obtained by inciting the patient to *re-live* the events which caused his illness. Perhaps my uncle's outburst of the previous night had served the same purpose, or at least, so I thought, for by that time I had worked out new ideas on his abnormal behaviour. I reasoned that if he had been having recurrent nightmares and had been in the middle of one on that fateful night of the earthquake, when his friends and colleagues were killed, it was only natural that his mind should temporarily become somewhat unhinged upon waking and discovering the carnage. And if my theory were correct, it also explained his seismic obsessions...

IV

A week later came another grim reminder of Sir Amery's condition. He had seemed so much improved, though he still occasionally rambled in his sleep, and had gone out into the garden "to do a bit of trimming." It was well into September and quite chill, but the sun was shining and he spent the entire morning working with a rake and hedge clippers. We were doing for ourselves and I was just thinking about preparing the mid-day meal when a singular thing happened. I distinctly felt the ground *move* fractionally under my feet and heard a low rumble. I was sitting in the living room when it happened and the next moment the door to the garden burst open and my uncle rushed in. His face was deathly white and his eyes bulged horribly as he fled past me to his rooms. I was so stunned by his wild appearance that I had barely moved from my chair by the time he shakily came back into the room. His hands trembled as he lowered himself into an easy chair.

"It was the *ground*…I thought for a minute that the ground…" He was mumbling, more to himself than to me, and visibly trembling from head to toe as the after-effect of the shock hit him. Then he saw the concern on my face and tried to calm himself. "The ground. I was sure I felt a tremor—but I was mistaken. It must be this place. All that open space…I fear I'll really have to make an effort and get away from here. There's altogether too much soil and not enough cement! Cement surroundings are the thing…"

I had had it on the tip of my tongue to say that I too had felt the shock but upon learning that he believed himself mistaken I kept quiet. I did not wish to needlessly add to his already considerable disorders.

That night, after Sir Amery had retired, I went through into his study— a room which, though he had never said so, I knew he considered inviolate— to have a look at the seismograph. Before I looked at the machine, however, I saw the *notes* spread out on the table beside it. A glance was sufficient to tell me that the sheets of white foolscap were covered by fragmentary jottings in my uncle's heavy handwriting and when I looked closer I was sickened to discover that they were a rambling jumble of seemingly disassociated—yet apparently *linked*—occurrences connected in some way with his weird delusions. These notes have since been delivered permanently into my possession and are as reproduced here:

HADRIAN'S WALL.

AD 122–128. Limestone Bank. (Gn'yah of the *Fragments*)??? *Earth tremors* interrupted the diggings and that is why cut, basalt blocks were left in the uncompleted ditch with wedge holes ready for splitting

W'nyal-Shash (MITHRAS).

Romans had their own deities *but it wasn't Mithras* that the disciples of Commodus, the Blood Maniac, sacrificed to at Limestone Bank! And that was the same area where, fifty years earlier, a great block of stone was unearthed and discovered to be covered with *inscriptions* and *engraven pictures*! Silvanus the centurion defaced it and buried it again. A skeleton, positively identified as Silvanus's by the signet ring on one of its fingers, has been lately found *beneath the ground (deep)* where once stood a Vicus Tavern at Housesteads Fort—but we don't know *how* he vanished! Nor were Commodus's followers any too careful. According to Caracalla they also vanished overnight— *during an earthquake!*

AVEBURY.

(Neolithic *A'byy* of the *Fragments* and *Pnakotic Mss???*) Reference Stukeley's book, *A Temple to the British Druids*, incredible…Druids, indeed… But Stukeley nearly had it when he said Snake Worship! *Worms, more like it!*

COUNCIL OF NANTES.

(9th century) The council didn't know what they were doing when they said: "Let the *stones* also which, deceived by the derision of the *demons*, they worship amid ruins and in wooded places, where they both make their vows and bestow their *offerings*, be *dug up* from the very foundations, and let them be cast into such places as never will their devotees be able to find them again…" I've read that paragraph so many times that it's become imprinted upon my mind! *God only knows what happened to the poor devils who tried to carry out the Council's orders…*

DESTRUCTION OF GREAT STONES.

In the 13th and 14th centuries the Church also attempted the removal of certain stones from Avebury because of local superstitions which caused the country folk to take part in *heathen worship* and *witchcraft* around them! In fact some of the stones *were* destroyed—by fire and douching—"because of the *devices* upon them."

INCIDENT.

1920–25. Why was a big effort made to bury one of the great stones? An *earth-tremor* caused the stone to slip, trapping a workman. *No effort appears to have been made to free him...* The "accident" happened at dusk and two other men *died of fright!* Why did other diggers flee the scene? And what was the titanic *thing* which one of them saw wriggling away *into the ground?* Allegedly the thing left monstrous *smell* behind it... *By their SMELL shall ye know them...* Was it a member of another nest of the timeless ghouls?

THE OBELISK.

Why was Stukeley's huge obelisk broken up? The pieces were buried in the early 18th century but in 1833 Henry Browne found burnt *sacrifices* at the site... And nearby, at Silbury Hill... *My God! That devil-mound!* There are some things, even amidst these horrors, which don't bear thinking of—and while I've still got my sanity Silbury Hill better remain one of them!

AMERICA: INNSMOUTH.

1928. What actually happened and why did the Federal government drop depth charges off Devil Reef in the Atlantic coast just out of Innsmouth? Why were half Innsmouth's citizens banished? What was their connection with Polynesia and what also lies buried in the lands *beneath the sea?*

WIND WALKER.

(Death-Walker, Ithaqua, Wendigo etc....) yet *another* horror—though of a different *type!* And such *evidence!* Alleged *human sacrifices* in Manitoba. Unbelievable circumstances surrounding *Norris Case!* Spencer of Quebec University literally *affirmed* the validity of the case...And at...

But that is as far as the notes go and when I first read them I was glad that such was the case. It was quickly becoming all too apparent that my uncle was far from well and still not quite right in his mind. Of course, there was always the chance that he had written those notes *before* his seeming improvement, in which case his plight was not necessarily as bad as it appeared.

Having put the notes back exactly as I found them I turned my attention to the seismograph. The line on the graph was straight and true and when I dismantled the spool and checked the chart I saw that it had followed that almost unnaturally unbroken smoothness for the last twelve days. As I have said, that machine and my uncle's condition were directly related and this proof of the quietness of the earth was undoubtedly the reason for his comparative well-being of late. But here was yet another oddity… Frankly I was astonished at my findings for I was certain I had felt a tremor—indeed I had *heard* a low rumble—and it seemed impossible that both Sir Amery and myself should suffer the same, simultaneous sensory illusion. I rewound the spool and then, as I turned to leave the room, I noticed that which my uncle had missed. It was a small brass screw lying on the floor. Once more I unwound the spool and saw the counter-sunk hole which I *had* noticed before but which had not made an impression of any importance upon my mind. Now I guessed that it was meant to house that screw. I am nothing where mechanics are concerned and could not tell what part that small integer played in the workings of the machine; nevertheless I replaced it and again set the instrument in order. I stood then, for a moment, to ensure that everything was working correctly and for a few seconds noticed nothing abnormal. It was my ears which first warned of the change. There had been a low, clockwork hum and a steady, sharp scraping noise before. The hum was still attendant but in place of the scraping sound was a jerky scratching which drew my fascinated eyes to the stylus.

That small screw had evidently made all the difference in the world. No wonder the shock we had felt in the afternoon, which had so disturbed my uncle, had gone unrecorded. The instrument had not been working correctly *then—but now it was… Now it could be plainly seen that every few minutes the ground was being shaken by tremors which, though they were not so severe as to be felt, were certainly strong enough to cause the stylus to wildly zigzag over the surface of the revolving graph paper…*

I felt in a far more shaken state than the ground when I finally retired that night. Yet I could not really decide the cause of my nervousness. Just why should I feel so apprehensive about my discovery? True, I knew the effect of the now—correctly?—working machine upon my uncle would probably be unpleasant and might even cause another of his "outbursts" but was that knowledge all that unsettled me? On reflection I could see no reason whatever why any particular area of the country should receive more than its usual quota of earth-tremors. Eventually I concluded that the machine was either faulty or far too sensitive and went to sleep assuring myself that the strong shock we had felt had been merely coincidental to my uncle's condition. Still, I noticed before I dozed off that the very air itself seemed charged with a strange tension and the slight breeze which had wafted the late leaves during the day had gone completely, leaving in its passing an absolute quiet in which, during my slumbers, I fancied all night that the ground trembled beneath my bed...

V

The next morning I was up early. I was short of writing materials and had decided to catch the lone morning bus into Radcar. I left before Sir Amery was awake and during the journey I thought back on the events of the previous day and decided to do a little research while I was in the town. In Radcar I had a bite to eat and then I called at the offices of the *Radcar Recorder* where a Mr. McKinnen, a sub-editor, was particularly helpful. He spent some time on the office telephones making extensive enquiries on my behalf. Eventually I was told that for the better part of a year there had been no tremors of any importance in England, a point I would obviously have argued had not further information been forthcoming. I learned that there *had* been some *minor shocks* and that these had occurred at places as far as Goole, a few miles away (that one within the last twenty-four hours) and at Tenterden near Dover. There had also been a very minor tremor at Ramsey in Huntingdonshire. I thanked Mr. McKinnen profusely for his help and would have left then—but, as an afterthought, he asked me if I would be interested in checking through the paper's international files. I gratefully accepted and was left on my own to study a great pile of interesting translations. Of course, most of it was useless to me but it did not take me long to sort out what I was after. At first I had difficulty believing the evidence of my own eyes. I read that in August there had been 'quakes in Aisne of such severity that one or two houses had collapsed and a number of people had been injured. These shocks had been likened to those of a few weeks earlier at Agen in that they seemed to be caused more by some *settling of the ground* than by an actual tremor. In early July there had also been shocks in Calahorra, Chinchon and Ronda in Spain. The trail went as straight as the flight of an arrow and lay across—*or rather under*—the Straits of Gibralter to Xauen in Spanish Morocco, where an entire street of houses had collapses. Farther yet, to... But I had had enough. I dared look no more; I did not wish to know—not even remotely—the whereabouts of dead G'harne...

Oh! I had seen more than sufficient to make me forget about my original errand. My book could wait, for now there were more important things to do. My next port of call was the town library where I took down

Nicheljohn's *World Atlas* and turned to that page with a large, folding map of the British Isles. My geography and knowledge of England's counties are passable and I had noticed what I considered to be an oddity in the seemingly unconnected places where England had suffered those *minor 'quakes*. I was not mistaken. Using a second book as a straight edge I lined up Goole in Yorkshire and Tenterden on the south coast and saw, with a tingle of monstrous forboding, that the line passed very close to, if not directly through, Ramsey in Huntingdonshire. With dread curiosity I followed the line north and, through suddenly fevered eyes, saw that it passed *within only a mile or so of the cottage on the moors*! I turned more pages with unfeeling, rubbery fingers until I found the leaf showing France. For a moment I paused—then I fumblingly found Spain and finally Africa. For a long while I just sat there in numbed silence, occasionally turning the pages, automatically checking names and locations... My thoughts were in a terrible turmoil when I eventually left the library and I could feel upon my spine the chill, hopping feet of some abysmal dread from the beginning of time. My previously wholesome nervous system had already started to crumble...

During the journey back across the moors in the evening bus, the drone of the engine lulled me into a kind of half-sleep in which I heard again something Sir Amery had mentioned—something he had murmured aloud while sleeping and presumably dreaming. He had said:

"They don't like water... England's safe... Have to go too deep..." The memory of those words shocked me back to wakefulness and filled me with a further icy chill which got into the very marrow of my bones. Nor were these feelings of horrid foreboding misleading, for awaiting me at the cottage was that which went far to completing the destruction of my entire nervous system...

As the bus came round the final wooded bend which hid the cottage from sight *I saw it*! The place had collapsed. I simply could not take it in! Even knowing all I knew—with all my slowly accumulating evidence—it was too much for my tortured mind to comprehend; I left the bus and waited until it had threaded its way through the parked police cars before crossing the road. The fence to the cottage had been knocked down to allow an ambulance to park in the queerly *tilted* garden. Spotlights had been set up, for it was almost dark, and a team of rescuers were toiling frantically at the incredible ruins. As I stood there, aghast, I was approached by a police officer and having stumblingly identified myself was told the following story.

A passing motorist had actually seen the collapse and the tremors attendant to it had been felt in nearby Marske. The motorist had realised there was little he could do on his own and had speeded into Marske to report the thing. Allegedly the house had gone down like a pack of cards. The police and an ambulance had been on the scene within minutes and rescue operations had begun immediately. Up to now it appeared that my uncle had been *out* when the collapse occurred for as of yet there had been no trace of him. There had been a strange, poisonous *odour* about the place but this had vanished soon after the work had started. The rescuers had cleared the floors of all the rooms except the study and during the time it took the officer to bring me up to date even more debris was being frantically hauled away.

Suddenly there was a lull in the excited babble of voices. I saw that the gang of rescue workers were standing looking down at something. My heart gave a wild leap and I scrambled over the debris to see what they had found.

There, where the floor of the study had been, was that which I had feared and more than half expected. It was simply a hole. A gaping hole in the floor—*but from the angles at which the floorboards lay, and the manner in which they were scattered about, it looked as though the ground, rather than sinking, had been pushed up from below.*

VI

Nothing has since been seen or heard of Sir Amery Wendy-Smith and though he is listed as being *missing* I know in fact that he is dead. He is gone to worlds of ancient wonder and my only prayer is that his soul wanders on *our* side of the threshold. For in our ignorance we did Sir Amery a great injustice—I and all the others who thought he was out of his mind. All his queer ways—I understand them all now, but the understanding has come hard and will cost me dear. No, he was not mad. He did the things he did out of self-preservation and though his precautions came to nothing in the end, it was fear of a nameless evil and not madness which prompted them.

But the worst is still to come. I myself have yet to face a similar end. I know it, for no matter what I do the tremors haunt me. Or is it only in my mind? No! There is little wrong with my mind. My nerves are gone but my mind is intact. I *know* too much! *They* have visited me in dreams, as I believe *they* must have visited my uncle, and what *they* have read in my mind has warned *them* of *their* danger. *They* dare not allow me to investigate, for it is such meddling which may one day fully reveal *them* to men—*before they are ready*... God! Why has that ancient fool Wilmarth at Miskatonic not answered my telegrams? There must be a way out! Even now *they* dig—those dwellers in darkness...

But no! This is no good. I must get a grip of myself and finish this narrative. I have not had time to try to tell the authorities the truth but even if I had I know what the result would have been. "There's something wrong with all the Wendy-Smith blood" they would say. But this manuscript will tell the story for me and will also stand as a warning to others. Perhaps when it is seen how my—*passing*—so closely parallels that of Sir Amery, people will be curious; with this manuscript to guide them perhaps men will seek out and destroy Earth's elder madness before it destroys them...

A few days after the collapse of the cottage on the moors, I settled here in this house on the outskirts of Marske to be close at hand if—though I could see little hope of it—my uncle should turn up again. But now some dread power keeps me here. I *cannot* flee... At first *their* power was not so strong, but now...I am no longer able even to leave this desk and I know the end must be coming fast. I am rooted to this chair as if grown here and it is as much as I can do to type! But I must...I must... And the ground movements are much stronger now. That hellish, damnable, mocking stylus—leaping so crazily over the paper...

I had been here only two days when the police delivered to me a dirty, soil-stained envelope. It had been found in the ruins of the cottage—near the lip of that curious hole—and was addressed to me. It contained those notes I have already copied and a letter from Sir Amery which, if its awful ending is anything to go on, he must have still been writing when the horror came for him. When I consider, it is not surprising that the envelope survived the collapse. *They* would not have known what it was, and so would have had no interest in it. *Nothing* in the cottage was purposely damaged—nothing *inanimate*, that is—and so far as I have been able to discover the only missing items are those terrible spheres, *or what remained of them...* But I must hurry. I cannot escape and all the time the tremors are increasing in strength and frequency... No! I will not have time. No time to write all I wanted to say... The shocks are too heavy... To o hea vy... Int erfer in g with m y t yping...I will finis h this i n th e only way rem ain ing to me and staple S ir Amer y's lette r to this man usc ript...now...

Dear Paul,

In the event of this letter ever getting to you, there are certain things I must ask you to do for the safety and sanity of the world. It is absolutely necessary that these things be explored and *dealt with*—though how that may be done I am at a loss to say. It was my intention, for the sake of my own sanity, to forget what happened at

G'harne. I was wrong to try to hide it. At this very moment there are men digging in strange, forbidden places and who knows what they may unearth? Certainly all these horrors must be tracked down and rooted out—but not by bumbling amateurs. It must be done by men who are ready for the ultimate in hideous, cosmic horror. Men with weapons. Perhaps flame-throwers would do the trick... Certainly a scientific knowledge of war would be a necessity... Devices could be made to track the enemy...I mean specialized seismological instruments... If I had the time I would prepare a dossier, detailed and explicit, but it appears that this letter will have to suffice as a guide to tomorrow's horror hunters. You see, *I now know for sure that they are after me*! And there's nothing I can do about it. It's too late! At first even I, just like so many others, believed myself to be just a little bit mad. I refused to admit to myself that what I had *seen* happen had ever happened at all! To admit *that* was to admit lunacy! But it's real all right... It *did* happen—*and will again*!

Heaven only knows what's been wrong with my seismograph but the damn thing's let me down in the worst possible way! Oh, *they* would have got me eventually, but I might at least have had time to prepare a proper warning... I ask you to think, Paul... Think of what has happened at the cottage... I can write of it as though it had *already happened*; because I know *it must! It will!* It is Shudde-M'ell, come for his spheres... Paul, look at the manner of my death, for if you are reading this then I am either dead or disappeared—which means the same thing. Read the enclosed notes carefully, I beg you. I haven't the time to be more explicit but these old notes of mine should be of some help... If you are only half so enquiring as I believe you to be, you will surely soon come to recognize a fantastic horror which, I repeat, the whole world must be *made* to believe in... The ground is really shaking now but, knowing it is the end, I am steady in my horror... Not that I expect my present calm state of mind to last... I think that by the time *they* actually come for me my mind will have snapped completely. I can imagine it now...The floor splintering, erupting, to admit *them*. Why! Even *thinking* of it my senses recoil at the terror of the thought... There will be a hideous *smell, a slime, a chanting* and gigantic *writhing* and... And then...

Unable to escape, I await the thing... I am trapped by the same hypnotic power that claimed the others at G'harne. What monstrous memories! How I awoke to see my friends and companions sucked dry of their life's blood by wormy, vampirish *things* from the cesspools of time! Gods of alien dimensions... I was hypnotized then by this same terrible force, unable to move to the aid of my friends or even to save myself! Miraculously, with the passing of the moon behind some wisps of cloud, the hypnotic effect was broken. Then, screaming and sobbing, temporarily out of my mind, I fled; hearing behind me the vile and slobbering *sucking* sounds and the droning, demoniac chanting of Shudde-M'ell and his hordes.

Not knowing that I did it, in my mindlessness I carried with me those hell-spheres... Last night I dreamed of them. And in my dreams I saw again the inscriptions on that stone box. Moreover, *I could read them!* All the fears and ambitions of those hellish things were there to be read as clearly as the headlines in a daily newspaper! "Gods" they may or may not be but one thing is sure; the greatest setback to their plans for conquest of the Earth *is their terribly long and complicated reproductory cycle!* Only a handful of young are born every thousand years; but, considering how *long* they have been here, the time must be drawing ever nearer when their numbers will be *sufficient!* Naturally, this tedious build up of their numbers makes them loath to lose even a single member of their hideous spawn. *And that is why they have tunnelled these many thousands of miles, even under deep oceans, to retrieve the spheres!* I had wondered why they could be following me—and now I know. I also know *how.* Can you not guess how they know where I am, Paul, or why they are coming? Those spheres are like a beacon to them; a siren voice calling. *And just as any other parent—though more out of awful ambition, I fear, than any type of emotion we could understand—they are merely answering the call of their young!*

But they are too late! A few minutes ago, just before I began this letter, the things *hatched...* Who would have guessed that they were *eggs*—or that the container they were in *was an incubator?* I can't blame myself for not knowing it. I even tried to have the spheres X-rayed once, damn them, but they reflected the rays! And the shells were so *thick!* Yet at the time of hatching they just splintered into tiny fragments. The creatures inside were no bigger than walnuts... Taking into account the *size* of an adult they must have a fantastic growth rate. Not that those two will ever grow! I shrivelled them with a cigar... *And you should have heard the mental screams from those beneath!*

If only I could have known earlier, *definitely*, that it was not madness, there might have been a way to escape this horror... But no use now... My notes—look into them, Paul, and do what I should have done. Complete a detailed dossier and present it to the authorities. Wilmarth may help and perhaps Spencer of Quebec University... Haven't much time now... Cracks in ceiling...

That last shock...ceiling coming away in chunks...coming up. Heaven help me, they're coming up...I can feel them groping inside my mind as they come—

Sir,

Reference this manuscript found in the ruins of number 17 Anwick Street, Marske, Yorkshire, following the earth tremors of September this year and believed to be a "fantasy" which the writer, Paul Wendy-Smith, had completed for publication. It is more than possible that the so-called disappearances of both Sir Amery Wendy-Smith and his nephew, the writer, were nothing more than promotion stunts for this story... It is well known that Sir Amery is/was interested in seismography and perhaps some prior intimation of the two 'quakes supplied the inspiration for his nephew's tale. Investigations continuing...

Sgt J. Williams.
Yorks. County Constabulary.
2nd October 1933.

THE HOUSE OF CTHULHU

This one was written in November 1971. It was supposed to appear in a magazine called Pulp *(just that?) which to my knowledge promptly disappeared—an all-too-regular occurrence! But then Kirby McCauley sold it to a brand-new magazine, Stuart Schiff's* Whispers. *In fact it was the very first story in the very first issue in July 1973; following which it took off. This tale has now seen more reprints and translations than anything else I've ever written: in DAW's* Year's Best Horror; *in the first* Orbit Book of Horror; *in Doubleday's* Whispers *anthology; in Jove's paperback* Whispers; *in Josh Pacter's* Top Fantasy, *and so forth; until, in 1984, W. Paul Ganley used it in (and as the title of) my Weirdbook Press Volume,* The House of Cthulhu And Other Tales of the Primal Land, *in both hardcover and paperback editions. Not to be outdone, in 1991 Headline in the UK published the book in paperback, and most recently (2005) TOR Books in the USA have done a lovely little hardback, with fabulous jacket art by my good friend Bob Eggleton. All in all, a very long (and very satisfying) road for this short Mythos story.*

> Where Weirdly angled ramparts loom,
> Gaunt sentinels whose shadows gloom
> Upon an undead hell-beast's tomb—
> And gods and mortals fears to tread.
> Where gateways to forbidden spheres
> And times are closed, but monstrous fears
> Await the passing of strange years—
> When that will wake which is not dead...

"Arlyeh"—A fragment from Teh Atht's *Legends of the Olden Runes.*
As translated by Thelred Gustau from the Theem'hdra manuscripts.

N ow it happened aforetime that Zar-thule the Conqueror, who is called Reaver of Reavers, Seeker of Treasures and Sacker of Cities, swam out of the East with his dragonships; aye, even beneath the snapping sails of his dragonships. The wind was but lately turned favorable, and now the weary rowers nodded over their shipped oars while sleepy steersmen held the course. And there Zar-thule descried him in the sea the island Arlyeh, whereon loomed tall towers builded of black stone whose tortuous twinings were of angles unknown and utterly beyond the ken of men; and this island was redly lit by the sun sinking down over its awesome black crags and burning behind the aeries and spires carved therefrom by other than human hands.

And though Zar-thule felt a great hunger and stood sore weary of the wide sea's expanse behind the lolling dragon's tail of his ship Redfire, and even though he gazed with red and rapacious eyes upon the black island, still he held off his reavers, bidding them that they ride at anchor well out to sea until the sun was deeply down and gone unto the Realm of Cthon, even unto Cthon, who sits in silence to snare the sun in his net beyond the edge of the world. Indeed, such were Zar-thule's raiders as their deeds were best done by night, for then Gleeth the blind Moon God saw them not, nor heard in his celestial deafness the horrible cries which ever attended unto such deeds.

For notwithstanding his cruelty, which was beyond words, Zar-thule was no fool. He knew him that his wolves must rest before a whelming, that if the treasures of the House of Cthulhu were truly such as he imagined them—then that they must likewise be well guarded by fighting men who would not give them up easily. And his reavers were fatigued even as Zar-thule himself, so that he rested them all down behind the painted bucklers lining the decks, and furled him up the great dragon-dyed sails. And he set a watch that in the middle of the night he might be roused, when, rousing in turn the men of his twenty ships, he would sail in unto and sack the island of Arlyeh.

Far had Zar-thule's reavers rowed before the fair winds found them, far from the rape of the Yaht-Haal, the Silver City at the edge of the frostlands. Their provisions were all but eaten, their swords all ocean rot in rusting sheaths; but now they ate all of their remaining regimen and drank of the liquors thereof; and they cleansed and sharpened their dire blades before taking themselves into the arms of Shoosh, Goddess of the Still Slumbers. They well knew them, one and all, that soon they would be at the sack, each for himself and loot to that sword's wielder whose blade drank long and deep.

And Zar-thule had promised them great treasures from the House of Cthulhu; for back there in the sacked and seared city at the edge of the frost-lands, he had heard from the bubbling, anguished lips of Voth Vehm the name of the so-called "forbidden" isle of Arlyeh. Voth Vehm, in the throes of terrible tortures, had called out the name of his brother priest, Hath Vehm, who guarded the House of Cthulhu in Arlyeh. And even in the hour of his dying Voth Vehm had answered to Zar-thule's additional tortures, crying out that Arlyeh was indeed forbidden and held in thrall by the sleeping but yet dark and terrible god Cthulhu, the gate to whose House his brother-priest guarded.

Then had Zar-thule reasoned that Arlyeh must contain riches indeed, for he knew it was not meet that brother priests betray one another; and aye, surely had Voth Vehm spoken exceedingly fearfully of this dark and terrible god Cthulhu only that he might thus divert Zar-thule's avarice from the ocean sanctuary of his brother priest, Hath Vehm. Thus reckoned Zar-thule, even brooding on the dead and disfigured hierophant's words, until he bethought him to leave the sacked city. Then, with the flames leaping brightly and reflected in his red wake, Zar-thule put to sea in his dragon-ships. All loaded down with silver booty he put to sea, in search of Arlyeh and the treasures of the House of Cthulhu. And thus came he to this place.

Shortly before the midnight hour the watch roused Zar-thule up from the arms of Shoosh, aye, and all the freshened men of the dragonships; and then beneath Gleeth the blind Moon God's pitted silver face, seeing that the wind had fallen, they muffled their oars and dipped them deep and so closed in with the shoreline. A dozen fathoms from beaching, out rang Zar-thule's plunder cry, and his drummers took up a stern and steady beat by which the trained but yet rampageous reavers might advance to the sack.

Came the scrape of keel on grit, and down from his dragon's head leapt Zar-thule to the sullen shallow waters, and with him his captains and men, to wade ashore and stride the night-black strand and wave their swords…and all for naught! Lo, the island stood quiet and still and seemingly untended…

Only now did the Sacker of Cities take note of this isle's truly awesome aspect. Black piles of tumbled masonry festooned with weeds from the tides rose up from the dark wet sand, and there seemed inherent in these gaunt and immemorial relics a foreboding not alone of bygone times; great crabs scuttled in and about the archaic ruins and gazed with stalked ruby eyes upon the intruders; even the small waves broke with an eerie *hush, hush, hush* upon the sand and pebbles and primordial exuviae of crumbled yet seemingly sentient towers and tabernacles. The drummers faltered, paused and finally silence reigned.

Now many of them among these reavers recognised rare gods and supported strange superstitions, and Zar-thule knew this and had no liking for their silence. It was a silence that might yet yield to mutiny!

"Hah!" quoth he, who worshipped neither god nor demon nor yet lent ear to the gaunts of night. "See—the guards knew of our coming and are all fled to the far side of the island—or perhaps they gather ranks at the House of Cthulhu." So saying, he formed him up his men into a body and advanced into the island.

And as they marched they passed them by other prehuman piles not yet ocean-sundered, striding through silent streets whose fantastic façades gave back the beat of the drummers in a strangely muted monotone.

And lo, mummied faces of coeval antiquity seemed to leer from the empty and oddly-angled towers and craggy spires, fleet ghouls that flitted from shadow to shadow apace with the marching men, until some of those hardened reavers grew sore afraid and begged them of Zar-thule, "Master, let us get us gone from here, for it appears that there is no treasure, and this place is like unto no other. It stinks of death—even of death and of them that walk the shadow-lands."

But Zar-thule rounded on one who stood close to him muttering thus, crying, "Coward!—Out on you!" Whereupon he lifted up his sword and hacked the trembling reaver in two parts, so that the sundered man screamed once before falling with twin thuds to the black earth. But now Zar-thule perceived that indeed many of his men were sore afraid, and so he had him torches lighted and brought up, and they pressed on quickly into the island.

There, beyond low dark hills, they came to a great gathering of queerly carved and monolithic edifices, all of the same confused angles and surfaces and all with the stench of the pit, even the fetor of the *very* pit about them. And in the centre of these malodorous megaliths there stood the greatest tower of them all, a massive menhir that loomed and leaned windowless to a great height, about which at its base squat pedestals bore likenesses of blackly carven krakens of terrifying aspect.

"Hah!" quoth Zar-thule. "Plainly is this the House of Cthulhu, and see— its guards and priests have fled them all before us to escape the reaving!"

But a tremulous voice, odd and mazed, answered from the shadows at the base of one great pedestal, saying, "No one has fled, O reaver, for there are none here to flee, save me—and I cannot flee for I guard the gate against those who may utter The Words."

At the sound of this old voice in the stillness the reavers started and peered nervously about at the leaping torch-cast shadows, but one stout captain stepped forward to drag from out of the dark an old, old man. And lo, seeing the mien of this mage, all the reavers fell back at once. For he bore upon his face and hands, aye, and upon all visible parts of him, a grey and furry lichen that seemed to crawl upon him even as he stood crooked and trembling in his great age!

"Who are you?" demanded Zar-thule, aghast at the sight of so hideous a spectacle of afflicted infirmity; even Zar-thule, aghast!

"I am Hath Vehm, brother-priest of Voth Vehm who serves the gods in the temples of Yaht-Haal; I am Hath Vehm, Keeper of the Gate at the House of Cthulhu, and I warn you that it is forbidden to touch me." And he gloomed with rheumy eyes at the captain who held him, until that raider took away his hands.

"And I am Zar-thule the Conqueror," quoth Zar-thule, less in awe now. "Reaver of Reavers, Seeker of Treasures and Sacker of Cities. I have plundered Yaht-Haal, aye, plundered the Silver City and burned it low. And I have tortured Voth Vehm unto death. But in his dying, even with hot coals eating at his belly; he cried out a name. And it was *your* name! And he was truly a brother unto you, Hath Vehm, for he warned me of the terrible god Cthulhu and of this 'forbidden' isle of Arlyeh. But I knew he lied, that he sought him only to protect a great and holy treasure and the brother-priest who guards it, doubtless with strange runes to frighten away the superstitious reavers! But Zar-thule is neither afraid nor credulous, old one. Here I stand, and I say to you on your life that I'll know the way into this treasure house within the hour!"

And now, hearing their chief speak thus to the ancient priest of the island, and noting the old man's trembling infirmity and hideous disfigurement, Zar-thule's captains and men had taken heart. Some of them had gone about and about the beetling tower of obscure angles until they found a door. Now this door was great, tall, solid and in no way hidden from view; and yet at times it seemed very indistinct, as though misted and distant. It stood straight up in the wall of the House of Cthulhu, and yet looked as if to lean to one side…and then in one and the same moment to lean to the other! It bore leering, inhuman faces and horrid hieroglyphs, all carved into its surface, and these unknown characters seemed to writhe about the gorgon faces; and aye, those faces too moved and grimaced in the light of the flickering torches.

The ancient Hath Vehm came to them where they gathered in wonder of the great door, saying: "That is the gate of the House of Cthulhu, and I am its guardian."

"So," spake Zar-thule, who was also come there, "and is there a key to this gate? I see no means of entry."

"Aye, there is a key; but none such as you might readily imagine. It is not a key of metal, but of words."

"Magic?" asked Zar-thule, undaunted. He had heard aforetime of similar thaumaturgies.

Zar-thule put the point of his sword to the old man's throat, observing as he did so the furry grey growth moving upon the elder's face and scrawny neck, saying: "Then say those words now and let's have done!"

"Nay, I cannot say The Words—I am sworn to guard the gate that The Words are *never* spoken, neither by myself nor by any other who would foolishly or mistakenly open the House of Cthulhu. You may kill me—even take my life with that very blade you now hold to my throat—but I will not utter The Words…"

"And I say that you will—eventually!" quoth Zar-thule in an exceedingly cold voice, in a voice even as cold as the northern sleet. Whereupon he put down his sword and ordered two of his men to come forward, commanding that they take the ancient and tie him down to thonged pegs made fast in the ground. And they tied him down until he was spread out flat upon his back, not far from the great and oddly-fashioned door in the wall of the House of Cthulhu.

Then a fire was lighted of dry-shrubs and of driftwood fetched from the shore; and others of Zar-thule's reavers went out and trapped certain great nocturnal birds that knew not the power of flight; and yet others found a spring of brackish water and filled them up the waterskins. And soon tasteless but satisfying meat turned on the spits above a fire; and in the same fire sword-points glowed red, then white. And after Zar-thule and his captains and men had eaten their fill, then the Reaver of Reavers motioned to his torturers that they should attend to their task. These torturers had been trained by Zar-thule himself, so that they excelled in the arts of pincer and hot iron.

But then there came a diversion. For some little time a certain captain— his name was Cush-had, the man who first found the old priest in the shadow of the great pedestal and dragged him forth—had been peering most strangely at his hands in the firelight and rubbing them upon the hide of his jacket. Of a sudden he cursed and leapt to his feet, springing up from the remnants of his meal. He danced about in a frightened manner, beating wildly at the tumbled flat stones about with his hands.

Then of a sudden he stopped and cast sharp glances at his naked forearms. In the same second his eyes stood out in his face and he screamed as were he pierced through and through with a keen blade, and he rushed to the fire and thrust his hands into its heart, even to his elbows. Then he drew his arms from the flames, staggering and moaning and calling upon certain trusted gods. And he tottered away into the night, his ruined arms steaming and dripping redly upon the ground.

Amazed, Zar-thule sent a man after Cush-had with a torch, and this man soon returned trembling and with a very pale face in the firelight to tell how the madman had fallen or leapt to his death in a deep crevice. But before he fell there had been visible upon his face a creeping, furry greyness; and as he had fallen, aye, even as he crashed down to his death, he had screamed: "Unclean...unclean...unclean!"

Then, all and all when they heard this, they remembered the old priest's words of warning when Cush-had dragged him out of hiding, and the way he had gloomed upon the unfortunate captain, and they looked at the ancient where he lay held fast to the earth. The two reavers whose task it had. been to tie him down looked them one to the other with very wide eyes, their faces whitening perceptibly in the firelight, and they took up a quiet and secret examination of their persons; even a *minute* examination...

Zar-thule felt fear rising in his reavers like the east wind when it rises up fast and wild in the Desert of Sheb. He spat at the ground and lifted up his sword, crying: "Listen to me! You are all superstitious cowards, all and all of you, with your old wives' tales and fears and mumbo-jumbo. What's there to be frightened of? An old man, alone, on a black rock in the sea?"

"But I saw Cush-had's face—" began the man who had followed the demented captain.

"You only *thought* you saw something;" Zar-thule cut him off. "It was only the flickering of your torch-fire and nothing more. Cush-had was a madman!"

"But—"

"Cush-had was a madman!" Zar-thule said again, and his voice turned very cold. "Are you, too, insane? Is there room for you, too, at the bottom of that crevice?" But the man shrank back and said no more, and yet again Zar-thule called his torturers forward that they should be about their work.

The hours passed...

Blind and coldly deaf Gleeth the old Moon God surely was, and yet perhaps he had sensed something of the agonised screams and the stench of roasting human flesh drifting up from Arlyeh that night. Certainly he seemed to sink down in the sky very quickly.

Now, however, the tattered and blackened figure stretched out upon the ground before the door in the wall of the House of Cthulhu was no longer strong enough to cry out loudly, and Zar-thule despaired for he saw that soon the priest of the island would sink into the last and longest of slumbers. And still The Words were not spoken. Too, the reaver king was perplexed by the ancient's stubborn refusal to admit that the door in the looming menhir concealed treasure; but in the end he put this down to the effect of certain vows Hath Vehm had no doubt taken in his inauguration to priesthood.

The torturers had not done their work well. They had been loath to touch the elder with anything but their hot swords; they *would not*—not even when threatened most direly—lay their hands upon him, or approach him more closely than absolutely necessary to the application of their agonising art. The two reavers responsible for tying the ancient down were dead, slain by former comrades upon whom they had inadvertently lain hands of friendship; and those they had touched, their slayers, they too were shunned by their companions and stood apart from the other reavers.

As the first grey light of dawn began to show beyond the eastern sea, Zar-thule finally lost all patience and turned upon the dying priest in a veritable fury. He took up his sword, raising it over his head in two hands…and then Hath Vehm spoke:

"Wait!" he whispered, his voice a low, tortured croak, "wait, O reaver—I will say The Words."

"What?" cried Zar-thule, lowering his blade. "You will open the door?"

"Aye," the cracked whisper came, "I will open the Gate. But first, tell me; did you truly sack Yaht-Haal, the Silver City? Did you truly raze it down with fire, and torture my brother-priest to death?"

"I did all that," Zar-thule callously nodded.

"Then come you close," Hath Vehm's voice sank low. "Closer, O reaver king, that you may hear me in my final hour."

Eagerly the Seeker of Treasures bent him down his ear to the lips of the ancient, kneeling down beside him where he lay—and Hath Vehm immediately lifted up his head from the earth and spat upon Zar-thule!

Then, before the Sacker of Cities could think or make a move to wipe the slimy spittle from his brow, Hath Vehm said The Words. Aye, even in a loud and clear voice he said them—words of terrible import and alien cadence that only an adept might repeat—and at once there came a great rumble from the door in the beetling wall of weird angles.

Forgetting for the moment the tainted insult of the ancient priest, Zar-thule turned to see the huge and evilly carven door tremble and waver and then, by some unknown power, move or slide away until only a great black hole yawned where it had been. And lo, in the early dawn light, the reaver horde pressed forward to seek them out the treasure with their eyes; even to seek out the treasure beyond the open door. Likewise Zar-thule made to enter the House of Cthulhu, but again the dying heirophant cried out to him:

"Hold! There are more words, O reaver king!"

"More words?" Zar-thule turned with a frown. The old priest, his life quickly ebbing, grinned mirthlessly at the sight of the furry grey blemish that crawled upon the barbarian's forehead over his left eye.

"Aye, more words. Listen: long and long ago, when the world was very young, before Arlyeh and the House of Cthulhu were first sunken into the sea, wise elder gods devised a rune that should Cthulhu's House ever rise and be opened by foolish men, it might be sent down again—even Arlyeh itself, sunken deep once more beneath the salt waters. *Now I say those other words!*"

Swiftly the king reaver leapt, his sword lifting, but ere that blade could fall Hath Vehm cried out those other strange and dreadful words and lo, the whole island shook in the grip of a great earthquake. Now in awful anger Zar-thule's sword fell and hacked off the ancient's whistling and spurting head from his ravened body; but even as the head rolled free, so the island shook itself again, and the ground rumbled and began to break open.

From the open door in the House of Cthulhu, whereinto the host of greedy reavers had rushed to discover the treasure, there now came loud and singularly hideous cries of fear and torment, and of a sudden an even more hideous stench. And now Zar-thule knew truly indeed that there was no treasure.

Great ebony clouds gathered swiftly and livid lightning crashed; winds rose up that blew Zar-thule's long black hair over his face as he crouched in horror before the open door of the House of Cthulhu. Wide and wide were his eyes as he tried to peer beyond the reeking blackness of that nameless, ancient aperture—but a moment later he dropped his great sword to the ground and screamed; even the Reaver of Reavers, screamed most terribly.

For two of his wolves had appeared from out the darkness, more in the manner of whipped puppies than true wolves, shrieking and babbling and scrambling frantically over the queer angles of the orifice's mouth...but they had emerged only to be snatched up and squashed like grapes by titanic tentacles that lashed after them from the dark depths beyond! And these rubbery appendages drew the crushed bodies back into the inky blackness, from

which there instantly issued forth the most monstrously nauseating slobber-
ings and suckings before the writhing members once more snaked forth into
the dawn light. This time they caught at the edges of the opening, and from
behind them pushed forward—*a face*!

Zar-thule gazed upon the enormously bloated visage of Cthulhu and he
screamed again as that terrible Being's awful eyes found him where he
crouched—found him and lit with an hideous light!

The reaver king paused, frozen, petrified, for but a moment, and yet long
enough that the ultimate horror of the thing framed in the titan threshold
seared itself upon his brain forever. Then his legs found their strength. He
turned and fled, speeding away and over the low black hills, and down to
the shore and into his ship, which he somehow managed, even single-handed
and in his frantic terror, to cast off. And all the time in his mind's eye there
burned that fearful sight—the awful *Visage* and *Being* of Lord Cthulhu.

There had been the tentacles, springing from a greenly pulpy head about
which they sprouted like lethiferous petals about the heart of an obscenely
hybrid orchid; a scaled and amorphously elastic body of immense proportions, with clawed feet fore and hind; long, narrow wings ill-fitting the horror that bore them in that it seemed patently impossible for any wings to lift
so fantastic a bulk—and then there had been the eyes! Never before had
Zar-thule seen such evil, rampant and expressed, as in the ultimately leering
malignancy of Cthulhu's eyes!

And Cthulhu was not finished with Zar-thule, for even as the king
reaver struggled madly with his sail the monster came across the low hills
in the dawn light, slobbering and groping down to the very water's edge.
Then, when Zar-thule saw against the morning the mountain that was
Cthulhu, he went mad for a period; flinging himself from side to side of his
ship so that he was like to fall into the sea, frothing at the mouth and babbling horribly in pitiful prayer—aye, even Zar-thule, whose lips never before uttered prayers—to certain benevolent gods of which he had heard.
And it seems that these kind gods, if indeed they exist, must have
heard him.

With a roar and a blast greater than any before, there came the final
shattering that saved Zar-thule for a cruel future, and the entire island split
asunder; even the bulk of Arlyeh breaking into many parts and settling into
the sea. And with a piercing scream of frustrated rage and lust—a scream
which Zar-thule heard with his mind as well as his ears—the monster
Cthulhu sank Him down also with the island and His House beneath the
frothing waves.

A great storm raged then such as might attend the end of the world. Banshee winds howled and demon waves crashed over and about Zar-thule's dragonship, and for two days he gibbered and moaned in the rolling, shuddering scuppers of crippled Redfire before the mighty storm wore itself out.

Eventually, close to starvation, the one-time Reaver of Reavers was discovered becalmed upon a flat sea not far from the fair strands of bright Theem'hdra; and then, in the spicy hold of a rich merchant's ship, he was borne in unto the wharves of the city of Klühn, Theem'hdra's capital.

With long oars he was prodded ashore, stumbling and weak and crying out in his horror of living—for he had gazed upon Cthulhu! The use of the oars had much to do with his appearance, for now Zar-thule was changed indeed, into something which in less tolerant parts of that primal land might certainly have expected to be burned. But the people of Klühn were kindly folk; they burned him not but lowered him in a basket into a deep dungeon cell with torches to light the place, and daily bread and water that he might live until his life was rightly done. And when he was recovered to partial health and sanity, learned men and physicians went to talk with him from above and ask him of his strange affliction, of which all and all stood in awe.

I, Teh Atht, was one of them that went to him, and that was how I came to hear this tale. And I know it to be true, for oft and again over the years I have heard of this Loathly Lord Cthulhu that seeped down from the stars when the world was an inchoate infant. There are legends and there are legends, and one of them is that when times have passed and the stars are right Cthulhu shall slobber forth from His House in Arlyeh again, and the world shall tremble to His tread and erupt in madness at His touch.

I leave this record for men as yet unborn, a record and a warning; leave well enough alone, for that is not dead which deeply dreams, and while perhaps the submarine tides have removed forever the alien taint which touched Arlyeh—that symptom of Cthulhu, which loathsome familiar grew upon Hath Vehm and transferred itself upon certain of Zar-thule's reavers—Cthulhu Himself yet lives on and waits upon those who would set Him free. I know it is so. In dreams…I myself have heard His call!

And when dreams such as these come in the night to sour the sweet embrace of Shoosh, I wake and tremble and pace the crystal-paved floors of my rooms above the Bay of Klühn, until Cthon releases the sun from his net to rise again, and ever and ever I recall the aspect of Zar-thule as last I saw him in the flickering torchlight of his deep-dungeon cell:

A fumbling grey mushroom thing that moved not of its own volition but by reason of the parasite growth which lived upon and within it…

THE NIGHT *SEA-MAID* WENT DOWN

I wrote a handful of stories while serving as a recruiting Sergeant in Leicester. "Sea-Maid" was one of them and I completed it in mid-December 1969. Derleth liked it and found it suitable for inclusion in The Caller of The Black. *Like quite a few other tales of mine, it hints strongly of my fascination with the sea—and with the Cthulhu Mythos, of course.*

J. H. Grier (Director)
Grier & Anderson,
Seagasso,
Sunderland,
Co. Durham.

"Queen of the Wolds Inn,"
Cliffside,
Bridlington,
Yorks.
Nov. 29th

Dear Johnny;

By now I suppose you'll have read my "official" report, sent off to you from this address on the fourteenth of the month, three days after the old *Sea-Maid* went down. How I managed that report I'll never know—but anyway, I've been laid up ever since, so if you've been worried about me or wondering why I haven't let on about my whereabouts till now, well, it's not really been my fault. I just haven't been up to doing much writing since the disaster. Haven't been up to much of anything for that matter. But, as you'll have seen from my report, I've made up my mind to quit, and suppose it's only right I give you what I can of an explanation for my decision. After all, you've been paying me good money to gang-boss your rigs these last four years, and no complaints there. In fact I've no complaints period—nothing *Seagasso* could sort out at any rate—but I'm damned if I'll sink sea-wells again. In fact I'm finished for good with *all* prospecting—sea, land...it makes no difference. Why!— when I think of what *might* have happened at any time in the last four years—

And now it *has* happened!

But there I go stalling again. I'll admit right now that I've torn up three versions of this letter, pondering the results of them reaching you; but now, having thought it all out, frankly I don't give a damn what you do with what I'm going to tell you. You can send an army of head-shrinkers after me if you like. One thing I'm sure of though…whatever I say you won't suspend the North Sea operations—"The country's economy", and all that.

At least my story will give old Anderson a laugh; the hard, unimaginative, stoic old bastard; and no doubt about it the story I have to tell is fantastic enough. I suppose it could be argued that I was "in my cups" that night (and it's true enough, I'd had a few) but I can hold my drink, as you well know. Still, the facts—*as I know them*—drunk or sober, remain simply fantastic.

Now, you'll remember that right from the start there was something funny about the "site" off Hunterby Head. The divers had trouble; the geologists, too, with their instruments; and it was the very devil of a job to float *Sea-Maid* down from Sunderland and get her anchored there; but nevertheless the preliminaries were all completed by late in September. Which, where I'm concerned, was where the trouble started.

We hadn't drilled more than six-hundred feet into the sea-bed when we brought up that first star-shaped thing. Now, Johnny, you know something?—I wouldn't have given two damns for the thing—except I'd seen one before. Old Chalky Grey (who used to be with the "Lescoil" rig *Ocean-Jem*, out of Liverpool) had sent me one only a few weeks before his platform and all the crew, including Chalky himself, went down twelve miles out from Withnersea. Somehow, when I saw what came up in the big core—that same star-shape—well, I couldn't help but think of Chalky and see some sort of nasty parallel. The one he'd sent me came up in a core, too, you see? And *Ocean-Jem* wasn't the only rig lost last year in so-called "freak storms"!

But anyway, regards those star-shaped stones, something more: I wasn't the only one to escape with my life on the night *Sea-Maid* went down. No, that's not strictly true, I was the only one to live through *that night*—but there was a certain member of the team who saw what was coming and got out before it happened—and it was mainly because of the star-shaped things that he went!

Joe Borszowski was the man—superstitious as hell, panicky, spooked at the sight of a mist on the sea—and when he saw the star-thing…!

It happened like this:

We'd drilled that first difficult bore through some very hard stuff down to a depth of some six hundred feet when a core-sample produced the first of the stars. Now, Chalky had reckoned the one he sent me to be a fossilized star-fish of sorts from some time when the North Sea was warm, a very ancient thing; and I must admit that with its five-pointed shape and being the size of a small star-fish I believed him to be correct. Anyway, when I showed the *Sea-Maid* star to old Borszowski he nearly went crackers. He swore we were in for trouble and demanded we all stop drilling and head for land right away. He insisted that our location was "accursed" and generally carried on like a mad thing without attempting to offer anything like a real explanation.

Well, of course I couldn't just leave it at that. If one of the lads was round the twist, as it were (meaning Borszowski) he could well affect the whole operation, jeopardize the whole thing, especially if his madness caught him at an important time. My immediate reaction was to want him off the rig; but the radio had been giving us a bit of bother so that I couldn't call in Wes Atlee, the chopper pilot. Yes, I'd seriously considered having the Pole lifted off by chopper. Riggers can be damned superstitious, as you well know, and I didn't want Joe "infecting" the others. As it turned out, that sort of action wasn't necessary, for in no time at all old Borszowski was round apologising for his outburst and trying to show he was sorry about all the fuss he'd made. Something told me, though, that he'd been quite serious about his fears— whatever they were. And so, to put the Pole's mind at rest (if I possibly could) I decided to have the rig's geologist, Carson, take the star to bits and have a closer look at it and let me know what the thing actually was.

Of course, he'd tell me it was simply a fossilised star-fish—I'd report the fact to Borszowski—things would be back to normal. So naturally when Carson told me that the thing wasn't a fossil, that he didn't know exactly *what* it was, well, I kept that bit of information to myself and told Carson to do the same. I was sure that whatever the trouble had been with Borszowski it wouldn't be helped any by telling him that the star-thing was not a perfectly ordinary, completely explicable object.

The drilling brought up two or three more of the stars down to about a thousand feet but nothing after that, so for a period I forgot all about them. As it happened I should have listened a bit more willingly to old Joe—and I would have, too, if I'd followed my intuition. You see, I'd been spooked myself right from the start. The mists were too heavy, the sea too quiet—things were altogether too queer all the way down the line. Of course, I didn't experience any of the early troubles the divers and geologists had known—I didn't join the rig till she was in position, ready to chew—but I was certainly in on it from then on. It had really started with the sea-phones, even before those stars came along.

Now you know I'm not knocking your 'phones, Johnny, they've been a damn good thing ever since *Seagasso* developed them, giving readings right down to the inch almost, so's we could tell just exactly when the drill was going through into gas or oil. And they didn't let us down this time either—we just failed to recognize or heed their warning, that's all.

In fact there were lots of warnings, but, as I've said, it started out with the sea-phones. We'd put a 'phone down inside each leg of the rig, right onto the sea-bed where they sat listening to the drill as it cut its way through the rocks, picking up the echoes as the bit worked its way down and the sounds of the cutting rebounded from the strata below. And of course, everything they heard we picked up on the surface—duplicated electronically and fed out to us through our computer. Which was why we believed initially that either the computer was on the blink or one of the 'phones was dicky. You see, even when we weren't drilling—when we were changing bits, joining up lengths or lining the bore—we were still getting readings from the computer!

Oh, the trouble was there all right, whatever it was, but it was showing up so regularly that we were fooled into believing the fault to be mechanical. On the seismograph it showed as a regular blip in an otherwise perfectly normal line; a blip that came up bang on time once every five seconds or so—blip…blip…blip—very odd! But, seeing that in every other respect the information coming out of the computer was spot on, no one worried over much about those inexplicable deviations. And, as you'll see, it wasn't till the very end I found a reason for them. Oh, yes, those blips were there right to the finish—but in between there came other difficulties; one of them being the trouble with the fish.

Now, if that sounds a bit funny, well, it was a funny business. The lads had rigged up a small platform, slung twenty feet or so below the main platform and about the same height above the water, and in their off-duty hours when they weren't resting or knocking back a pint in the mess, you could usually see one or two of them down there fishing. First time we found anything odd in the habits of the fish around the rig was one morning when Nick Adams hooked a beauty. All of three feet long, the fish was, wriggling and yellow in the cold November sunlight. Nick just about had the fish docked when the hook came out of its mouth so that it fell among some support-girders down near where leg number four was being washed by a slight swell. It just lay there, flopping about a bit, writhing around in the girders. Nick scrambled down after it with a rope round his waist while his brother Dave hung on to the other end. And what do you think?—when he got down to it, damned if the fish didn't go for him! It actually made to *bite* him, flopping after him on the girders and snapping its jaws until he had to yell for Dave to haul him up. Later he told us about it—how the damned thing hadn't even tried to get back into the sea, seeming more interested in setting its teeth in him than preserving its own life! Now, you'd expect that sort of reaction from a great eel, Johnny, wouldn't you?—but hardly from a cod—not from a North-Sea cod!

From then on Spelmann, the diver, couldn't go down—not *wouldn't* mind you, *couldn't*—the fish simply would not let him! They'd chew on his suit, his air-hose—he got so frightened of them he became literally useless to us. I can't see as I blame him though, especially when I think of what later happened to Davies.

But of course, before Davies' accident, there was that further trouble with Borszowski. It was in the sixth week, when we were expecting to break through at any time, that Joe failed to come back off shore-leave. Instead he sent me a long, rambling letter—a supposedly "explanatory" letter—and to be truthful, when I read it I figured we were better off without him.

The man had quite obviously been cracking up for a long time. He went on about monsters (yes, *monsters!*), sleeping in great caverns underground and especially under the seas, waiting for a chance to take over the surface world. He said that those stone, star-shaped things were seals or barriers that kept these beings ("gods", he called them) imprisoned; that these gods could control the weather to a degree; that they were even capable of influencing the actions of lesser creatures—such as fish, or, occasionally, men—and that he believed one of them must he lying there, locked in the ground beneath the sea, pretty close to where we were drilling. He was afraid we were "going to set it loose"! The only thing that had stopped him pressing the matter earlier (when he'd carried on so about that first star-thing), was that then, as now, he believed we'd all think he was mad! Finally, though, and particularly since the trouble with the fish, he had *had* to warn me. As he put it: "If anything *should* happen, I would never be able to forgive myself if I had not at least tried."

Well, as I've said, Borszowski's letter was rambling and disjointed—but he'd written it in a rather convincing manner, hardly what you'd expect from a real madman. He quoted references from the Holy Bible (particularly Exodus 20:4) and emphasized again his belief that the star-shaped things were nothing more or less than prehistoric pentacles (pentagrams?), laid down by some great race of alien scientists many millions of years ago. He reminded me of the heavy, unusual mists we'd had and of the queer way the cod had gone for Nick Adams. He even brought up again the question of the dicky sea-phones and computer—making, in toto, an altogether disturbing assessment of *Sea-Maid*'s late history as applicable to his own odd fancies.

I did some checking on Joe's background that same afternoon, discovering that he'd travelled far in his earlier years and had also been a bit of a scholar in his time. Too, it had been noticed on occasion—whenever the mists were heavier than usual—that he crossed himself with a certain sign over his left breast. A number of the lads had seen him do it and they all told the same tale of that sign; it was pointed with one point straight up, two down and wide, two more still lower and closer together; yes, his sign was a five-pointed star!

In fact, Borszowski's letter so disturbed me I was still thinking about it that evening after we'd shut down for the day. That was why I was out on the main platform having a quiet pipeful—I can concentrate, you know, with a bit of 'baccy. Dusk was only a few minutes away when the *accident* happened.

Davies, the steel-rigger, was up tightening a few loosened nuts near the top of the rig. Don't ask me where the mist came from, I wouldn't know, but suddenly it was there; swimming up from the sea, a thick, grey blanket that cut visibility down to no more than a few feet. I'd just shouted up to Davies that he better pack it in for the night when I heard his yell and saw his lantern come blazing down out of the greyness. The light disappeared through an open hatch and a second later Davies followed it. He went straight through the hatchway, missing the sides by inches, and then there came the splashes as first the lantern, then the man, hit the sea. In two shakes of a dog's tail Davies was splashing about down there in the mist and yelling fit to ruin his lungs—proving to me and the others who'd rushed from the mess at my call that his fall had done him little harm. We lowered a raft immediately, getting two of the men down to the water in less than a minute, and no one gave it a second thought that Davies wouldn't be picked up. He was, after all, an excellent swimmer. In fact the lads on the raft thought the whole episode was a big laugh—that is, until Davies started to scream.

I mean, there are screams and there are screams, Johnny! Davies wasn't drowning—he wasn't making noises like a drowning man! He wasn't picked up, either.

No less quickly than it had settled, the mist lifted, so that by the time the raft touched water visibility was normal for a November evening—but there was no sign of the rigger. There was something, though, for the whole surface of the sea was silver with fish; big and little, of almost every indigenous species you could imagine; and the way they were acting, apparently trying to throw themselves aboard the raft, I had the lads haul themselves and the raft back up to the platform as soon as it became evident that Davies was gone for good. Johnny!—I swear I'll never eat fish again.

That night I didn't sleep very well at all. Now you know I'm not being callous. I mean, aboard an ocean-going rig after a hard day's work, no matter what has happened during the day, a man usually manages to sleep. Yet that night I just couldn't drop off. I kept going over in my mind all the...well, the *things*. The occurrences, the happenings on the old *Sea-Maid*; the trouble with the instruments; Borszowski's letter; and finally, of course, the queer way we lost Davies—until I thought my head must burst with the burden of wild notions and imaginings going around and around inside it.

Next afternoon the chopper came in (with Wes Atlee complaining about having had to make two runs in two days), and delivered all the booze and goodies for the party the next day or whenever. As you know, we always have a blast when we strike it rich—and this time we figured we were going to. We'd been out of booze a few days by that time (bad weather had stopped Wes from bringing in anything heavier than mail) and so I was running pretty high and dry. Well, you know me, Johnny. I got in the back of the mess with all those bottles and cracked a few. I could see the gear turning from the window, and, over the edge of the platform, the sea all grey and eerie looking, and somehow the idea of getting a load of drink inside me seemed a good one.

I'd been in there topping-up for over an hour when Jeffries, my 21C, got through to me on the 'phone. He was in the instrument-cabin and said he reckoned the drill would go through to pay-dirt within a few minutes. He sounded worried, though, sort of shaky, and when I asked him why this was he didn't rightly seem able to answer—mumbled something about the seismograph mapping those strange blips again; as regular as ever but somehow stronger, closer...

About that time I first noticed the mist swirling up from the sea, a real pea-souper, billowing in to smother the rig and turn the men on the platform to grey ghosts. It muffled the sound of the gear, too, altering the metallic clank and rattle of pulleys and chains to distant, dull *noises* such as I might have expected to hear from the rig if I'd been in a suit deep down under the sea.

It was warm enough in the back room of the mess there, yet unaccountably I found myself shivering as I looked out over the rig and listened to the ghostly sounds of the shrouded men and machinery.

That was when the wind came up. First the mist, then the wind—but I'd never before seen a mist that a good strong wind couldn't blow away! Oh,

I've seen freak storms before, Johnny, but believe me this was *the* freak storm! She came up out of nowhere—not breaking the blanket of grey but driving it round and round like a great mad ghost—blasting the already choppy sea against the old *Sea-Maid*'s supporting legs, flinging up spray to the platform's guard-rails and generally (from what I could see from the window) creating havoc. I'd no sooner recovered from my initial amazement when the 'phone rang again. I picked up the receiver to hear Jimmy Jeffries' somewhat distorted yell of triumph coming over the wires:

"We're *through*, Pongo!" he yelled. "We're through and there's juice on the way up the bore right now!" Then his voice took the shakes again, turning in tone from wild excitement to terror in a second, as the whole rig wobbled on her four great legs. "Holy Heaven!—what...?" the words crackled into my ear. "*What was that*, Pongo? The rig...wait..." I heard the clatter as the 'phone at the other end banged down, but a moment later Jimmy was back. "It's not the rig—the legs are steady as rocks—*it's the whole sea-bed*! Pongo, what's going on. Holy Heaven—!"

This time the 'phone went completely dead as the rig moved again, jerking up and down three or four times and shaking everything loose inside the mess store-room. I still held on to the instrument, though, and just for a second or two it came back to life. Jimmy was screaming incoherently into the other end. I remember then that I yelled for him to get into a life-jacket, that there was something terribly wrong and we were in for big trouble, but I'll never know if he heard me. The rig rocked again, throwing me down on the floor-boards among the debris of bottles, crates, cans and packets; and there, skidding wildly about the tilting floor, I collided with a life-jacket. God only knows what the thing was doing there in the store-room; they were normally kept in the equipment shed and only taken out following storm-warnings (which, it goes without saying, we hadn't had) but somehow I managed to struggle into it and make my way into the mess proper before the next upheaval.

By that time, over the roar of the wind and waves outside (the broken crests of the waves were actually slapping against the outer walls of the mess by then) I could hear a whipping of free-running pulleys and a high-pitched screaming of revving, uncontrolled gears—and there was another sort of screaming....

In a blind panic I was crashing my way through the tumble of tables and chairs in the mess towards the door leading out onto the platform when the greatest shock so far tilted the floor to what must have been thirty degrees and saved me my efforts. In a moment—as I flew against the door, bursting it open and floundering out into the storm—I knew for sure that *Sea-Maid* was going down. Before, it had only been a possibility; a mad, improbable possibility; but now—now I knew for sure. Half stunned from my collision with the door I was thrown roughly against the platform rails, to cling there for dear life in the howling, tearing wind and chill, rushing mist and spray.

And that was when I saw it.

I saw it—and in my utter disbelief—in one crazy moment of understanding—I relaxed my hold on the rails and slid under them into the throat of that banshee, demon storm that howled and tore at the trembling girders of the old *Sea-Maid*.

Even as I fell, a colossal wave smashed into the rig, breaking two of the legs as though they were nothing stronger than match-sticks, and the next instant I was in the sea, picked up and swept away on the great crest of that same wave. Even in the dizzy, sickening rush as the great wave hurled me aloft, I tried to spot *Sea-Maid* in the maelstrom of wind, mist and ocean. It was futile, and I gave it up in order to put all effort to my own battle f or survival.

I don't remember much after that—at least, not until I was picked up, and even that's not too clear. I do remember, though, while fighting the icy water, a dreadful fear of being eaten alive by fish; but so far as I know there were none about. I remember, too, being hauled aboard the life-boat from the mainland in a sea that was flat as a pancake and calm as a mill-pond.

The next really lucid moment came when I woke up to find myself between clean sheets in a Bridlington hospital.

But there, I've held off from telling the important part—and for the same reason Joe Borszowski held off: I don't want to be thought a madman. Well, I'm not mad, Johnny, but I don't suppose for a single moment that you'll take my story seriously—nor, for that matter, will *Seagasso* suspend any of its North-Sea commitments—but at least I'll have the satisfaction of knowing I tried to warn you.

Now I ask you to remember what Borszowski said about great, alien beings lying asleep and imprisoned beneath the bed of the sea; "gods" capable of controlling the actions of lesser creatures, capable of bending the very weather to their wills—and then explain the sight I saw before I found myself floundering in that mad ocean as the old *Sea-Maid* went down.

It was simply a gusher, Johnny, a gusher—but one such as I'd never seen before in my whole life and hope never to have to see again. For instead of reaching to the heavens in one solid black column—it *pulsed* upwards, pumping up in short, strong jets at a rate of about one spurt in every five seconds—

and it wasn't oil, Johnny—oh God!—it wasn't oil! Booze or none I swear I wasn't drunk; not so drunk as to make me *colour-blind*, at any rate!

Like I said, old Borszowski was right, he *must* have been right. There *was* one of those great god-creatures down there, *and our drill had chopped right into the thing!*

Whatever it was it had blood pretty much like ours—good and thick and red—and a great heart strong enough to pump that blood up the borehole right to the surface!

Think of it, that monstrous heart beating down there in the rocks beneath the sea! *How could we have guessed that right from the beginning our instruments had been working at maximum efficiency—that those odd, regular blips recorded on the seismograph had been nothing more than the beating of a great submarine heart?*

All of which explains, I hope, my resignation.

Bernard "Pongo" Jordan,
Bridlington,
Yorks.

NAME AND NUMBER

In the tradition of a good many writers of weird fiction before me (E. A. Poe, Seabury Quinn, and Manly Wade Wellman spring most easily to mind) I created my own"occult investigator" in the shape of Titus Crow. He featured first in "The Caller of The Black", (the first story in this current volume) but was destined for greater adventures in many a story (not to mention several novels) that were still to come. "Name and Number" is one such story. Written in 1981, just one month after I left the Army (following twenty-two years' service), it first appeared in Francesco Cova's excellent glossy Anglo-Italian fanzine (Kadath), in the 5th issue, dated July 1982. Nominated for a British Fantasy Award, which it didn't win, its most recent appearance was in TOR Books' Harry Keogh: Necroscope, & Other Weird Heroes. But the best (in my opinion) Titus Crow story, "Lord of the Worms", can be found in this book's companion volume…

I

Of course, nothing now remains of Blowne House, the sprawling bungalow retreat of my dear friend and mentor Titus Crow, destroyed by tempestuous winds in a freak storm on the night of 4 October 1968, but…

Knowing all I know, or knew, of Titus Crow, perhaps it has been too easy for me to pass off the disastrous events of that night simply as a vindictive attack of dark forces; and while that is exactly what they were, I am now given to wonder if perhaps there was not a lot more to it than met the eye.

Provoked by Crow's and my own involvement with the Wilmarth Foundation (that vast, august and amazingly covert body, dedicated to the detection and the destruction of Earth's elder evil, within and outside of Man himself, and working in the sure knowledge that Man is but a small and comparatively recent phenomenon in a cosmos which has known sentience, good and evil, through vast and immeasurable cycles of time), dark forces did indeed destroy Blowne House. In so doing they effectively removed Titus Crow from the scene, and as for myself…I am but recently returned to it.

But since visiting the ruins of Crow's old place all these later years (perhaps because the time flown in between means so very little to me?), I have come to wonder more and more about the *nature* of that so well-remembered attack, the nature of the very winds themselves—those twisting, rending, tearing winds—which fell with such intent and purpose upon the house and bore it to the ground. In considering them I find myself casting my mind back to a time even more remote, when Crow first outlined for me the facts in the strange case of Mr. Sturm Magruser V.

Crow's letter—a single hand-written sheet in a blank, sealed envelope, delivered by a taxi driver and the ink not quite dry—was at once terse and cryptic, which was not unusual and did not at all surprise me. When Titus Crow was idling, then all who wished anything to do with him must also bide their time, but when he was in a hurry—

> Henri,
> Come as soon as you can, midnight would be fine. I expect you will stay the night. If you have not eaten, don't—there is food here. I have something of a story to tell you, and in the morning we are to visit a cemetery!
> Until I see you—
> Titus

The trouble with such invitations was this: I had never been able to refuse them! For Crow being what he was, one of London's foremost occultists, and my own interest in such matters amounting almost to obsession—why, for all its brevity, indeed by the very virtue of that brevity—Crow's summons was more a royal command!

And so I refrained from eating, wrote a number of letters which could not wait, enveloped and stamped them, and left a note for my housekeeper, Mrs. Adams, telling her to post them. She was to expect me when she saw me, but in any matter of urgency I might be contacted at Blowne House.

Doubtless the dear lady, when she read that address, would complain bitterly to herself about the influence of "that dreadful Crow person," for in her eyes Titus had always been to blame for my own deep interest in darkling matters. In all truth, however, my obsession was probably inherited, sealed into my personality as a permanent stamp of my father, the great New Orleans mystic Etienne-Laurent de Marigny.

Then, since the hour already approached twelve and I would be late for my "appointment", I phoned for a taxi and double-checked that my one or two antique treasures were safely locked away; and finally I donned my overcoat. Half an hour or so later, at perhaps a quarter to one, I stood on Crow's doorstep and banged upon his heavy oak door; and having heard the arrival of my taxi, he was there at once to greet me. This he did with his customary grin (or enigmatic smile?), his head cocked slightly to one side in an almost inquiring posture. And once again I was ushered into the marvellous Aladdin's cave which was Blowne House.

Now, Crow had been my friend ever since my father sent me out of America as a child in the late '30s, and no man knew him better than I; and yet his personality was such that whenever I met him—however short the intervening time—I would always be impressed anew by his stature, his leonine good looks, and the sheer weight of intellect which seemed invariably to shine out from behind those searching, dark eyes of his. In his flame-red, wide-sleeved dressing gown, he might easily be some wizard from the pages of myth or fantasy.

In his study he took my overcoat, bade me sit in an easy chair beside a glowing fire, tossed a small log onto ruddy embers and poured me a customary brandy before seating himself close by. And while he was thus engaged I took my chance to gaze with fascination and unfeigned envy all about that marvellous room.

Crow himself had designed and furnished that large room to contain most of what he considered important to his world, and certainly I could have spent ten full years there in constant study of the contents without absorbing or even understanding a fifth part of what I read or examined. However, to give a brief and essentially fleshless account of what I could see from my chair:

His "library", consisting of one entire wall of shelves, contained such works as the abhorrent *Cthaat Aquadingen* (in a binding of human skin!), Feery's *Original Notes on the Necronomicon* (the complete book, as opposed to my own abridged copy), Wendy-Smith's translation of the *G'harne Fragments*, a possibly faked but still priceless copy of the *Pnakotic Manuscripts*,

Justin Geoffrey's *People of the Monolith*, a literally fabulous *Cultes des Goules* (which, on my next birthday, having derived all he could from it, he would present to me), the *Geph Transcriptions*, Wardle's *Notes on Nitocris*, Urbicus' *Frontier Garrison*, circa A.D. 183, Plato's *Atlantis*, a rare, illustrated, pirated and privately printed *Complete Works of Poe* in three sumptuous volumes, the far more ancient works of such as Josephus, Magnus, Levi and Erdschluss, and a connected set of volumes on oceanic lore and legend which included such works as Gantley's *Hydrophinnae* and Konrad von Gerner's *Fischbuch* of 1598. And I have merely skimmed the surface…

In one dim corner stood an object which had been a source of fascination for me, and no less for Crow himself: a great hieroglyphed, coffin-shaped monstrosity of a grandfather clock, whose tick was quite irregular and abnormal, and whose four hands moved independently and without recourse to any time system with which I was remotely familiar. Crow had bought the thing in auction some years previously, at which time he had mentioned his belief that it had once belonged to my father—of which I had known nothing, not at that time.

As for the general decor and feel of the place:

Silk curtains were drawn across wide windows; costly Boukhara rugs were spread on a floor already covered in fine Axminister; a good many Aubrey Beardsley originals—some of them most erotic—hung on the walls in equally valuable antique rosewood frames; and all in all the room seemed to exude a curiously mixed atmosphere of rich, warm, Olde World gentility on the one hand, a strange and alien chill of outer spheres on the other.

And thus I hope I have managed to convey something of the nature of Titus Crow and of his study—and of his studies—in that bungalow dwelling on Leonard's Heath known as Blowne House… As to why I was there—

"I suppose you're wondering," Crow said after a while, "just why I asked you to come? And at such an hour on such a chilly night, when doubtless you've a good many other things you should be doing? Well, I'll not keep you in suspense—but first of all I would greatly appreciate your opinion of something." He got up, crossed to his desk and returned with a thick book of newspaper cuttings, opening it to a previously marked page. Most of the cuttings were browned and faded, but the one Crow pointed out to me was only a few weeks old. It was a photograph of the head and shoulders of a man, accompanied by the following legend:

> Mr. Sturm Magruser, head of Magruser Systems UK, the weapons manufacturing company of world repute, is on the point of winning

for his company a £2,000,000 order from the Ministry of Defence in respect of an at-present "secret" national defence system. Mr. Magruser, who himself devised and is developing the new system, would not comment when he was snapped by our reporter leaving the country home of a senior Ministry of Defence official, but it has been rumoured for some time that his company is close to a breakthrough on a defence system which will effectively make the atom bomb entirely obsolete. Tests are said to be scheduled for the near future, following which the Ministry of Defence is expected to make its final decision...

"Well?" Crow asked as I read the column again.

I shrugged. "What are you getting at?"

"It makes no impression?"

"I've heard of him and his company, of course," I answered, "though I believe this is the first time I've actually seen a picture of him—but apart from—"

"Ah!" Crow cut in. "Good! This is the first time you've seen his picture: and him a prominent figure and his firm constantly in the news and so on. Me too."

"Oh?" I was still puzzled.

"Yes, it's important, Henri, what you just said. In fact, I would hazard a guess that Mr. Magruser is one of the world's least-photographed men."

"So? Perhaps he's camera shy."

"Oh, he is, he is—and for a very good reason: We'll get to it—eventually. Meanwhile, let's eat!"

Now, this is a facet of Crow's personality which did annoy me: his penchant for leaping from one subject to another, willy-nilly, with never a word of explanation, leaving one constantly stumbling in the dark. He could only do it, of course, when he knew that his audience was properly hooked. But in my case I do not expect he intended any torment; he merely offered me the opportunity to use my mind. This I seized upon, while he busied himself bringing out cold fried chicken from his kitchen.

II

Sturm Magruser...A strange name, really. Foreign, of course. Hungarian, perhaps? As the "Mag" in "Magyar"? I doubted it; even though his features were decidedly Eastern or Middle Eastern; for they were rather pale, too. And what of his first name, Sturm? If only I were a little more proficient in tongues, I might make something of it. And what of the man's reticence, and of Crow's comment that he stood amongst the least-photographed of men?

We finished eating. "What do you make of the *V* after his name?" Crow asked.

"Hmm? Oh, it's a common enough vogue nowadays," I answered, "particularly in America. It denotes that he's the fifth of his line, the fifth Sturm Magruser."

Crow nodded and frowned. "You'd think so, wouldn't you? But in this case it can't possibly be. No, for he changed his name by deed poll after his parents died." He had grown suddenly intense, but before I could ask him why, he was off again. "And what would you give him for nationality, or rather origin?"

I took a stab at it. "Romanian?"

He shook his head. "Persian."

I smiled. "I was way out, wasn't I?"

"What about his face?" Crow pressed.

I picked up the book of cuttings and looked at the photograph again. "It's a strange face, really. Pale somehow…"

"He's an albino."

"Ah!" I said. "Yes, pale and startled—at least, in this picture—displeased at being snapped, I suppose."

Again he nodded. "You suppose correctly… All right, Henri, enough of that for the moment. Now I'll tell you what I made of this cutting—Magruser's picture and the story when first I saw it. Now, as you know I collect all sorts of cuttings from one source or another, tidbits of fact and fragments of information which interest me or strike me as unusual. Most occultists, I'm told, are extensive collectors of all sorts of things. You yourself are fond of antiques, old books and outré bric-a-brac, much as I am, but as yet without my dedication. And yet if you examine all of my scrapbooks you'll probably discover that this would appear to be the most mundane cutting of them all. At least on the surface. For myself, I found it the most frightening and disturbing."

He paused to pour more brandy and I leaned closer to him, fascinated to find out exactly what he was getting at. "Now," he finally continued, "I'm an odd sort of chap, as you'll appreciate, but I'm not eccentric—not in the popular sense of the word. Or if I am," he hurried on, "it's of my choosing. That is to say, I believe I'm mentally stable."

"You are the sanest man I ever met," I told him.

"I wouldn't go that far," he answered, "and you may soon have reason for reevaluation, but for the moment I *am* sane. How then might I explain the loathing, the morbid repulsion, the absolute shock of horror which struck me almost physically upon opening the pages of my morning newspaper and coming upon that picture of Magruser? I could not explain it—not immediately…" He paused again.

"Presentiment?" I asked. "A forewarning?"

"Certainly!" he answered. "But of what, and from where? And the more I looked at that damned picture, the more sure I became that I was on to something monstrous! Seeing him—that face, startled, angered, trapped by the camera—and despite the fact that I could not possibly know him, I *recognised* him."

"Ah!" I said. "You mean that you've known him before, under his former name?"

Crow smiled, a trifle wearily I thought. "The world has known him before under several names," he answered. Then the smile slipped from his face. "Talking of names, what do you make of his forename?"

"Sturm? I've already considered it. German, perhaps?"

"Good! Yes, German. His mother was German, his father Persian, both nationalized Americans in the early 1900s. They left America to come here during McCarthy's Unamerican Activities witch-hunts. Sturm Magruser, incidentally, was born on first April 1921. An important date, Henri, and not just because it was April Fool's Day."

"A fairly young man," I answered, "to have reached so powerful a position."

"Indeed." Crow nodded. "He would have been forty-three in a month's time."

"Would have been?" I was surprised by Crow's tone of finality. "Is he dead then?"

"Mercifully, yes," he answered, "Magruser and his project with him! He died the day before yesterday, on fourth March 1964, also an important date. It was in yesterday's news, but I'm not surprised you missed it. He wasn't given a lot of space, and he leaves no mourners that I know of. As to his 'secret weapon'"—and here Crow gave an involuntary little shudder— "the secret has gone with him. For that, too, we may be thankful."

"Then the cemetery you mentioned in your note is where he's to be interred?" I guessed.

"Where he's to be cremated," he corrected me. "Where his ashes are to be scattered to the winds."

"Winds!" I snapped my fingers. "Now I have it! *Sturm* means 'storm'— it's the German word for storm!"

Crow nodded. "Again correct," he said. "But let's not start to add things up too quickly."

"Add things up?" I snorted. "My friend, I'm completely lost!"

"Not completely," he denied. "What you have is a jigsaw puzzle without a picture to work from. Difficult, but once you have completed the frame the rest will slowly piece itself together. Now, then, I was telling you about the time three weeks ago when I saw Magruser's picture.

"I remember I was just up, still in my dressing gown, and I had just brought the paper in here to read. The curtains were open and I could see out into the garden. It was quite cold but relatively mild for the time of the year. The morning was dry and the heath seemed to beckon me, so that I made up my mind to take a walk. After reading the day's news and after breakfast, I would dress and take a stroll outdoors. Then I opened my newspaper—and Sturm Magruser's face greeted me!

"Henri, I dropped the paper as if it were a hot iron! So shaken was I that I had to sit down or risk falling. Now, I'm a fairly sturdy chap, and you can well imagine the sort of shock my system would require so to disturb it. Then as I sat down in my chair and stooped to recover the newspaper—the other thing.

"Out in the garden, a sudden stirring of wind. The hedgerow trembling and last year's leaves blowing across my drive. And birds startled to flight, as by the sudden presence of someone or thing I could not see. And the sudden gathering and rushing of spiralling winds, dust devils that sucked up leaves and grit and other bits of debris and shot them aloft. Dust devils, Henri, in March—in England—half a dozen of them that paraded all about Blowne House for the best part of thirty minutes! In any other circumstance, a marvellous, fascinating phenomenon."

"But not for you?"

"No." He shook his head. "Not then. I'll tell you what they signified for me, Henri. They told me that just as I had recognised *something*, so I had been recognised! Do you understand?"

"Frankly, no," and it was my turn to shake my head.

"Let it pass," he said after a moment. "Suffice it to say that there were these strange spiralling winds, and that I took them as a sign that indeed my psychic sense had detected something unutterably dangerous and obscene in this man Sturm Magruser. And I was so frightened by my discovery that I at once set about to discover all I could of him, so that I should know what the threat was and how best to deal with it."

"Can I stop you for a moment?" I requested.

"Eh? Oh, certainly."

"Those dates you mentioned as being important, Magruser's birth and death dates. In what way important?"

"Ah! We shall get to that, Henri." He smiled. "You may or may not know it, but I'm also something of a numerologist."

Now it was my turn to smile. "You mean like those fellows who measure the Great Pyramid and read in their findings the secrets of the universe?"

"Do not be flippant, de Marigny!" he answered at once, his smile disappearing in an instant. "I meant no such thing. And in any case, don't be in too great a hurry to discredit the pyramidologists. Who are you to say what may or may not be? Until you have studied a thing for yourself, treat it with respect."

"Oh!" was all I could say.

"As for birth and death dates, try these: 1889, 1945."

I frowned, shrugged, said: "They mean nothing to me. Are they, too, important?"

"They belong to Adolf Hitler," he told me; "and if you add the individual numbers together you'll discover that they make five sets of nine. Nine is an important number in occultism, signifying death. Hitler's number, 99999, shows him to have been a veritable Angel of Death, and no one could deny that! Incidentally, if you multiply five and nine you get forty-five, which are the last two numbers in 1945—the year he died. This is merely one example of an ancient science. Now, please, Henri, no more scoffing at numerology…"

Deflated, still I was beginning to see a glimmer of light in Crow's reasoning. "Ah!" I said again. "And Sturm Magruser, like Hitler, has dates which add up to forty-five? Am I right? Let me see: the 1st of the 4th 1921—that's eighteen—and the 4th of the 3rd 1964. That's forty-five!"

Crow nodded, smiling again. "You're a clever man, Henri, yes—but you've missed the most important aspect of the thing. But never mind that for now, let me get back to my story…

"I have said that I set about to discover all I could of this fellow with the strange name, the camera-shy manner, the weight of a vast international concern behind him—and the power to frighten the living daylights out of me, which no other man ever had before. And don't ask me how, but I knew I had to work fast. There wasn't a great deal of time left before…before whatever was coming came.

"First, however, I contacted a friend of mine at the British Museum, the curator of the Special Books Department, and asked him to search something out for me in the *Necronomicon*. I must introduce you one day, Henri. He's a marvellous chap. Not quite all there, I fancy—he can't be, to work in that place—but so free of vice and sin, so blindly naive and innocent, that the greatest possible evils would bounce right off him, I'm sure. Which is just as well, I suppose. Certainly I would never ask an inquiring or susceptible mind that it lay itself open to the perils of Alhazred's book.

"And at last I was able to concentrate on Magruser. This was about midday and my mind had been working frantically for several hours, so that already I was beginning to feel tired—mentally if not physically. I was also experiencing a singular emotion, a sort of morbid suspicion that I was being watched, and that the observer lurked somewhere in my garden!

"Putting this to the back of my mind, I began to make discreet telephone inquiries about Magruser, but no sooner had I voiced his name than the feeling came over me again, more strongly than before. It was as if a cloud of unutterable malignity, heavy with evil, had settled suddenly over the entire house. And starting back from the telephone, I saw once again the shadow of a nodding dust devil where it played with leaves and twigs in the centre of my drive.

III

"Now my fear turned to anger. Very well, if it was war…then I must now employ weapons of my own. Or if not weapons, defences, certainly.

"I won't go into details, Henri, but you know the sort of thing I mean. I have long possessed the necessary knowledge to create barriers of a sort against evil influences; no occultist or student of such things worth his salt would ever be without them. But it had recently been my good fortune to obtain a certain—shall we call it 'charm'?—allegedly efficacious above all others.

"As to how this 'charm' happened my way:

"In December Thelred Gustau had arrived in London from Iceland, where he had been studying Surtsey's volcanic eruption. During that eruption, Gustau had fished from the sea an item of extreme antiquity—indeed, a veritable time capsule from an age undreamed of. When he contacted me in mid-December, he was still in a high fever of excitement. He needed my skills, he said, to help him unravel a mystery 'predating the very dinosaurs'. His words.

"I worked with him until mid-January, when he suddenly received an offer from America in respect of a lecture tour there. It was an offer he could not refuse—one which would finance his researches for several years to come—and so, off he went. By that time I had become so engrossed with the work I almost went with him. Fortunately I did not." And here he paused to refill our glasses.

"Of course," I took the opportunity to say, "I knew you were extremely busy with something. You were so hard to contact, and then always at Gustau's Woolwich address. But what exactly were you working on?"

"Ah!" he answered. "That is something which Thelred Gustau himself will have to reveal—which I expect he'll do shortly. Though who'll take him seriously, heaven only knows. As to what I may tell you of it—I'll have to have your word that it will be kept in the utmost secrecy."

"You know you have it," I answered.

"Very well… During the course of the eruption, Surtsey ejected a…a *container*, Henri, the 'time capsule' I have mentioned. Inside—fantastic!

"It was a record from a prehistoric world, Theem'hdra, a continent at the dawn of time, and it had been sent to us down all the ages by one of that continent's greatest magicians, the wizard Teh Atht, descendant of the mighty Mylakhrion. Alas, it was in the unknown language of that primal land, in Teh Atht's own hand, and Gustau had accidentally lost the means of its translation. But he did have a key, and he had his own great genius, and—"

"And he had you." I smiled. "One of the country's greatest paleographers."

"Yes," said Crow, matter-of-factly and without pride, "second only to Professor Gordon Walmsley of Goole. Anyway, I helped Gustau where I could, and during the work I came across a powerful spell against injurious magic and other supernatural menaces. Gustau allowed me to make a copy for myself, which is how I came to be in possession of a fragment of elder magic from an age undreamed of. From what I could make of it, Theem'hdra had existed in an age of wizards, and Teh Atht himself had used this very charm or spell to ward off evil.

"Well, I had the thing, and now I decided to employ it. I set up the necessary paraphernalia and induced within myself the required mental state. This took until well into the afternoon, and with each passing minute the sensation of impending doom deepened about the house, until I was almost prepared to flee the place and let well alone. And, if I had not by now been certain that such flight would be a colossal dereliction of duty, I admit I would have done so.

"As it was, when I had willed myself to the correct mental condition, and upon the utterance of certain words—the effect was instantaneous!

"Daylight seemed to flood the whole house; the gloom fled in a moment; my spirits soared, and outside in the garden a certain ethereal watchdog collapsed in a tiny heap of rubbish and dusty leaves. Teh Atht's rune had proved itself effective indeed..."

"And then you turned your attention to Sturm Magruser?" I prompted him after a moment or two.

"Not that night, no. I was exhausted, Henri. The day had taken so much out of me. No, I could do no more that night. Instead I slept, deeply and dreamlessly, right through the evening and night until the jangling of my telephone awakened me at nine o'clock on the following morning."

"Your friend at the Rare Books Department?" I guessed.

"Yes, enlisting my aid in narrowing down his field of research. As you'll appreciate, the *Necronomicon* is a large volume—compared to which Feery's *Notes* is a pamphlet—and many of its sections appear to be almost repetitious in their content. The trouble was, I wasn't even certain that it contained what I sought; only that I believed I had read it there. If not—" and he waved an expansive hand in the direction of his own more than appreciable occult library "—then the answer must be here somewhere—whose searching out would form an equally frustrating if not utterly impossible task. At least in the time allowed."

"You keep hinting at this urgency." I frowned. "What do you mean, 'the time allowed?'"

"Why," he answered, "the time in which Magruser must be disposed of, of course!"

"Disposed of?" I could hardly believe my ears.

Crow sighed and brought it right out in the open: "The time in which I must kill him!" he said.

I tried to remain calm, tried not to seem too flippant when I said, "So, you had resolved to do away with him. This was necessary?"

"Very. And once my enquiries began to produce results, why, then his death became more urgent by the minute! For over the next few days I turned up some very interesting and very frightening facts about our Mr. Magruser, not the least of them concerning his phenomenal rise from obscurity and the amount of power he controlled here and abroad. His company extended to no less than seven different countries, with a total of ten plants or factories engaged in the manufacture of weapons of war. Most of them conventional weapons—for the moment. Ah, yes! And those numbers too, Henri, are important.

"As for his current project—the completion of this 'secret' weapon or 'defence system', in this I was to discover the very root and nature of the evil, after which I was convinced in my decision that indeed Magruser must go!"

The time was now just after three in the morning and the fire had burned very low. While Crow took a break from talking and went to the kitchen to prepare a light snack, I threw logs on the fire and shivered, not merely because of the chill the night had brought. Such was Crow's story and his method of delivery that I myself was now caught up in its cryptic strangeness, the slowly strangling threads of its skein. Thus I paced the floor and pondered all he had told me, not least his stated intention to—murder?—Sturm Magruser, who now apparently was dead.

Passing Crow's desk I noticed an antique family Bible in two great volumes, the New Testament lying open, but I did not check book or chapter. Also littering his desk were several books on cryptology, numerology, even one on astrology, in which "science" Crow had never to my knowledge displayed a great deal of faith or interest. Much in evidence was a well-thumbed copy of Walmsley's *Notes on Deciphering Codes, Cryptograms, and Ancient Inscriptions*, also an open notebook of obscure jottings and diagrams. My friend had indeed been busy.

Over cheese and crackers we carried on, and Crow took up his tale once more by hinting of the awesome power of Magruser's "secret" weapon.

"Henri," he began, "there is a tiny island off the Orkneys which, until mid-1961, was green, lovely, and a sanctuary for seabirds. Too small and isolated to settle, and far too cold and open to the elements in winter, the place was never inhabited and only rarely visited. Magruser bought it, worked there, and by February '62—"

"Yes?"

"A dustbowl!"

"A dustbowl?" I repeated him. "Chemicals, you mean?"

Crow shrugged. "I don't know how his weapon works exactly, only what it produces. Also that it needs vast amounts of energy to trigger it. From what I've been able to discover, he used the forces of nature to fuel his experiment in the Orkneys, the enormous energies of an electrical storm. Oh, yes, and one other thing: the weapon was not a defense system!"

"And of course you also know," I took a stab at it, "what he intended to do with this weapon?"

"That too, yes." He nodded. "He intended to destroy the world, reduce us to savagery, return us to the Dark Ages. In short, to deliver a blow from which the human race would never recover."

"But—"

"No, let me go on. Magruser intended to turn the world into a desert, start a chain reaction that couldn't be stopped. It may even have been worse than I suspected. He may have aimed at total destruction—no survivors at all!"

"You had proof?"

"I had evidence… As for proof: he's dead, isn't he?"

"You did kill him, then?"

"Yes."

After a little while I asked, "What evidence did you have?"

"Three types of evidence, really," he answered, relaxing again in his chair. "One: the evidence of my own five senses—and possibly that sixth sense by which I had known him from the start. Two: the fact that he had carried out his experiments in other places, several of them, always with the same result. And three—"

"Yes?"

"That too was information I received through government channels. I worked for MOD as a very young man, Henri. Did you know that? It was the War Department in those days. During the war I cracked codes for them, and I advised them on Hitler's occult interests."

"No," I said, "I never knew that."

"Of course not," he replied. "No man has my number, Henri," and he smiled. "Did you know that there's supposed to be a copy of the *Necronomicon* buried in a filled-in bunker just across the East German border in Berlin? And did you know that in his last hour Hitler was approached in his own bunker by a Jew—can you imagine that?—a Jew who whispered something to him before he took his life? I believe I know what that man whispered, Henri. I think he said these words: 'I know you, Adolf Hitler!'"

"Titus," I said, "there are so many loose ends here that I'm trying to tie together. You've given me so many clues, and yet—"

"It will all fit, Henri," he calmed me. "It will fit. Let me go on…"

"When I discovered that Magruser's two-million-pound 'order' from the MOD was not an order at all but merely the use of two million pounds' worth of equipment—and as soon as I knew what that equipment was— then I guessed what he was up to. To clinch matters there finally came that call from the British Museum, and at last I had all the information I needed. But that was not until after I had actually met the man face-to-face.

"First, the government 'equipment' Magruser had managed to lay his hands on: two million pounds' worth of atomic bombs!"

IV

"What?" I was utterly astonished. "You're joking!"

"No," he answered, "I am not joking. They were to provide the power he needed to trigger his doomsday weapon, to start the chain reaction. A persuasive man, Magruser, and you may believe that there's hell to pay right now in certain government circles. I have let it be known—anonymously, of course—just exactly what he was about and the holocaust the world so narrowly escaped. Seven countries, Henri, and seven atomic bombs. Seven simultaneous detonations powering his own far more dreadful weapon, forging the links in a chain reaction which would spread right across the world!"

"But…how…when was this to happen?" I stammered.

"Today," he answered, "at ten o'clock in the morning, a little more than five hours from now. The bombs were already in position in his plants, waiting for the appointed time. By now of course they have been removed and the plants destroyed. And now too, Britain will have to answer to the heads of six foreign powers; and certain lesser heads will roll, you may be sure. But very quietly, and the world as a whole shall never know."

"But what was his purpose?" I asked. "Was he a madman?"

He shook his head. "A madman? No. Though he was born of human flesh, he was not even a man, not completely. Or perhaps he was more than a man. A force? A power…

"A week ago I attended a party at the home of my friend in the MOD. Magruser was to be there, which was why I *had* to be there—and I may tell you that took a bit of arranging. And all very discreetly, mind you, for I could not let any other person know of my suspicions. Who would have believed me anyway?

"At the party, eventually I cornered Magruser—as strange a specimen as ever you saw—and to come face-to-face with him was to confirm my quarry's identity. I now knew beyond any question of doubt that indeed he was the greatest peril the world has ever faced! If I sound melodramatic, Henri, it can't be helped.

"And yet to look at him…any other man might have felt pity. As I have said, he was an albino, with hair white as snow and flesh to match, so that his only high points seemed to lie in pallid pulses beating in his throat and forehead. He was tall and spindly, and his head was large but not overly so; though his cranium did display a height and width which at one and the same time hinted of imbecility and genius. His eyes were large, close together, pink, and their pupils were scarlet. I have known women—a perverse group at best—who would call him attractive, and certain men who might envy him his money, power, and position. As for myself, I found him repulsive! But of course my prejudice was born of knowing the truth.

"He did not wish to be there, that much was plain, for he had that same trapped look about him which came through so strongly in his photograph. He was afraid, Henri, afraid of being stopped. For of course he knew that someone, somewhere, had recognized him. What he did not yet know was that I was that someone.

"Oh, he was nervous, this Magruser. Only the fact that he was to receive his answer that night, the go-ahead from the ministry, had brought him out of hiding. And he did receive that go-ahead, following which I cornered him, as I have said."

"Wait," I begged him. "You said he knew that someone had recognised him. How did he know?"

"He knew at the same moment I knew, Henri, at the very instant when those spinning winds of his sprang up in my garden! But I had destroyed them, and fortunately before he could discover my identity. Oh, you may be sure he had tried to trace me, but I had been protected by the barriers I had placed about Blowne House. Now, however, I too was out in the open…

"But I still can't see how the British government could be tricked into giving him a handful of atomic bombs!" I pressed. "Are we all in the hands of lunatics?"

Crow shook his head. "You should know by now," he said, "that the British give nothing for nothing. What the government stood to gain was far greater than a measly two million pounds. Magruser had promised to deliver a power screen, Henri, a dome of force covering the entire land, to be switched on and off at will, making the British Isles totally invulnerable!"

"And we believed him?"

"Oh, there had been demonstrations, all faked, and it had been known for a long time that he was experimenting with a 'national defence system'. And remember, my friend, that Magruser had never once stepped out of line. He was the very model of a citizen, a man totally above suspicion who supported every welfare and charity you could name. Why, I believe that on occasion he had even funded the government itself; but for all this he had not the means of powering his damnable weapons. And now you begin to see something of the brilliance of the man, something of his fiendishness.

"But to get back to what I was saying: I finally cornered him, we were about to be introduced, I even stuck out my hand for him to shake, and—

"At that very moment a window blew in and the storm which had been blowing up for over an hour rushed into the room. Rushing winds, Henri, and fifty ladies and gentlemen spilling their drinks and hanging on to their hats—and a whirling dervish of a thing that sucked up invitation cards and flowers from vases and paper napkins and flew *between* Magruser and myself like…like one of hell's own devils!

"How his pink eyes narrowed and glared at me then, and in another moment he had stepped quickly out of my reach. By the time order was restored Magruser was gone. He had rushed out of the house to be driven away, probably back to his plant outside Oxford.

"Well, I too left in something of a hurry, but not before my friend had promised not to tell Magruser who I was. Later, Magruser did indeed call him, only to be fobbed off with the answer that I must have been a gate-crasher. And so I was safe from him—for the moment.

"When I arrived home my telephone was ringing, and at first I was of a mind not to pick it up but…it was the information I had been waiting for, a quotation from the Mad Arab himself, Abdul Alhazred." Here Crow paused to get up, go to his desk, rummage about for a second or two and return with a scrap of paper. He seated himself once more and said: "Listen to this, Henri:

'Many and multiform are ye dim horrors of Earth, infesting her ways from ye very prime. They sleep beneath ye unturned stone; they rise with ye tree from its root; they move beneath ye sea, and in subterranean places they dwell in ye inmost adyta. Some there are long known to man, and others as yet unknown, abiding ye terrible latter days of their revealing. One such is an evil born of a curse, for ye Greatest Old One, before He went Him down into His place to be sealed therein and sunken under ye sea, uttered a cry which rang out to ye very corners of ye All; and He cursed this world then and forever. And His curse was this: that whosoever inhabit this world which was become his prison, there should breed amongst them and of their flesh great traitors who would ever seek to destroy them and so leave ye world cleared off for ye day of His return. And when they heard this great curse, them that held Him thrust Him down where He could do no more harm. And because they were good, they sought to eradicate ye harm He had willed, but could not do so. Thus they worked a counter spell, which was this: that there would always be ones to know the evil ones when they arose and waxed strong, thus protecting ye innocents from His great curse. And this also did they arrange: that in their fashion ye evil ones would reveal themselves, and that any man with understanding might readily dispose of such a one by seizing him and saying unto him, "I know you," and by revealing his number…'

"And in the end it was as simple as that, Henri…

"Late as the evening had grown, still I set about to strengthen those psychic or magical protections I had built about Blowne House. Also, I placed about my own person certain charms for self-protection when I was abroad and outside the safety of these stout walls; all of which took me until the early hours of the morning. That day—that very day—Sturm Magruser would be collecting his deadly detonators, the triggers for his devilish device; and in my mind's eye I pictured a vehicle pulling up at some innocuous-seeming but well-guarded and lethally supplied establishment, and the driver showing a pass, and documents being signed in triplicate and the subsequent very careful loading of seven heavy crates.

"There would be a pair of executive jets waiting on the private runway inside Magruser's Oxford plant, and these would take six of the atomic bombs off to their various destinations around the globe. And so it can be seen that my time was running down. Tired as I was, worn down by worry and work, still I must press on and find the solution to the threat."

"But surely you had the solution?" I cut in. "It was right there in that passage from Alhazred."

"I had the means to destroy him, Henri, yes—but I did not have the means of delivery! The only thing I could be sure of was that he was still in this country, at his centre of operations. But how to get near him, now that he knew me?"

"He knew you?"

Crow sighed. "My face, certainly, for we had now met. Or almost. And if I knew my quarry, by now he might also have discovered my name and particulars. Oh, yes, Henri. For just as I have my means, be sure Magruser had his. Well, obviously I could not stay at Blowne House, not after I realised how desperate the man must be to find me. I must go elsewhere, and quickly.

"And I did go, that very night. I drove up to Oxford."

"To Oxford?"

"Yes, into the very lion's den, as it were. In the morning I found a suitable hotel and garaged my car, and a little later I telephoned Magruser."

"Just like that?" Again I was astonished. "You telephoned him?"

"No, not just like that at all," he answered. "First I ordered and waited for the arrival of a taxi. I dared not use my Mercedes for fear that by now he knew both the car and its number." He smiled tiredly at me. "You are beginning to see just how important numbers really are, eh, Henri?"

I nodded. "But please go on. You said you phoned him?"

"I tried the plant first and got the switchboard, and was told that Mr. Magruser was at home and could not be disturbed. I said that it was important, that I had tried his home number and was unable to obtain him, and that I must be put through to him at once."

"And they fell for that? Had you really tried his home number?"

"No, it's not listed. And to physically go near his estate would be sheer lunacy, for surely the place would be heavily guarded."

"But then they *must* have seen through your ruse," I argued. "If his number was ex-directory, how could you possibly tell them that you knew it?"

Again Crow smiled. "If I was the fellow I pretended to be, I would know it," he answered.

I gasped. "Your friend from the ministry! You used his name."

"Of course," said Crow. "And now we see again the importance of names, eh, my friend? Well, I was put through and eventually Magruser spoke to me, but I knew that it was him before ever he said a word. The very sound of his breathing came to me like exhalations from a tomb! 'This is Magruser,' he said, his voice full of suspicion. 'Who is speaking?'

"'Oh, I think you know me, Sturm Magruser,' I answered. "Even as I know you!'"

V

"There was a sharp intake of breath. Then: 'Mr. Titus Crow,' he said. 'You are a most resourceful man. Where are you?'

"'On my way to see you, Magruser,' I answered.

"'And when may I expect you?'

"'Sooner than you think. I have your number!'

"At that he gasped again and slammed the phone down; and now I would discover whether or not my preliminary investigation stood me in good stead. Now, too, I faced the most danger-fraught moments of the entire business.

"Henri, if you had been Magruser, what would you do?"

"Me? Why, I'd stay put, surrounded by guards—and they'd have orders to shoot you on sight as a dangerous intruder."

"And what if I should come with more armed men than you? And would your guards, if they were ordinary chaps, obey that sort of order in the first place? How could you be sure to avoid any encounter with me?"

I frowned and considered it. "I'd put distance between us, get out of the country, and—"

"Exactly!" Crow said. "Get out of the country."

I saw his meaning. "The private airstrip inside his plant?"

"Of course," Crow nodded. "Except I had ensured that I was closer to the plant than he was. It would take me fifteen to twenty minutes to get there by taxi. Magruser would need between five and ten minutes more than that…

"As for the plant itself—proudly displaying its sign, Magruser Systems, UK—it was large, set in expansive grounds and surrounded by a high, patrolled wire fence. The only entrance was from the main road and boasted an electrically operated barrier and a small guardroom sort of building to house the security man. All this I saw as I paid my taxi fare and approached the barrier.

"As I suspected, the guard came out to meet me, demanding to know my name and business. He was not armed that I could see, but he was big and heavy. I told him I was MOD and that I had to see Mr. Magruser.

"'Sorry, sir,' he answered. 'There must be a bit of a flap on. I've just had orders to let no one in, not even pass-holders. Anyway, Mr. Magruser's at home.'

"'No, he's not,' I told him, 'he's on his way here right now, and I'm to meet him at the gate.'

"'I suppose that'll be all right then, sir,' he answered, 'just as long as you don't want to go in.'

"I walked over to the guardroom with him. While we were talking, I kept covert watch on the open doors of a hangar spied between buildings and installations. Even as I watched, a light aircraft taxied into the open and mechanics began running to and fro, readying it for flight. I was also watching the road, plainly visible from the guardroom window, and at last was rewarded by the sight of Magruser's car speeding into view a quarter mile away.

"Then I produced my handgun."

"What?" I cried. "If all else failed you planned to shoot him?"

"Not at all. Oh, I might have tried it, I suppose, but I doubt if a bullet could have killed him. No, the gun had another purpose to serve, namely the control of any merely human adversary."

"Such as the security man?"

"Correct. I quickly relieved him of his uniform jacket and hat, gagged him and locked him in a small back room. Then, to make absolutely certain, I drove the butt of my weapon through the barrier's control panel, effectively ruining it. By this time Magruser's car was turning off the road into the entrance, and of course it stopped at the lowered barrier. There was Magruser, sitting on my side and in the front passenger seat, and in the back a pair of large young men who were plainly bodyguards.

"I pulled my hat down over my eyes, went out of the guardroom and up to the car, and as I had prayed Magruser himself wound down his window. He stuck out his hand, made imperative, flapping motions, said, 'Fool! I wish to be in. Get the barrier—'

"But at that moment I grabbed and held on to his arm, lowered my face to his, and said, 'Sturm Magruser, I know you—and I know your number!'

"'What? What?' he whispered—and his eyes went wide in terror as he recognised me.

"Then I told him his number, and as his bodyguards leapt from the car and dragged me away from him, he waved them back. 'Leave him be,' he said, 'for it's too late now.' And he favoured me with such a look as I shall never forget. Slowly he got out of the car, leaning heavily upon the door, facing me. 'That is only half my number,' he said, 'but sufficient to destroy me. Do you know the rest of it?'

"And I told him the rest of it.

"What little colour he had drained completely from him and it was as if a light had gone out behind his eyes. He would have collapsed if his men hadn't caught and supported him, seating him back in the car. And all the time his eyes were on my face, his pink and scarlet eyes which had started to bleed.

"'A very resourceful man,' he croaked then, and, 'So little time.' To his driver he said, 'Take me home…'

"Even as they drove away I saw him slump down in his seat, saw his head fall on one side. He did not recover."

After a long moment I asked, "And you got away from that place?" I could think of nothing else to say, and my mouth had gone very dry.

"Who was to stop me?" Crow replied. "Yes, I got away, and returned here. Now you know it all."

"I know it," I answered, wetting my lips, "but I still don't understand it. Not yet. You must tell me how you—"

"No, Henri." He stretched and yawned mightily. "The rest is for you to find out. You know his name and you have the means to discover his number.

The rest should be fairly simple. As for me: I shall sleep for two hours, then we shall take a drive in my car for one hour; following which we shall pay, as it were, our last respects to Sturm Magruser V."

Crow was good as his word. He slept, awakened, breakfasted and drove—while I did nothing but rack my brains and pore over the problem he had set me. And by the time we approached our destination I believed I had most of the answers.

Standing on the pavement outside the gardens of a quiet country crematorium between London and Oxford, we gazed in through spiked iron railings across plots and headstones at the pleasant-seeming, tall-chimneyed building which was the House of Repose, and I for one wondered what words had been spoken over Magruser. As we had arrived, Magruser's cortege, a single hearse, had left. So far as we were aware, none had remained to join us in paying "our last respect".

Now, while we waited, I told Crow, "I think I have the answers."

Tilting his head on one side in that old-fashioned way of his, he said, "Go on."

"First his name," I began. "Sturm Magruser V. The name Sturm reveals something of the nature of his familiar winds, the dust devils you've mentioned as watching over his interests. Am I right?"

Crow nodded. "I have already allowed you that, yes," he said.

"His full name stumped me for a little while, however," I admitted, "for it has only thirteen letters. Then I remembered the V, symbolic for the figure five. That makes eighteen, a double nine. Now, you said Hitler had been a veritable Angel of Death with his 99999…which would seem to make Magruser the very Essence of Death itself!"

"Oh? How so?"

"His birth and death dates," I reminded. "The 1st April 1921, and 4th March 1964. They, too, add up to forty-five, which, if you include the number of his name, gives Magruser 9999999. Seven nines!" And I gave myself a mental pat on the back.

After a little while Crow said, "Are you finished?'" And from the tone of his voice I knew there was a great deal I had overlooked.

VI

I sighed and admitted: "I can't see what else there could be."

"Look!" Crow said, causing me to start.

I followed his pointing finger to where a black-robed figure had stepped out onto the patio of the House of Repose. The bright wintry sun caught his white collar and made it a burning band about his neck. At chest height he carried a bowl, and began to march out through the garden with measured tread. I fancied I could hear the quiet murmur of his voice carrying on the still air, his words a chant or prayer.

"Magruser's mortal remains," said Crow, and he automatically doffed his hat. Bareheaded; I simply stood and watched.

"Well," I said after a moment or two, "where did my calculations go astray?"

Crow shrugged. "You missed several important points, that's all. Magruser was a 'black magician' of sorts, wouldn't you say? With his demonic purpose on Earth and his 'familiar winds', as you call them? We may rightly suppose so; indeed the Persian word *magu* or *magus* means magician. Now, then, if you remove Magus from his name, what are you left with?"

"Why," I quickly worked it out, "with R, E, R. Oh, yes and with V."

"Let us rearrange them and say we are left with R, E, V and R," said Crow. And he repeated, "R, E, V and R. Now, then, as you yourself pointed out, there are thirteen letters in the man's name. Very well, let us look at—"

"Rev. 13!" I cut him off. "And the family Bible you had on your desk. But wait! You've ignored the other R."

Crow stared at me in silence for a moment. "Not at all," he finally said, "for R is the *eighteenth* letter of the alphabet. And thus Magruser, when he changed his name by deed poll, revealed himself!"

Now I understood, and now I gasped in awe at this man I presumed to call friend, the vast intellect which was Titus Crow. For clear in my mind I could read it all in the eighteenth verse of the thirteenth chapter of the Book of Revelations.

Crow saw knowledge written in my dumbfounded face and nodded. "His birthdate, Henri, adds up to eighteen—666, the Number of the Beast!"

"And his ten factories in seven countries," I gasped. "The ten horns upon his seven heads! And the Beast in Revelations rose up *out of the sea!*"

"Those things, too," Crow grimly nodded.

"And his death date, 999!"

Again, his nod and, when he saw that I was finished: "But most monstrous and frightening of all, my friend, his very name—which, if you read it in reverse order—"

"Wh-what?" I stammered. But in another moment my mind reeled and my mouth fell open.

"Resurgam!"

"Indeed," and he gave his curt nod. "I shall rise again!"

Beyond the spiked iron railings the priest gave a sharp little cry and dropped the bowl, which shattered and spilled its contents. Spiralling winds, coming from nowhere, took up the ashes and bore them away…

RECOGNITION

By January 1977 my military career had moved on somewhat. Into my last four years, I had become the Initial Training Sergeant-Major—the DI—at the Royal Military Police HQ in Chichester, Sussex; an establishment which has only recently relocated all these years later. While my work didn't leave me a great deal of spare time, still I managed to write a few stories in the evenings. Recognition *was one of them, and four years later it saw print in W. Paul Ganley's* Weirdbook 15. *In the next half decade Paul would become the most regular of my very few literary outlets; for by then my agent in the US, Kirby McCauley, was more or less obliged to concentrate his efforts on a guy called Stephen King. Perhaps it's a good job I was in the Army and didn't have to support my family with my writing! The narrator of this story could easily be mistaken for a psychic investigator similar to Titus Crow; in fact I almost made it a Crow story. But no, that wasn't to be, for Crow's nature was far more bold, daring and...inquisitive? I'm sure that you'll understand my meaning at the story's very end.*

I

"As to why I asked you all to join me here, and why I'm making it worth your while by paying each of you five hundred pounds for your time and trouble, the answer is simple. The place appears to be haunted, and I want rid of the ghost."

The speaker was young, his voice cultured, his features fine and aristocratic. He was Lord David Marriot, and the place of which he spoke was a Marriot property: a large, ungainly, mongrel architecture of dim and doubtful origins, standing gaunt and gloomily atmospheric in an acre of brooding oaks. The wood itself stood central in nine acres of otherwise barren moors borderland.

Lord Marriot's audience numbered four: the sprightly octogenarian Lawrence Danford, a retired man of the cloth; by contrast the so-called "mediums" Jonathan Turnbull and Jason Lavery, each a "specialist" in his own right; and myself, an old friend of the family whose name does not really matter since I had no special part to play. I was simply there as an observer—an adviser, if you like—in a matter for which, from the beginning, I had no great liking.

Waiting on the arrival of the others, I had been with David Marriot at the old house all afternoon. I had long known something of the history of the place...and a little of its legend. There I now sat, comfortable and warm as our host addressed the other three, with an excellent sherry in my hand while logs crackled away in the massive fireplace. And yet suddenly, as he spoke, I felt chill and uneasy.

"You two gentlemen," David smiled at the mediums, "will employ your special talents to discover and define the malignancy, if indeed such an element exists; and you, sir," he spoke to the elderly cleric, "will attempt to exorcise the unhappy—creature?—once we know who or what it is." Attracted by my involuntary agitation, frowning, he paused and turned to me. "Is something troubling you, my friend...?"

"I"m sorry to have to stop you almost before you've started, David," I apologised, "but I've given it some thought and—well, this plan of yours worries me."

Lord Marriot's guests looked at me in some surprise, seeming to notice me for the first time, although of course we had been introduced; for after all they were the experts while I was merely an observer. Nevertheless, and while I was never endowed with any special psychic talent that I know of (and while certainly, if ever I had been, I never would have dabbled), I did know a little of my subject and had always been interested in such things.

And who knows?—perhaps I do have some sort of sixth sense, for as I have said, I was suddenly and quite inexplicably chilled with a sensation of foreboding that I knew had nothing at all to do with the temperature of the library. The others, for all their much-vaunted special talents, apparently felt nothing.

"My plan worries you?" Lord Marriot finally repeated. "You didn't mention this before."

"I didn't know before just how you meant to go about it. Oh, I agree that the house requires some sort of exorcism, that something is quite definitely wrong with the place, but I'm not at all sure that you should concern your-self with finding out exactly what it is you're exorcising."

"Hmm, yes, I think I might agree," Old Danford nodded his grey head. "Surely the essence of the, *harumph*, matter, is to be rid of the thing—whatever it is. Er, not," he hastily added, "that I would want to do these two gentlemen out of a job—however much I disagree with, *harumph*, spiritualism and its trappings." He turned to Turnbull and Lavery.

"Not at all, sir," Lavery assured him, smiling thinly. "We've been paid in advance, as you yourself have been paid, regardless of results. We will therefore—*perform*—as Lord Marriot sees fit. We are not, however, spiritualists. But in any case, should our services no longer be required…" He shrugged.

"No, no question of that," the owner of the house spoke up at once. "The advice of my good friend here has been greatly valued by my family for many years, in all manner of problems, but he would be the first to admit that he's no expert in matters such as these. I, however, am even less of an authority, and my time is extremely short; I never have enough time for anything! That is why I commissioned him to find out all he could about the history of the house, in order to be able to offer you gentlemen something of an insight into its background.

"And I assure you that it's not just idle curiosity than prompts me to seek out the source of the trouble here. I wish to dispose of the property, and prospective buyers just will not stay in it long enough to appreciate its many good features! And so, if we are to lay something to rest here, something which ought perhaps to have been laid to rest long ago, then I want to know what it is. Damn me, the thing's caused me enough trouble!

"So let's please have no more talk about likes and dislikes or what should or should not be done. It will be the way I've planned it." He turned again to me. "Now, if you'll be so good as to simply outline the results of your research…?"

"Very well," I shrugged in acquiescence. "As long as I've made my feelings in the matter plain…" Knowing David the way I did, further argument would be quite fruitless: his mind was made up. I riffled through the notes lying in my lap, took a long pull on my pipe, and commenced: "Oddly enough, the house as it now stands is comparatively modern, no more than two hundred and fifty years old, but it was built upon the shell of a far older structure, one whose origin is extremely difficult to trace. There are local legends, however, and there have always been chroniclers of tales of strange old houses. The original house is given brief mention in texts dating back almost to Roman times, but the actual site had known habitation—possibly a

Druidic order or some such—much earlier. Later it became part of some sort of fortification, perhaps a small castle, and the remnants of earthworks in the shape of mounds, banks and ditches can be found even today in the surrounding countryside.

"Of course the present house, while large enough by modern standards, is small in comparison with the original: it's a mere wing of the old structure. An extensive cellar—a veritable maze of tunnels, rooms, and passages—was discovered during renovation some eighty years ago, when first the Marriots acquired the property, and then several clues were disclosed as to its earlier use.

"This wing would seem to have been a place of worship of sorts, for there was a crude altar-stone, a pair of ugly, font-like basins, a number of particularly repugnant carvings of gargoyles or 'gods', and other extremely ancient tools and bric-a-brac. Most of this incunabula was given into the care of the then curator of the antiquities section of the British Museum, but the carved figures were defaced and destroyed. The records do not say why…

"But let's go back to the reign of James I.

"Then the place was the seat of a family of supposed nobility, though the line must have suffered a serious decline during the early years of the seventeenth century—or perhaps fallen foul of the authorities or the monarch himself—for its name simply cannot be discovered. It would seem that for some reason, most probably serious dishonour, the family name has been erased from all contemporary records and documents!

"Prior to the fire which razed the main building to the ground in 1618, there had been a certain intercourse and intrigue of a similarly undiscovered nature between the nameless inhabitants, the de la Poers of Exham Priory near Anchester, and an obscure esoteric sect of monks dwelling in and around the semi-ruined Falstone Castle in Northumberland. Of the latter sect: they were wiped out utterly by Northern raiders—a clan believed to have been outraged by the 'heathen activities' of the monks—and the ruins of the castle were pulled to pieces, stone by stone. Indeed, it was so well destroyed that today only a handful of historians could even show you where it stood!

"As for the de la Poers: well, whole cycles of ill-omened myth and legend revolve around that family, just as they do about their Anchester seat. Suffice it to say that in 1923 the Priory was blown up and the cliffs beneath it dynamited, until the deepest roots of its foundations were obliterated. Thus the Priory is no more, and the last of that line of the family is safely locked away in a refuge for the hopelessly insane.

"It can be seen then that the nameless family that lived here had the worst possible connections, at least by the standards of those days, and it is not at all improbable that they brought about their own decline and disappearance through just such traffic with degenerate or ill-advised cultists and demonologists as I have mentioned.

"Now then, add to all of this somewhat tenuously connected information the local rumours, which have circulated on and off in the villages of this area for some three hundred years—those mainly unspecified fears and old wives' tales that have sufficed since time immemorial to keep children and adults alike away from this property, off the land and out of the woods—and you begin to understand something of the aura of the place. Perhaps you can feel that aura even now? I certainly can, and I'm by no means psychic..."

"Just what is it that the locals fear?" Turnbull asked. "Can't you enlighten us at all?"

"Oh, strange shapes have been seen on the paths and roads; luminous nets have appeared strung between the trees like great webs, only to vanish in daylight; and, yes, in connection with the latter, perhaps I had better mention the bas-reliefs in the cellar."

"Bas-reliefs?" queried Lavery.

"Yes, on the walls. It was writing of sorts, but in a language no one could understand—glyphs almost."

"My great-grandfather had just bought the house," David Marriot explained. "He was an extremely well-read man, knowledgeable in all sorts of peculiar subjects. When the cellar was opened and he saw the glyphs, he said they had to do with the worship of some strange deity from an obscure and almost unrecognized myth cycle. Afterwards he had the greater area of the cellar cemented in—said it made the house damp and the foundations unsafe."

"Worship of some strange deity?" Old Danford spoke up. "What sort of deity? Some lustful thing that the Romans brought with them, d'you think?"

"No, older than that," I answered for Lord Marriot. "Much older. A spider-thing."

"A spider?" This was Lavery again, and he snorted the words out almost in contempt.

"Not quite the thing to sneer at," I answered. "Three years ago an ageing but still active gentleman rented the house for a period of some six weeks. An anthropologist and the author of several books, he wanted the place for its solitude; and if he took to it he was going to buy it. In the fifth week he was taken away raving mad!"

"Eh? *Harumph!* Mad, you say?" Old Danford repeated after me.

I nodded. "Yes, quite insane. He lived for barely six months, all the while raving about a creature named Atlach-Nacha—a spider-god from the

Cthulhu Cycle of myth—whose ghostly avatar, he claimed, still inhabited the house and its grounds."

At this Turnbull spoke up. "Now really!" he spluttered. "I honestly fear that we're rapidly going from the sublime to the ridiculous!"

"Gentlemen, please!" There was exasperation now in Lord Marriot's voice. "What does it matter? You know as much now as there is to know of the history of the troubles here—more than enough to do what you've been paid to do. Now. then, Lawrence—" he turned to Danford. "Have you any objections?"

"*Harumph!* Well, if there's a demon here—that is, something other than a creature of the Lord—then of course I'll do my best to help you. *Harumph!* Certainly."

"And you, Lavery?"

"Objections? No, a bargain is a bargain. I have your money, and you shall have your noises."

Lord Marriot nodded, understanding Lavery's meaning. For the medium's talent was a supposed or alleged ability to speak in the tongue of the ghost, the possessing spirit. In the event of a non-human ghost, however, then his mouthings might well be other than speech as we understand the spoken word. They might simply be—noises.

"And that leaves you, Turnbull."

"Do not concern yourself, Lord Marriot," Turnbull answered, flicking imagined dust from his sleeves. "I, too, would be loath to break an honourable agreement. I have promised to do an automatic sketch of the intruder, an art in which I'm well practised, and if all goes well I shall do just that. Frankly, I see nothing at all to be afraid of. Indeed, I would appreciate some sort of explanation from our friend here—who seems to me simply to be doing his best to frighten us off." He inclined his head inquiringly in my direction.

I held up my hands and shook my head. "Gentlemen, my only desire is to make you aware of this feeling of mine of…yes, premonition! The very air seems to me imbued with an aura of—" I frowned. "Perhaps disaster would be too strong a word."

"Disaster?" Old Danford, as was his wont, repeated after me. "How do you mean?"

"I honestly don't know. It's a feeling, that's all, and it hinges upon this desire of Lord Marriot's to know his foe, to identify the nature of the evil here. Yes, upon that, and upon the complicity of the rest of you."

"But—" the young Lord began, anger starting to make itself apparent in his voice.

"At least hear me out," I protested. "Then—" I paused and shrugged. "Then…you must do as you see fit."

"It can do no harm to listen to him," Old Danford pleaded my case. "I for one find all of this extremely interesting. I would like to hear his argument." The others nodded slowly, one by one, in somewhat uncertain agreement.

"Very well," Lord Marriot sighed heavily. "Just what is it that bothers you so much, my friend?"

"Recognition," I answered at once. "To recognise our—opponent?—that's where the danger lies. And yet here's Lavery, all willing and eager to speak in the thing's voice, which can only add to our knowledge of it; and Turnbull, happy to fall into a trance at the drop of a hat and sketch the thing, so that we may all know exactly what it looks like. And what comes after that? Don't you see? The more we learn of it, the more it learns of us!

"Right now, this *thing*—ghost, demon, 'god', apparition, whatever you want to call it—lies in some deathless limbo, extra-dimensional, manifesting itself rarely, incompletely, in our world. But to know the thing, as our lunatic anthropologist came to know it and as the superstitious villagers of these parts think they know it—that is to draw it from its own benighted place into this sphere of existence. That is to give it substance, to participate in its materialisation!"

"Hah!" Turnbull snorted. "And you talk of superstitious villagers! Let's have one thing straight before we go any further. Lavery and I do *not* believe in the supernatural, not as the misinformed majority understand it. We believe that there are other planes of existence, yes, and that they are inhabited; and further, that occasionally we may glimpse alien areas and realms beyond the ones we were born to. In this we are surely nothing less than scientists, men who have been given rare talents, and each experiment we take part in leads us a little further along the paths of discovery. No ghosts or demons, sir, but scientific phenomena which may one day open up whole new vistas of knowledge. Let me repeat once more: there is nothing to fear in this, nothing at all!"

"There I cannot agree," I answered. "You must be aware, as I am, that there are well-documented cases of—"

"Self-hypnotism!" Lavery broke in. "In almost every case where medium experimenters have come to harm, it can be proved that they were the victims of self-hypnosis."

"And that's not all," Turnbull added. "You'll find that they were all believers in the so-called supernatural. We, on the other hand, are not—"

"But what of these well-documented cases you mentioned?" Old Danford spoke up. "What sort of cases?"

"Cases of sudden, violent death!" I answered. "The case of the medium who slept in a room once occupied by a murderer, a strangler, and who was found the next morning strangled—though the room was windowless and locked from the inside! The case of the exorcist," (I paused briefly to glance at Danford) "who attempted to seek out and put to rest a certain grey thing which haunted a Scottish graveyard. Whatever it was, this monster was legended to crush its victims' heads. Well, his curiosity did for him: he was found with his head squashed flat and his brains all burst from his ears!"

"And you think that all of—" Danford began.

"I don't know what to think," I interrupted him, "but certainly the facts seem to speak for themselves. These men I've mentioned, and many others like them, all tried to understand or search for things which they should have left utterly alone. Then, too late, each of them recognised…something…and it recognised them! What *I* think really does not matter; what matters is that these men are no more. And yet here, tonight, you would commence just such an experiment, to seek out something you really aren't meant to know. Well, good luck to you. I for one want no part of it. I'll leave before you begin."

At that Lord Marriot, solicitous now, came over and laid a hand on my arm. "Now you promised me you'd see this thing through with me."

"I did not accept your money, David," I reminded him.

"I respect you all the more for that," he answered. "You were willing to be here simply as a friend. As for this change of heart… At least stay a while and see the thing under way."

I sighed and reluctantly nodded. Our friendship was a bond sealed long ago, in childhood. "As you wish—but if and when I've had enough, then you must not try to prevent my leaving."

"My word on it," he immediately replied, briskly pumping my hand. "Now then: a bite to eat and a drink, I think, another log on the fire, and then we can begin…"

II

The late autumn evening was setting in fast by the time we gathered around a heavy, circular oak table set centrally upon the library's parquet flooring, in preparation for Lavery's demonstration of his esoteric talent. The other three guests were fairly cheery, perhaps a little excited—doubtless as a result of David's plying them unstintingly with his excellent sherry—and our host himself seemed in very good spirits; but I had been little affected and the small amount of wine I had taken had, if anything, only seemed to heighten the almost tangible atmosphere of dread which pressed in upon me from all sides. Only that promise wrested from me by my friend kept me there; and by it alone I felt bound to participate, at least initially, in what was to come.

Finally Lavery declared himself ready to begin and asked us all to remain silent throughout. The lights had been turned low at the medium's request and the sputtering logs in the great hearth threw red and orange shadows about the spacious room.

The experiment would entail none of the usual paraphernalia beloved of mystics and spiritualists; we did not sit with the tips of our little fingers touching, forming an unbroken circle; Lavery had not asked us to concentrate or to focus our minds upon anything at all. The antique clock on the wall ticked off the seconds monotonously as the medium closed his eyes and lay back his head in his high-backed chair. We all watched him closely.

Gradually his breathing deepened and the rise and fall of his chest became regular. Then, almost before we knew it and coming as something of a shock, his hands tightened on the leather arms of his chair and his mouth began a silent series of spastic jerks and twitches. My blood, already cold, seemed to freeze at the sight of this, and I had half risen to my feet before his face grew still. Then Lavery's lips drew back from his teeth and he opened and closed his mouth several times in rapid succession, as if gnashing his teeth through a blind, idiot grin. This only lasted for a second or two, however, and soon his face once more relaxed. Suddenly conscious that I still crouched over the table, I forced myself to sit down.

As we continued to watch him, a deathly pallor came over the medium's features and his knuckles whitened as he gripped the arms of his chair. At this point I could have sworn that the temperature of the room dropped sharply, abruptly. The others did not seem to note the fact, being far too fascinated with the motion of Lavery's exposed Adam's apple to be aware of anything else. That fleshy knob moved slowly up and down the full length of his throat, while the column of his windpipe thickened and contracted in a sort of slow muscular spasm. And at last Lavery spoke. He spoke—and at the sound I could almost feel the blood congealing in my veins!

For this was in no way the voice of a man that crackled, hissed and gibbered from Lavery's mouth in a—language?—which surely never originated in this world or within our sphere of existence. No, it was the voice of…something else. Something monstrous!

Interspaced with the insane cough, whistle and stutter of harshly alien syllables and cackling cachinnations, occasionally there would break through a recognisable combination of sounds which roughly approximated our pronunciation of "Atlach-Nacha": but this fact had no sooner made itself plain to me than, with a wild shriek, Lavery hurled himself backwards—or was *thrown* backwards—so violently that he overturned his chair, rolling free of it to thrash about upon the floor.

Since I was directly opposite Lavery at the table, I was the last to attend him. Lord Marriot and Turnbull on the other hand were at his side at once, pinning him to the floor and steadying him. As I shakily joined them I saw that Old Danford had backed away into the furthest corner of the room, holding up his hands before him as if to ward off the very blackest of evils. With an anxious inquiry I hurried towards him. He shook me off and made straight for the door.

"Danford!" I cried. "What on earth is—" But then I saw the way his eyes bulged and how terribly he trembled in every limb. The man was frightened for his life, and the sight of him in this condition made me forget my own terror in a moment. "Danford," I repeated in a quieter tone of voice. "Are you well?"

By this time Lavery was sitting up on the floor and staring uncertainly about. Lord Marriot joined me as Danford opened the library door to stand for a moment facing us. All the blood seemed to have drained from his face; his hands fluttered like trapped birds as he stumbled backwards out of the room and into the passage leading to the main door of the house.

"Abomination!" he finally croaked, with no sign of his customary *"Harumph!"* "A presence—monstrous—ultimate abomination—*God help us…!*"

"Presence?" Lord Marriot repeated, taking his arm. "What is it, Danford? What's wrong, man?"

The old man tugged himself free. He seemed now somewhat recovered, but still his face was ashen and his trembling unabated. "A presence, yes," he hoarsely answered, "a monstrous presence! I could not even try to exorcise…*that*!" And he turned and staggered along the corridor to the outer door.

"But where are you going, Danford?" Marriot called after him.

"Away," came the answer from the door. "Away from here. I'll—I'll be in touch, Marriot—but I cannot stay here now." The door slammed behind him as he stumbled into the darkness and a moment or two later came the roar of his car's engine.

When the sound had faded into the distance, Lord Marriot turned to me with a look of astonishment on his face. He asked: "Well, what was that all about? Did he see something, d'you think?"

"No, David," I shook my head, "I don't think he *saw* anything. But I believe he sensed something—something perhaps apparent to him through his religious training—and he got out before it could sense him!"

We stayed the night in the house, but while bedrooms were available we all chose to remain in the library, nodding fitfully in our easy chairs around the great fireplace. I for one was very glad of the company, though I kept this fact to myself, and I could not help but wonder if the others might not now be similarly apprehensive.

Twice I awoke with a start in the huge quiet room, on both occasions feeding the red-glowing fire. And since that blaze lasted all through the night, I could only assume that at least one of the others was equally restless…

In the morning, after a frugal breakfast (Lord Marriot kept no retainers in the place; none would stay there, and so we had to make do for ourselves), while the others prowled about and stretched their legs or tidied themselves up, I saw and took stock of the situation. David, concerned about the aged clergyman, rang him at home and was told by Danford's housekeeper that her master had not stayed at home overnight. He had come home in a tearing rush at about nine o'clock, packed a case, told her that he was off "up North" for a few days' rest, and had left at once for the railway station. She also said that she had not liked his colour.

The old man's greatcoat still lay across the arm of a chair in the library where he had left it in his frantic hurry of the night before. I took it and hung it up for him, wondering if he would ever return to the house to claim it.

Lavery was baggy-eyed and dishevelled and he complained of a splitting headache. He blamed his condition on an overdose of his host's sherry, but I knew for a certainty that he had been well enough before his dramatic demonstration of the previous evening. Of that demonstration, the medium said he could remember nothing; and yet he seemed distinctly uneasy and kept casting about the room and starting at the slightest unexpected movement, so that I believed his nerves had suffered a severe jolt.

It struck me that he, surely, must have been my assistant through the night; that he had spent some of the dark hours tending the fire in the great hearth. In any case, shortly after lunch and before the shadows of afternoon began to creep, he made his excuses and took his departure. I had somehow known that he would. And so three of us remained…three of the original five.

But if Danford's unexplained departure of the previous evening had disheartened Lord Marriot, and while Lavery's rather premature desertion had also struck a discordant note, at least Turnbull stood straight and strong on the side of our host. Despite Old Danford's absence, Turnbull would still go ahead with his part in the plan; an exorcist could always be found at some later date, if such were truly necessary. And certainly Lavery's presence was not prerequisite to Turnbull's forthcoming performance. Indeed, he wanted no one at all in attendance, desiring to be left entirely alone in the house. This was the only way he could possibly work, he assured us, and he had no fear at all about being on his own in the old place. After all, what was there to fear? This was only another experiment, wasn't it?

Looking back now I feel a little guilty that I did not argue the point further with Turnbull—about his staying alone in the old house overnight to sketch his automatic portrait of the unwanted tenant—but the man was so damned arrogant to my way of thinking, so sure of his theories and principles, that I offered not the slightest opposition. So we three all spent the evening reading and smoking before the log fire, and as night drew on Lord Marriot and I prepared to take our leave.

Then, too, as darkness fell over the oaks crowding dense and still beyond the gardens, I once again felt that unnatural oppressiveness creeping in upon me, that weight of unseen energies hovering in the suddenly sullen air.

Perhaps, for the first time, Lord Marriot felt it too, for he did not seem at all ill-disposed to leaving the house; indeed, there was an uncharacteristic quickness about him, and as we drove away in his car in the direction of the local village inn, I noticed that he involuntarily shuddered once or twice. I made no mention of it; the night was chill, after all…

At The Traveller's Rest, where business was only moderate, we inspected our rooms before making ourselves comfortable in the snug. There we played cards until about ten o'clock, but our minds were not on the game. Shortly after 10:30 Marriot called Turnbull to ask if all was going well. He returned from the telephone grumbling that Turnbull was totally ungrateful. He had not thanked Lord Marriot for his concern at all. The man demanded absolute isolation, no contact with the outside world whatever, and he complained that it would now take him well over an hour to go into his trance. After that he might begin to sketch almost immediately, or he might not start until well into the night, or there again the experiment could prove to be completely fruitless. It was all a matter of circumstance, and his chances would not be improved by useless interruptions.

We had left him seated in his shirt-sleeves before a roaring fire. Close at hand were a bottle of wine, a plate of cold beef sandwiches, a sketch pad and pencils. These lay upon an occasional table which he would pull into a position directly in front of himself before sleeping, or, as he would have it, before "going into trance". There he sat, alone in that ominous old house.

Before retiring we made a light meal of chicken sandwiches, though neither one of us had any appreciable appetite. I cannot speak for Marriot, but as for me…it took me until well into the wee small hours to get to sleep…

In the morning my titled friend was at my door while I was still halfway through washing. His outward appearance was ostensibly bright and breezy, but I sensed that his eagerness to get back to the old house and Turnbull was more than simply a desire to know the outcome of the latter's experiment; he was more interested in the man's welfare than anything else. Like my own, his misgivings with regard to his plan to learn something of the mysterious and alien entity at the house had grown through the night; now he would be more than satisfied simply to discover the medium well and unharmed.

And yet what could there possibly be at the place to harm him? Again, that question.

The night had brought a heavy frost, the first of the season, and hedgerows and verges were white as from a fall of snow. Half-way through the woods, on the long gravel drive winding in towards the house, there the horror struck! Manoeuvring a slight bend, Lord Marriot cursed, applied his brakes and brought the car skidding to a jarring halt. A shape, white and grey—and hideously red—lay huddled in the middle of the drive.

It was Turnbull, frozen, lying in a crystallised pool of his own blood, limbs contorted in the agony of death, his eyes glazed orbs that stared in blind and eternal horror at a sight Lord Marriot and I could hardly imagine. A thousand circular holes of about half an inch in diameter penetrated deep into his body, his face, all of his limbs; as if he had been the victim of some maniac with a brace and bit! Identical holes formed a track along the frosted grass verge from the house to this spot, as did Turnbull's flying footprints.

Against all my protests—weakened by nausea, white and trembling with shock as he was—still Lord Marriot raced his car the remainder of the way to the house. There we dismounted and he entered through the door which hung mutely ajar. I would not go in with him but stood dumbly wringing my hands, numb with horror, before the leering entrance.

A minute or so later he came staggering to the door. In his hand he carried a leaf from Turnbull's sketch pad. Before I could think to avert my eyes he thrust the almost completed sketch toward me, crying, "Look! Look!"

I caught a glimpse of something bulbous and black, hairy and red-eyed—a tarantula, a bat, a dragon—whose jointed legs were tipped with sharp, chitinous darts. A mere glimpse, without any real or lasting impression of detail, and yet—

"No!" I cried, throwing up my hands before my face, turning and rushing wildly back down the long drive. "No, you fool, don't let me see it! I don't want to know! *I don't want to know!*"

CURSE OF THE GOLDEN GUARDIANS

My "Primal Land" trilogy is set in a forgotten prehistoric Age of Man when Ma Nature hasn't yet decided what talents men should or should not have: an age of wizards and weirdlings! The semi-barbarian Tarra Khash is an itinerant Hrossak, an adventurous steppesman whose wanderings carry him far and wide across the Primal Land. In that most ancient period our Earth was that much closer to Cthulhu's era; the facts of His being were not nearly so esoteric; indeed certain of the darker mages of the era studied Him and His legends most assiduously, especially in their quest for immortality. They even built temples to Cthulhu and others of His cycle, some of which—like the tombs of the Pharaohs in far more recent times—were lost. In "Curse of the Golden Guardians", Tarra Khash comes across just such a place, and then meets up with the ones who watch over it. The Primal Land tales were written in the early 1980s, this one in February 1984. W. Paul Ganley's Weirdbook Press first published it, in Vol. 1 of The Compleat Khash *(1991) along with five other stories.*

Thin to the point of emaciation and burned almost black by a pitiless sun, Tarra Khash came out of the Nameless Desert into dawn-grey, forbidding foothills which, however inarticulate, nevertheless spoke jeeringly of a once exact sense of direction addled by privation and dune blindness. For those misted peaks beyond the foothills could only be the southern tip of the Mountains of Lohmi, which meant that the Hrossak had been travelling a little north of due east, and not as he had intended south-east toward his beloved and long-forsaken steppes.

Another might have cursed at sight of those distantly looming spires of rock in the pale morning light, but Tarra Khash was a true Hrossak for all his wanderlust and not much given to bemoaning his fate. Better to save his breath and use the time taking stock and planning afresh. Indeed, it could well prove providential that he had stumbled this way instead of that, for here at least there was water, and an abundance of it if his ears played him not false. Surely that was the thunder of a cataract he heard?—Aye, and just as surely his desiccated nostrils seemed to suck at air suddenly moist and sweet as the breath of his own mother, as opposed to the desert's arid, acrid exhalations.

Water, yes!—and Tarra licked his parched lips.

Moreover, where there's water there are beasts to drink it, fish to swim in it and frogs to croak in the rushes at its rim; and birds to prey upon frogs and fishes both. But even as thoughts such as these brought a grin to haggard Hrossak features, others, following hard and fast upon their heels, fetched on a frown. What he envisioned was nothing less than an oasis, and never a one-such without its lawful (or often as not unlawful) masters and protectors. Mountain men, probably, well known for their brute natures; or polyglot nomads from the desert, settled here in what to them must surely be a land of plenty.

Or...or perhaps he made too much of a mere sound, a touch of moisture in the morning air. For after all he had ventured here by chance; perchance he was the first such to venture here. Still, better safe than sorry.

Tarra had several small sacks of gold tethered to a thong about his waist. Other than these he wore a loincloth and carried a scabbard slung diagonally across his back, in which was fixed the jewelled hilt of a curved ceremonial sword; but just the hilt and a few inches of blade, for the rest had been shivered to shards in battle. Tarra kept the broken sword not for its value as a weapon but for the jewels in its hilt, which were worth a small fortune and therefore held high barter value. A man could buy his life many times over with those gemstones. Moreover, anyone seeing that hilt stuck in its scabbard would picture an entire sword there, and a Hrossak with a scimitar has always been a force to be reckoned with.

Jewels and gold both, however, might well prove too much of a temptation, for which reason Tarra now removed the sacklets from their thong and buried them beside an oddly carved rock. That was better; few men would risk their necks for a sweaty breech-clout, and scarcer still one who'd attempt the removal of a man's personal weapon!

And so Tarra climbed rocks and escarpments toward sound of rushing water and taste of spray, and along the way ate a lizard he killed with a rock, until after half a mile an oft-glimpsed glimmer and sparkle was grown to a shining spout of water descending from a high, sheer cliff. By then, too, the sun was up, and the way grown with grasses however coarse and bushes of thorn, then flowers and a scattering of trees with small fruits, and some with carobs and others with nuts. Here a small bird sang, and there the coarse grasses rustled, and somewhere a wild piglet squealed as it rooted in soil now loamy. A place of plenty indeed, and as yet no signs of Man or of his works, unless—

—Unless that was firesmoke Tarra's eager nostrils suspicioned, and a moment later more than suspicioned: the tangy reek of a wood fire, and the mouthwatering aroma of pork with its juices dripping and sputtering on smoking, red-glowing embers.

By all that was good!—sweet pork for breakfast, and a pool of clear water to draw the sting from sandpapered skin and soothe the stiffness from creaking joints. Tarra went more swiftly now, lured on irresistibly; and yet he went with caution, until at last he reached the rim of a great bowl-like depression in a wide terrace of rock beneath beetling cliffs. And there, lying flat upon his belly, he slowly craned forth his neck until the cataract-carved pool below, and its sandy margins, lay visible in every aspect to his desert-weary eyes. And a sight for sore eyes it was:

The pool was round as a young girl's navel, and its waters clear and sparkly as her blue eyes. Fish there were in small shoals that Tarra could plainly see, and reeds along one curve of bank, giving way to a species of wide, low-hanging willow which grew in a clump where the rock was cleft. And there sat one who looked like an old man half-in, half-out of the sweet green shade, at his feet a fire whose smoke rose near vertical to the sky, except where gusts of spume from the waterfall caused it to eddy.

Even as Tarra watched, the old man (if such he was) baited a hook and tossed it on a line into the pool, where fish at once came speeding to investigate. The Hrossak glanced back over one shoulder, then the other. Nothing back there: the foothills and mountains on one hand, the shimmering desert on the other. And between the two this hidden pool, or rather this lake, for certainly the basin was a big one. He relaxed; he scanned the scene again; his mouth watered at the delicious, drifting odour of roasting meat. Down below a fish took the hook, was hauled in a frenzy of flexing body and flash of scales dripping from the water. It joined several more where they glittered silver in a shallow hole close to where the old man sat. He baited his hook again, turned the spit, swigged from a wineskin. Tarra could stand no more.

Here the descent would be too steep; he would break a leg or even his neck; but over there, close to where the waterfall plunged and turned the lake to milk, were rounded terraces or ledges like steps cut in the rock, and projecting boulders for handholds. No problem…

He wriggled back from the rim, stood up, loped around the edge of the bowl toward the waterfall. Almost there he stopped, used his broken sword's scant inches of blade to cut a bow, strung it with the thong from his middle. Two straight, slender stems for flightless arrows—crude but effective at short range—and he was ready. Except...

It is never a wise move to come upon a man suddenly, when he may well be shocked into precipitous and possibly violent reaction. Tarra went to the head of the water-carved steps, leaned casually upon a great boulder and called down, "Halloo, there!"

The basin took up his call, adding it to the thunder of plummeting waters: "Halloo, there—*halloo, halloo, halloo—there, there, there!*"

Down below the lone fisherman scrambled to his feet, saw Tarra Khash making his way down slippery terraces of stone toward him. Tarra waved and, however uncertainly, the man by the pool waved back. "Welcome!" he called up in a tremulous croak. "Welcome, stranger..."

Tarra was half-way down. He paused, yelled: "Be at your ease, friend. I smelled your meat and it aroused a small hunger in me, that's all. I'll not beg from you though, but merely borrow your hook, if I may, and catch a bite of my own."

"No need, no need at all," the other croaked at once, seemingly reassured. "There's more than enough here for both of us. A suckling pig and a skin of wine...which way have you come? It's a strange place for wanderers, and that's no lie!"

Tarra was down. Stepping forward he said, "Across the Nameless Desert—which is just a smidgeon dusty this time of year!" He gave his head a shake and dust formed a drifting cloud about his shoulders. "See?"

"Sit, sit!" the other invited, fully at his ease now. "You'll be hungry as well as thirsty. Come, take a bite to eat and a swig of sweet wine."

"I say gladly to both!" answered Tarra Khash. "But right now, the sweetest thing I can imagine is a dip in these crystal waters. What?—I could drink the lake dry! It'll take but a moment." He tossed his makeshift bow and arrows down, stepped to pool's rim. The scabbard and hilt of sword stayed where they were, strapped firmly to his back.

"Careful, son!" the oldster cautioned, his voice like dry dice rattling in a cup—but the Hrossak was already mid-dive, his body knifing deep in cool, cleansing waters. "Careful!" came the warning again as his head broke the surface. "Don't swim out too far. The water whirls toward the middle and will drag you down quick as that!" He snapped his fingers.

Tarra laughed, swilled out his gritty mouth, turned on his back and spouted like a whale. But the oldster was right: already he could feel the tug of a strong current. He headed for the shelf, called: "Peace! I've no lust for swimming, which seems to me a fruitless exercise at best. No, but the dust was so thick on me I grew weary from carrying it around! *Ho!*" And he hauled himself from the water.

A moment later, seated on opposite sides of the fire, each silently appraised the other. The old man—a civilized man by his looks, what Tarra could see of them; possibly out of Klühn, though what such as he could want here the Hrossak found hard to guess—was blocky turning stout, short of stature and broken of voice. He wore loose brown robes that flowed in the nomad fashion, cowled to keep the sun from his head. Beneath that cowl rheumy grey eyes gazed out from behind a veil of straggling white hair; they were deep-set in a face much seamed and weathered. His hands were gnarled, too, and his calves and feet withered and grey where he shuffled his open leather sandals to scuff at the pebbles. Oh, he was a grandfather, little doubt, and yet—

Tarra found himself distracted as the other teased a smoking chunk of pork as big as his fist from the spit and passed it over the fire on a sharp stick. "Eat," he growled. "The Nameless Desert is no friend to an empty belly."

Feeling the sun steaming water from his back, Tarra wolfed at the meat, gazed out over the lake, dangled a toe languidly in its water. And while he munched on crisp crackling and tore at soft flesh, so the other studied him.

A Hrossak, plainly, who beneath his blisters and cracked skin would be bronze as the great gongs in the temples of Khrissa's ice-priests. Not much known for guile, these men of the steppes, which was to say that they were generally a trustworthy lot. Indeed, it was of olden repute in Klühn that if a Hrossak befriends you he's your friend for life. On the other hand, best not to cross one. Not unless you could be sure of getting away with it...

The old man checked Tarra over most minutely:

Standing, he'd be a tall one, this Hrossak, and despite his current leanness his muscles rippled beneath sun- and sand-tortured skin. Hair a shiny, tousled brown (now that dust and dirt were washed away) and eyes of a brown so deep that it was almost black; long arms and legs, and shoulders broad as those of any maned and murderous northern barbarian; strong white teeth set in a wide, ofttimes laughing mouth—aye, he was a handsome specimen, this steppeman—but doubtless as big a fool as any. Or if not yet a fool, then shortly.

"Hadj Dyzm," he informed now, "sole survivor of a caravan out of Eyphra. We had almost made it through a mountain pass and were headed for Chlangi—our planned watering place, you understand—on our way to Klühn. Mountain scum ambushed us in the eastern foothills. I played dead, as did two others…" (Tarra, still munching, glanced quickly about and to the rear, his keen eyes missing nothing.) Dyzm nodded: "Oh yes, there *were* three of us, myself and two young bucks." Tarra could almost taste him biting his lip. Well, he wouldn't pry. The old man could keep his secrets. Anyway, it was easier to change the subject.

"Khash," he said."Tarra, to my friends. I'm heading for Hrossa—or should be! Now—I suppose I'll rest up here for a day or two, then get on my way again. Go with me if you will, or is your aim still set on Chlangi the Doomed?"

The other shrugged. "Undecided. Chlangi is a place of brigands, I'm told, and your Hrossa is likewise somewhat…wild?"

"You'd be safe enough with me, and there's sea trade with Klühn—though not much, I'll admit. Again, I've been away for many a year; relations may well have improved. One thing's certain: if a man can pay his way, then he's welcome in Hrossa."

"Pay my way!" The other laughed gratingly."Oh, I can do that all right. I could even pay you—to be my protection on the way to Chlangi—if you were of a mind." He dipped into his robes and came out with several nuggets of gold, each big as a man's thumb.

Tarra blinked."Then you're a rich merchant, Hadj Dyzm, or at any rate a man of means! Well, I wish I could be of assistance. But no, I believe it's Hrossa for me. I'll think it over, though."

Dyzm nodded. "Fair enough!" he barked in that strange rough voice. "And in my turn I shall give some thought to your own kind offer. But let me say this: of all my treasure—of the veritable *lumps* of gold which are mine—those nuggets I have shown you are the merest motes. For your help I would pay you ten, nay twenty times what you have seen!"

"Ware, man!" Tarra cautioned. "Men have been killed for a toothful! Speak not of lumps—at least not so carelessly!" It was a true statement and a sobering thought.

They sat in silence then, eating their fill for a long while, until the pork was finished and the wineskin empty. By then, too, the sun was riding high in a sky so blue it hurt, and Tarra was weary nigh unto death.

"I'm for sleeping," he finally said."I'll be happy to find you here when I awaken, Hadj Dyzm, and if you are gone I'll not forget you. Peace."

Then he climbed to a shady ledge almost certainly inaccessible to the oldster, and with a single half-speculative glance at Dyzm where he sat in the shade of the willows below, and another out across the glittery pool, he settled himself down to sleep...

II

Tarra Khash was not much given to dreaming, but now he dreamed. Nor was his dream typical, for he was not a greedy man; and yet he dreamed of gold.

Gold, and a great deal of it. Heaps of it, ruddily reflecting the flickering light of a torch held high in Tarra's trembling fist. Trembling, aye, for the dream was not a pleasurable thing but a nightmare, and the treasure cave where the dreaming Hrossak waded ankle deep in bright dust not merely a cave but—

—*A tomb!*

The tomb of Tarra Khash! And as behind him its great stone slab of a door pivoted, shutting him in forever—

—Tarra came awake in a moment, jerking bolt upright with hoarse cry and banging his head on jutting rim of rock whose bulk had kept the sun from him. But now...the sun already three parts down the sky and shadows stretching; and already the chill of evening in the air, where overhead kites wheeled against a blue degrees darker, their keen eyes alert for carrion; and the great pool grey now where it lay in the shade of the basin, and the spray from the cataract a veil of milk drifting above the fall.

Tarra lay down again, fingering his skull. He shivered, not so much from chilly flesh as a chill of the spirit. A dream such as that one were surely ill-omened, whose portent should not be ignored. Tarra touched his bump again and winced, then grinned however ruefully. What? A Hrossak full-grown and troubled by a dream? Terrors enough in this primal land without conjuring more from surfeit of swine-flesh!

"Ho!" came a gritty, coughing shout from below. "Did you call me? I was sleeping."

Tarra cloaked himself in his wits and sat up—this time more carefully, "I wondered if you were still there," he called down. "I couldn't see you in the shade of your tree, and the fire appears to be dead."

"What?" Hadj Dyzm came from cover, stretched and yawned. He poked for a moment at dull embers, then snorted a denial. "No, not dead but sleeping like us. There—" and he propped a dry branch over hot ashes. By the time Tarra had climbed stiffly down, smoke was already curling.

"Fish for supper," said Dyzm. "If I may depend on you to see to it, I'll go tend my beasts."

"Beasts?" Tarra was surprised. "Beasts of burden? Here?" He stared hard at the other in the dying light. "You said nothing of this before. Things take a turn for the better!"

"Listen," said Dyzm. "While you slept I thought things over. I've a tale to tell and a proposition to make. I'll do both when I get back. Now, will you see to the fish?"

"Certainly!" the Hrossak answered, kneeling to blow a tiny flame to life. "Beasts of burden, hey? And now maybe I'll reconsider your offer—my protection, I mean, en route for Chlangi—for it's a shorter way by far to the so-called Doomed City by yak, than it is to the steppes on foot! And truth to tell, my feet are sore weary of—" But Hadj Dyzm was no longer there. Humped up a little and wheezing, he made his way carefully upward, from one rock terrace to the next higher; and he needed his wind for breathing, not chattering to a suddenly gossipy Hrossak.

Tarra, however, chattered only for effect: chiefly to hide his hurried reappraisal of this "stranded merchant". Stranded, indeed! How so? With beasts of burden at his command? There were deep waters here for sure, and not alone in this crystal pool!

Using his broken blade the Hrossak quickly gutted the fishes, spitted them together on a green stick and set it over the stinging smoke, then checked on Dyzm's progress up the side of the bowl. And…he could climb surprisingly well, this old man! Already he was at the rim, just disappearing over the top. Tarra let him get right out of sight, then sprang to his feet and raced up the terraces. At the top he followed Dyzm's trail beneath the cliffs to where the water came down in a near-solid sheet from above, its shining tongue lunging sheer down the slippery face of the rock. No need for stealth here, where the thunder of the fall deadened all else to silence.

Then he spotted the oldster, but—

On the other side of the fall? Now how had he managed to get across? And so speedily! The old fellow was full of surprises, and doubtless there were more to come; Tarra must try to anticipate them.

He watched from the shelter of a leaning rock, his gaze half-obscured by rising spray from the lake. Dyzm's animals were not yaks but two pairs of small camels, which he now tended in the pale evening light. Tethered to a tree in the lee of the cliff, three of them had saddles and small bags, the other was decked more properly as a pack animal. Dyzm put down a large bundle of green branches and coarse grasses collected along the way and the camels at once commenced to feed. While they did so, the old man checked their saddlebags. And furtive was old Hadj Dyzm as he went about his checking, with many a glance over his brown-robed shoulders, which seemed a little less humped now and, oddly, less venerable. But perhaps that was only an effect of the misty light...

Keeping low and melding with the lengthening shadows, Tarra retraced his steps to the bowl, down the terraces to the lake, and was just in time to keep the fishes from ruin as the fire's flames blazed higher. So that a short while later, when Dyzm returned, supper was ready and the fire crackled a bright yellow welcome, its light reflecting in the water along with night's first stars.

Seeing that all was well, Dyzm handed Tarra a blanket he'd brought back with him from his camel-tending; Tarra threw it gratefully across his shoulders, drawing it to him like a robe. Hunching down, they ate in silence; and then, with the last rays of the sun glancing off the western rim of the bowl, the old man shoved a little more wood on the fire and began to talk:

"Tarra Khash, I like you and believe that you're a trustworthy man. Most steppemen are, individually. Oh, it's true I know little enough about you, but we've eaten together and talked a little, and you've given me no cause to suspect that you're anything but a right-minded, fair-dealing, strong-limbed and hardy Hrossak. Which are all the qualifications you need to be my partner. Hear me out:

"If you hadn't come on the scene when you did—indeed, only half an hour later—then I'd have been long gone from here and even now on my way to Klühn via Chlangi, and to all the many hells with trail brigands and bandits! And fifty-fifty I would make it unscathed, for I'm a survivor, d'you see? Not that I'd normally complain, even if I didn't make it: a man has a life to live and when it's done it's done. Being a Hrossak, you'd agree with that, I know.

"Ah! But that's a poor man's philosophy, Tarra Khash—the philosophy of defeat. For a poor man has nothing to lose, and what's life itself but a burdensome, lingering thing? When a man becomes rich, however, his viewpoint changes. And the richer he becomes, the greater the change. Which tells you this: that since coming here I have grown rich. So rich that I am no longer willing to risk a fifty-fifty chance of hying myself to Chlangi all in one piece. Aye, for what's wealth if you're not alive to enjoy it?

"Wait!—let me say on. Now, I can see your first question writ clear across your face. It is this: how, by what means, have I, Hadj Dyzm, a poor man all my life, suddenly grown wealthy? Well, this much I'll tell you—" He brought out a weighty saddlebag from beneath his robe, spread the hem of Tarra's blanket over the smooth rock, tipped out contents of bag.

Tarra's jaw dropped and his eyes opened wide, reflecting the glow and glitter and gleam of the heap of gold and jade and jewels which now lay scintillant in the fire's flickering. And: "By all that's—" he gasped, stretching forth a hand. But before his fingers could touch, Dyzm grasped them in his own wrinkled paw.

"Hold!" he cautioned again. "Wait! You have not heard all. This is but a twelfth part of it. Eleven more bags there are, where this one came from. Aye, and an hundred, a thousand times more where *they* came from!"

"Treasure trove!" Tarra hissed. "You've found a cache!"

"*Shh!*" said Dyzm sharply. "A cache? A hoard? Treasure long lost and buried in the desert's drifting sands?" Slowly he shook his head. "Nay, lad, more than that. I have discovered the tombs of a line of ancient kings, who in their time were wont to take with them to the grave all the treasures gathered up in all the days of their long, long lives!" And chuckling hoarsely, he patted Tarra's knee through the blanket.

The tombs of kings! Treasures beyond avarice! Tarra's head whirled with the sudden greed, the poisonous *lust* he felt pulsing in his veins—until a cooling breeze blew upon his brain from dark recesses of memory. In his mind's eye he saw a huge slab of stone pivoting to block a portal, heard the shuddering reverberations as that massive door slammed immovably into place, felt the weight of a million tons of rock and sand pressing down on him, keeping him from the blessed air and light.

He drew back his hand and stopped licking his lips. His eyes narrowed and he stared hard at Hadj Dyzm.

The oldster gave a harsh, hoarse chuckle. "That's a rare restraint you show, lad. Don't you want to touch it?"

"Aye," Tarra nodded. "Touch it? I'd like to wash my face in it!—but not until you've told me where it comes from."

"Ho-ho!" cried Dyzm. "What? But we haven't settled terms yet!"

Again Tarra nodded. "Well, since you're so good at it, let's hear what you've to say. What are your terms?"

Dyzm stroked his gnarly chin. "The way I see it, with you along especially in Chlangi my chances for survival go up from fifty-fifty to, oh, say three out of four?"

"Go on."

"So let's settle for that. For your protection I'll pay you one fourth part of all I've got."

Tarra sat back, frowned. "That doesn't sound much of a partnership to me."

Dyzm chuckled, low and throaty. "Lad, these are early days. After all, we can only take so much with us—*this* time!"

Tarra began to understand. "As I prove myself—that is, as you continue to survive, which with my protection you will—so my percentage will improve; is that it?"

"Exactly! We'll return—trip after trip until the vaults are emptied—by which time you'll be earning a full half-share and there'll be men enough in our employ to keep all the brigands in Theem'hdra at bay!"

"But where are these vaults you speak of?" Tarra asked, and got exactly the answer he'd expected.

"Man, if I told you that at this juncture…why, what need of me would you have then? Anyway, the vaults are impossible to find; I myself found them only by dint of sheerest accident. Aye, and I have sealed up the hole again, so that it's now doubly impossible."

Tarra grinned, however mirthlessly. "It would seem," he said, "for all your high opinion of Hrossaks, that this one is only trustworthy up to a point!"

"If there's one thing I've learned in life," Dyzm answered, "it's this: that *all* men are trustworthy—up to a point." He pointed at the fortune nestling in the corner of Tarra's blanket, tossed down the saddlebag. "But keep them," he said."Why not? And take them up with you to your ledge to sleep the night, where a poor old lad with a pot belly and bandy legs can't reach you and choke your life out in the dark. But don't talk to me of trust and mistrust, Tarra Khash…"

Tarra reddened but said nothing. Truth to tell, old Dyzm's arrow had struck home: the Hrossak *had* taken his precautions before sleeping, and he'd done a fair bit of suspicioning, too. (Only thank goodness the old fox hadn't seen him following him, else were there a real tongue-lashing in the offing!)

At any rate Tarra said no more, nor old Dyzm, and after sitting awhile in silence they each began to make their arrangements for the night. The Hrossak found himself a smooth hollow in the stone close by—but far enough away from spouting water to be bone dry, and still retaining the sun's heat—and there curled up in his blanket. Hadj Dyzm retired yawning to an arbor in the willows, rustling about a bit amongst the branches until settled. Only then, before sleeping, was there more talk, and brief at that:

"When do you want my answer?" Tarra softly called in the night.

"Tomorrow at latest—else by noon I move on alone. But for goodwill, if that's what you seek, keep that saddlebag anyway—if only to remind you of a once-in-a-lifetime chance missed. You have a molehill; you could have a mountain."

And on that they settled down, except…neither one slept.

III

For Tarra it was like this: the old man had seemingly dealt with him fairly, and yet still something—many things, perhaps—bothered him. The yellowish texture of Dyzm's wrinkled skin, for instance, though why simple signs of age and infirmity should bother Tarra he couldn't imagine. And the old boy's voice, croaking like Khrissan crotala. A disease, maybe? His name, too: for "Hadj Dyzm" as name was more likely found attached to a man of cold Khrissa or Eyphra, and men of those parts rarely stray. They are rigidly cold, such men, brittle as the ice which winters down on them from the Great Ice Barrier and across the Chill Sea. And merchants they scarcely ever are, who by their natures are self-sufficient. And yet this one, at his time of life, alleged a longing for Klühn, city of sophisticates, warm in the winter and the temperate currents of the Eastern Ocean even as Khrissa in mid-summer. Or perhaps, weary of ice and frozen wastes, Dyzm would simply see out his life there, dotage-indulgent of luxuries and soft sea strands?

But what of the two who'd fled the beleaguered caravan with him? Old Dyzm had mentioned precious little of them, and had seemed to regret even that! Anyway, if he were so enamoured of Klühn (via Chlangi) why come this way around the southern tip of Lohmi's mountains, in precisely the wrong direction in the first place?

Lastly, why show Tarra *any* of his treasure? Why not simply make him a decent offer for his assistance in crossing unscathed the badlands twixt here and Chlangi, and thence to Klühn? Surely that were wisest…

These were the thoughts which kept Tarra awake, but Hadj Dyzm's were something else. For where the Hrossak's were vague, curious, inquiring things, Dyzm's were cunning-sharp and dire indeed. At any rate, he had not long settled before stirring, however furtively, and rising up in the night like a hunched blot on rocks white in the moonlight. Then, pausing only to listen to Tarra's deep breathing and so ensure he slept (which still he did not, and which Dyzm knew well enough), the old man made his way up the terraces and quickly became one with the shadows.

Tarra watched him go through slitted eyes, then replaced his sword-stump in its scabbard, rose up and followed silently behind. And no hesitation this time, no feeling of guilt or question of "trust" to bother his mind. No, for his thoughts on Hadj Dyzm had commenced to come together, and the puzzle was beginning to take on form. How the last pieces of that puzzle would fall into place, Tarra could not yet say, but he had an idea that his immediate future—perhaps his entire future—might depend upon it.

Straight to the waterfall went Hadj Dyzm's shadow in the night, with that of Hrossak fleeting not too far behind; so that this time Tarra saw the old man pass *behind* that shining spout of water, his back to the cliff, feet shuffling along a projecting ledge, and so out of sight. Tarra waited for long moments, but no sign of the oldster emerging from the other side. The Hrossak scratched impatiently at an itch on his shoulder, scuffed his feet and adjusted the scabbard across his back. Still no sign of Hadj.

Taking jewelled hilt of sword with its precious inches of steel in hand, finally Tarra ventured onto the ledge and behind the fall—and saw at once whereto the wily old tomb-looter had disappeared. Behind the fall, hollowed by water's rush through untold centuries, a moist cavern reached back into forbidding gloom. But deep within was light, where a flickering torch sputtered in a bracket fixed to the wall. Tarra went to the torch and found others prepared where they lay in a dry niche. Taking one up and holding it to the flame until it caught sputtering life of its own, he followed a trail of footprints in the dust of the floor, moving ever deeper into the heart of the cliff. And always ahead a coil of blue smoke hanging in the musty air, by which he was doubly sure that Dyzm had passed this way.

Now the passage grew narrow, then wider; here it was high-ceilinged, there low; but as the light of the flambeau behind him grew fainter and fainter with distance, until a bend shut it off entirely, and as Tarra burrowed deeper and deeper, so he became aware of more than the work of nature here, where ever increasingly the walls were carved with gods and demons, with stalactites cut in the likenesses of kings and queens seated upon dripstone thrones. A gallery of the gods, this place—of an entire mythology long-forgotten, or almost forgotten—and of them that worshipped, or used to worship, the Beings of that paleogaean pantheon.

Tarra gave an involuntary shudder as he crept silently twixt grinning gargoyles and doomful demons, past looming, tentacled krakens and pschent-crowned, wide-mouthed *things* not so much men as long-headed lizards; and it was here, coming round a second bend in the passage and suddenly into a great terminal chamber, that he reached the very heart of this secret, once-sacred place.

Or was it the heart?

For here—where the ceiling reached up beyond the limits of torchlight, from which unsighted dome massy, morbidly carven daggers of rock depended, and where the stalagmites formed flattened pedestals now for teratological grotesques beyond the Hrossak's staggered imagination—here the footprints in the dust led directly to a central area where blazed another faggot, this one thrust callously into the talon of a staring stone man-lizard. And at this idol's clawed feet lay more bound bundles of dry wood, their knobs all coated with pitch.

Tarra lit a second torch and followed Dyzm's trail a few paces more, to the exact center of the chamber. Which was where the trail ended—or rather, descended!

Between the twin stalagmite thrones of winged, tentacled krakens (images of loathly Lord Cthulhu, Tarra knew from olden legends of his homeland) steps cut from the very rock commenced what seemed a dizzy spiral dive into unknown bowels of earth. And up from that yawning pit came the reek of Dyzm's torch, and from vaults unguessed came clatter of pebbles inadvertently dislodged.

Now Tarra knew at this stage that he had come far enough. He felt it in his water: common sense advising that he now retrace his steps. But to what end? No use now to plead ignorance of the oldster's secret, for certes Dyzm would note the absence or use of two of his tarry torches. And anyway, 'twas curiosity had led the Hrossak on, not greed for more than he'd been offered. In no way did he wish any harm upon the other (not at this stage of the adventure, anyway), but by the same token he saw no good reason why he should remain, as it were, in the dark in respect of the subterranean treasure vaults. Also he desired to know why, in the dead of night, any man should require to venture down into this place. What was it that lured the oldster? More treasure? But surely there would be time enough for that later? Alas, Tarra failed to take into account the greed of some men, which is limitless. To them those fabulous regions "Beyond the Dreams of Avarice" do not exist!

And so he set foot upon the first step, then the second, and by yellow light of flaring brand descended but not very far. At the end of a single steep twist the corkscrew ended in a smaller chamber, where once again two stony sons of Cthulhu sat facing each other this time across a circular shaft whose sides fell smooth and sheer into darkness. And here, too, some curious machinery: a drum of rope with pulleys, a winding handle and large copper bucket, all made fast to the weighty pedestal of one of the Cthulhu images. And tied to the other pedestal, a rope ladder whose rungs went down into gloom. Tarra peered over the rim and saw down there at some indeterminate depth the flickering light of Hadj Dyzm's torch.

Now the Hrossak examined the rope ladder more carefully, and satisfied himself that it was made of pretty stout stuff. Seating himself on the rim of the shaft, he leaned his weight on the ladder's rungs and they supported him effortlessly. He began to lower himself and paused.

Again that niggling mini-Tarra, the one that dwelled in the back of his mind, was whispering cautionary things to him. But cautioning of what? If an old man dared venture here at this hour, surely there could be little of any real danger here? Tarra silenced the frantic whisperer in his head and peered about.

Seated there at pit's rim, he aimed his torch in all directions. There were unexplored niches and recesses in the walls here, true, and also he had this sensation of hooded eyes, of something watching. But how possibly? By whom, watched? These stony idols, perhaps! And Tarra snorted his abrupt dismissal of the idea. At any rate, Hadj Dyzm was below, as witness the flare of his torch. Ah, well, only one thing for it—

And clenching the thin end of the faggot between his teeth, he once more set feet to rope rungs and began to descend. Up until which time, Tarra had not erred…

The flue swiftly widened out, like the neck of a jar, and at a count of only thirty rungs Tarra touched floor. There was the torch he had seen from above, guttering now on this cavern's floor, but of Hadj Dyzm—

The Hrossak stood with one hand on the ladder and turned in a slow circle, holding high his torch. Over there…more statues of Cthulhu and others of his pantheon. And over here…an open box carved from solid rock, its heaped contents spilling over onto the floor. But *such* contents!

Tarra stepped as in a dream toward that fabulous hoard, and reaching it heard Dyzm's hoarse, echoing chuckle—*from above*!

He fell into a crouch, spun on his heel, leaped back toward the ladder— in time to see it whisked up, out of sight. And more important, far out of reach. So that now Tarra knew how sorely he'd been fooled, and how surely he was trapped.

"Hrossak?" came Dyzm's guttural query from overhead. "You, Tarra Khash—do you hear me?"

"Loud and clear, trustworthy one!" Tarra almost choked on the words.

"Then hearken awhile," the other chortled, "and I'll tell you *all* the tale, for I've seen what a curious lad you are and I'm sure you'll be enthralled."

"By all means," Tarra growled. "Why, you might say I'm a captive audience!" And he too laughed, but a trifle bitterly.

"In all truth," said Dyzm, "I really did come out of Eyphra with a cara-van—but of sheerest necessity, I assure you. Mayhap you've heard of the sul-phur pits twixt Eyphra and Chill Sea?"

Tarra had: effluvium of extinct blowholes, the pits were worked by a penal colony under the watchful, cruel eyes of guards little better than crim-inals themselves. It was said that men aged ten years for every one spent in those hellholes, and that their skins rapidly grew withered and yellow from…the…work!

Withered and yellow, aye. Which was a fair description of the way Tarra's brain felt right now.

He sighed, shook his head in dismay, sat down in the dust. He looked up. "You escaped, hey?"

"Not so fast, Hrossak! Oh, you're right, I was there, indeed I was—for three long years! And all that time spent planning my escape, which is all anyone does in that place, until finally it became imperative. You see, there was a ragged bone of a man in that place with me, and before he died he spoke to me of these vaults. His directions couldn't be simpler: come around the southern tip of the Mountains of Lohmi until you find a waterfall and pool, and so on. He had been here, you see, coming upon this place (quite genuinely) by accident. Later, weighed down with treasure, he'd fallen into the hands of mountain men. They were so awed by what he had with him that they let him live, even let him keep a bauble or two before cuffing him about a bit and pointing him in the direction of Eyphra. Aye, and weeks later he'd stumbled into that suspicious city a ragged starveling, filthy and ver-minous, so that when the people saw his few paltry nuggets and gems… Why! What else could he be but a thief? And so they'd taken away the last of his trove and sent him to dig in the sulphur pits, which was where I met him when they sent me there for murder. Ah!—but he'd already been there for four years, and it was something of a legend how long Death had fruit-lessly stalked him. However that may be, all men must die in the end. And he was no exception…

"Now then: oft and again he'd told me the tale of these treasure vaults, but never how to get here until the very end, with the last gasp of his dying. And by then I knew he told the truth, for dying, what use would he have for lies? He knew he was finished, you see, and so had nothing to lose.

"For that matter, neither had I much to lose; which was why, at first op-portunity, I ran off. No easy task, Tarra Khash, flight from the sulphur pits. I left three guards dead in my wake, and a fourth crippled, but at last I was free and running. Aye, and now I had somewhere to run.

"Bits of jewellery I'd taken from the dead guards bought me third-class passage with a caravan I met with where it entered the pass through Lohmi's peaks, following which I spent a deal of my time with a pair of guides, converting them from their loyalty to the caravan's master to my own cause. Ah!—but it's a powerful lure, treasure, as you've discovered."

Here Tarra gruffly interrupted: "What? *Hah!* You can have all your much-vaunted tomb-loot, Hadj Dyzm. Keep it and good luck to you. Nothing more than cursed curiosity caused me to follow you, and more fool me for that!"

Again Dyzm's chuckle, but darker now. "Well, and doubtless you've heard what curiosity did for the cat?"

Tarra nodded, almost groaning in his frustration. But then he took a deep breath, clenched his fists until the muscles of his arms bulged, and said: "But I've also heard how cats have nine lives. Be sure, Hadj Dzym, that in one of them, this mouser will catch up with a certain rat!"

"Come now, Hrossak!" gurgled the other. "What's this I detect in your tone? Do you dare, in your unenviable position, to threaten? It bodes not well for our future dealings, I think! Be careful what you say. Better let me finish before you drop yourself even deeper in the mire. You see, I'm not an unreasonable man, and for all your treachery, I—"

"*My* treachery!" Tarra once more cut in, unable to believe his ears.

"Certainly! Didn't you follow me when I tended my camels in the dusk, spying on me all the way? I had thought you might discover the cave behind the falls there and then. But no, you needed more encouragement. And so I gave it to you—tonight! Aye, and haven't you admitted following me here, as I'd known you would? Curiosity, you say? But should I believe that? Am I as great a fool as you, then?"

"Amazing!" Tarra gasped. "And I'm talking to a self-confessed murderer?"

"Several times over!" Dyzm emphatically agreed. "And they needed killing all—but in any case, that's quite another matter, part of an entirely separate set of circumstances. Now hear me out:

"Where was I ? Ah, yes—

"—So, there I was journeying with the caravan, putting a deal of distance twixt myself and sulphur pits, and along the way recruiting for my treasure hunt. And half-way down Lohmi's eastern flank, lo! the mountain men struck. In great numbers, too. Now, perhaps on other occasion my converted guides might have stayed and fought and died for their rightful master, but now they had a new master and he had promised them riches. Once more the old principle surfaces, Tarra Khash. Namely: a poor man will risk his all for very little gain, but a rich man's lust for life is that much stronger. Hasn't he more to live for? So it was with the guides: my whispers had set deepest desires in motion, creating a conflict of loyalties. The choice was this: stay and remain poor and perhaps die—or flee and live and grow fat and rich. Need I say more? I doubt it…"

"You lured the traitors here," Tarra nodded, "leaving caravan and all to tender mercy of mountain-bred barbarians. Very well, and where are your disciples now?"

"Alas, I know not," said Dyzm, and the Hrossak sensed his shrug. "Except that you are closer to them than I am."

"What?" Tarra gave a start, peering all about at the flickering shadows cast by his dying torch. (Hadj's, upon the floor, had long since expired.) "Are you saying that they're down here?"

"Aye, somewhere. More than that I can't say; I've not seen them for a bit…" And this time Dyzm's chuckle was deep and doomful indeed.

"You mean some harm's befallen them, and you've made no effort to find and save them?"

"What? Lower myself down there?" the other feigned shock at the very suggestion. "Haven't I explained? You speak to a man who toiled three long years in the sulphur pits, remember? And you think I would willingly incarcerate myself in another of Earth's dark holes? For be sure such would be prison to me and surely drive me mad! No, not I, Tarra Khash."

And now the Hrossak, for all that he was a hard man, felt genuinely sickened to his stomach. "You let them starve down here!" he accused, spitting out the sour bile of his mouth into the dust.

"I did not!" Dyzm denied. "Indeed I would have fed them well. Meat and fishes aplenty—water, too, if they'd needed it. My promise was this: a meal each time they half-filled this bucket here with gold and jewels. Any more than that and the rope might break, d'you see? And given a stouter rope they'd doubtless swarm up it. Anyway, starve they did not and my promise was, after all, redundant…"

"And that was their only incentive, that so long as they worked you would feed them?" Tarra shook his head in disgust. "'Young bucks,' you called them. Frightened pups, it seems to me."

"Ah, no," answered Dyzm. "More than hunger goaded them, that has to be admitted."

His words—the way he spoke them, low and phlegmy, almost lingeringly—set Tarra's skin to tingling. After a while, in as steady a voice as he could muster, he said: "Well, then, say on, old fox: what other incentives goaded them? Or better still get straight to the point and tell me how they died."

"Two things I'll tell you—" Dyzm's voice was light again, however throaty, "about incentives. And one other thing about my age, for this fox is in no way old. 'Aged' I am, aye—by dint of sulphur steam in my throat and lungs, and my skin all yellowed from its sting—but not aged, if you see the distinction. And my belly puffed and misshapen from years of hunger, and likewise my limbs gnarly from hard labour. But my true years can't number a great many more than your own, Tarra Khash, and that's a bitter fact."

"I'd marked all that for myself," said Tarra, "but—"

"—But let me speak!" Dyzm's turn to interrupt. And: "Incentives, you wanted. Very well. One: I would take four half-buckets of treasure—only four—and then lower the ladder and let them up, and all three of us would get our share. Two: the quicker they got to work and began filling the bucket, the better for them, for their time would likely be...limited."

Limited? Tarra liked not the word. "By the amount of food you could provide?"

"No, game is plentiful in and around the lake, as you've seen. Guess again."

"By the number of torches you could readily prepare, whose light the two would need in order to do your bidding?"

"No, the preparation of torches proved in no way inconvenient."

Tarra frowned. "Then in what way limited?"

He heard Dyzm's gurgly, self-satisfied sigh. "I cannot be sure," he finally said. "It was only...something that my friend in the sulphur pits warned me about."

"Oh?"

"Aye, for I also had it from him—in his dying breath, mind you, which was a deep one—that the ancient race of kings whose tombs and treasures these were, had set certain guardians over their sepulchres and sarcophagi, and that even now the protective spells of long-dead wizards were morbidly extant and active. Which is to say that the place is cursed, Tarra Khash, and that the longer you stay down there—in what you will shortly discover to be a veritable labyrinth of tombs—the more immediate the horror!"

IV

Horror? And the Hrossak cared for *that* word not at all! Nor on this occasion did he doubt the veracity of what Dyzm had said: it would explain why the pool and country around had not been settled. Nomads and hill men alike were wary of such places, as well they might be. Finally he found voice: "And the nature of this doom?"

"Who can say?" Dyzm replied. "Not I, for the two who went before you did not live to tell me. But they did tell me this: that in a certain tomb are twin statues of solid gold, fashioned in the likeness of winged krakens not unlike the dripstone idols of these cavern antechambers. And having loaded three half-buckets of treasure for me, they went off together to fetch me one of these statues; their last trip, as would have been. Alas, they returned not... But you need a fresh torch, Hrossak, for that one dies." He let fall a fat faggot and Tarra quickly fired it.

"Now then," Dyzm continued in a little while, "this is what I propose. Find for me that tomb and fetch me a kraken of gold, and that will suffice."

"Suffice?"

"I shall then be satisfied that you are a sincere man and worthy to be my partner in future ventures. And when I have the statue, then shall I lower the ladder and we'll be off to Chlangi together, and so on to Klühn."

Tarra could not keep from laughing, albeit a mite hysterically. "Am I to believe this? Fool I am, Hadj Dyzm—great fool, as you've well proved—but *such* a fool?"

"Hmm!" Dyzm gruffly mused. He dropped more torches. "Well, think it over. I can wait awhile. How long the demon guardians will wait is a different matter. Meanwhile: 'ware below!—I lower the bucket." And down came the bucket on the end of its rope.

Tarra at once tugged at the rope, testing it, and as the bucket came to rest upon the floor he swung himself aloft, climbing by strength of his arms alone. Man-high he got—and not an inch higher. With soft, twangy report rope parted, and down crashed Hrossak atop bucket and all. "*Ow!*" he complained, getting upon his feet.

Above, Dyzm chuckled. "Ow, is it?" he said. "Worse than that, Tarra Khash, if the rope had held! Did you think I'd sit here and do nothing until you popped up out of the hole? I've a knife here you could shave with, to cut you or rope or both. Oh, I know, 'twas desperation made you try it. Well, you've tried and failed, so an end to tomfooleries, eh? Now I'll lower the rope some and you can make a knot; after which you can get off and find me my kraken statue. But a warning: any more heroics and I'll make you fetch both!"

"Very well," Tarra answered, breathing heavily, "—but first tell me something. Right here, a pace or two away, lies a great stone box of treasure.

Doubtless your two dragged it here for you. Now tell me: why were its contents never hauled aloft?"

"Ah!" said Dyzm. "That would be their fourth haul, when they told me about the statues. I had forgotten."

"So," said the Hrossak, nodding, "returning with this box—their *fourth* haul and not the third, as you first alleged—these idiots told you about the golden, winged kraken idols, so that you spurned this latest haul in favour of the greater marvel they described. Is that it?"

"Something like that, aye. I'm glad you reminded me. Perhaps before you get off searching you'd like to—"

"I would *not* like to!" answered Hrossak hotly. "It's either contents of this box *or* one of these damned idols—if I can find 'em—but not both. Which, I rather fancy, is what they told you, too."

Hadj Dyzm was peeved. "Hmm!" he grumbled. "Perhaps you're not so daft after all, Hrossak. But…I've set my heart on an idol, and so you'd better be off, find and fetch it."

"Not so fast," said Tarra. "Your word before I go: you *will* fetch me up, when I return with the statue?" (Even though he knew very well that Hadj Dyzm would not.)

"My word," said the other, very gravely.

"So be it," said the Hrossak. "Now, which way do I go?"

"I was right after all," said Dyzm. "You are daft—and deaf to boot! How should I know which way you must go? I would suggest you follow prints on dusty floor, as so recently you followed mine…"

V

A little while later Tarra knew exactly what the fox had meant by a labyrinth. Following sandal prints in the dust, he moved from cavern to cavern, and all of them alike as cells in a comb of honey. A veritable necropolis, this place, where bones were piled about the walls in terrible profusion, and skulls heaped high as a man's waist. Not all dead kings, these ossified remains; no, for most wore fetters about their ankles, or heaps of rust where ages had eaten the metal away. And about their shoulders small wooden yokes turned almost to stone; and each skeleton right hand with its little finger missing, to mark him (or her) as property of the king.

Tarra wrinkled his nose. They had been savages in those days, he thought, for all their trappings of civilization, their carving and metal-moulding, their love of jewellery, their long-forgotten death-rituals, of which these bones formed the merest crumbling relics. Still, no time to ponder the ways of men whose race was old when the desert was young; there was much to be done, and not all of Hrossak's searching concerned with golden idols, either!

Tarra Khash remembered all too clearly the years he'd spent trapped in Nud Annoxin's well-cell in Thinhla. Hah!—he'd never thought to be in just such predicament again. And yet now…? Well, life is short enough; it was not Tarra's intention to spend the rest of his down here. Ideas were slowly dawning, taking shape in his brain like wraiths of mist over fertile soil as he pondered the problem.

Shuddering a little (from the cold of the place, he told himself, for he had not brought his blanket with him), he passed through more of the domed caves, always following the print tracks where they were most dense—but to one side of them, so that his own trail would be clear and fresh—and knowing that these ways had been explored before. At least he had something of an advantage in that; but they, his predecessors, had had each other's company. Company?—in this place of death Tarra would be satisfied right now by sight of rat, let alone fellow man!

His predecessors… He wondered what fate had overtaken them. Aye, and perhaps he'd soon enough find that out, too.

But for now—if he could only find something to use as grapple. And something else as rope. For the fox couldn't sit up there forever. He too must eat and drink. Grapple and rope, aye—but what to use? A long golden chain, perhaps? No, too soft and much too heavy, and all other metal doubtless rotten or rusted utterly away. And Tarra aware with every passing moment, as ideas were first considered, then discarded, that the "guardians" of this place—*if* they weren't merely frighteners conjured out of Hadj Dyzm's own imagination—might even now be waking.

Such were his thoughts as he came by light of flaring fagot into a central chamber large by comparison as that of a queen at the centre of her hive. A queen, or a king, or many such. For here the walls had been cut into deep niches, and each niche containing a massy sarcophagus carved from solid rock, and all about these centuried coffins the floor strewn with wealth untold!

But in the middle of this circular, high-domed cavern, there reposed the mightiest tomb of all: a veritable mausoleum, with high marble ceiling of its own held up by fluted marble columns, and an entrance guarded by—

Guarded? The word was too close to "guardian" to do a lot for Tarra's nerves. But like it or not the tomb *was* guarded—by a pair of golden krakens, wings and all, seated atop onyx pedestals, one on each side of the leering portal. Somewhat awed (for this must surely be the last resting place of the greatest of all these ancient monarchs) the Hrossak moved forward and stuck his torch in the rib-cage of a skeleton where it lay at the foot of the pedestal on the left…stuck it there and slowly straightened up, felt gooseflesh crawl on naked arms and thighs and back—and leapt backward as if fanged by viper!

Long moments Tarra stood there then, in torchlight flickering, with heart pounding, longing to flee full tilt but nailed to the spot as if his feet had taken root in solid rock. And all the while his gaze rapt upon that cadaver whose ribs supported the hissing brand, *that skeleton which even now wore ragged robe, upon whose bony feet were leather sandals of the sort that had made those recent prints in dust of ages*!

The Hrossak took a breath—and another—and forced his hammering heart to a slower pace and the trembling of his limbs to marble stillness. And breathing deeply a third time, he slowly crouched and leaned forward, studying morbid remains more closely. The bones were burned as from some mordant acid. In places their surfaces were sticky and shiny-black with tarry traces, possibly burnt and liquefied marrow. Tatters of skin still attached, but so sere and withered as to be parchment patches, and the skull…that was worst of all.

Yawning jaws gaped impossibly wide in frozen scream, and torch-flung shadows shifted in empty sockets like frightened ghosts of eyes. Still crouching, shuddering, Tarra took up his torch and held it out at arm's length toward the other pedestal. As he had suspected (without, as yet, knowing *why* he suspected), a second skeleton, in much the same condition, sprawled beneath the other kraken. And again the word "guardians" seemed to echo in Hrossak's head.

But the images were only of gold, not loathsome flesh and alien ichor, and even were they alive—if they were, indeed, *the* guardians—their size would hardly make them a threat. Why, they were little more than octopuses, for all the goldsmith's loathsome skill!

Tarra gazed into sightless golden eyes, glanced at wings folded back, laid his hands upon tentacles half-lifted, apparently in groping query. Cold gold, in no wise threatening. And yet it seemed to the Hrossak there was a film of moisture, of some nameless tomb-slime, on the surface of the metal, making it almost slippery to the touch. That wouldn't be much help when it came to carrying the thing. And if he could not find means to manufacture grapnel and rope, then for certain he must put his faith in Hadj Dyzm—initially, anyway.

He moved round behind the pedestal, closed his arms about the belly of the idol until his hands clasped his elbows, lifted. Heavy, aye, but he thought it would fit into the bucket. Only…would the rope be strong enough?

Rope! And again a picture of rope and grapple burned on the surface of his mind's eye. Tarra eased the idol back onto its pedestal, bent down and tore at the tatters which clothed the mysteriously slain cadaver. At his touch they crumbled away. Whatever it was seared the bones—seared the flesh *from* those bones—it had also worked on the coarse cloth. No, he could hardly make a rope out of this rotten stuff; but now he had a better idea. Dyzm himself would furnish the rope!

First, however—

He checked his torch, which was beginning to burn a trifle low, then turned toward the open door of the sepulchre. This was sheer curiosity, he knew—and he minded what Hadj Dyzm had said of curiosity—but still he had to know what sort of king it was whose incarceration in some dim by-gone age had warranted mass slaughter in and about these tomb-caves.

Pausing before the high, dark portal, he thrust out torch before him and saw within—

No carven coffin here but a massive throne, and seated thereon a shriv-elled mummy all of shiny bone and leather, upright and proud and fused to marble seat by nameless ages. Indeed, the very fossil of a thing. A *thing*, aye, for the huge creature was not and never had been human.

Entering, Tarra approached a throne whose platform was tall as his chest, staring up at what in its day must have been a fearsome sight. Even now the thing was terrifying. But…it was dead, and dead things can hurt no one. Can they?

He held his torch high.

The mummy was that of a lizard-man, tall, thin and long headed; with fangs curving down from fleshless jaws, and leathern chin still sprout-ing a goatlike beard of coarse hair; and upon its head a jewelled pschent, and in its talon of a hand a sceptre or knobby wand of ebony set with precious stones.

So this had been the living creature whose likeness Tarra had seen carved from the dripstone of the upper caves. Also, it had been a king of kings, and crueller far than any merely human king. He looked again at the wand. A fas-cinating thing. The Hrossak reached up his hand to jewelled, ebony rod, giv-ing it a tug. But it was now one with dry claw, welded there by time. He tugged harder—and heard from behind him a low rumble!

In the next split second several things…

First: Tarra remembered again his dream of a great slab door slamming shut. Then: he saw that in fact the wand was not held fast in claw but attached by golden link to a lever in the arm of the throne. Finally: even thinking these thoughts he was hurling himself backward, diving, slithering out of tomb on his belly as the door, falling in an arc from the inner ceiling, came thundering down. Then Tarra feeling that monstrous counterbalanced slab brushing his heels, and its gongy reverberations exactly as he had dreamed them!

His torch had gone flying, skittering across the floor in a straight line; but now, its impetus spent, it rolled a little in the dust. This had the effect of damping the flame. Still rolling, it flickered lower, came to rest smoking hugely from a dull red knob. The darkness at once crept in...

Ignoring his fear (snarling like a great hound at his back) Hrossak leapt to the near-extinguished brand, gathered it up, spun with it in a rushing, dizzy circle. This had the double effect of creating a protective ring about himself in the sudden, gibbering darkness, and of aerating the hot heart of the faggot, which answered by bursting into bright light. The shadows slunk back, defeated.

Panting, fighting to control mind and flesh alike, for this last close call had near unmanned him, the Hrossak suddenly found himself angry. Now berserker he was not—not in the way of the blood-crazy Northmen of the fjords—but when Tarra Khash was roused he really *was* roused. Right now he was mad at himself for ignoring his own instincts in the first place, mad at whichever ancient architect had designed this place as death-trap, mad at his predicament (which might yet prove permanent), but most of all mad at the miserable and much-loathed Hadj Dyzm, who must now be made to pay for all. Nor was Hrossak temper improved much by the fact that the skin of his hands, arms and chest had now commenced to itch and burn terribly, an affliction for which he could find no good cause or reason unless—

—unless nothing!—for these were precisely the areas of his person which he had pressed against the golden kraken idol!

Was that vile metallic sweat he had noticed upon the thing some sort of stinging acid, then? Some poison? If so, patently the centuries had detracted from its potency. Before striding from the main chamber and following his own trail toward the entrance shaft, Tarra stooped, scooped up dust, layered it upon the stinging areas. Also, he glanced once more at the golden idols.

They crouched, gleaming, upon their pedestals exactly as before...and yet somehow—different? Were they not, perhaps, more upright? Did their eyes not seem about to pop open? Had their tentacles not stretched outward fractionally, perhaps threateningly, and was not the sheen of slime upon their metal surfaces that much thicker and slimier?

The Hrossak snorted. So much for a wild imagination! But enough of that, now he must put his plan into action without delay. This place was dangerous; something hideous had happened to the men who came here before him; time was wasting and there could well be other horrors down here which as yet Tarra knew nothing about. He returned quickly to where the bucket lay upon the floor at the end of its rope.

"Ho!" came Hadj Dyzm's harsh greeting as Tarra fired a fresh torch. "And where's my idol, Hrossak?"

Tarra looked up. Dyzm's evil face peered down from the ceiling hole, but anxiously, Tarra thought. "Oh, I've found your damned idols, foxy one," he called up, "and nearly came to grief doing it! This place is booby trapped, and I was very nearly the booby!"

"But the idol," Dyzm pressed, "Where is it?"

Tarra thought fast. "Three things," he said. "First: the kraken idols lie on a lower level. Not deep, but impossible to scale carrying idol. Second: I have a solution for first. Third: as you've seen, I had to return for a fresh torch."

"Clown!" snapped Dyzm. "Waster of time! Why did you not take spare faggots with you?"

"An oversight," Tarra agreed. "Do you want to hear my solution?"

"Get on with it."

"I need hauling gear—namely, a rope."

"What's this?" Dyzm was suspicious.

"To hoist idol up from below," Tarra lied again. "Also, 'twere a good test: a chance to see if the rope is strong enough."

"Explain."

"Easy: if the rope breaks from weight of kraken alone, certainly it will break with bucket and idol both."

"Ah!" Dyzm's suspicion seemed confirmed. "You want me to toss down the bucket rope in order to make yourself a grappling hook."

Tarra feigned exasperation. "What? Have I not already tried to climb, and did not the rope break? The idol, however, is fairly small, not quite the weight of a man."

"Hmm! How much rope do you need?"

Enough to hang you! Tarra thought, but out loud he said: "Oh, about ten man-lengths."

"What?" Dyzm spluttered. "You're surely mad, Hrossak! Am I then to give you a length *twice* as long as the distance between us? Now surely you plan to make a grapnel!"

"Of what?" Tarra sighed. "Crumbling bones for hook, or soft gold, perhaps? Now who's wasting time? Even if it were possible, how could I climb with you up there to cut me or rope or both with your sharp knife. 'Twas you pointed that out in the first place, remember? And anyway, I have your promise to let down the ladder—or had you forgotten that, too?"

"Now, now, lad—don't go jumping to hasty conclusions." Tarra could hear him shuffling about a little; a thin trickle of dust drifted down from above; finally:

"Very well, assume I give you the length of rope you say you need. What then?"

"First I fetch the idol. Then you lower what rope you have left, and I tie mine to it. Ah!—and to be certain it won't break, we use a double length. You then haul up idol in bucket. And if you're worried about me swarming up the rope, well, you still have your knife, right? *Then*—you toss down rope ladder for me. And the last quickly, for already I've had enough of this place!"

Dyzm considered it again, said: "Done!"

A moment later and the rope began coiling in the bottom of the bucket, and as it coiled so Tarra gazed avidly at the heavy *handle* of that container, which he knew he could bend into a perfect hook for hurling! Finally Dyzm cut the rope, let its end fall.

"There!" he called down. "Ten man-lengths."

Tarra loosened the rope from the bucket handle, coiled it in loops over one shoulder. He must now play out the game to its full. Obviously he could neither make nor use grapple with Dyzm still up there, and so must first ensure his departure.

"Incidentally," he said, in manner casual, "those booby-traps I mentioned. It wasn't one such which killed your last two partners."

"Eh?" from above, in voice startled. "How do you mean? Did you find them?"

"Aye, what's left of them. Obviously the work of your unknown 'guardians', Hadj. But these caves are extensive, possibly reaching out for many miles under the desert. The guardians—whatever they are—must be elsewhere. If they were here…then were we both dead in a trice!"

"Then were *you* dead in a trice, you mean," the other corrected.

But Tarra only shook his head. "Both of us," he insisted. "I found one of your lads on a high, narrow ledge near-inaccessible. He was all broken in parts and the flesh slurped off him. The other, in like condition, lay in narrow niche no more than a crack in the wall—but the horrors had found him there, for sure. And would the funnel of this well stop them? I doubt it."

The other was silent.

Tarra started away, keeping his head down and grinning grimly to himself; but Dyzm at once called him to a halt. "Hrossak—do you have any idea of the true nature of these guardians?"

"Who can say?" Tarra was mysterious. "Perhaps they slither, or flop. Likely, they fly! One thing for sure: they suck flesh from bones easy as leeches draw blood!" And off he went.

Now this was the Hrossak's plan: that he wait a while, then cause a loud commotion of screaming and such, and shrieking, "The guardians! The guardians!" And gurgling most horribly until Hadj Dyzm must surely believe him dead. All of which to be performed, of course, right out of sight of him above. Then utter silence (in which Tarra hoped to detect sounds of fox's frenzied flight), and back to break handle from bucket, form grapnel, attach double length of rope, and so escape. Then to track villain down and break his scrawny neck!

That had been his first plan…

But now, considering it again, Tarra had second thoughts. Since he must wait down here for at least a little while, why not turn the interval to his own advantage? For even now, if things went wrong—if, for instance, the real guardians came on the scene—he might still have to rely on Hadj Dyzm to get him out of here quickly. His chance of the latter happening, especially now, after putting the fears up the fox, were slim, he knew; but any port in a storm. Better slim chance than no chance at all. And so it were best if he *appeared* to be following Hadj's instructions right up to the very end. Anyway, the thought of stealing one of the idols was somehow appealing.

With these thoughts on his mind, he rapidly retraced his steps to the cave of the golden krakens where they waited on their pedestals before the tomb of the lizard-king, and—

By light of flaring torch the Hrossak gaped at the transformation taken place in the idols. For they did *not* wait atop their pedestals—not exactly. And now, truth slowly dawning, Tarra began to discern the real nature of the curse attaching to these subterranean tombs. Doubtless the alien monarchs of this long-extinct race had been great wizards, whose spells and maledictions had reached down through dim and terrible centuries. But in the end even the most powerful spells lose their potency, including this one. What must in its primordial origin have been a swift metamorphosis indeed was now turned to a tortuously slow thing—but a deadly thing for all that, as witness the pair of charred cadavers.

With creep impossibly slow—so slow the eye could scarce note it—the kraken idols were moving. And doubtless the process was gradually speeding up even as the spell persisted. For they had commenced to slither down the length of their pedestals, sucker arms clinging to the tops as they imperceptibly lowered themselves. Their eyes were half-open now, and gemstone orbs gleamed blackly and evilly beneath lids of beaten gold. Moreover, the acid ooze which their bodies seemed to exude had thickened visibly, smoking a little where it contacted the onyx of the pedestals.

Tarra's first thought was of flight, but where to flee? Go back and tell Hadj Dyzm and the fiend would doubtless leave him here till krakens were fully transformed. And would there be sufficient time remaining to make and use grapnel? Doubtful...

Doom descended on the Hrossak's shoulders like an icy cloak; he felt weighed down by it. Was this to be the end, then? Must he, too, succumb to kraken kiss, be turned to bag of scorched and tarry bones?

Aye, possibly—but not alone!

Filled now with dreams of red revenge, which strengthened him, Tarra ran forward and fastened a double loop of rope about the belly of the kraken on the left, yanking until its tentacle tips slipped free from rim of pedestal. And back through shadow-flickered caves he dragged the morbid, scarcely mobile thing, while acrid smoke curled up from rope, where an as yet sluggish acid ate into it. But the rope held and at last sweaty Hrossak emerged beneath the spot where Hadj Dyzm waited.

"Have you got it?" the fox eagerly, breathlessly called down.

"Aye," panted Tarra, "at the end of my rope. Now send down your end and prepare to wind away." And he rolled the bucket out of sight as if in preparation.

Down came Hadj's rope without delay, and Tarra knotting it to the middle of *his* length, and Hadj taking up the slack. Then the Hrossak hauled kraken into view, and fox's gasp from above. "Beautiful!" he croaked, for he saw only the gold and not the monstrous mutation, the constantly accelerating mobility of the thing.

The rope where it coiled kraken's belly was near burned through now, so Tarra made fresh loops under reaching tentacles and back of wings. Once he inadvertently touched the golden flesh of the monster—and had to bite his lip to keep from shouting his agony, as the skin of his knuckles blackened and cracked!

But at last, "Haul away!" he cried; and chortling greatly the fox took the strain and commenced turning the handle of his gear. And such was his greed that the bucket was now forgotten. But Tarra had not forgotten it.

And so, as the mass of transmuting gold-flesh slowly ascended in short jerks, turning like a plumb bob on its line, Hrossak stepped into shadow and tore the handle from the bucket, quickly bending it into a hook. Stepping back, he thrust hook through loop of rope before it was drawn up too high, and standing beneath the suspended idol cried: "Now let down the ladder, Hadj Dyzm, as agreed, lest I impede your progress with my own weight. For it's a fact you can't lift idol and me both!"

"One thing at a time," the other answered. "First the idol."

"Damn you, Hadj!" cried Tarra, hanging something of his weight on the hook to let the other see he was in earnest—only to have the hook straighten out at once and slip from the loop, leaving Tarra to fall to his knees. And by the time he was back on his feet, rope and idol and all had been dragged up well beyond his reach, and Hadj's chuckle echoing horribly on high—for a little while.

Then, while Hrossak stood clenching and unclenching his fists and scowling, came Hadj's voice in something of a query: "Hrossak—what's this nasty reek I smell?" (and idol slowly turning on its line, disappearing up the flue).

"The reek of my sweat," answered Tarra, "mingled with smoke of torch's dying—aye, and in all likelihood my dying, too!" He stepped out of harm's way as droplets hissed down from above, smoking where they struck the floor. And now the idol almost as high as the rim, and droplets of acid slime falling faster in a hissing rain.

Tarra kept well back, listening to fox's grunting as he worked the gear—his grunting, then his squawk of surprise, and at last his shriek of sheerest horror!

In his mind's eye Tarra could picture it all in great detail:

The gear turning, winding up the rope, a ratchet holding it while Hadj Dyzm rested his muscles before making the next turn. And the kraken coming into view, a thing of massy, gleamy gold. Another turn, and eyes no longer glazed glaring into Hadj's—and tentacles no longer leaden reaching—and acid no longer dilute squirting and hissing!

Then—

Still screaming to burst his heart—fat bundle of rags entwined in golden nightmare of living, lethal tentacles—Hadj and kraken and all came plummeting down the shaft. Even the rope ladder, though that fell only part way, hanging there tantalizingly beyond Hrossak's reach.

And Hadj's body broken but not yet dead, flopping on the floor in terrible grip, his flesh melting and steaming away, as Tarra bent the bucket's handle back into a hook and snatched up a length of good rope. And horror of horrors, now the *other* kraken slithering into view from out the dark, reaching to aid its evil twin!

Now the Hrossak cast for dear life, cast his hook up to where the lower rungs of the ladder dangled. Missed!—and another cast.

Hideous, hissing tentacles reaching for his ankles; vile vapour boiling up from no longer screaming fox; the entire chamber filled with loathsome reek and the hook catching at last, dragging ladder with it to slime-puddled floor.

Then Tarra was aloft, and later he would not remember his hands on rungs at all. Only the blind panic and shrieking terror that seemed to hurl him up and out of the hole and up the spiral steps and down the long tunnel of carven stalactites to the waterfall and so out into the night. And no pause even to negotiate the ledge behind the fall, but a mighty dive which took him through that curtain of falling water, out and down under the stars to strike the lake with hardly a splash; and then the exhausting swim back to shore against the whirlpool's pull, to where a fire's embers smouldered and guttered still.

After that—

Morning found a rich, rich man following the foothills east with his camels. And never a backward glance from Tarra Khash…

AUNT HESTER

This one was written in December, 1971 and saw first publication in The Satyr's Head *(1975), an anthology edited by Dave Sutton, published in the UK by Corgi Books. Since when it has seen several reprints, most recently in* Great Ghost Stories—*a Carroll and Graf anthology, 2004—edited by R. Chetwynd Hayes and Stephen Jones. At the time of its writing I was an Operational Platoon Commander, in what was then West Germany. On publication, however, I had become the RMP Unit Quartermaster at our Scotland HQ in Edinburgh Castle. "Aunt Hester" is, of course, a Cthulhu Mythos story, in its way similar to Lovecraft's "The Thing on the Doorstep". But while HPL's Mythos backdrop is clearly evident, his actual style of writing is nowhere to be found.*

I suppose my Aunt Hester Lang might best be described as the "black sheep" of the family. Certainly no one ever spoke to her, or of her—none of the elders of the family, that is—and if my own little friendship with my aunt had been known I am sure that would have been stamped on too; but of course that friendship was many years ago.

I remember it well: how I used to sneak round to Aunt Hester's house in hoary Castle-Ilden, not far from Harden on the coast, after school when my folks thought I was at Scouts, and Aunt Hester would make me cups of cocoa and we would talk about newts ("efts", she called them), frogs, conkers and other things—things of interest to small boys—until the local Scouts' meeting was due to end, and then I would hurry home.

We (father, mother and myself) left Harden when I was just twelve years old, moving down to London where the Old Man had got himself a good job. I was twenty years old before I got to see my aunt again. In the intervening years I had not sent her so much as a postcard (I've never been much of a letter-writer) and I knew that during the same period of time my parents had neither written nor heard from her; but still that did not stop my mother warning me before I set out for Harden not to "drop in" on Aunt Hester Lang.

No doubt about it, they were frightened of her, my parents—well, if not frightened, certainly they were apprehensive.

Now to me a warning has always been something of a challenge. I had arranged to stay with a friend for a week, a school pal from the good old days, but long before the northbound train stopped at Harden my mind was made up to spend at least a fraction of my time at my aunt's place. Why shouldn't I? Hadn't we always got on famously? Whatever it was she had done to my parents in the past, I could see no good reason why *I* should shun her.

She would be getting on in years a bit now. How old, I wondered? Older than my mother, her sister, by a couple of years—the same age (obviously) as her twin brother, George, in Australia—but of course I was also ignorant of his age. In the end, making what calculations I could, I worked it out that Aunt Hester and her distant brother must have seen at least one hundred and eight summers between them. Yes, my aunt must be about fifty-four years old. It was about time someone took an interest in her.

It was a bright Friday night, the first after my arrival in Harden, when the ideal opportunity presented itself for visiting Aunt Hester. My school friend, Albert, had a date—one he did not really want to put off—and though he had tried his best during the day it had early been apparent that his luck was out regards finding, on short notice, a second girl for me. It had been left too late. But in any case, I'm not much on blind dates—and most dates are "blind" unless you really know the girl—and I go even less on doubles; the truth of the matter was that I had wanted the night for my own purposes. And so, when the time came for Albert to set out to meet his girl, I walked off in the opposite direction, across the autumn fences and fields to ancient Castle-Ilden.

I arrived at the little old village at about eight, just as dusk was making its hesitant decision whether or not to allow night's onset, and went straight to Aunt Hester's thatch-roofed bungalow. The place stood (just as I remembered it) at the Blackhill end of cobbled Main Street, in a neat garden framed by cherry trees with the fruit heavy in their branches. As I approached the gate the door opened and out of the house wandered the oddest quartet of strangers I could ever have wished to see.

There was a humped-up, frenetically mobile and babbling old chap, ninety if he was a day; a frumpish fat woman with many quivering chins; a skeletally thin, incredibly tall, ridiculously wrapped-up man in scarf, pencil-slim overcoat, and fur gloves; and finally, a perfectly delicate old lady with a walking-stick and ear-trumpet. They were shepherded by my Aunt Hester, no different it seemed than when I had last seen her, to the gate and out into the street. There followed a piped and grunted hubbub of thanks and general genialities before the four were gone—in the direction of the leaning village pub—leaving my aunt at the gate finally to spot me where I stood in the shadow of one of her cherry trees. She knew me almost at once, despite the interval of nearly a decade.

"Peter?"

"Hello, Aunt Hester."

"Why, Peter Norton! My favourite young man—and tall as a tree! Come in, come in!"

"It's bad of me to drop in on you like this," I answered, taking the arm she offered, "all unannounced and after so long away, but I—"

"No excuses required," she waved an airy hand before us and smiled up at me, laughter lines showing at the corners of her eyes and in her unpretty face. "And you came at just the right time—my group has just left me all alone."

"Your 'group'?"

"My séance group! I've had it for a long time now, many a year. Didn't you know I was a bit on the psychic side? No, I suppose not; your parents wouldn't have told you about *that*, now would they? That's what started it all originally—the trouble in the family, I mean." We went on into the house.

"Now I had meant to ask you about that," I told her. "You mean my parents don't like you messing about with spiritualism? I can see that they wouldn't, of course—not at all the Old Man's cup of tea—but still, I don't really see what it could have to do with them."

"Not, *your* parents, Love," (she had always called me "Love"), "mine—and yours later; but especially George, your uncle in Australia. And not just spiritualism, though that has since become part of it. Did you know that my brother left home and settled in Australia because of me?" A distant look came into her eyes. "No, of course you didn't, and I don't suppose anyone else would ever have become aware of my power if George hadn't walked me through a window…"

"Eh?" I said, believing my hearing to be out of order. "Power? Walked you through a window?"

"Yes," she answered, nodding her head, "he walked me through a window! Listen, I'll tell you the story from the beginning."

By that time we had settled ourselves down in front of the fire in Aunt Hester's living-room and I was able to scan, as she talked, the paraphernalia her "group" had left behind. There were old leather-bound tomes and treatises, tarot cards, a ouija board shiny brown with age, oh, and several other items beloved of the spiritualist. I was fascinated, as ever I had been as a boy, by the many obscure curiosities in Aunt Hester's cottage.

"The first I knew of the link between George and myself," she began, breaking in on my thoughts, "as apart from the obvious link that exists between all twins, was when we were twelve years old. Your grandparents had taken us, along with your mother, down to the beach at Seaton Carew. It was July and marvellously hot. Well, to cut a long story short, your mother got into trouble in the water.

"She was quite a long way out and the only one anything like close to her was George—who couldn't swim! He'd waded out up to his neck, but he didn't dare go any deeper. Now, you can wade a long way out at Seaton. The bottom shelves off very slowly. George was at least fifty yards out when we heard him yelling that Sis was in trouble…

"At first I panicked and started to run out through the shallow water, shouting to George that he should swim to Sis, which of course he couldn't—*but he did*! Or at least, *I did*! Somehow, I'd swapped places with him, do you see? Not physically but mentally. I'd left him behind me in the shallow water, in my body, and I was swimming for all I was worth for Sis in his! I got her back to the shallows with very little trouble—she was only a few inches out of her depth—and then, as soon as the danger was past, I found my consciousness floating back into my own body.

"Well, everyone made a big fuss of George; he was the hero of the day, you see? How had he done it?—they all wanted to know; and all he was able to say was that he'd just seemed to stand there watching himself save Sis. And of course he *had* stood there watching it all—through my eyes!

"I didn't try to explain it; no one would have believed or listened to me anyway, and I didn't really understand it myself—but George was always a bit wary of me from then on. He said nothing, mind you, but I think that even as early as that first time he had an idea…"

Suddenly she looked at me closely, frowning. "You're not finding all this a bit too hard to swallow, Love?"

"No," I shook my head. "Not really. I remember reading somewhere of a similar thing between twins—a sort of Corsican Brothers situation."

"Oh, but I've heard of many such!" she quickly answered. "I don't suppose you've read Joachim Feery on the *Necronomicon*?"

"No," I answered. "I don't think so."

"Well, Feery was the illegitimate grandson of Baron Kant, the German 'witch-hunter'. He died quite mysteriously in 1934 while still a comparatively young man. He wrote a number of occult limited editions—mostly published at his own expense—the vast majority of which religious and other authorities bought up and destroyed as fast as they appeared. Unquestionably—though it has never been discovered where he saw or read them— Feery's source books were very rare and sinister volumes; among them the *Cthaat Aquadingen*, the *Necronomicon,* von Junzt's *Unspeakable Cults*, Prinn's *De Vermis Mysteriis* and others of that sort. Often Feery's knowledge in respect of such books has seemed almost beyond belief. His quotes, while apparently genuine and authoritative, often differ substantially when compared with the works from which they were supposedly culled. Regarding such discrepancies, Feery claimed that most of his occult knowledge came to him 'in dreams'!" She paused, then asked: "Am I boring you?"

"Not a bit of it," I answered. "I'm fascinated."

"Well, anyhow," she continued, "as I've said, Feery must somewhere have seen one of the very rare copies of Abdul Alhazred's *Necronomicon*, in one translation or another, for he published a slim volume of notes concerning that book's contents. I don't own a copy myself but I've read one belonging to a friend of mine, an old member of my group. Alhazred, while being reckoned by many to have been a madman, was without doubt the world's foremost authority on black magic and the horrors of alien dimensions, and he was vastly interested in every facet of freakish phenomena, physical and metaphysical."

She stood up, went to her bookshelf and opened a large modern volume of Aubrey Beardsley's fascinating drawings, taking out a number of loose white sheets bearing lines of her own neat handwriting.

"I've copied some of Feery's quotes, supposedly from Alhazred. Listen to this one:

"'Tis a veritable & attestable Fact, that between certain related Persons there exists a Bond more powerful than the strongest Ties of Flesh & Family, whereby one such Person may be *aware* of all the Trials & Pleasures of the other, yea, even to experiencing the Pains or Passions of one far distant; & further, there are those whose Skills in such Matters are aided by forbidden Knowledge or Intercourse through dark Magic with Spirits & Beings of outside Spheres. Of the latter: I have sought them out, both Men & Women, & upon Examination have in all Cases discovered them to be Users of

Divination, Observers of Times, Enchanters, Witches, Charmers, or Necromancers. All claimed to work their Wonders through Intercourse with dead & departed Spirits, but I fear that often such Spirits were evil Angels, the Messengers of the Dark One & yet more ancient Evils. Indeed, among them were some whose Powers were prodigious, who might at Will *inhabit* the Body of another even at a great Distance & against the Will & often unbeknown to the Sufferer of such Outrage…"

She put down the papers, sat back and looked at me quizzically.

"That's all very interesting," I said after a moment, "but hardly applicable to yourself."

"Oh, but it is, Love," she protested. "I'm George's twin, for one thing, and for another—"

"But you're no witch or necromancer!"

"No, I wouldn't say so—but I am a 'User of Divinations', and I do 'work my Wonders through Intercourse with dead & departed Spirits'. That's what spiritualism is all about."

"You mean you actually take this, er, Alhazred and spiritualism and all seriously?" I deprecated.

She frowned. "No, not Alhazred, not really," she answered after a moment's thought. "But he is interesting, as you said. As for spiritualism: yes, I *do* take it seriously. Why, you'd be amazed at some of the vibrations I've been getting these last three weeks or so. *Very* disturbing, but so far rather incoherent; frantic, in fact. I'll track him down eventually, though—the spirit, I mean…"

We sat quietly then, contemplatively for a minute or two. Frankly, I didn't quite know what to say; but then she went on: "Anyway, we were talking about George and how I believed that even after that first occasion he had a bit of an idea that I was at the root of the thing. Yes, I really think he did. He said nothing, and yet…

"And that's not all, either. It was some time after that day on the beach before Sis could be convinced that she hadn't been saved by me. She was sure it had been me, not George, who pulled her out of the deep water.

"Well, a year or two went by, and school-leaving exams came up. I was all right, a reasonable scholar—I had always been a bookish kid—but poor old George…" She shook her head sadly. My uncle, it appeared, had not been too bright.

After a moment she continued. "Dates were set for the exams and two sets of papers were prepared, one for the boys, another for the girls. I had no trouble with my paper, I knew even before the results were announced that I was through easily—but before that came George's turn. He'd been worrying and chewing, cramming for all he was worth, biting his nails down to the elbows...and getting nowhere. I was in bed with flu when the day of his exams came round, and I remember how I just lay there fretting over him. He was my brother, after all.

"I must have been thinking of him just a bit too hard, though, for before I knew it there I was, staring down hard at an exam paper, sitting in a class full of boys in the old school!

"...An hour later I had the papers all finished, and then I concentrated myself back home again. This time it was a definite effort for me to find my way back to my own body.

"The house was in an uproar. I was downstairs in my dressing-gown; mother had an arm round me and was trying to console me; father was yelling and waving his arms about like a lunatic. 'The girl's gone *mad!*' I remember him exploding, red faced and a bit frightened.

"Apparently I had rushed downstairs about an hour earlier. I had been shouting and screaming tearfully that I'd miss the exam, and I had wanted to know what I was doing home. And when they had called me *Hester* instead of *George!* Well, then I had seemed to go completely out of my mind!

"Of course, I had been feverish with flu for a couple of days. That was obviously the answer: I had suddenly reached the height of a hitherto unrecognised delirious fever, and now the fever had broken I was going to be all right. That was what they said . . .

"George eventually came home with his eyes all wide and staring, frightened-looking, and he stayed that way for a couple of days. He avoided me like the plague! But the next week—when it came out about how good his marks were, how easily he had passed his examination papers—well—"

"But surely he must have known," I broke in. What few doubts I had entertained were now gone forever. She was plainly not making all of this up.

"But why should he have known, Love? He knew he'd had two pretty nightmarish experiences, sure enough, and that somehow they had been connected with me; but he couldn't possibly know that they had their origin in me—that I formed their focus."

"He did find out, though?"

"Oh, yes, he did," she slowly answered, her eyes seeming to glisten just a little in the homely evening glow of the room. "And as I've said, that's why he left home in the end. It happened like this:

"I had never been a pretty girl—no, don't say anything, Love. You weren't even a twinkle in your father's eye then, he was only a boy himself, and so you wouldn't know. But at a time of life when most girls only have to pout to set the boys on fire, well, I was only very plain—and I'm probably giving myself the benefit of the doubt at that.

"Anyway, when George was out nights—walking his latest girl, dancing, or whatever—I was always at home on my own with my books. Quite simply, I came to be terribly jealous of my brother. Of course, you don't know him, he had already been gone something like fifteen years when you were born, but George was a handsome lad. Not strong, mind you, but long and lean and a natural for the girls.

"Eventually he found himself a special girlfriend and came to spend all his time with her. I remember being furious because he wouldn't tell me anything about her…"

She paused and looked at me and after a while I said "Uhhuh?" inviting her to go on.

"It was one Saturday night in the spring, I remember, not long after our nineteenth birthday, and George had spent the better part of an hour dandying himself up for this unknown girl. That night he seemed to take a sort of stupid, well, *delight* in spiting me; he refused to answer my questions about his girl or even mention her name. Finally, after he had set his tie straight and slicked his hair down for what seemed like the thousandth time, he dared to wink at me—maliciously, I thought, in my jealousy—as he went out into the night.

"That did it. Something *snapped*! I stamped my foot and rushed upstairs to my room for a good cry. And in the middle of crying I had my idea—"

"You decided to, er, swap identities with your brother, to have a look at his girl for yourself," I broke in. "Am I right?"

She nodded in answer, staring at the fire; ashamed of herself, I thought, after all this time. "Yes, I did," she said. "For the first time I used my power for my own ends. And mean and despicable ends they were.

"But this time it wasn't like before. There was no instantaneous, involuntary flowing of my psyche, as it were. No immediate change of personality. I had to force it, to concentrate and concentrate and *push* myself. But in a short period of time, before I even knew it, well, there I was."

"There you were? In Uncle George's body?"

"Yes, in his body, looking out through his eyes, holding in his hand the cool, slender hand of a very pretty girl. I had expected the girl, of course, and yet…

"Confused and blustering, letting go of her hand, I jumped back and bumped into a man standing behind me. The girl was saying: "George, what's wrong?" in a whisper, and people were staring. We were in a second-show picture-house queue. Finally I managed to mumble an answer, in a horribly hoarse, unfamiliar, frightened voice—George's voice, obviously, and my fear—and then the girl moved closer and kissed me gently on the cheek!

"She did! But of course she would, wouldn't she, if I were George? 'Why, you jumped then like you'd been stung—' she started to say; but I wasn't listening, Peter, for I had jumped again, even more violently, shrinking away from her in a kind of horror. I must have gone crimson, standing there in that queue, with all those unfamiliar people looking at me—*and I had just been kissed by a girl*!

"You see, I wasn't thinking like George, at all! I just wished with all my heart that I hadn't interfered, and before I knew it I had George's body in motion and was running down the road, the picture-house queue behind me and the voice of this sweet little girl echoing after me in pained and astonished disbelief.

"Altogether my spiteful adventure had taken only a few minutes, and, when at last I was able to do so; I controlled myself—or rather, George's self—and hid in a shop doorway. It took another minute or two before I was composed sufficiently to manage a, well, a 'return trip', but at last I made it and there I was back in my room.

"I had been gone no more than seven or eight minutes all told, but I wasn't back to *exactly* where I started out from. Oh, George hadn't gone rushing downstairs again in a hysterical fit, like that time when I sat his exam for him—though of course the period of *transition* had been a much longer one on that occasion—but he had at least moved off the bed. I found myself standing beside the window…" She paused.

"And afterwards?" I prompted her, fascinated.

"Afterwards?" she echoed me, considering it. "Well, George was very quiet about it… No, that's not quite true. It's not that he was quiet, rather that he avoided me more than ever, to such an extent that I hardly ever saw him—no more than a glimpse at a time as he came and went. Mother and father didn't notice George's increased coolness towards me, but I certainly did. I'm pretty sure it was then that he had finally recognised the source of this thing that came at odd times like some short-lived insanity to plague him. Yes, and looking back, I can see how I might easily have driven George completely insane! But of course, from that time on he was forewarned…"

"Forewarned?" I repeated her. "And the next time he—"

"The next time?" She turned her face so that I could see the fine scars on her otherwise smooth left cheek. I had always wondered about those scars. "I don't remember a great deal about the next time—shock, I suppose, a 'mental block', you might call it—but anyway, the next time was the *last* time!...

"There was a boy who took me out once or twice, and I remember that when he stopped calling for me it was because of something George had said to him. Six months had gone by since my shameful and abortive experiment, and now I deliberately put it out of my mind as I determined to teach George a lesson. You must understand, Love, that this boy I mentioned, well...he meant a great deal to me.

"Anyway, I was out to get my own back. I didn't know how George had managed to make it up with his girl, but he had. I was going to put an end to their little romance once and for all.

"It was a fairly warm, early October, I remember, when my chance eventually came. A Sunday afternoon, and George was out walking with his girl. I had it planned minutely. I knew exactly what I must say, how I must act, what I must do. I could do it in two minutes flat, and be back in my own body before George knew what was going on. For the first time my intentions were *deliberately* malicious..."

I waited for my aunt to continue, and after a while again prompted her: "And? Was this when—"

"Yes, this was when he walked me through the window. Well, he didn't exactly walk me through it—I believe I leapt; or rather, he leapt me, if you see what I mean. One minute I was sitting on a grassy bank with the same sweet little girl, and the next there was this awful pain— My whole body hurt, and it was *my* body, for my consciousness was suddenly back where it belonged. Instantaneously, inadvertently, I was—myself!

"*But I was lying crumpled on the lawn in front of the house!* I remember seeing splinters of broken glass and bits of yellow-painted wood from my shattered bedroom window, and then I went into a faint with the pain.

"George came to see me in the hospital—once. He sneered when my parents had their backs turned. He leaned over my bed and said: "*Got* you, Hester!" Just that, nothing more.

"I had a broken leg and collarbone. It was three weeks before they let me go home. By then George had joined the Merchant Navy and my parents knew that somehow I was to blame. They were never the same to me from that time on. George had been the Apple of the Family Eye, if you know what I mean. They knew that his going away, in some unknown way, had been my fault. I did have a letter from George—well, a note. It simply warned me 'never to do it again', that there were worse things than falling through windows!"

"And you never did, er, do it again?"

"No, I didn't dare; I haven't dared since. There *are* worse things, Love, than being walked through a window! And if George hates me still as much as he might…

"But I've often *wanted* to do it again. George has two children, you know?"

I nodded an affirmation: "Yes, I've heard mother mention them. Joe and Doreen?"

"That's right," she nodded. "They're hardly children any more, but I think of them that way. They'll be in their twenties now, your cousins. George's wife wrote to me once many years ago. I've no idea how she got my address. She did it behind George's back, I imagine. Said how sorry she was that there was 'trouble in the family'. She sent me photographs of the kids. They were beautiful. For all I know there may have been other children later—even grandchildren."

"I don't think so," I told her. "I think I would have known. They're still pretty reserved, my folks; but I would have learned that much, I'm sure. But tell me: how is it that you and mother aren't closer? I mean, she never talks about you, my mother, and yet you are her sister."

"Your mother is two years younger than George and me," my aunt informed me. "She went to live with her grandparents down South when she was thirteen. Sis, you see, was the brilliant one. George was a bit dim; I was clever enough; but Sis, she was really clever. Our parents sent Sis off to live with Granny, where she could attend a school worthy of her intelligence. She stayed with Gran from then on. We simply drifted apart…

"Mind you, we'd never been what you might call close, not for sisters. Anyhow, we didn't come together again until she married and came back up here to live, by which time George must have written to her and told her one or two things. I don't know what or how much he told her, but—well, she never bothered with me—and anyway I was working by then and had a flat of my own.

"Years passed, I hardly ever saw Sis, her little boy came along—you, Love—I fell in with a spiritualist group, making real friends for the first time in my life; and, well, that was that. My interest in spiritualism, various other ways of mine that didn't quite fit the accepted pattern, the unspoken thing I had done to George…we drifted apart. You understand?"

I nodded. I felt sorry for her, but of course I could not say so. Instead I laughed awkwardly and shrugged my shoulders. "Who needs people?"

She looked shocked. "We all do, Love!" Then for a while she was quiet, staring into the fire.

"I'll make a brew of tea," she suddenly said, then looked at me and smiled in a fashion I well remembered. "Or should we have cocoa?"

"Cocoa!" I instinctively laughed, relieved at the change of subject.

She went into the kitchen and I lit a cigarette. Idle, for the moment, I looked about me, taking up the loose sheets of paper that Aunt Hester had left on her occasional table. I saw at once that many of her jottings were concerned with extracts from exotic books. I passed over the piece she had read out to me and glanced at another sheet. Immediately my interest was caught; the three passages were all from the Holy Bible:

"Regard not them that have familiar spirits, neither seek after wizards, to be defiled by them." Lev. 19:31.

"Then said Saul unto his servants, Seek me a woman that hath a familiar spirit, that I may go to her and enquire of her. And his servants said to him, Behold, there is a woman that hath a familiar spirit at En-dor." I Sam. 28:6,7.

"Many of them also which used curious arts brought their books together, and burned them before all men." Acts 19:19.

The third sheet contained a quote from *Today's Christian*:

"To dabble in matters such as these is to reach within demoniac circles, and it is by no means rare to discover scorn and scepticism transformed to hysterical possession in persons whose curiosity has led them merely to attend so-called 'spiritual séances'. These things of which I speak are of a nature as serious as any in the world today, and I am only one among many to utter a solemn warning against any intercourse with 'spirit forces' or the like, whereby the unutterable evil of demonic possession could well be the horrific outcome."

Finally, before she returned with a steaming jug of cocoa and two mugs, I read another of Aunt Hester's extracts, this one again from Feery's *Notes on the Necronomicon*:

"Yea, & I discovered how one might, be he an Adept & his

174

familiar Spirits powerful enough, control the Wanderings or Migration of his Essence into all manner of Beings & Persons—even from beyond the Grave of Sod or the Door of the Stone Sepulchre…"

I was still pondering this last extract an hour later, as I walked Harden's night streets towards my lodgings at the home of my friend.

Three evenings later, when by arrangement I returned to my aunt's cottage in old Castle-Ilden, she was nervously waiting for me at the gate and whisked me breathlessly inside. She sat me down, seated herself opposite and clasped her hands in her lap almost in the attitude of an excited young girl.

"Peter, Love, I've had an idea—such a simple idea that it amazes me I never thought of it before."

"An idea? How do you mean, Aunt Hester—what sort of idea? Does it involve me?"

"Yes, I'd rather it were you than any other. After all, you know the story now…"

I frowned as an oddly foreboding shadow darkened latent areas of my consciousness. Her words had been innocuous enough as of yet, and there seemed no reason why I should suddenly feel so—*uncomfortable*, but—

"The story?" I finally repeated her. "You mean this idea of yours concerns—Uncle George?"

"Yes, I do!" she answered. "Oh, Love, I can *see* them; if only for a brief moment or two, I can see my nephew and niece. You'll help me? I know you will."

The shadow thickened darkly, growing in me, spreading from hidden to more truly conscious regions of my mind. "Help you? You mean you intend to—" I paused, then started to speak again as I saw for sure what she was getting at and realised that she meant it: "But haven't you said that this stuff was too dangerous? The last time you—"

"Oh, yes, I know," she impatiently argued, cutting me off. "But now, well, it's different. I won't stay more than a moment or two—just long enough to see the children—and then I'll get straight back…*here*. And there'll be precautions. It can't fail, you'll see."

"Precautions?" Despite myself I was interested.

"Yes," she began to talk faster, growing more excited with each passing moment. "The way I've worked it out, it's perfectly safe. To start with,

George will be asleep—he won't know anything about it. When his sleeping mind moves into my body, why, it will simply stay asleep! On the other hand, when *my* mind moves into *his* body, then I'll be able to move about and—"

"And use your brother as a keyhole!" I blurted, surprising even myself. She frowned, then turned her face away. What she planned was wrong. I knew it and so did she, but if my outburst had shamed her it certainly had not deterred her—not for long.

When she looked at me again her eyes were almost pleading. "I know how it must look to you, Love, but it's not so. And I know that I must seem to be a selfish woman, but that's not quite true either. Isn't it natural that I should want to see my family? They are mine, you know. George, my brother; his wife, my sister-in-law; their children, my nephew and niece. Just a—yes—a 'peep', if that's the way you see it. But, Love, I *need* that peep. I'll only have a few moments, and I'll have to make them last me for the rest of my life."

I began to weaken. "How will you go about it?"

"First, a glance," she eagerly answered, again reminding me of a young girl. "Nothing more, a mere glance. Even if he's awake he won't ever know I was there; he'll think his mind wandered for the merest second. If he *is* asleep, though, then I'll be able to, well, 'wake him up', see his wife—and, if the children are still at home, why, I'll be able to see them too. Just a glance."

"But suppose something does go wrong?" I asked bluntly, coming back to earth. "Why, you might come back and find your head in the gas oven! What's to stop him from slashing your wrists? That only takes a second, you know."

"That's where you come in, Love." She stood up and patted me on the cheek, smiling cleverly. "You'll be right here to see that nothing goes wrong."

"But—"

"And to be doubly sure," she cut me off, "why, *I'll be tied in my chair*! You can't walk through windows when you're tied down, now can you?"

Half an hour later, still suffering inwardly from that as yet unspecified foreboding, I had done as Aunt Hester directed me to do, tying her wrists to the arms of her cane chair with soft but fairly strong bandages from her medicine cabinet in the bathroom.

She had it all worked out, reasoning that it would be very early morning in Australia and that her brother would still be sleeping. As soon as she was comfortable, without another word, she closed her eyes and let her head fall slowly forward onto her chest. Outside, the sun still had some way to go to setting; inside, the room was still warm—yet I shuddered oddly with a deep, nervous chilling of my blood.

It was then that I tried to bring the thing to a halt, calling her name and shaking her shoulder, but she only brushed my hand away and hushed me. I went back to my chair and watched her anxiously.

As the shadows seemed visibly to lengthen in the room and my skin cooled, her head sank even deeper onto her chest, so that I began to think she had fallen asleep. Then she settled herself more comfortably yet and I saw that she was still awake, merely preparing her body for her brother's slumbering mind.

In another moment I knew that something had changed. Her position was as it had been; the shadows crept slowly still; the ancient clock on the wall ticked its regular chronological message; but I had grown inexplicably colder, and there was this feeling that *something* had changed…

Suddenly there flashed before my mind's eye certain of those warning jottings I had read only a few nights earlier, and there and then I was determined that this thing should go no further. Oh, she had warned me not to do anything to frighten or disturb her, but this was different. Somehow I knew that if I didn't act now—

"Hester! Aunt Hester!" I jumped up and moved toward her, my throat dry and my words cracked and unnatural-sounding. And she lifted her head and opened her eyes.

For a moment I thought that everything was all right—then…

She cried out and stood up, ripped bandages falling in tatters from strangely strong wrists. She mouthed again, staggering and patently disorientated. I fell back in dumb horror, knowing that something was very wrong and yet unable to put my finger on the trouble.

My aunt's eyes were wide now and bulging, and for the first time she seemed to see me, stumbling toward me with slack jaw and tongue protruding horribly between long teeth and drawnback lips. It was then that I knew what was wrong, that this frightful *thing* before me was not my aunt, and I was driven backward before its stumbling approach, warding it off with waving arms and barely articulate cries.

Finally, stumbling more frenziedly now, clawing at empty air inches in front of my face, she—it—spoke: "No!" the awful voice gurgled over its wriggling tongue. "No, Hester, you…you *fool*! I warned you…"

And in that same instant I saw not an old woman, but the horribly alien figure of *a man in a woman's form*!

More grotesque than any drag artist, the thing pirouetted in grim, constricting agony, its strange eyes glazing even as I stared in a paralysis of horror. Then it was all over and the frail scarecrow of flesh, purple tongue still protruding from frothing lips, fell in a crumpled heap to the floor.

That's it, that's the story—not a tale I've told before, for there would have been too many questions, and it's more than possible that my version would not be believed. Let's face it, who *would* believe me? No, I realised this as soon as the thing was done, and so I simply got rid of the torn bandages and called in a doctor. Aunt Hester died of a heart attack, or so I'm told, and perhaps she did—straining to do that which, even with her powers, should never have been possible.

During this last fortnight or so since it happened, I've been trying to convince myself that the doctor was right (which I was quite willing enough to believe at the time), but I've been telling myself lies. I think I've known the real truth ever since my parents got the letter from Australia. And lately, reinforcing that truth, there have been the dreams and the daydreams—*or are they?*

This morning I woke up to a lightless void—a numb, black, silent void—wherein I was incapable of even the smallest movement, and I was horribly, hideously frightened. It lasted for only a moment, that's all, but in that moment it seemed to me that I was dead—or that the living ME inhabited a dead body!

Again and again I find myself thinking back on the mad Arab's words as reported by Joachim Feery: "...even from beyond the Grave of Sod..." And in the end I know that this is indeed the answer.

That is why I'm flying tomorrow to Australia. Ostensibly I'm visiting my uncle's wife, my Australian aunt; but really I'm only interested in him, in Uncle George himself. I don't know what I'll be able to do, or even if there is anything I *can* do. My efforts may well be completely useless, and yet I must try to do something.

I *must* try, for I know now that it's that or find myself once again, perhaps permanently, locked in that hellish, nighted—place?—of black oblivion and insensate silence. In the dead and rotting body of my Uncle George, already buried three weeks when Aunt Hester put her mind in his body—*the body she's now trying to vacate in favour of mine!*

THE KISS OF BUGG-SHASH

In 1972 in the UK, Sphere Books had published an anthology titled New Writings in Horror and the Supernatural, Vol 2, *which contained among others a story called "Demoniacal" by David Sutton. This story seemed to me so very much a Mythos-story that I obtained David's permission to write a sequel. The sequel was/is the following story. Both tales would later (1978) appear in tandem in a pamphlet from Jon M. Harvey's small press (Spectre Press), under the title* Cthulhu 3. *I believe they've subsequently seen print in* The Crypt of Cthulhu, *edited by Robert M. Price, and likewise in Price's Fedogan & Bremer anthology,* The New Lovecraft Circle, *1995.*

I

"You let it out?" Thomas Millwright incredulously repeated Ray Nuttall's obliquely offered admission. Alan Bart, Nuttall's somewhat younger companion, nodded in eager if apprehensive agreement, shivering despite the warmth of the Londoner's city flat.

"Yes, we did, sir," he blurted. "But not intentionally, you must understand that. God, never that and certainly not if we'd known what we were doing, but—"

"Christ, Alan, but you're gibbering!" Nuttall's disgusted exclamation cut Bart off in mid-sentence, his weak eyes peering nervously about the flat and giving the lie to his cool controlled tone of voice. "I'm sure Mr. Millwright understands everything we've told him. There's really no need to go on so."

Alan Bart's cynical-seeming friend had pulled himself together somewhat. He had accepted the horror of the thing far more readily than the younger man, since that series of events which three nights earlier had culminated when the two, albeit unwittingly, had indeed called up a demon, or demonic device, from nameless nether-gulfs into the world of men.

"Oh yes, I understand perfectly what you've told me," answered the saturnine, dark-eyed occult scholar, "though I must admit to finding some difficulty in believing that—"

"That a couple of rank amateurs, bungling about with a rather weird and esoteric gramophone record and an evocation from some old eccentric's book of spells, could actually conjure such a being?" Nuttall finished it for him.

"In a nutshell, yes…exactly." The occultist made no bones of it. "Mind you, I can readily enough understand how you might have convinced yourselves that it was so. Self-hypnosis is the basis of many so-called cases of demonic possession."

"We thought you might say something like that," Nuttall told him, "but we can prove our story very easily." His voice was suddenly trembling; he plainly fought to maintain a grip on himself. "However, it's not a pleasant experience…"

"It's horrible, horrible!" The younger man, Bart, jumped up. His normally sallow features were suddenly many shades lighter. "Don't make us prove it, Mr. Millwright! Not that again, God, not that!" his voice began to rise hysterically.

"You needn't stay for it, Alan," Nuttall took pity on the weaker man. "I can stand it on my own, I think, and anyway it will only be for a second. And I won't really be alone, as Mr. Millwright will be with me."

Millwright frowned and rose to his feet from the couch where he had been reclining. His face plainly showed his interest. "Just what would this 'proof' of yours consist of?"

"We would simply turn off the lights for a moment," Nuttall answered, reaching his hand out to the light switch on the wall.

"Wait!" Bart screamed, grabbing his companion's arm. "Wait," he gulped, his eyes wide and fearful. He turned to the occultist: "Is there a light in your bathroom?"

"Of course," Millwright answered, frowning again. He showed Bart to the bathroom door and watched bemused as the young man tremblingly entered. He noticed how Bart made sure that the light in the small room was on before he went in. Then he heard the catch go home on the inside of the door.

Suddenly Millwright began to believe. These two night visitors, with their arsenal of pocket torches and their patently psychotic fear of darkness, were not really pulling his leg. But most probably it was as he had diagnosed; the odds were all in favour of self-hypnosis. They had desired so badly that their experiment should work and they had probably been in such a state of self-induced hysteria at the time, through the music and their esoteric chantings, that they actually believed they had called up a demon from hell.

On the other hand...well, Millwright was not inexperienced in the darker mysteries. Black Magic, practised with a degree of discretion, and the various carefully edited works he had written in the same vein, had made life very easy for him for the past fifteen years. Now, though, he had to see for himself—or, at least, experience—this "proof" that these young men had offered him. Such proof would not be pleasant, the man called Nuttall had warned him. Well, very few magical or necromantic experiences were pleasant; but of course, Nuttall would hardly be willing to demonstrate the thing—whatever it was—if it were really dangerous...

They had not explained exactly what they believed they had released from its nether habitation, but possibly they did not know: They had told him, however, that they knew he was an "expert" in this sort of thing, which was why they had approached him for his help.

And now...there was one easy way to find out what the truth of the matter really was. Millwright returned to his study and into the presence of the olive-skinned man called Nuttall. He saw that his visitor was sweating in anticipation, though he still maintained the vestiges of self-assurance.

"All right, Mr. Nuttall," Millwright said, closing the study door behind him. "Let's have your demonstration."

Nuttall's Adam's apple was visibly bobbing. "I have to stay right here," he muttered, "beside the light switch, so that I can switch it on again. And you'll need to hold my hand, I think, to really—appreciate—the thing. Are you ready?"

Despite his few remaining doubts regards the veracity of their story, the occultist nevertheless felt a thrill of unseen energies, weird forces, building in the air. He almost called a halt to the experiment there and then. Later, he wished that he had....

Instead, he nodded his readiness and, at that, Nuttall switched off the light.

In the brightly lit bathroom, huddled fearfully in one corner with his face screwed up in dread expectation, Alan Bart heard Millwright's high-pitched scream and, seconds later, his sobbing accusations and vicious swearing. He knew then that Ray had "demonstrated". Weak-kneed, he let himself out of the bathroom and made his way unsteadily back to the occultist's study.

There he found what he knew he would find: the horror which he himself had experienced twice already. The two men, his friend Nuttall and the still steadily swearing, bulge-eyed occultist, were hastily removing their outer garments. All the while, they were frenziedly wiping at their faces, shaking their arms and hands and kicking their legs in a concerted effort to be rid of the viscous, clear jelly that covered them head to toe in shiny, gluey envelopes. This was the snail-trail, the residue of the Black One—the Filler of Space—He Who Comes in the Dark!—that creature or power of outer dimensions which only the purity of the light might disperse!

Nuttall sat wrapped in a towel, pale, drawn and shivering beside the warmth of a gas fire whose glowing logs looked so very nearly real. He and the occultist had showered to cleanse themselves of the obnoxious, slimy coverings and now Millwright sat, listening, while Bart explained the most intricate details of what had gone on before.

Bart narrated how he and Nuttall had stumbled across the means of drawing the horror of the jelly-substance through the fabric of alien dimensions to their own world; how they had discovered that light held this creature of darkness, this fly-the-light, at bay; and how thereafter, whenever they found themselves in darkness, the thing that lived and chittered in darkness would return to try to drown them in its exuded essence. At this mention, all eyes flickered towards that thick liquid which even now slimed the floor in stinking, drying puddles, that juice which not one of the three could as yet bring himself to touch or clear away.

"And you actually have a copy of *Mad Berkley's Book?*" The shaken occultist asked, the silver tassels of his oriental dressing-gown moving to the shudders of his body.

"Yes, it belonged to Ray's grandfather," Bart agreed. "We've brought it with us." He crossed the room to where his coat hung and tremulously removed from a large inner pocket a leather-bound volume in iron clasps. He handed the book to the occultist who opened it, studied its contents for a few moments, then snapped it decisively shut.

"Oh yes, that's *Mad Berkley's Book* all right. And, indeed, it's in better condition than my own copy. Old Berkley's believed to have combined all the worst elements of a score of esoteric volumes in this work—the *Necronomicon*, the *Cthaat Aquadingen*, the German *Unaussprechlichen Kulten*—and, by God, I can readily enough believe it now! I myself have never used the book. I knew that a lot of the stuff Old Berkley put down on paper was damnably dangerous, of course, but *this*! This is a monstrous evil!"

He paused for a moment, his hands shaking terribly; then his eyes hardened as he turned them upon Nuttall by the gas fire. "You bloody fool!

You've damned me with the same hideous curse! Didn't you realise that once I had experienced that—thing—that I, too, would be subject to such visitations?"

Nuttall looked up, a shadow of his previous cynical control returning to drawn, haggard features. "I guessed it might be so, yes," he admitted, then hastily went on; "but don't you see it had to be this way? How else could I be sure you'd help us? Now that you're in the same boat, you have to help. If you can…exorcise…this horror, then we'll all be safe. At least you have an incentive…now!"

"Why, you damned young—" Millwright rose in a fury, but Bart caught at his sleeve.

"What use to fight about it, Mr. Millwright? Don't you see that there's no time for that? Sooner or later, unless we find…well…an antidote, one by one, accidentally, we'll all be caught in the dark. When that happens…then…" Bart's voice trailed ominously away as he left the sentence unfinished.

"But I don't know of any 'antidote' as you put it," the occultist rounded on him, his voice harsh.

"Then we'd better start looking for one right away," Ray Nuttall snapped, the situation finally getting the better of his nerves. "Surely you have some idea of what the thing is? I mean, you're the expert, after all. Are there no other occultists we can consult?"

"I know of three or four others in England of more than ordinary power, yes," Millwright answered, pondering their problem. Then he shook his head. "No use to contact them, however. They wouldn't help me. I might as well admit it right now—my reputation in occult circles is not good. I've used what I know of the dark powers to my own ends far too often for the liking of certain lily-livered contemporaries, I'm afraid. There are so-called 'ethics' even in matters such as these. The only men I know who might have helped—though even that is doubtful—have also fallen foul of some evil, I fear.

"You've heard of Titus Crow and Henri-Laurent de Marigny? Yes? Well, they disappeared together some months ago, when Crow's home was destroyed in a freak lightening storm. That rules them out. No, if I'm to beat this thing, then I'm to do it on my own…but you two will help me. Now, we've much to do. There'll be no sleep for us tonight. Personally, I doubt if I shall ever sleep again!"

II

With all the lights of the flat ablaze, midnight found the three in various attitudes of uneasy study. Millwright had heard their story through once more in all its detail before deciding on a definite course of action. At the mention of the newspaper article that quoted Millwright and had sparked off Nuttall's interest in the progressive group, Fried Spiders, the occultist admitted that his only interest at the time had been in gaining publicity for his recent book on occult themes. In fact, he had never so much as heard the LP in question.

Millwright concluded that the two accidentally hit upon the perfect atmosphere and setting, leading up to the conjuration. Doubtless the soft drugs Nuttall had access to had helped bring about a proper connection with outside spheres, had contributed in forming a link, as it were, with alien dimensions. When the group had finished their few lines of intoned invocation, Nuttall had taken up the chant to its conclusion... And then came the Black One! Never guessing that any such visitation might actually occur, Nuttall had failed to take the traditional precaution of prisoning the horror in a pentagram.

And it *was* a horror! A thing with invisible, evil eyes that saw in the dark, with mouths and lips that sucked and slobbered. They had driven it off simply by switching on the light. If they had not...then soon they would have drowned in its hideous residual slime, the juices it exuded from alien agglutinous pores.

Having driven the thing off, they had thought that they were rid of it. However, later that night, after cleaning up, when Bart sought to leave Nuttall's place to return home, out in the dark the thing had come to him again. He had barely been able to make it back to Nuttall's door and the sanctuary of the blessed light within.

Now, unseen, the Black One waited for the summons of its beloved darkness, when it could return again with its sucking mouths to drown its liberators in loathsome slime. And now, too, it waited for Millwright...

The occultist was only too well aware of the horror of living with this nightmare—of never knowing when the lights might fail; the constant fear of accidentally knocking oneself unconscious and waking at night in a darkened room, or perhaps not waking at all! Now, at the midnight hour, tired as he was, he patiently turned the leaves of a great and anciently esoteric textbook, hopeful of finding some clue as to the nature of the thing his visitors had called up from the darker spheres.

Nuttall and Bart were similarly employed, albeit with lesser works of reference. Only the dry rustles of flipped pages, the occasional muttered curse as a promising stream of research went dry and the ticking of Millwright's wall-clock disturbed the silence. Their task seemed impossible; and yet by morning, through sheer diligence and hard work—engendered of a dreadful fear—they had learned much of the horror that even now stalked the dark places and awaited them hungrily. Though what they had discovered had only served to increase their terror.

This creature, being or power, had been known in the predawn world to the earliest Black Magicians and Necromancers. Records had come down even from predeluge Atlantis of "The Night Thing"— "The Black One"— "The Filler of Space"— "Bugg-Shash the Terrible"—a demon whom Eibon of Mhu Thulan himself had written of as being:

> One of the darkest Beings of the Netherworld, whose Trail is as that of a monstrous Snail, who hails from the blackest Pits of the most remote Spheres. Cousin to Yibb-Tstll, Bugg-Shash, too is a Drowner; His lips do suck and lick; His Kiss is the slimy Kiss of the hideous Death. He wakes the very Dead to His Command, and encased in the horror of His Essence even the worm-ravaged Lich hastens to His Bidding…

This from that tome so carefully scrutinized and guarded from the view of his two assistants by Millwright.

And from Feery's *Notes On The Cthaat Aquadingen*—though Millwright had warned that Feery's reconstructions and translations were often at fault or fanciful in their treatment of the original works—Bart had culled the following cryptic information:

> Lest any brash or inexperienced Wizard be tempted to call forth one of ye Drowners—be it Yibb-Tstll or Bugg-Shash—this Warning shall guide him & inform him of his Folly. For ye Drowners are of a like treacherous & require even ye most delicate Handling & minutest Attention to thaumaturgic Detail. Yibb-Tstll may only be controlled by use of ye Soul-searing Barrier of Naach-Tith, & Bugg-Shash may only be contained in ye Pentagram of Power. Too, ye Drowners must be sent early about ye Business of them, which is Death, lest they find ways to turn upon ye Caller. Call NOT upon Bug-Shash for ye sake of mere idle curiosity; for ye Great Black One,

neither Him nor His Cousin, will return of His own Accord to His Place, but will seek out by any Means a Victim, being often that same Wizard which uttered ye Calling. Of ye two is Bugg-Shash most treacherous & vilely cunning, for should no Sacrifice or Victim be prepared for His Coming, He will not go back without He takes His Caller with Him, must needs He stay an hundred Years to accomplish His Purpose…

Nuttall supplied the smallest contribution towards their knowledge of the horror lurking in the darkness. This fragment was from a heavy, handwritten tome whose title had been carefully removed from its spine by burning with a hot iron—and it *was* a fragment. Of the Filler of Space, the book related only this:

Bugg-Shash is unbearable! His lips suck; He knows not defeat but brings down His victim at the last; aye, even though He follows that victim unto Death and beyond to achieve His purpose. And there was a riddle known to my forefathers:

What evil wakes that should lie dead,
Swathed in horror toe to head?

"That's from the *Necronomicon*!" Millwright cried when, towards dawn, Nuttall found this piece and read it aloud in the brightly lit study. "It is Alhazred!" The occultist snatched the book from the other's hands to pore eagerly over the page—then threw it down in disgust.

"Only that," he grumbled, "nothing more. But it's a clue! This book is simply a hodge-podge of occult lore and legend, but perhaps the Mad Arab's *Necronomicon*—in which I'm sure those lines have their origin—perhaps *that* book contains more on the same subject. It's certainly worth a try. Fortunately, the blacker side of my reputation has not yet reached the authorities at the British Museum. They recognise me as an 'authority' in my own right—as a genuine scholar. Through them, I have access to archives forbidden to most others. I admit that these scraps we've found worry me…horribly! But we must remember that every magical conjuration has its dangers. So far in this business I have—well, I've escaped justice, so to speak. Yes, and I hope to do so again.

"If there is a way to…deflect…this horror, then I now believe I stand every chance of finding it, though that may take some time. This clue is the one I needed." He tapped the book with a fingernail. "If not...at least we know what we're up against. Personally, well, you will never find my home wanting for a gross of candles; I will always have a store of dry batteries and electric light bulbs; I will always carry on my person at least one cigarette lighter and a metal box of fresh, dry matches. Bugg-Shash will not find me unprepared when darkness falls..."

Through the morning, Bart and Nuttall slept and, even though daylight streamed in across Millwright's balcony and through his windows, still the electric lights burned while candles sank down slowly on their wicks. In mid-afternoon, when the occultist returned in cautious triumph, the two were up and about.

"I have it," he said, closing the door of the sumptuous flat behind him. "At least, I think so. It is the Third Sathlatta. There was more on Bugg-Shash in the *Necronomicon*, and that in turn led me to the *Cthaat Aquadingen*," he shuddered. "It is a counterspell to be invoked—as with many of the Sathlat-tae—at midnight. Tonight we'll free ourselves of Bugg-Shash forever... unless..." As he finished the occultist frowned. Despite his words, there was uncertainty in his tone.

"Yes?" Nuttall prompted him. "Unless what? Is something wrong?"

"No, no," Millwright shook his head angrily, tiredly. "It's just that...again I've come across this peculiar warning!"

"What warning is that?" Bart worriedly asked, his face twitching nervously.

"Oh, there are definite warnings, of sorts," Millwright answered, "but they're never clearly stated. Confound that damned Arab! It seems he never once wrote a word without that he wrapped it in a riddle!" He collapsed into a chair.

"Go on," prompted Nuttall, "explain. How does this 'counterspell' of yours work...and what are these 'warnings' that you're so worried about?"

"As to your first question: I don't believe there's any need to explain more than I've done already. But to enlighten you, albeit briefly; the Sath-lattae consist of working spells and counterspells. The third Sathlatta is of the latter order. As to what I'm frightened of, well..."

"Yes?" Nuttall impatiently prompted him again.

"As applicable to our present situation," Millwright finally went on, "—in this predicament we're in—the third Sathlatta is...incomplete!"

"You mean it won't work?" Bart demanded, his eyes wide and fearful.

"Oh, yes, it'll work all right. But—"

"For God's sake!" Nuttall cried, his usually disciplined nerves stretched now to the breaking point, evidence of which shoved clearly in his high, quavering voice. "Get on, man!"

"How do I explain something which I can't readily understand myself?" Millwright snarled, rounding on the frightened man. "And you'd better not start shouting at me, my friend. Why, but for your meddling, none of us would be in this position...and remember that, without my help, you're stuck with it forever!"

At that, Nuttall s face went very white and he began a stuttered apology. The occultist cut him short. "Forget it. I'll tell you why I'm worried. To put it simply, the third Sathlatta carries a clause!"

"A clause?" Bart repeated the word wonderingly, plainly failing to understand.

"To quote Alhazred," Millwright ignored him,"the counterspell's protection lasts 'only unto death'!"

For a moment there was silence; then Bart gave a short, strained laugh. "Only unto death? Why, who could ask fairer than that? I really don't see—"

"And one other-thing," the occultist continued. "The third Sathlatta is not irrevocable. Its action may be reversed simply by uttering the Sathlatta itself in reverse order."

Millwright's guests stared at him for a few moments without speaking; then Nuttall said: "Does anyone else know of our...problem?"

"Not unless you've told someone else," the occultist answered, a deep frown creasing his forehead. "Have you?"

"No," Nuttall answered, "we haven't...but you see what I mean, don't you? What is there to worry about, if it's all as simple as you say? We, certainly, will never mess about with this sort of thing again...and who else is there to know what's happened? Even if someone was aware that we'd conjured up a devil, it's unlikely he'd know how to reverse this process of yours. It's doubtful anyone would even want or dare to, isn't it?"

Millwright considered it and gradually his manner became more relaxed. "Yes, you're right, of course," he answered. "It's just that I don't like complications in these things. You see, I know something of the Old Adepts. They didn't issue the sort of warnings I've seen here for nothing. This Bugg-Shash—whatever he is—must be the very worst order of demons. Everything about him is...demoniacal!"

III

That same evening, from copious notes copied in the rare books department of the British Museum, Millwright set up all the paraphernalia of his task. He cleared the floor of his study. Then, in what appeared to Nuttall and Bart completely random positions—which were, in fact, carefully measured, if in utterly alien tables—upon the naked floor, he placed candles, censers and curious copper bowls. When he was satisfied with the arrangement of these implements, leaving the centre of the floor clear, he chalked on the remaining surrounding floor-space strange and disturbing magical symbols in a similarly confusing and apparently illogical over-all design. Central to all these preparatory devices, he drew a plain white circle and, as the midnight hour approached, he invited his guests to enter with him into this protective ring.

During the final preparations the candles had been lit. The contents of the censers and bowls, too, now sent up to the ceiling thinly wavering columns of coloured smoke and incense. Moreover, the purely electrical lights of the room had been switched off—very much to the almost hysterical Bart's dislike—so that only the candles gave a genuine, if flickering, light while the powders and herbs in their bowls and censers merely glowed a dull red.

As the first stroke of midnight sounded from the clock on the wall, Millwright drew from his pocket a carefully folded sheet of paper. In a voice dead of emotion—devoid, almost, of all human inflection—he read the words so carefully copied earlier that day from a near-forgotten tome in the dimmer reaches of the British Museum.

It is doubtful whether Bart or Nuttall could ever have recalled the jumble of alien vowels, syllables and discordants that rolled in seemingly chaotic disorder off Millwright's tongue in that dimly lit room. Certainly, it would have been impossible for any mere mortal, unversed in those arts with which Millwright had made himself familiar, to repeat that hideously jarring, incredible sequence of sounds. To utter the thing backwards, then—"in reverse order," as Millwright had had it—must plainly be out of the question. This thought, if not the uppermost in their minds, undoubtedly occurred to the two initiates as the occultist came to the end of his performance and the echoes of his hellish liturgy died away...but, within the space of seconds, this and all other thoughts were driven from their minds by sheer terror!

Even Millwright believed, at first, that he had made some terrible mistake, for now there fell upon the three men in the chalked circle a tangible weight of horror and impending doom! Bart screamed and would have fled the circle and the room at once—doubtless to his death—but the occultist grabbed him and held him firmly.

Slowly but surely, the candles dimmed as their flames inexplicably lowered. Then, one by one, they began to flicker out, apparently self-extinguished. Bart's struggles and screaming became such that Nuttall, too, had to hold on to him to prevent his rushing from the circle. Suddenly, there came to the ears of the three—as if from a thousand miles away—the merest whisper at first, a susurration, as heard in a sounding shell. The rustling chitterings of what could only be…a presence!

Bart promptly fainted. Millwright and Nuttall lowered him to the floor and crouched beside his unconscious form, still holding him tightly in their terror, staring into the surrounding shadows. The hideously evil chitterings, madly musical in an indefinable alien manner, grew louder. And then… something slimy and wet moved gelatinously in the darker shadows of the room's corners!

"Millwright!" Nuttall's voice cracked on that one exclamation. The word had been an almost inarticulate utterance, such as a child might make, crying out for its mother in the middle of a particularly frightening nightmare.

"Stay still! And be quiet!" Millwright commanded, his own voice no less cracked and high-pitched.

Only two candles burned now, so low and dim that they merely pushed back the immediate shadows. As the occultist reached out a tremulous hand to draw one of these into the circle…so the other blinked out, leaving only a spiral of grey smoke hanging in the near-complete darkness.

At this, the abominable chittering grew louder still. It surrounded the circle completely now and, for the first time, the two conscious men clearly saw that which the single, tiny remaining flame held at bay. Creeping up on all sides, to the very line of the chalked circle, the Thing came; a glistening, shuddering wall of jelly-like ooze in which many mouths gaped and just as many eyes monstrously ogled! This was Bugg-Shash the Drowner, The Black One, The Filler of Space. Indeed, the bulk of this…Being?…did seem to fill the entire study! All bar the blessed sanctuary of the circle.

The eyes were…beyond words, but worse still were those mouths. Sucking and whistling with thickly viscous lips, the mouths glistened and slobbered and, from out of those gluttonous orifices poured the lunatic chitterings of alien song—the Song of Bugg-Shash—as His substance towered up and leaned inwards to form a slimy ceiling over their very heads!

Nuttall closed his eyes and began to pray out loud, while Millwright simply moaned and groaned in his terror, unable to voice prayers to a God he had long forsaken; but though it seemed that all was lost, the Third Sathlatta had not failed them. Even as the ceiling of jelly began an apparently inexorable descent, so the remaining candle flared up and, at that, the bulk of Bugg-Shash broke and ran like water through a shattered dam. The wall and ceiling of quivering protoplasm with its loathsome eyes and mouths seemed to waver and shrink before Millwright's eyes as the awful Black One drew back to the darker shadows.

Then, miraculously, the many extinct candles flared up, returning to life one by one and no less mysteriously than they had snuffed themselves out. The occultist knew then that what he had seen had merely been an immaterial visitation, a vision of what *might* have been, but for the power of the Third Sathlatta.

Simultaneously with Bart's return to consciousness, Millwright shouted: "We've won!"

As Nuttall ventured to open incredulous eyes the occultist stepped out of the circle, crossed to the light switch and flooded the room with light. The thing he and Nuttall had witnessed must indeed have been merely a vision—a demon-inspired hallucination—for no sign of the horror remained. The floor, the walls and bookshelves, the pushed-aside furniture, all were clean and dry, free of the horrid Essence of Bugg-Shash. No single trace of His visit showed in any part of the room; no single crack or crevice of the pine floor knew the morbid loathsomeness of His snail-trail slime...

IV

"Ray!" Alan Bart cried, shouldering his way through the long-haired, tassel-jacketed patrons of The Windsor's smokeroom. Nuttall saw him, waved him in the direction of a table and ordered another drink. With a glass in each hand he then made his way from the bar, through the crush of regulars, to where Bart now sat with his back to the wall, his fist wrapped tightly around an evening newspaper.

Over a week had passed since their terrifying experience at the London flat of Thomas Millwright. Since then, they had started to grow back into their old creeds and customs. Although they still did not quite trust the dark, they had long since proved for themselves the efficacy of Millwright's Third Sathlatta. Ever the cynic, and despite the fact that he still trembled in dark places, Nuttall now insisted upon taking long walks along lone country lanes of an evening, usually ending up at The Windsor before closing time. Thus Bart had known where to find him.

"What's up?" Nuttall questioned as he took a seat beside the younger man. He noted with a slight tremor of alarm the drawn, worried texture of his friend's face.

"Millwright's dead!" Bart abruptly blurted, without preamble. "He's dead—a traffic accident—run down by a lorry not far from his flat. He was identified in the mortuary. It's all in the paper." He spread the newspaper before Nuttall who hardly glanced at it.

If the olive-skinned man was shocked, it did not show; his weak eyes had widened slightly at Bart's disclosure, nothing more. He let the news sink in, then shrugged his shoulders.

Bart was completely taken aback by his friend's negative attitude. "We did *know* him!" he protested.

"Briefly," Nuttall acknowledged; and then, to Bart's amazement, he smiled. "That's a relief," he muttered.

Bart drew away from him. "What? Did I hear you say—"

"It's a relief, yes," Nuttall snapped. "Don't you see? He was the only one we knew who could ever have brought that…*thing*…down on us again. And now he's gone."

For a while they sat in silence, tasting their drinks, allowing the human noises of the crowded room to close in and impinge upon their beings. Then Bart said: "Ray, do you suppose that…?"

"Hmm?" Nuttall looked at him. "Do I suppose what, Alan?"

"Oh, nothing really. I was just thinking about what Millwright told us; about the protection of that spell of his lasting 'only unto death'!"

"Oh?" Nuttall answered. "Well, if I were you, I shouldn't bother. It's something I don't intend to find out about for a long time."

"And there's something else bothering me," Bart admitted, not really listening to Nuttall's perfunctory answer. "It's something I can't quite pin down—part of what we discovered that night at Millwright's place, when we were going through all those old books. Damned if I can remember what it is, though!"

"Then forget it!" Nuttall grinned. "And while you're at it, how about a drink? It's your round."

Against his better instincts, but not wanting Nuttall to see how desperately he feared the darkness still, Bart allowed himself to be talked into walking home. Nuttall lived in a flat in one of the rather more "flash" areas of the city, but walking they would have to pass Bart's place first. Bart did not mind the dark so much—he said—so long as he was not alone.

Low, scudding clouds obscured the stars as they walked and a chill autumn wind blew discarded wrappers, the occasional leaf and loose, eerily-flapping sheets of evening "racing specials" against their legs.

Nuttall's flat was city-side of a suburban estate, while Bart's place lay more on the outskirts of the city proper. The whole area, though, was still quite new, so that soon the distances between welcome lamp-posts increased; there was no need for a lot of light way out here. With the resultant closing-in of darkness, Bart shuddered and pressed closer to his apparently fearless friend. He did not know it, but Nuttall was deep in worried thought. Bart's words in the smokeroom of The Windsor had brought niggling doubts flooding to the forefront of his consciousness; he could quite clearly recall all that they had uncovered at Millwright's home—including that which Bart had forgotten…

At the city end of Bart's road, almost half-way to Nuttall's flat and within half a mile of Bart's door, they saw a man atop a ladder attending to an apparently malfunctioning street lamp. The light flickered, flared, then died as they approached the lamp-post and the base of the ladder.

"These people," Bart asserted with a little shudder, "are the grafters. Out here all hours of the night—just to make sure that we have…light."

Without a breath of warning, simultaneous with Bart's shivery uttering of the word "light", the great bowl of the street lamp crashed down from above to shatter into a million glass fragments at their feet.

"My God!" Nuttall shouted up at the black silhouette clambering unsteadily down the ladder. "Take it easy, old chap. You bloody near dropped that thing right on our heads!"

The two men stopped in the dark street to steady the precarious-looking ladder and, as they did so, a splattering of liquid droplets fell from above, striking their hands and upturned faces. In the darkness they could not see those liquid droplets…but they could feel the clinging sliminess of them! Frozen in spontaneous horror, they stared at each other through the shrouding night as the figure on the ladder stepped down between them.

Bart's pocket torch cut a jerky swath of light across Nuttall's frozen features until it played upon the face of the man from the ladder. That face—stickily wet and hideously vacant, dripping nightmare slime as it was—*was nevertheless the face of Millwright!*

Millwright, the pawn of the Black One, fled from the mortuary—where Bugg-Shash had found his body in the dark—to accomplish that Being's purpose, the purpose He must pursue before He could return to His own hellish dimension!

Only blind instinct, the instinct of self-preservation, had caused Bart to reach for his torch; but the sight revealed by its beam had completely unnerved him. His torch fell from uselessly twitching fingers, clattering on the pavement, and the dead man's heel came down upon it with shattering force. Again the darkness closed in.

Then the slimy figure between the two men moved and they felt fingers like bands of iron enclosing their wrists. The zombie that was Millwright exerted fantastic strength to hold them—or rather, Bugg-Shash exerted His strength through the occultist's corpse—as dead lips opened to utter the ghastly, soul-destroying strains of the *reversed* Third Sathlatta!

In the near-distant darkness faint, delighted chitterings commenced; and the weird trio thrashed about across the road, to and fro in a leaping, twisting, screaming tug-o'-war of death as, at last, the thing that Bart had forgotten came back to his collapsing, nightmare-blasted mind:

> He wakes the very Dead to His Command, and encased in the horror of his Essence even the worm-ravaged Lich hastens to His bidding…

The hellish dance lasted, as did the screaming, until they felt the lips of Bugg-Shash and his monstrous kisses…

DE MARIGNY'S CLOCK

In May to June 1979, when I was a recently promoted Sergeant and had been at the recruiting office for just a few months, I found the time to write "De Marigny's Clock", a story that August Derleth liked at first sight. It would fit right into The Caller of The Black, *he said, which it did, two years later. It's another one of those stories with quite a long printing history, but I won't go into it here. Suffice it to say that it features Titus Crow and the world's strangest timepiece, a sort of longcase clock that you might even call a "space-timepiece". The clock wasn't my invention; it belonged to Lovecraft and E. Hoffman Price long before me, but Titus Crow and his ward, Henri Laurent De Marigny would later borrow it to take them on some of their weirdest adventures: even to frozen Borea, and beyond that to the home of the Elder Gods themselves—in far Elysia!*

Any intrusions, other than those condoned or invited, upon the privacy of Titus Crow at his bungalow retreat, Blowne House, on the outskirts of London, were almost always automatically classified by that gentleman as open acts of warfare. In the first place for anyone to make it merely to the doors of Crow's abode without an invitation—often even *with* one—was a sure sign of the appearance on the scene of a forceful and dogmatic character; qualities which were almost guaranteed to clash with Crow's own odd nature. For Blowne House seemed to exude an atmosphere all its own; an exhalation of impending *something* which usually kept the place and its grounds free even from birds and mice; and it was quite unusual for Crow himself to invite visitors. He kept strange hours and busied himself with stranger matters and, frankly, was almost antisocial even in his most "engaging" moments. Over the years the reasons for this apparent inhospitality had grown, or so it seemed to Crow, increasingly clear-cut.

For one thing, his library contained quite a large number of rare and highly costly books, many of them long out of print and some of them never officially in print, and London apparently abounded with unscrupulous "collectors" of such items. For another his studies, usually in occult matters and obscure archaeological, antiquarian or anthropological research, were such as required the most concentrated attention and personal involvement, completely precluding any disturbances from outside sources.

Not that the present infringement came while Crow was engaged with any of his many and varied activities—it did not; it came in the middle of the night, rousing him from deep and dreamless slumbers engendered by a long day of frustrated and unrewarding work on de Marigny's clock. And Titus Crow was not amused.

"What the hell's going on here? Who are you and what are you doing in my house?" He had sat bolt upright in bed almost as soon as the light went on. His forehead had come straight into contact with a wicked-looking automatic held in the fist of a most unbeautiful thug. The man was about five feet eight inches in height, thickset, steady on legs which were short in comparison with the rest of his frame. He had a small scar over his left eye and a mouth that slanted downward—cynically, Crow supposed—from left to right. Most unbeautiful.

"Just take it easy, guv', and there'll be no bother," the thug said, his voice soft but ugly. Crow's eyes flicked across the room to where a second hoodlum stood, just within the bedroom door, a nervous grin twisting his pallid features. "Find anything, Pasty?" the man with the pistol questioned, his eyes never leaving Crow's face for a second.

"Nothing, Joe," came the answer, "a few old books and a bit of silver, nothing worth our while—yet. He'll tell us where it is, though, won't you, chum?"

"Pasty!" Crow exclaimed. "Powers of observation, indeed! I was just thinking, before hearing your name, what a thin, pasty creature you look—Pasty." Crow grinned, got out of bed and put on his flame-red dressing-gown. Joe looked him up and down appraisingly. Crow was tall and broad-shouldered and it was plain to see that in his younger days he had been a handsome man. Even now there was a certain tawniness about him, and his eyes were still very bright and more than intelligent. Overall his aspect conveyed an impression of hidden power, which Joe did not particularly care much for. He decided it would be best to show his authority at the earliest opportunity. And Crow obligingly supplied him with that opportunity in the next few seconds.

The jibe the occultist had aimed at Pasty had meanwhile found its way home. Pasty's retaliation was a threat: "Lovely colour, that dressing-gown," he said, "it'll match up nicely if you bleed when I rap you on your head." He laughed harshly, slapping a metal cosh into his open palm. "But before that, you will tell us where it is, won't you?"

"Surely," Crow answered immediately, "it's third on the left, down the passage…*ugh*!" Joe's pistol smacked into Crow's cheek, knocking him sprawling. He carefully got up, gingerly fingering the red welt on his face.

"Now that's just to show you that we don't want any more funnies, see?" Joe said.

"Yes, I see," Crow's voice trembled with suppressed rage. "Just what do you want?"

"Now is that so difficult to figure out?" Pasty asked, crossing the room. "Money…we want your money! A fine fellow like you, with a place like this—" the lean man glanced appraisingly about the room, noting the silk curtains, the boukhara rugs; the original erotic illustrations by Aubrey Beardsley in their rosewood frames—"ought to have a good bit of ready cash lying about…we want it!"

"Then I'm sorry to have to disappoint you," Crow told him happily, seating himself on his bed, "I keep my money in a bank—what little I've got."

"Up!" ordered Joe briefly. "Off the bed." He pulled Crow to one side, nodding to Pasty, indicating some sort of action involving the bed. Crow stepped forward as Pasty yanked back the covers from the mattress and took out a sharp knife.

"Now wait—" he began, thoroughly alarmed.

"Hold it, guv', or I might just let Pasty use his blade on you!" Joe waved his gun in Crow's face, ordering him back. "You see, you'd be far better off to tell us where the money is without all this trouble. This way you're just going to see your little nest wrecked around you." He waited, giving Crow the opportunity to speak up, then indicated to Pasty that he should go ahead.

Pasty went ahead!

He ripped open the mattress along both sides and one end, tearing back the soft outer covering to expose the stuffing and springs beneath, then pulling out the interior in great handfuls, flinging them down on the floor in total disregard of Crow's utter astonishment and concern.

"See, gov', you're a recluse—in our books, anyway—and retiring sorts like you hide their pennies in the funniest places. Like in mattresses…or behind wall-pictures!" Joe gave Pasty a nod, waving his pistol at the Beardsleys.

"Well for God's sake, just *look* behind them," Crow snarled, again starting forward. "There's no need to rip them off the walls!"

"Here!" Pasty exclaimed, turning an enquiring eye on the outraged householder. "These pictures worth anything then?"

"Only to a collector—you'd never find a fence for stuff like that," Crow replied.

"Hah! Not so stupid, our recluse!" Joe grinned. "But being clever won't get you anywhere, guv', except hospital maybe... Okay, Pasty, leave the man's dirty pictures alone. You—" he turned to Crow "—your study; we've been in there, but only passing through. Let's go, guv'; you can give us a hand to, er, shift things about." He pushed Crow in the direction of the door.

Pasty was last to enter the study. He did so shivering, an odd look crossing his face. Pasty did not know it but he was a singularly rare person, one of the world's few truly "psychic" men. Crow was another—one who had the *talent* to a high degree—and he sensed Pasty's sudden feeling of apprehension.

"Snug little room, isn't it?" he asked, grinning cheerfully at the uneasy thug.

"Never mind how pretty the place is—try the panelling, Pasty," Joe directed.

"Eh?" Pasty's mind obviously was not on the job. "The panelling?" His eyes shifted nervously round the room.

"Yes, the panelling!" Joe studied his partner curiously. "What's wrong with you, then?" His look of puzzlement turned to one of anger. "Now come on, Pasty boy, get a grip! At this rate we'll be here all bleeding night!"

Now it happened that Titus Crow's study was the pride of his life, and the thought of the utter havoc his unwelcome visitors could wreak in there was a terrifying thing to him. He determined to help them in their abortive search as much as he could; they would not find anything—there was nothing to find!—but this way he could at least ensure as little damage as possible before they realised there was no money in the house and left. They were certainly unwilling to believe anything he said about the absence of substantive funds! But then again, to anyone not knowing him reasonably well—and few did—Crow's home and certain of its appointments might certainly point to a man of considerable means. Yet he was merely comfortable, not wealthy, and, as he had said, what money he did have was safe in a bank. The more he helped them get through with their search the quicker they would leave. He had just made up his mind to this effect when Pasty found the hidden recess by the fireside.

"Here!" The nervous look left Pasty's face as he turned to Joe. "Listen to this." He rapped on a square panel. The sound was dull, hollow. Pasty swung his cosh back purposefully.

"No, wait—I'll open is for you." Crow held up his hands in protest.

"Go on then, get it open." Joe ordered. Crow moved over to the wall and expertly slid back the panel to reveal a dim shelf behind. On the shelf was a single book. Pasty pushed Crow aside, lifted out the book and read off its title:

"The…what?…Cthaat Aquadingen! Huh!" Then his expression quickly turned to one of pure disgust and loathing. "Ughhh!" He flung the book away from him across the room, hastily wiping his hands down his jacket. Titus Crow received a momentary but quite vivid mental message from the mind of the startled thug. It was a picture of things rotting in vaults of crawling darkness, and he could well understand why Pasty was suddenly trembling.

"That…that damn book's wet!" the shaken crook exclaimed nervously.

"No, just sweating!" Crow informed. "The binding is, er, human skin, you see. Somehow it still retains the ability to sweat—a sure sign that it's going to rain."

"Claptrap!" Joe snapped. "And you get a grip of yourself," he snarled at Pasty. "There's something about this place I don't like either; but I'm not letting it get me down." He turned to Crow, his mouth strained and twisting in anger: "And from now on you speak when you're spoken to." Then carefully, practicedly, he turned his head and slowly scanned the room, taking in the tall bookshelves with their many volumes, some ancient, others relatively modern; and he glanced at Pasty and grinned knowingly. "Pasty," Joe ordered, "get them books off the shelves—I want to see what's behind them. How about it, recluse, you got anything behind there?"

"Nothing, nothing at all," Crow quickly answered. "For goodness sake don't go pulling them down; some of them are coming to pieces as it is. No!"

His last cry was one of pure protestation; horror at the defilement of his collection. The two thugs ignored him.

Pasty, seemingly over his nervousness, happily went to work, scattering the books left, right and centre. Down came the collected works of Edgar Allan Poe, the first rare editions of Machen's and Lovecraft's fiction; then the more ancient works, of Josephus, Magnus, Levi, Borellus, Erdschluss and Wittingby; closely followed by a connected set on oceanic evil: Gaston Le Fe's Dwellers in the Depths, Oswald's Legends of Liqualia, Gantley's Hydrophinnae, the German Unter-Zee Kulten and Hartrack's In Pressured Places…

Crow could merely stand and watch it all, a black rage growing in his heart; and Joe, not entirely insensitive to the occultist's mood, gripped his pistol a little tighter and unsmilingly cautioned him: "Just take it easy, hermit. There's still time to speak up—just tell us where you hide your money and it's all over. No? Okay, what's next?" His eyes swept the now littered room again, coming to rest in a dimly lighted corner where stood a great clock.

In front of the clock—an instrument apparently of the "grandfather" class; at least, from a distance of that appearance—stood a small occasional table bearing an adjustable reading-lamp, one or two books and a few scattered sheets of notepaper. Seeing the direction in which Joe's actions were leading him, Crow smiled inwardly and wished his criminal visitor all the best. If Joe could make anything of that timepiece, then he was a cleverer man than Titus Crow; and if he could actually open it, as is possible and perfectly normal with more orthodox clocks, then Crow would be eternally grateful to him. For the sarcophagus-like thing in the dim corner was that same instrument with which Crow had busied himself all the previous day and on many, many other days since first he purchased it more than ten years earlier. And none of his studies had done him a bit of good! He was still as unenlightened with regard to the clock's purpose as he had been a decade ago.

Allegedly the thing had belonged to one Etienne-Laurent de Marigny, once a distinguished student of occult and oriental mysteries and antiquities, but where de Marigny had come by the coffin-shaped clock was yet another mystery. Crow had purchased it on the assurance of its auctioneer that it was, indeed, that same timepiece mentioned in certain of de Marigny's papers as being "a door on all space and time; one which only certain adepts—not all of this world—could use to its intended purpose!" There were, too, rumours that a certain Eastern mystic, the Swami Chandraputra, had vanished forever from the face of the Earth after squeezing himself into a cavity hidden beneath the panel of the lower part of the clock's coffin shape. Also, de Marigny had supposedly had the ability to open at will that door into which the Swami vanished—but that was a secret he had taken with him to the grave. Titus Crow had never been able to find even a keyhole; and while the clock weighed what it should for its size, yet when one rapped on the lower panel the sound such rappings produced were not hollow as might be expected. A curious fact—a curious history altogether—but the clock itself was even more curious to gaze upon or listen to.

Even now Joe was doing just those things: looking at and listening to the clock. He had switched on and adjusted the reading-lamp so that its light fell upon the face of the peculiar mechanism. At first sight of that clock-face

Pasty had gone an even paler shade of grey, with all his nervousness of a few minutes earlier instantly returned. Crow sensed his perturbation; he had had similar feelings while working on the great clock, but he had also had the advantage of understanding where such fears originated. Pasty was experiencing the same sensations he himself had known when first he saw the clock in the auction rooms. Again he gazed at it as he had then; his eyes following the flow of the weird hieroglyphs carved about the dial and the odd movements of the four hands, movements coinciding with no chronological system of earthly origin; and for a moment there reigned an awful silence in the study of Titus Crow. Only the strange clock's enigmatic and oddly paced ticking disturbed a quiet which otherwise might have been that of the tomb.

"That's no clock like any I've ever seen before!" exclaimed an awed Joe. "What do you make of *that*, Pasty?"

Pasty gulped, his Adam's apple visibly bobbing. "I...I don't like it! It...it's shaped like a damned *coffin*! And why has it four hands, and how come they move like that?" He stopped to compose himself a little, and with the cessation of his voice came a soft whispering from beyond the curtained windows. Pasty's eyes widened and his face went white as death. *"What's that?"* His whisper was as soft as the sounds prompting it.

"For God's sake get a grip, will you?" Joe roared, shattering the quiet. He was completely oblivious to Pasty's psychic abilities. "It's rain, that' s what it is—what did you bleeding think it was, spooks? I don't know what's come over you, Pasty, damned if I do. You act as if the place was haunted or something."

"Oh, but it is!" Crow spoke up. "At least the garden is. A very unusual story, if you'd care to hear it."

"We don't care to hear it," Joe snarled. "And I warned you before—speak when you're spoken to. Now, this...*clock*! Get it open, quick."

Crow had to hold himself to stop the ironic laughter he felt welling inside. "I can't," he answered, barely concealing a chuckle. "I don't know how!"

"You what?" Joe shouted incredulously. "You don't know how? What the hell d'you mean?"

"I mean what I say," Crow answered. "So far as I know that clock's not been opened for well over thirty years!"

"Yes? S...so where does it p...plug in?" Pasty enquired, stuttering over the words.

"Should it plug in?" Crow answered with his own question. Joe, however, saw just what Pasty was getting at; as, of course, had the "innocent" Titus Crow.

"Should it plug in, he asks!" Joe mimed sarcastically. He turned to Pasty. "Good point, Pasty boy—now," he turned back to Crow, menacingly, "tell us something, recluse. If your little toy here isn't electric, and if you can't get it open—*then just how do you wind it up?*"

"I don't wind it up—I know nothing whatsoever of the mechanical principles governing it," Crow answered. "You see that book there on the occasional table? Well, that's Walmsley's *Notes on Deciphering Codes, Cryptograms and Ancient Inscriptions*; I've been trying for years merely to understand the hieroglyphs on the dial, let alone *open* the thing. And several notable gentlemen students of matters concerning things not usually apparent or open to the man in the street have opinionated to the effect that yonder *device* is not a clock at all! I refer to Etienne-Laurent de Marigny, the occultist Ward Phillips of Rhode Island in America, and Professor Gordon Walmsley of Goole in Yorkshire; all them believe it to be a space-time-machine—*believed* in the case of the first two mentioned, both those gentlemen now being dead—and I don't know enough about it yet to decide whether or not I agree with them! There's no money in it, if that's what you're thinking."

"Well, I warned you, guv'," Joe snarled, "space-time machine!—My God!—H.G. bloody Wells, he thinks he is! Pasty, tie him up and gag him. I'm sick of his bleeding claptrap. He's got us nervous as a couple of cats, he has!"

"I'll say no more," Crow quickly promised, "you carry on. If you can get it open I'll be obliged to you; I'd like to know what's inside myself."

"Come off it, guv'," Joe grated, then: "Okay, but one more word—you end up immobile, right?" Crow nodded his acquiescence and sat on the edge of his great desk to watch the performance. He really did not expect the thugs to do much more than make fools of themselves. He had not taken into account the possibility—the probability—of violence in the solution of the problem. Joe, as a child, had never had much time for the two-penny wire puzzles sold in the novelty shops. He tried them once or twice, to be sure, but if they would not go first time—well, you could usually *make* them go— with a hammer! As it happened such violence was not necessary.

Pasty had backed up to the door. He was still slapping his cosh into his palm, but it was purely a reflex action now; a nervous reflex action. Crow got the impression that if Pasty dropped his cosh he would probably faint.

"The panels, Pasty," Joe ordered. "The panels in the clock."

"You do it," Pasty answered rebelliously. "That's no clock and I'm not touching it. There's something wrong here."

Joe turned to him in exasperation. "Are you crazy or something? It's a clock and nothing more! And this joker just doesn't want us to see inside.

Now what does that suggest to you?"

"Okay, okay—but you do it this time. I'll stay out of the way and watch funnyman here. I've got a feeling about that thing, that's all." He moved over to stand near Crow who had not moved from his desk. Joe took his gun by the barrel and rapped gently on the panel below the dial of the clock at about waist height. The sound was sharp, solid. Joe turned and grinned at Titus Crow. There certainly seemed to be *something* in there. His grin rapidly faded when he saw Crow grinning back. He turned again to the object of his scrutiny and examined its sides, looking for hinges or other signs pointing to the thing being a hollow container of sorts. Crow could see from the crook's puzzled expression that he was immediately at a loss. He could have told Joe before he began that there was not even evidence of jointing; it was as if the body of the instrument was carved from a solid block of timber— timber as hard as iron.

But Crow had underestimated the determined thug. Whatever Joe's shortcomings as a human being, as a safecracker he knew no peer. Not that de Marigny's clock was in any way a safe, but apparently the same principles applied! For as Joe's hands moved expertly up the sides of the panelling there came a loud click and the mad ticking of the instrument's mechanism went totally out of kilter. The four hands on the carven dial stood still for an instant of time before commencing fresh movements in alien and completely inexplicable sequences. Joe stepped nimbly back as the large panel swung silently open. He stepped just a few inches too far back, jolting the occasional table. The reading-lamp went over with a crash, momentarily breaking the spell of the wildly oscillating hands and crazy ticking of de Marigny's clock. The corner was once more thrown in shadow and for a moment Joe stood there undecided, put off stroke by his early success. Then he gave a grunt of triumph, stepped forward and thrust his empty left hand into the darkness behind the open panel.

Pasty sensed the *outsideness* at the same time as Crow. He leapt across the room shouting: "Joe, Joe—for God's sake, leave it alone...*leave it alone!*" Crow, on the other hand, spurred by no such sense of comradeship, quickly stood up and backed away. It was not that he was in any way a coward, but he knew something of Earth's darker mysteries—and of the mysteries of other spheres—and besides, he sensed the danger of interfering with an action having origin far from the known side of nature.

Suddenly, the corner was dimly illuminated by an eerie, dappled light from the open panel; and Joe, his arm still groping beyond that door, gave a yell of utter terror and tried to pull back. The ticking was now insanely aberrant, and the wild sweeps of the four hands about the dial were completely confused and orderless. Joe had braced himself against the frame of the opening, fighting some unseen menace within the strangely lit compartment, trying desperately to withdraw his arm. Against all his efforts his left shoulder abruptly jammed forward, into the swirling light, and at the same moment he stuck the barrel of his gun into the opening and fired six shots in rapid succession.

By this time Pasty had an arm round Joe's waist, one foot braced against the base of the clock, putting all his strength into an attempt to haul his companion away from whatever threatened in the swirling light of the now fearsome opening. He was fighting a losing battle. Joe was speechless with terror, all his energies concentrated on escape from the clock; great veins stuck out from his neck and his eyes seemed likely at any moment to pop from his head. He gave one bubbling scream as his head and neck jerked suddenly forward into the maw of the mechanical horror…and then his body went limp.

Pasty, still wildly struggling with Joe's lower body, gave a last titanic heave at that now motionless torso and actually managed to retrieve for a moment Joe's head from the weirdly lit door.

Simultaneously Pasty and Titus Crow saw something—something that turned Pasty's muscles to water, causing him to relax his struggle so that Joe's entire body bar the legs vanished with a horrible *hisss* into the clock— something that caused Crow to throw up his hands before his eyes in the utmost horror!

In the brief second or so that Pasty's efforts had partly freed the sagging form of his companion in crime, the fruits of Joe's impulsiveness had made themselves hideously apparent. The cloth of his jacket near the left shoulder and that same area of the shirt immediately beneath had been *removed*, seemingly *dissolved* or burnt away by some unknown agent; and in place of the flesh which should by all rights have been laid bare by this mysterious vanishment, *there had been a great blistered, bubbling blotch of crimson and brown—and the neck and head had been in the same sickening state!*

Surprisingly, Pasty recovered first from the shock. He made one last desperate, fatal, grab at Joe's disappearing legs—and the fingers of his right hand crossed the threshold of the opening into the throbbing light beyond. Being in a crouching position and considerably thinner than his now completely vanished friend; Pasty did not stand a chance. Simultaneous with Crow's cry of horror and warning combined, he gave a sobbing shriek and seemed simply to dive headlong into the leering entrance.

Had there been an observer what happened next might have seemed something of an anticlimax. Titus Crow, as if in response to some agony beyond enduring, clapped his hands to his head and fell writhing to the floor. There he stayed, legs threshing wildly for some three seconds, before his body relaxed as the terror of his experience drove his mind to seek refuge in oblivion.

Shortly thereafter, of its own accord, the panel in the clock swung smoothly back into place and clicked shut; the four hands steadied to their previous, not quite so deranged motions, and the ticking of the hidden mechanism slowed and altered its rhythm from the monstrous to the merely abnormal…

Titus Crow's first reaction on waking was to believe himself the victim of a particularly horrible nightmare; but then he felt the carpet against his cheek and, opening his eyes, saw the scattered books littering the floor. Shakily he made himself a large jug of coffee and poured himself a huge brandy, then sat, alternately sipping at both until there was none of either left. And when both the jug and the glass were empty he started all over again.

It goes without saying that Crow went nowhere near de Marigny's clock! For the moment, at least, his thirst for knowledge in *that* direction was slaked.

As far as possible he also kept from thinking back on the horrors of the previous night; particularly he wished to forget the hellish, psychic impressions received as Pasty went into the clock. For it appeared that de Marigny, Phillips and Walmsley had been right! The clock was, in fact, a space-time machine of sorts. Crow did not know *exactly* what had caused the hideous shock to his highly developed psychic sense; but in fact, even as he had felt that shock and clapped his hands to his head, somewhere out in the worlds of Aldebaran, at a junction of forces neither spatial, temporal, nor of any intermediate dimension recognised by man except in the wildest theories, the Lake of Hali sent up a few streamers of froth and fell quickly back into silence.

And Titus Crow was left with only the memory of the feel of unknown acids burning, of the wash of strange tides outside nature, and of the rushing and tearing of great beasts designed in a fashion beyond man's wildest conjecturing…

MYLAKHRION THE IMMORTAL

In 1977 I was the DI at the RMP HQ. As stated elsewhere, time was short. I'd even had to give up hang-gliding—something I had done for kicks all over the Scottish hills from my base in Edinburgh—and I'd sold my "kites" to other Military Policemen who were equally crazy! A sad state of affairs; I missed the rush of adrenalin, but at least I had managed to purchase myself some spare time in which to write. "Mylakhrion the Immortal" was one of a handful of stories written in that spare time. It's another tale set in the Primal Land; for by then (and ever since the not unreasonable success of The House of Cthulhu*) I had decided to write an entire bookful of them. Not a bad idea, because, as elsewhere stated, in 1984 Paul Ganley would publish that very book in both paper and hardcover, with the obvious title,* The House of Cthulhu.*

There was a time when I, Teh Atht, marvelling at certain thaumaturgical devices handed down to me from the days of my wizard ancestor, Mylakhrion of Tharamoon (dead these eleven hundred years), thought to question him with regard to the nature of his demise; with that, and with the reason for it. For Mylakhrion had been, according to all manner of myths and legends, the greatest wizard in all Theem'hdra, and it concerned me that he had not been immortal. Like many another wizard before me I, too, had long sought immortality, but if the great Mylakhrion himself had been merely mortal…surely my own chance for self-perpetuity must be slim indeed.

Thus I went up once more into the Mount of the Ancients, even to the very summit, and there smoked the Zha-weed and repeated rare words by use of which I might seek Mylakhrion in dreams. And lo!—he came to me. Hidden in a grey mist so that only the conical outline of his sorcerer's cap and the slow billowing of his dimly rune-inscribed gown were visible, he came, and in his doomful voice demanded to know why I had called him up from the land of shades, disturbing his centuried sleep.

"Faceless one, ancestor mine, o mighty and most omniscient sorcerer," I answered, mindful of Mylakhrion's magnitude. "I call you up that you may answer for me a question of ultimate importance. A question, aye, and a riddle."

"There is but one question of ultimate importance to men," gloomed Mylakhrion, "and its nature is such that they usually do not think to ask it until they draw close to the end of their days. For in their youth men cannot foresee the end, and in their middle span they dwell too much upon their lost youth; ah, but in their final days, when there is no future, then they give mind to this great question. And by then it is usually too late: For the question is one of life and death, and the answer is this: yes, Teh Atht, by great and sorcerous endeavour, a man might truly make himself immortal…

"As to your riddle, that is easy. The answer is that *I am indeed immortal!* Even as the great Ones, as the mighty furnace stars, as Time itself, am I immortal. For ever and ever. Here you have called me up to answer your questions and riddles, knowing full well that I am eleven hundred years dead. But do I not take on the aspect of life? Do my lips not speak? And is this not immortality? Dead I am, but I say to you that I can never truly die."

Then Mylakhrion spread his arms wide, saying; "All is answered. Farewell…"And his outline, already misted and dim, began to recede deeper still into Zha-weed distances, departing from me. Then, greatly daring, I called out:

"Wait, Mylakhrion my ancestor, for our business is not yet done."

Slowly he came back, reluctantly, until his silhouette was firm once more; but still, as always, his visage was hidden by the swirling mists and only his dark figure and the gold-glowing runes woven into his robes were visible. Silently he waited, as silently as the tomb of the universe at the end of time, until I spoke yet again:

"This immortality of yours is not the sort I seek, Mylakhrion, which I believe you know well enow. Fleshless, bodiless, except for that shape given you by my incantations and the smoke of the Zha-weed, voiceless other than when called up from the land of shades to answer my questions…what is that for immortality? No, ancestor mine, I desire much more from the future than that. I want my body and all of its sensations. I want volition and sensibility, and all normal lusts and passions. In short, I want to be eternal, remaining as I am now but incorruptible, indestructable! That is immortality!"

208

"There is no such future for you, Teh Atht!" he immediately gloomed, voice deeply sunken and ominous. "You expect too much. Even I, Mylakhrion of Tharamoon, could not—achieve—" And here he faltered and fell silent.

I perceived then a seeming agitation in the mist-wreathed phantom; he appeared to tremble, however slightly, and I sensed his eagerness to be gone. Thus I pressed him:

"Oh? And how much *did* you achieve, Mylakhrion? Is there more I should know? What were your experiments and how much did you discover in your great search for immortality? I believe you are hiding something from me, o mighty one, and if I must I'll smoke the Zha-weed again—aye, and yet again—leaving you no rest or peace until you have answered me as I would be answered!"

Hearing me speak thus, Mylakhrion's figure stiffened and swelled momentarily massive, but then his shoulders drooped and he nodded slowly, saying, "Have I come to this? That the most meagre talents have power to command me? A sad day indeed for Mylakhrion of Tharamoon, when his own descendant uses him so sorely. What is it you wish to know, Teh Atht of Klühn?"

"While you were unable to achieve immortality in your lifetime, ancestor mine," I answered, "mayhap nathless you can assist me in the discovery of the secret in mine. Describe to me the magicks you used and discarded in your search, the runes you unravelled and put aside, the potions imbibed and unctions applied to no avail, and these I shall take note of that no further time be wasted with them. Then advise me of the paths which you might have explored had time and circumstances permitted. For I *will* be immortal, and no power shall stay me from it."

"Ah, youth, it is folly," quoth he, "but if you so command—"

"I do so command."

"Then hear me out and I will tell all, and perhaps you will understand when I tell you that you cannot have immortality…not of the sort you so fervently desire."

And so Mylakhrion told me of his search for immortality. He described for me the great journeys he undertook—leaving Tharamoon, his island-mountain aerie, in the care of watchdog familiars—to visit and confer with other sorcerers and wizards; even journeys across the entire length and breadth of Theem'hdra. Alone he went out into the deserts and plains, the hills and icy wastes in pursuit of this most elusive of mysteries. He visited and talked with Black Yoppaloth of Yhemnis, with the ghost of Shildakor in lava-buried Bhur-esh, with Ardatha Ell, a traveller in space and time who lived for a while in the Great Circle Mountains and studied the featureless, vastly cubical houses of the long-gone Ancients, and with Mellatiquel Thom, a cousin-wizard fled to Yaht-Haal when certain magicks turned against him.

And always during these great wanderings he collected runes and cantrips, spells and philtres, powders, and potions and other devices necessary to his thaumaturgical experiments. But never a one to set his feet on the road to immortality. Aye, and using vile necromancy he called up the dead from their ashes, even the dead, for his purposes. And this is something I, Teh Atht, have never done, deeming it too loathsome and danger-fraught a deed. For to talk to a dream-phantom is one matter, but to hold intercourse with long-rotted liches…that is a vile, vile thing.

But for all his industry Mylakhrion found only frustration. He conversed with demons and lamias, hunted the legendary phoenix in burning deserts, near-poisoned himself with strange drugs and nameless potions and worried his throat raw with the chanting of oddly cacophonic invocations. And only then did he think to ask himself this question:

If a man desired immortality, what better way than to ask the secret of one *already* immortal? Aye, and there was just such a one…

Then, when Mylakhrion spoke the name of Cthulhu—the tentacled Great One who seeped down from the stars with his spawn in aeons past to build his cities in the steaming fens of a young and inchoate Earth—I shuddered and made a certain sign over my heart. For while I had not yet had to do with this Cthulhu, his legend was awful and I had heard much of him. And I marvelled that Mylakhrion had dared seek out this Great One, even Mylakhrion, for above all other evils Cthulhu was legended to tower like a menhir above mere gravestones.

And having marvelled I listened most attentively to all that my ancestor had to say of Cthulhu and the other Great Ones, for since their nature was in the main obscure, and being myself a sorcerer with a sorcerer's appetite for mysteries, I was most desirous of learning more of them.

"Aye, Teh Atht," Mylakhrion continued, "Cthulhu and his brethren: they must surely know the answer, for they are—"

"Immortal?"

For answer he shrugged, then said: "Their genesis lies in unthinkable abysses of the past, their end nowhere in sight. Like the cockroach they were here before men, and they will supersede man. Why, they were oozing like vile ichor between the stars before the sun spewed out her molten children, of which this world is one; and they will live on when Sol is the merest cinder. Do not attempt to measure their life-spans in terms of human life, nor even geologically. Measure them rather in the births and deaths of planets, which to them are like the tickings of vast clocks. Immortal? As near immortal as matters not. From them I could either beg, borrow or steal the secret—but how to go about approaching them?"

I waited for the ghost of my dead ancestor to proceed, and when he did not immediately do so cried out: "Say on then, forebear mine! Say on and be done with beguiling me!"

He sighed for reply and answered very low: "As you command…

"At length I sought me out a man rumoured to be well versed in the ways of the Great Ones; a hermit, dwelling in the peaks of the Eastern Range, whose visions and dreams were such as were best dreamed far removed from his fellow men. For he was wont to run amuck in the passion of his nightmares, and was reckoned by many to have bathed in the blood of numerous innocents, 'to the greater glory of Loathly Lord Cthulhu!'

"I sought him out and questioned him in his high cave, and he showed me the herbs I must eat and whispered the words I must howl from the peaks into the storm. And he told me when I must do these things, that I might then sleep and meet with Cthulhu in my dreams. Thus he instructed me…

"But as night drew nigh in this lonely place my host became drowsy and fell into a fitful sleep. Aye, and his ravings soon became such, and his strugglings so wild, that I stayed not but ventured back out into the steep slopes and thus made away from him. Descending those perilous crags only by the silver light of the Moon, I spied the madman above me, asleep yet rushing to and fro, howling like a dog and slashing with a great knife in the darkness of the shadows. And I was glad I had not stayed!

"Thus I returned to Tharmoon, taking a winding route and gathering of the herbs whereof the hermit had spoken, until upon my arrival I had with me all the elements required for the invocation, while locked in my mind I carried the Words of Power. And lo!—I called up a great storm and went out onto the balcony of my highest tower; and there I howled into the wind the Words, and I ate of the herbs mixed so and so, and a swoon came upon me so that I fell as though dead into a sleep deeper by far than the arms of Shoosh, Goddess of the Still Slumbers. Ah, but deep though this sleep was, it was by no means still!

"No, that sleep was—*unquiet!* I saw the sepulchre of Cthulhu in the Isle of Arlyeh, and I passed through the massive and oddly-angled walls of that alien stronghold into the presence of the Great One Himself!"

Here the outlines of my ancestor's ghost became strangely agitated, as if its owner trembled uncontrollably, and even the voice of Mylakhrion wavered and lost much of its doomful portent. I waited for a moment before crying: "Yes, go on—what did the awful Lord of Arlyeh tell you?"

"...Many things, Teh Atht. He told me the secrets of space and time; the legends of lost universes out beyond the limits of man's imagination; he outlined the hideous truths behind the N'tang Tapestries, the lore of dimensions other than the familiar three. And at last he told me the secret of immortality!

"But the latter he would not reveal until I had made a pact with him. And this pact was that I would be his priest ever and ever, even until his coming. And believing that I might later break free of any strictures Cthulhu could place upon me, I agreed to the pact and swore upon it. In this my fate was sealed, my doom ordained, for no man may escape the curse of Cthulhu once its seal is upon him...

"And lo, when I wakened, I did all as I had been instructed to attain the promised immortality; and on the third night Cthulhu visited me in dreams, for he knew me now and how to find me, and commanded me as his servant and priest to set about certain tasks. Ah, but these were tasks which would assist the Great One and his prisoned brethren in breaking free of the chains placed upon them in aeons past by the wondrous Gods of Eld, and what use to be immortal forever more in the unholy service of Cthulhu?

"Thus, on the fourth day, instead of doing as bidden, I set about protecting myself as best I could from Cthulhu's wrath, working a veritable frenzy of magicks to keep him from me...to no avail! In the middle of the fifth night, wearied nigh unto death by my thaumaturgical labours, I slept, and again Cthulhu came to me. And he came in great anger—even *great* anger!

"For he had broken down all of my sorcerous barriers, destroying all spells and protective runes, discovering me for a traitor to his cause. And as I slept he drew me up from my couch and led me through the labyrinth of my castle, even to the feet of those steps which climbed up to the topmost tower. He placed my feet upon those stone stairs and commanded me to climb, and when I would have fought him he applied monstrous pressures to my mind that numbed me and left me bereft of will. And so I climbed, slowly and like unto one of the risen dead, up to that high tower, where without pause I went out onto the balcony and threw myself down upon the needle rocks a thousand feet below...

"Thus was my body broken, Teh Atht, and thus Mylakhrion died."

As he finished speaking I stepped closer to the swirling wall of mist where Mylakhrion stood, black-robed and enigmatic in mystery. He did not seem so tall now, no taller than I myself, and for all the power he had wielded in life he no longer awed me. Should I, Teh Atht, fear a ghost? Even the ghost of the world's greatest sorcerer?

"Still you have not told me that which I most desire to know," I accused.

"Ah, you grow impatient," he answered. "Even as the smoke of the Zha-weed loses its potency and the waking world beckons to you, so your impatience grows. Very well, let me now repeat what Cthulhu told me of immortality:

"He told me that the only way a mere man, even the mightiest wizard among wizards, might perpetuate himself down all the ages was by means of reincarnation! But alas, such as my return would be it would not be complete; for I must needs inhabit another's body, another's mind, and unless I desired a weak body and mind I should certainly find resistance in the person of that as yet unborn other. In other words I must *share* that body, that mind! But surely, I reasoned, even partial immortality would be better than none at all. Would you not agree, descendant mine?

"Of course, I would want a body—or part of one—close in appearance to my own, and a mind to suit. Aye, and it must be a keen mind and curious of mysteries great and small: that of a sorcerer! And indeed it were better if my own blood should flow in the veins of—"

"Wait!" I then cried, searching the mist with suddenly fearful eyes, seeking to penetrate its greyness that I might gaze upon Mylakhrion's unknown face. "I…I find your story most…disturbing…my ancestor, and—"

"—and yet you must surely hear it out, Teh Atht," he interrupted, doom once more echoing in his voice. And as he spoke he moved flowingly forward until at last I could see the death-lights in his shadowy eyes. Closer still he came, saying:

"To ensure that this as yet unborn one would be all the things I desired of him, I set a covenant upon my resurrection in him. And this condition was that his curiosity and sorcerous skill must be such that he would first call me up from the Land of Shades ten times, and that only then would I make myself manifest in his person… *And how many times have you called me up, Teh Atht?*"

"Ten times—fiend!" I choked. And feeling the chill of subterranean pools flowing in my bones, I rushed upon him to seize his shoulders in palsied hands, staring into a face now visible as a reflection in the clear glass of a mirror. A mirror? Aye! For though the face was that of an old, old man—*it was nonetheless my own!*

And without more ado I fled, waking to a cold, cold morn atop the Mount of the Ancients, where my tethered yak watched me with worried eyes and snorted a nervous greeting…

❖ ❖ ❖

But that was long ago and in my youth, and now I no longer fear My-lakhrion, though I did fear him greatly for many a year. For in the end I was stronger than him, aye, and he got but a small part of me. In return I got all of his magicks, the lore of a lifetime spent in the discovery of dark secrets.

All of this and immortality, too, of a sort; and yet even now Mylakhrion is not beaten. For surely I will carry something of him with me down the ages. Occasionally I smile at the thought and feel laughter rising in me like wind over the desert…but rarely. The laughter hardly sounds like mine at all and its echoes seem to linger o'erlong.

THE SISTER CITY

With this one we're back to my first year as a writer, 1967, and one of the first half-dozen stories I sent to August Derleth at Arkham House. You know something, I'm still astonished that Derleth even gave me a shot. Not that my stories themselves were bad, but the way I presented them most definitely was. Try to picture it: sitting at his desk, Derleth opens the cardboard tube that I sent—surface mail, to save on postage—from Berlin. Inside he finds a story, or rather a scroll, that he has to nail to his desk top in order to read the damn thing! And it's typed single-space, sometimes on both sides of the military, scribble-pad sized sheets! It's a wonder he didn't go out of his mind! But no, he was gathering stories for Tales of the Cthulhu Mythos, *and this one was the right size and shape. "The Sister City" made it into* TOTCM, *since when it has seen many a reprint, not least as a chapter in my novel* Beneath the Moors.

This manuscript attached as
"Annex 'A'" to report number
M-Y-127/52, dated 7th August 1952.

Towards the end of the war, when our London home was bombed and both my parents were killed, I was hospitalised through my own injuries and forced to spend the better part of two years on my back. It was during this period of my youth—I was only seventeen when I left the hospital—that I formed, in the main, the enthusiasm which in later years developed into a craving for travel, adventure and knowledge of Earth's elder antiquities. I had always had a wanderer's nature but was so restricted during those two dreary years that when my chance for adventure eventually came I made up for wasted time by letting that nature hold full sway.

Not that those long, painful months were totally devoid of pleasures. Between operations, when my health would allow it, I read avidly in the hospital's library, primarily to forget my bereavement, eventually to be carried along to those worlds of elder wonder created by Walter Scott in his enchanting *Arabian Nights*.

Apart from delighting me tremendously, the book helped to take my mind off the things I had heard said about me in the wards. It had been put about that I was different; allegedly the doctors had found something strange in my physical make-up. There were whispers about the peculiar qualities of my skin and the slightly extending horny cartilage at the base of my spine. There was talk about the fact that my fingers and toes were ever so slightly webbed and being, as I was, so totally devoid of hair, I became the recipient of many queer glances.

These things plus my name, Robert Krug, did nothing to increase my popularity at the hospital. In fact, at a time when Hitler was still occasionally devastating London with his bombs, a surname like Krug, with its implications of Germanic ancestry, was probably more a hindrance to friendship than all my other peculiarities put together.

With the end of the war I found myself rich; the only heir to my father's wealth, and still not out of my teens. I had left Scott's Jinns, Ghouls and Efreets far behind me but was returned to the same *type* of thrill I had known with the *Arabian Nights* by the popular publication of Lloyd's *Excavations on Sumerian Sites*. In the main it was that book which was responsible for the subsequent awe in which I ever held those magical words "Lost Cities".

In the months that followed, indeed through all my remaining—formative—years, Lloyd's work remained a landmark, followed as it was by many more volumes in a like vein. I read avidly of Layard's *Nineveh and Babylon* and *Early Adventures in Persia, Susiana and Babylonia*. I dwelled long over such works as Budge's *Rise and Progress of Assyriology* and Burckhardt's *Travels in Syria and the Holy Land*.

Nor were the fabled lands of Mesopotamia the only places of interest to me. Fictional Shangri-La and Ephiroth ranked equally beside the reality of Mycenæ, Knossos, Palmyra and Thebes. I read excitedly of Atlantis and Chichén-Itzá; never bothering to separate fact from fancy, and dreamed equally longingly of the Palace of Minos in Crete and Unknown Kadath in the Colde Waste.

What I read of Sir Amery Wendy-Smith's African expedition in search of dead G'harne confirmed my belief that certain myths and legends are not far removed from historical fact. If no less a person than that eminent antiquarian and archaeologist had equipped an expedition to search for a jungle city considered by most reputable authorities to be purely mythological... Why! His failure meant nothing compared with the fact that he had *tried*...

While others, before my time, had ridiculed the broken figure of the demented explorer who returned alone from the jungles of the Dark Continent I tended to emulate his deranged fancies—as his theories have been considered—re-examining the evidence for Chyria and G'harne and delving ever deeper into the fragmentary antiquities of legendary cities and lands with such unlikely names as R'lyeh, Ephiroth, Mnar and Hyperborea.

As the years passed my body healed completely and I grew from a fascinated youth into a dedicated man. Not that I ever guessed what drove me to explore the ill-lit passages of history and fantasy. I only knew that there was something fascinating for me in the re-discovery of those ancient worlds of dream and legend.

Before I began those far-flung travels which were destined to occupy me on and off for four years I bought a house in Marske, at the very edge of the Yorkshire moors. This was the region in which I had spent my childhood and there had always been about the brooding moors a strong feeling of *affinity* which was hard for me to define. I felt closer to *home* there somehow—and infinitely closer to the beckoning past. It was with a genuine reluctance that I left my moors but the inexplicable lure of distant places and foreign names called me away, across the seas.

First I visited these lands that were within easy reach, ignoring the places of dreams and fancies but promising myself that later—later!!

Egypt, with all its mystery! Djoser's step-pyramid at Saggara, Imhotep's, Masterpiece; the ancient mastabas, tombs of centuries-dead kings; the inscrutably smiling sphinx; the Sneferu pyramid at Meidum and those of Chephren and Cheops at Giza; the mummies, the brooding Gods....

Yet in spite of all its wonder Egypt could not hold me for long. The sand and heat were damaging to my skin which tanned quickly and roughened almost overnight.

Crete, the Nymph of the beautiful Mediterranean...Theseus and the Minotaur; the Palace of Minos at Knossos.... All wonderful—but that which I sought was not there.

Salamis and Cyprus, with all their ruins of ancient civilizations, each held me but a month or so. Yet it was in Cyprus that I learned of yet another personal peculiarity—my queer abilities in water...

I became friendly with a party of divers at Famagusta. Daily they were diving for amphorae and other relics of the past offshore from the ruins at Salonica on the south-east coast. At first the fact that I could remain beneath the water three times as long as the best of them, and swim further without the aid of fins or snorkel, was only a source of amazement to my friends; but after a few days I noticed that they were having less and less to do with me. They did not care for the hairlessness of my body or the webbing, which seemed to have lengthened, between my toes and fingers. They did not like the bump low at the rear of my bathing-costume or the way I could converse with them in their own tongue when I had never studied Greek in my life.

It was time to move on. My travels took me all over the world and I became an authority on those dead civilisations which were my one joy in life. Then, in Phetri, I heard of the Nameless City.

Remote in the desert of Araby lies the Nameless City, crumbling and inarticulate, its low walls nearly hidden by the sands of uncounted ages. It was of this place that Abdul Alhazred the mad poet dreamed on the night before he sang his inexplicable couplet:

> "That is not dead which can eternal lie,
> And with strange aeons even death may die."

My Arab guides thought I, too, was mad when I ignored their warnings and continued in search of that city of Devils. Their fleet-footed camels took them off in more than necessary haste for they had noticed my skin's scaly strangeness and certain other unspoken things which made them uneasy in my presence. Also, they had been nonplussed, as I had been myself, at the strange fluency with which I used their tongue.

Of what I saw and did in Kara-Shehr I will not write. It must suffice to say that I learned of things which struck chords in my subconscious; things which sent me off again on my travels to seek Sarnath the Doomed in what was once the land of Mnar…

No man knows the whereabouts of Sarnath and it is better that this remains so. Of my travels in search of the place and the difficulties which I encountered at every phase of my journey I will therefore recount nothing. Yet my discovery of the slime-sunken city, and of the incredibly aged ruins of nearby Ib, were major links forged in the lengthening chain of knowledge which was slowly bridging the awesome gap between this world and my ultimate destination. And I, bewildered, did not even know where or what that destination was.

For three weeks I wandered the slimy shores of the still lake which hides Sarnath and at the end of that time, driven by a fearful compulsion, I once again used those unnatural aquatic powers of mine and began exploring beneath the surface of that hideous morass.

That night I slept with a small green figurine, rescued from the sunken ruins, pressed to my bosom. In my dreams I saw my mother and father—but dimly, as if through a mist—and they beckoned to me...

The nest day I went again to stand in the centuried ruins of Ib and as I was making ready to leave I saw the inscribed stone which gave me my first real clue. The wonder is that I could *read* what was written on that weathered, aeon-old pillar; for it was written in a curious cuneiform older even than the inscriptions on Geph's broken columns, and it had been pitted by the ravages of time.

It told nothing of the beings who once lived in Ib, or anything of the long-dead inhabitants of Sarnath. It spoke only of the destruction which the men of Sarnath had brought to the beings of Ib—and of the resulting Doom that came to Sarnath. This doom was wrought by the Gods of the beings of Ib but of those Gods I could learn not a thing. I only knew that reading that stone and being in Ib had stirred long-hidden memories, perhaps even *ancestral* memories, in my mind. Again that feeling of closeness to home, that feeling I always felt so strongly on the moors in Yorkshire, flooded over me. Then, as I idly moved the rushes at the base of the pillar with my foot, yet more chiselled inscriptions appeared. I cleared away the slime and read on. There were only a few lines but those lines contained my clue:

"Ib is gone but the Gods live on. Across the world is the Sister City, hidden in the earth, in the barbarous lands of Zimmeria. There The People flourish yet and there will The Gods ever be worshipped; even unto the coming of Cthulhu..."

Many months later in Cairo, I sought out a man steeped in elder lore, a widely acknowledged authority on forbidden antiquities and prehistoric lands and legends. This sage had never heard of Zimmeria but he did know of a land which had once had a name much similar. "And where did this Cimmeria lie?" I asked.

"Unfortunately," my erudite adviser answered, consulting a chart, "most of Cimmeria now lies beneath the sea but originally it lay between Vanaheim and Nemedia in ancient Hyborea."

"You say *most* of it is sunken?" I queried. "But what of the land which lies above the sea?" Perhaps it was the eagerness in my voice which caused him to glance at me the way he did. Again, perhaps it was my queer aspect; for the hot suns of many lands had hardened my hairless skin most peculiarly and a strong web now showed between my fingers.

"Why do you wish to know?" he asked. "What is it you are seeking?"

"Home," I answered instinctively, not knowing what prompted me to say it.

"Yes…" he said, studying me closely. "That might well be… You are an Englishman, are you not? May I enquire from which part?"

"From the North-East." I said, reminded suddenly of my moors. "Why do you want to know?"

"My friend, you have searched in vain," he smiled, "for Cimmeria, or that which remains of it, encompasses all of that North-Eastern part of England which is your home-land. Is it not ironic? In order to find your home you have left it…"

That night fate dealt me a card which I could not ignore. In the lobby of my hotel was a table devoted solely to the reading habits of the English residents. Upon it was a wide variety of books, paper-backs, newspapers and journals, ranging from *The Reader's Digest* to *The News of The World*, and to pass a few hours in relative coolness I sat beneath a soothing fan with a glass of iced water and idly glanced through one of the newspapers. Abruptly, on turning a page, I came upon a picture and an article which, when I had scanned the thing through, caused me to book a seat on the next flight to London.

The picture was poorly reproduced but was still clear enough for me to see that it depicted a small, green figurine—*the duplicate of that which I had salvaged from the ruins of Sarnath beneath the still pool…*

The article, as best I can remember, read like this:

"Mr. Samuel Davies, of 17 Heddington Crescent, Radcar, found the beautiful relic of bygone ages pictured above in a stream whose only known source is the cliff-face at Sarby-on-the-Moors. The figurine is now in Radcar Museum, having been donated by Mr. Davies, and is being studied by the curator, Prof. Gordon Walmsley of Goole. So far Prof. Walmsley had been unable to throw any light on the figurine's origin but the Wendy-Smith Test, a scientific means of checking the age of archaeological fragments, has shown it to be over ten thousand years old. The green figurine does not appear to have any connection with any of the better known civilisations of ancient England and is thought to be a find of rare importance. Unfortunately, expert pot-holers have given unanimous opinions that the stream, where it springs from the cliffs at Sarby, is totally untraversable."

The next day, during the flight, I slept for an hour or so and again, in my dreams, I saw my parents. As before they appeared to me in a mist—but their beckonings were stronger than in that previous dream and in the blanketing vapours around them were strange *figures*, bowed in seeming obeisance, while a chant of teasing familiarity rang from hidden and nameless throats…

I had wired my housekeeper from Cairo, informing her of my returning, and when I arrived at my house in Marske found a solicitor waiting for me. This gentleman introduced himself as being Mr. Harvey, of the Radcar firm of Harvey, Johnson and Harvey, and presented me with a large, sealed envelope. It was addressed to me, in my father's hand, and Mr. Harvey informed me his instructions had been to deliver the envelope into my hands on the attainment of my twenty-first birthday. Unfortunately I had been out of the country at the time, almost a year earlier, but the firm had kept in touch with my housekeeper so that on my return the agreement made nearly seven years earlier between my father and Mr. Harvey's firm might be kept. After Mr. Harvey left I dismissed my woman and opened the envelope. The manuscript within was not in any script I had ever learned at school. This was the language I had seen written on that aeon-old pillar in ancient Ib; nonetheless I knew instinctively that it had been my father's hand which had written the thing. And of course, I could read it as easily as if it were in English. The many and diverse contents of the letter made it, as I have said, more akin to a manuscript in its length and it is not my purpose to completely reproduce it. That would take too long and the speed with which The First Change is taking place does not permit it. I will merely set down the specially significant points which the letter brought to my attention.

In disbelief I read the first paragraph—but, as I read on, that disbelief soon became a weird amazement which in turn became a savage joy at the fantastic disclosures revealed by those timeless hieroglyphs of Ib. *My parents were not dead!* They had merely gone away, gone home…

That time nearly seven years ago, when I had returned home from a school reduced to ruins by the bombing, our London home had been purposely sabotaged by my father. A powerful explosive had been rigged, primed to be set off by the first air-raid siren, and then my parents had gone off in secrecy back to the moors. They had not known, I realised, that I was on my way home from the ruined school where I boarded. Even now they were unaware that I had arrived at the house just as the radar defences of England's military services had picked out those hostile dots in the sky. That plan which had been so carefully laid to fool men into believing that my parents were dead had worked well; but it had also nearly destroyed me. And all this time I, too, had believed them killed. But why had they gone to such extremes? What *was* that secret which it was so necessary to hide from our fellow men—and where were my parents now? I read on…

Slowly all was revealed. We were not *indigenous* to England, my parents and I, and they had brought me here as an infant from our homeland, a land quite near yet paradoxically far away. The letter went on to explain how *all* the children of our race are brought here as infants, for the atmosphere of our home-land is not conducive to health in the young and unformed. The difference in my case had been that my mother was unable to part with me. That was the awful thing! Though all the children of our race must wax and grow up *away* from their homeland, the elders can only rarely depart from their native clime. This fact is determined by their physical *appearance* throughout the greater period of their life-spans. *For they are not, for the better part of their lives, either the physical or mental counterparts of ordinary men.*

This means that children have to be left on doorsteps, at the entrances of orphanages, in churches and in other places where they will be found and cared for; for in extreme youth there is little difference between my race and the race of men. As I read I was reminded of those tales of fantasy I had once loved; of ghouls and fairies and other creatures who left their young to be reared by human beings and who stole human children to be brought up in their own likenesses.

Was *that*, then, my destiny? Was I to be a ghoul? I read on. I learned that the people of my race can only leave our native country twice in their lives; once in youth—when, as I have explained, they are brought here of necessity to be left until they attain the approximate age of twenty-one years—and once in later life, when *changes* in their appearances make them compatible to *outside* conditions. My parents had just reached this latter stage of their—development—when I was born. Because of my mother's devotion they had forsaken their *duties* in our own land and had brought me personally to England where, ignoring The Laws, they stayed with me. My father had brought certain treasures with him to ensure an easy life for himself and my mother until that time should come when they would be *forced* to leave me, the Time of the Second Change, when to stay would be to alert mankind of our existence.

That time had eventually arrived and they had covered up their departure back to our own, secret land by blowing up our London home; letting the authorities and I, (though it must have broken my mother's heart), believe them dead of a German bomb raid.

And how could they have done otherwise? They dared not take the chance of telling me *what I really was*; for who can say what effect such a disclosure would have had on me, I who had barely begun to show my *differences*? They had to hope I would discover the secret myself, or at least the greater part of it, which I had done! But to be doubly sure my father left his letter.

The letter also told how not many *foundlings* find their way back to their own land. Accidents claim some and others go mad. At this point I was reminded of something I had read somewhere of two inmates of Oakdeene Sanatorium near Glasgow who are so horribly mad *and so unnatural in aspect* that they are not even allowed to be seen and even their nurses cannot abide to stay near them for long. Yet others become hermits in wild and inaccessible places and, worst of all, still others suffer more hideous fates and I shuddered as I read what those fates were. But there *were* those few who did manage to get back. These were the lucky ones, those who returned to claim their rights; and while some of them were *guided* back—by adults of the race during second visits—others made it by instinct or luck. Yet horrible though this overall plan of existence seemed to be, the letter explained its logic. For my homeland could not support many of my kind and those perils of lunacy, brought on by inexplicable physical changes, and accidents and those *other fates* I have mentioned acted as a system of selection whereby only the fittest in mind and body returned to the land of their birth.

But there; I have just finished reading the letter through a second time— and already I begin to feel a stiffening of my limbs... My father's manuscript has arrived barely in time. I have long been worried by my growing *differences*. The webbing on my hands now extends almost to the small, first knuckles and my skin is fantastically thick, rough and ichthyic. The short tail which protrudes from the base of my spine is now not so much an oddity as an *addition*; an extra limb which, in the light of what I now know, is not an oddity at all but the most natural thing in my world! My hairlessness, with the discovery of my destiny, has also ceased to be an embarrassment to me. I am different from men, true, but is that not as it should be? *For I am not a man...*

Ah, the lucky fates which caused me to pick up that newspaper in Cairo! Had I not seen that picture or read that article I might not have returned so soon to my moors and I shudder to think what might have become of me then. What would I have done after The First Change had altered me? Would

I have hurried, disguised and wrapped in smothering clothes, to some distant land—there to live the life of a hermit? Perhaps I would have returned to Ib or the Nameless City, to dwell in ruins and solitude until my appearance was again capable of sustaining my existence among men. And what after that—after The Second Change?

Perhaps I would have gone mad at such inexplicable alterations in my person. Who knows but there might have been another inmate at Oakdeene? On the other hand my fate might have been worse than all these; for I may have been drawn to dwell in the depths, to be one with the Deep Ones in the worship of Dagon and Great Cthulhu, as have others before me.

But no! By good fortune, by the learning gained on my far journeys and by the help given me by my father's document I have been spared all those terrors which others of my kind have known. I will return to Ib's Sister City, to Lh-yib, in that land of my birth *beneath* these Yorkshire moors; that land from which was washed the green figurine which guided me back to these shores, that figurine which is the duplicate of the one I raised from beneath the pool at Sarnath. I will return to be worshipped by those whose ancestral brothers died at Ib on the spears of the men of Sarnath; those who are so aptly described on the Brick Cylinders of Kadatheron; these who chant voicelessly in the abyss. I will return to Lh-yib!

For even now I hear my mother's voice; calling me as she did when I was a child and used to wander these very moors. "Bob! Little Bo! Where are you?"

Bo, she used to call me and would only laugh when I asked her why. But why not? Was Bo not a fitting name? Robert—Bob—Bo? What odds? Blind fool that I have been! I never really pondered the fact that my parents were never quite like other people; not even towards the end…Were not my ancestors worshipped in grey stone Ib before the coming of men, in the earliest days of Earth's evolution? I should have guessed my identity when first I brought that figurine up out of the slime; *for the features of the thing were as my own features will be after The First Change, and engraved upon its base in the ancient letters of Ib—letters I could read because they were part of my native language, the precursor of all languages—was my own name!*

Bokrug:

Water-Lizard God of the people of Ib and Lh-yib, the Sister City!

Note:

Sir,

Attached to this manuscript, "Annex 'A'" to my report, was a brief note of explanation addressed to the NECB in Newcastle and reproduced as follows:

Robert Krug,
Marske,
Yorks.,
Evening—19 July '52

Secretary and Members,
NECB, Newcastle-on-Tyne.

Gentlemen of the North-East Coal-Board:

My discovery whilst abroad, in the pages of a popular science magazine, of your Yorkshire Moors Project, scheduled to commence next summer, determined me, upon the culmination of some recent discoveries of mine, to write you this letter. You will see that my letter is a protest against your proposals to drill deep into the moors in order to set off underground explosions in the hope of creating pockets of gas to be tapped as part of the country's natural resources. It is quite possible that the undertaking envisioned by your scientific advisors would mean the destruction of two ancient races of sentient life. The prevention of such destruction is that which causes me to break the laws of my race and thus announce the existence of them and their servitors. In order to explain my protest more fully I think it necessary that I tell my whole story. Perhaps upon reading the enclosed manuscript you will suspend indefinitely your projected operations.

Robert Krug…

POLICE REPORT M-Y-127/52
Alleged Suicide

Sir,

I have to report that at Dilham, on the 20th July 1952, at about four-thirty PM, I was on duty at the Police Station when three children (statements attached at Annex 'B') reported to the Desk Sgt. that they had seen a "funny man" climb the fence at "Devil's Pool," ignoring the warning notices, and throw himself into the stream where it vanishes into the hillside. Accompanied by the eldest of the children I went to the scene of the alleged occurrence, about three-quarters of a mile over the moors from Dilham, where the spot that the "funny man" allegedly climbed the fence was pointed out to me. There *were* signs that someone had recently gone over the fence; trampled grass and grass-stains on the timbers. With slight difficulty I climbed the fence myself but was unable to decide whether or not the children had told the truth. There was no evidence in or around the pool to suggest that anyone had thrown himself in—but this is hardly surprising as at that point, where the stream enters the hillside, the water rushes steeply downwards into the earth. Once in the water only an extremely strong swimmer would be able to get back out. Three experienced pot-holers were lost at this same spot in August last year when they attempted a partial reconnoiter of the stream's underground course.

When I further questioned the boy I had taken with me, I was told that a *second* man had been on the scene prior to the incident. This other man had been seen to limp as though he was hurt, into a nearby cave. This had occurred shortly before the "funny man"—described as being green and having a short, flexible tail—came out of the same cave, went over the fence and threw himself into the pool.

On inspecting the said cave I found what appeared to be an animal-hide of some sort, split down the arms and legs and up the belly, in the manner of the trophies of big-game hunters. This object was rolled up neatly in one corner of the cave and is now in the found-property room at the Police Station in Dilham. Near this hide was a complete set of good-quality gent's clothing, neatly folded and laid down. In the inside pocket of the jacket I found a wallet containing, along with fourteen pounds in one-pound notes, a card bearing the address of a house in Marske; namely, 11 Sunderland Crescent. These articles of clothing, plus the wallet, are also now in the found-property room.

At about six-thirty PM I went to the above address in Marske, and interviewed the housekeeper, one Mrs. White, who provided me with a statement (attached at Annex 'C') in respect of her partial employer, Robert Krug. Mrs. White also gave me two envelopes, one of which contained the manuscript attached to this report at Annex 'A'. Mrs. White had found this envelope, sealed, with a note asking her to deliver it, when she went to the house on the afternoon of the 20th about half an hour before I arrived. In view of the enquiries I was making and because of their nature, i.e.—an investigation into the possible suicide of Mr. Krug, Mrs. White thought it was best that the envelope be given to the police. Apart from this she was at a loss what to do with it because Krug had forgotten to address it. As there was the possibility of the envelope containing a suicide note or dying declaration I accepted it.

The other envelope, which was unsealed, contained a manuscript in a foreign language and is now in the property room at Dilham.

In the two weeks since the alleged suicide, despite all my efforts to trace Robert Krug, no evidence has come to light to support the hope that he may still be alive. This, plus the fact that the clothing found in the cave has since been identified by Mrs. White as being that which Krug was wearing the night before his disappearance, has determined me to request that my report be placed in the "unsolved" file and that Robert Krug be listed as missing.

Sgt. J. T. Miller,
Dilham, Yorks.

7 August 1952

Note:

Sir,
Do you wish me to send a copy of the manuscript at Annex 'A'—as requested of Mrs. White by Krug—to the Secretary of the North-East Coal-Board?

Inspector I. L. Ianson,
Yorkshire County Constabulary,
Radcar, Yorks.

Dear Sgt. Miller,
In answer to your note of the 7th. Take no further action on the Krug case. As you suggest, I have had the man posted as missing, believed a suicide. As for his *document*; well, the man was either mentally unbalanced or a monumental hoaxer; possibly a combination of both. Regardless of the fact that certain things in his story are

matters of indisputable fact, the majority of the thing appears to be the product of a diseased mind.

Meanwhile, I await your progress-report on that other case. I refer to the baby found in the church pews at Eely-on-the-Moor last June. How are you going about tracing the mother?

WHAT DARK GOD?

According to August Derleth he had "a thing about trains," which was one of the reasons he gave for paying me the fee of (wow!) thirty-five dollars for "What Dark God?"—which I seem to remember accepting in Arkham House books. (A nice move on my part, as I've stated elsewhere.) But I would have been happy with the payment anyway, mainly because the story was written in 1968, in the first few months of my newfound "skill" as an author. So in fact I was absolutely thrilled to be getting paid anything at all! The only drawback: Derleth could not guarantee a publication date and didn't even have a title for the anthology in which the story would appear. But the man wasn't well; three years later he was dead; "What Dark God?" had to wait until 1975 before seeing print in editor Jerry Page's anthology, Nameless Places. *Well, at least it was an Arkham House book.*

"…Summanus—whatever power he may be…"
Ovid's *Fasti*

The *Tuscan Rituals?* Now where had I heard of such a book or books before? Certainly very rare… Copy in the British Museum? Perhaps! Then what on earth were *these* fellows doing with a copy? And such a strange bunch of blokes at that.

Only a few minutes earlier I had boarded the train at Bengham. It was quite crowded for a night train and the boozy, garrulous, and vociferous "Jock" who had boarded it directly in front of me had been much upset by the fact that all the compartments seemed to be fully occupied.

"Och, they bleddy British trains," he had drunkenly grumbled, "either a'wiz emp'y or a'wiz fool. No orgynization whatsayever—ye no agree, ye sassenach?" He had elbowed me in the ribs as we swayed together down the dim corridor.

"Er, yes," I had answered. "Quite so!"

Neither of us carried cases and as we stumbled along, searching for vacant seats in the gloomy compartments, Jock suddenly stopped short.

"Noo what in hell's this—will ye look here? A compartment wi' the bleddy blinds doon: Prob'ly a young laddie an' lassie in there wi' six emp'y seats. Privacy be damned. Ah'm no standin' oot here while there's a seat in there..."

The door had proved to be locked—on the inside—but that had not deterred the "bonnie Scot" for a moment. He had banged insistently upon the wooden frame of the door until it was carefully, tentatively opened a few inches; then he had stuck his foot in the gap and put his shoulder to the frame, forcing the door fully open.

"No, no..." The scrawny, pale, pinstripe-jacketed man who stood blocking the entrance protested. "You can't come in—this compartment is reserved..."

"Is that so, noo? Well, if ye'll kindly show me the reserved notice," Jock had paused to tap significantly upon the naked glass of the door with a belligerent fingernail, "Ah'll bother ye no more—meanwhile, though, if ye'll hold ye're blether, *Ah'd appreciate a bleddy seat...*"

"No, no..." The scrawny man had started to protest again, only to be quickly cut off by a terse command from behind him:

"Let them in..."

I shook my head and pinched my nose, blowing heavily and puffing out my cheeks to clear my ears. For the voice from within the dimly lit compartment had sounded hollow, unnatural. Possibly the train had started to pass through a tunnel, an occurrence which never fails to give me trouble with my ears. I glanced out of the exterior corridor window and saw immediately that I was wrong; far off on the dark horizon I could see the red glare of coke-oven fires. Anyway, whatever the effect had been which had given that voice its momentarily peculiar—resonance?—it had obviously passed, for Jock's voice sounded perfectly normal as he said: "Noo tha's *better*, excuse a body, will ye?" He shouldered the dubious-looking man in the doorway to one side and slid clumsily into a seat alongside a second stranger. As I joined them in the compartment, sliding the door shut behind me, I saw that there were four strangers in all; six people including Jock and myself, we just made comfortable use of the eight seats which faced inwards in two sets of four.

I have always been a comparatively shy person so it was only the vaguest of perfunctory glances which I gave to each of the three new faces before I settled back and took out the pocket-book I had picked up earlier in the day in London. Those merest of glances, however, were quite sufficient to put me off my book and to tell me that the three friends of the pinstripe-jacketed man appeared the very strangest of travelling companions—especially the extremely tall and thin member of the three, sitting stiffly in his seat beside Jock. The other two answered to approximately the same description as Pin-Stripe—as I was beginning mentally to tag him—except that one of them wore a thin moustache; but that fourth one, the tall one, was something else again.

Within the brief duration of the glance I had given him I had seen that, remarkable though the rest of his features were, his mouth appeared decidedly odd—almost as if it had been painted onto his face—the merest thin red line, without a trace of puckering or any other depression to show that there was a hole there at all. His ears were thick and blunt and his eyebrows were bushy over the most penetrating eyes it has ever been my unhappy lot to find staring at me. Possibly that was the reason I had glanced so quickly away; the fact that when I had looked at him I had found *him* staring at *me*—and his face had been totally devoid of any expression whatsoever. *Fairies?* The nasty thought had flashed through my mind unbidden; nonetheless, that would explain why the door had been locked.

Suddenly Pin-Stripe—seated next to me and directly opposite Funny-Mouth—gave a start, and, as I glanced up from my book, I saw that the two of them were staring directly into each other's eyes.

"Tell them..." Funny-Mouth said, though I was sure his strange lips had not moved a fraction, and again his voice had seemed distorted, as though his words passed through weirdly angled corridors before reaching my ears.

"It's, er—almost midnight," informed Pin-Stripe, grinning sickly first at Jock and then at me.

"Aye," said Jock sarcastically, "happens every nicht aboot this time... Ye're very observant..."

"Yes," said Pin-Stripe, choosing to ignore the jibe, "as you say—but the point I wish to make is that we three, er, that is, we *four*," he corrected himself, indicating his companions with a nod of his head, "are members of a little-known, er, religious sect. We have a ceremony to perform and would appreciate it if you two gentlemen would remain quiet during the proceedings..." I heard him out and nodded my head in understanding and agreement—I am a tolerant person—but Jock was of a different mind.

"Sect?" he said sharply. "Ceremony?" He shook his head in disgust. "Well; Ah'm a member o' the Church O' Scotland and Ah'll tell ye noo—Ah'll hae no truck wi' bleddy heathen *ceremonies…*"

Funny-Mouth had been sitting ramrod straight, saying not a word, doing nothing, but now he turned to look at Jock, his eyes narrowing to mere slits; above them, his eyebrows meeting in a black frown of disapproval.

"Er, perhaps it would be better," said Pin-Stripe hastily, leaning across the narrow aisle towards Funny-Mouth as he noticed the change in that person's attitude, "if they, er, *went to sleep…?*"

This preposterous statement or question, which caused Jock to peer at its author in blank amazement and me to wonder what on earth he was babbling about, was directed at Funny-Mouth who, without taking his eyes off Jock's outraged face, nodded in agreement.

I do not know what happened then—it was as if I had been suddenly *unplugged*—I was asleep, yet not asleep—in a trance-like condition full of strange impressions and mind-pictures—abounding in unpleasant and realistic sensations, with dimly recollected snatches of previously absorbed information floating up to the surface of my conscious mind, correlating themselves with the strange people in the railway compartment with me…

And in that dream-like state my brain was still very active; possibly *fully* active. All my senses were still working; I could hear the clatter of the wheels and smell the acrid tang of burnt tobacco from the compartment's ash-trays. I saw Moustache produce a folding table from the rack above his head—saw him open it and set it up in the aisle, between Funny-Mouth and himself on their side and Pin-Stripe and his companion on my side— saw the designs upon it, designs suggestive of the more exotic work of Chandler Davies, and wondered at their purpose. My head must have fallen back, until it rested in the corner of the gently rocking compartment, for I saw all these things without having to move my eyes; indeed, I doubt very much if I *could* have moved my eyes and do not remember making any attempt to do so.

I saw that book—a queerly bound volume bearing its title, *The Tuscan Rituals*, in archaic, burnt-in lettering on its thick spine—produced by Pin-Stripe and opened reverently to lie on that ritualistic table, displayed so that all but Funny Mouth, Jock, and I could make out its characters. But Funny-Mouth did not seem in the least bit interested in the proceedings. He gave me the impression that he had seen it all before, many times…

Knowing I was dreaming—or was I?—I pondered that title, *The Tuscan Rituals*. Now where had I heard of such a book or books before? The *feel* of it echoed back into my subconscious, telling me I recognised that title—but in what connection?

I could see Jock, too, on the fixed border of my sphere of vision, lying with his head lolling towards Funny-Mouth—in a trance similar to my own, I imagined—eyes staring at the drawn blinds on the compartment windows. I saw the lips of Pin-Stripe, out of the corner of my right eye, and those of Moustache, moving in almost perfect rhythm, and imagined those of Other—as I had named the fourth who was completely out of my periphery of vision—doing the same, and heard the low and intricate liturgy which they were chanting in unison.

Liturgy? Tuscan Rituals? Now what dark "God" was this they worshipped? …And what had made *that* thought spring to my dreaming or hypnotised mind? And what was Moustache doing now?

He had a bag and was taking things from it, laying them delicately on the ceremonial table. Three items in all in one corner of the table, that nearest Funny-Mouth. Round cakes of wheat-bread in the shape of wheels with ribbed spokes. Now who had written about offerings of round cakes of—…?

Festus? Yes, *Festus*—but, again, in what connection?

Then I heard it. A *name*: chanted by the three worshippers, but not by Funny-Mouth who still sat aloofly upright. "Summanus, Summanus, Summanus…" They chanted; and suddenly, it all clicked into place.

Summanus! Of whom Martianus Capella had written as being The Lord of Hell…I remembered now. It was Pliny who, in his *Natural History*, mentioned the dreaded *Tuscan Rituals*, "books containing the Liturgy of Summanus…" Of course; Summanus—Monarch of Night—The Terror that Walketh in Darkness; Summanus, whose worshippers were so few and whose cult was surrounded with such mystery, fear, and secrecy that according to St. Augustine even the most curious enquirer could discover no particular of it.

So Funny-Mouth, who stood so aloof to the ceremony in which the others were participating, must be a priest of the cult.

Though my eyes were fixed—my centre of vision being a picture, one of three, on the compartment wall just above Moustache's head—I could still clearly see Funny-Mouth's face and, as a blur to the left of my periphery, that of Jock. The liturgy had come to an end with the calling of the "God's" name and the offering of bread. For the first time Funny-Mouth seemed to be taking an interest. He turned his head to look at the table and just as I was certain that he was going to reach out and take the breadcakes the train lurched and Jock slid sideways in his seat, his face coming into clearer perspective as it came to rest about half-way down Funny-Mouth's upper right arm. Funny-Mouth's head snapped round in a blur of motion. *Hate*, livid and pure, shone from those cold eyes, was reflected by the bristling eyebrows and tightening features; only the strange, painted-on mouth remained sterile of emotion. But he made no effort to move Jock's head.

It was not until later that I found out what happened then. Mercifully my eyes could not take in the whole of the compartment—or what was happening in it. I only knew that Jock's face, little more than an outline with darker, shaded areas defining the eyes, nose, and mouth at the lower rim of my fixed "picture", became suddenly contorted; twisted somehow, as though by some great emotion or pain. He said nothing, unable to break out of that damnable trance, but his eyes bulged horribly and his features writhed. If only I could have taken my eyes off him, or closed them even, to shut out the picture of his face writhing and Funny-Mouth staring at him so terribly. Then I noticed the change in Funny-Mouth. He had been a chalky-grey colour before; we all had, in the weak glow from the alternatively brightening and dimming compartment ceiling light. Now he seemed to be *flushed*; pinkish waves of unnatural colour were suffusing his outré features and his red-slit mouth was fading into the deepening blush of his face. It almost looked as though... *My God! He did not have a mouth.* With that unnatural reddening of his features the painted slit had vanished completely; his face was blank beneath the eyes and nose.

What a God-awful dream. I knew it must be a dream now—it *had* to be a dream—such things do not happen in real life. Dimly I was aware of Moustache putting the bread-cakes away and folding the queer table. I could feel the rhythm of the train slowing down. We must be coming into Grenloe. Jock's face was absolutely convulsed now. A white, twitching, jerking, bulge-eyed blur of hideous motion which grew paler as quickly as that of Funny-Mouth—if that name applied now—reddened. Suddenly Jock's face stopped its jerking. His mouth lolled open and his eyes slowly closed. He slid out of my circle of vision towards the floor.

The train was moving much slower and the wheels were clacking over those groups of criss-crossing rails which always warn one that a train is approaching a station or depot. Funny-Mouth had turned his monstrous, nightmare face towards me. He leaned across the aisle, closing the distance between us. I mentally screamed, physically incapable of the act, and strained with every fibre of my being to break from the trance which I suddenly knew beyond any doubting *was not a dream and never had been...*

The train ground to a shuddering halt with a wheeze of steam and a squeal of brakes. Outside in the night the station-master was yelling instructions to a porter on the unseen platform. As the train stopped Funny-Mouth was jerked momentarily back, away from me, and before he could bring his face close to mine again Moustache was speaking to him.

"There's no time, Master—this is our stop…" Funny-Mouth hovered over me a moment longer, seemingly undecided, then he pulled away. The others filed past him out into the corridor while he stood, tall and eerie, just within the doorway. Then he lifted his right hand and snapped his fingers.

I could move. I blinked my eyes rapidly and shook myself, sitting up straight, feeling the pain of the cramp between my shoulder-blades. "I say—" I began.

"*Quiet!*" ordered that echoing voice from unknown spaces—and of course, his painted, false mouth never moved. I was right; I had been hypnotised, not dreaming at all. That false mouth—Walker in Darkness—Monarch of Night—Lord of Hell—the Liturgy to Summanus…

I opened my mouth in amazement and horror, but before I could utter more than one word—*"Summanus…"*—something happened.

His waist-coat slid to one side near the bottom and a long, white, tapering tentacle with a blood-red tip slid into view. That tip hovered, snake-like, for a moment over my petrified face—and then struck. As if someone had taken a razor to it my face opened up and the blood began to gush. I fell to my knees in shock, too terrified even to yell out, automatically reaching for my handkerchief; and when next I coweringly looked up Funny-Mouth had gone.

Instead of seeing him—*It*—I found myself staring, from where I knelt dabbing uselessly at my face, into the slack features of the sleeping Jock.

Sleeping?

I began to scream. Even as the train started to pull out of the station I was screaming. When no one answered my cries I managed to pull the communication-cord. Then, until they came to find out what was wrong, I went right on screaming. Not because of my face—*because of Jock…*

A jagged, bloody, two-inch hole led clean through his jacket and shirt and into his left side—the side which had been closest to…to that *thing—and there was not a drop of blood in his whole, limp body.* He simply lay there—half on, half off the seat—victim of "a bleddy heathen ceremony"—substituted for the bread-cakes simply because the train had chosen an inopportune moment to lurch—a sacrifice to Summanus…

THE STATEMENT OF HENRY WORTHY

Even before "What Dark God?"—in fact in September 1967—
I had sent off this my, er, most ambitious story so far to August Der-
leth at Arkham House. He didn't turn it down flat but said it
needed work—which it did. When he saw my revision Derleth said
it would go into his Lumley File for publication at a later date, per-
haps in The Caller of The Black. *But it wasn't to be, for as with*
"What Dark God?" so with Statement. *After Derleth died, several*
stories by various authors had been left drifting in a literary limbo
without any foreseeable future. In my case: eventually Derleth's sur-
vivors at Arkham House collected my loose stories from the "Lum-
ley File", plus a handful of others I'd written, and sold elsewhere,
into a new book with the title The Horror at Oakdeene. *Thus in*
1977, all of ten years after I had written and revised it, at long last
"The Statement of Henry Worthy" saw print in my third and last
Arkham House book.

I

Difficult as it is to find a way in which to tell the truth of the hideous affair, I know that if I am to avoid later implication in the events leading up to and relevant to the disappearance of my poor nephew, Matthew Worthy, it is imperative that the tale be told. And yet…

The very nature of that alien and foulest of afflictions which contaminated Matthew is sufficient, merely thinking back on it in the light of what I know now, to cause me to look over my shoulder in apprehension and to shudder in an involuntary spasm—this in spite of the fact that it is far from chilly here in my study, and despite the effects of the large draught of whisky I have just taken, a habit rapidly grown on me over the last few days.

Better, I suppose, to start at the very beginning, at that time in early July of this Year of Our Lord, 1931, when Matthew came down from Edinburgh to visit. He was a fine young man: tall, with a strong, straight back and a good, wide-browed, handsome face. He had a shock of jet hair which took him straight to the hearts of the more eligible young ladies of Eeley-on-the-Moor, and of the neighbouring village of High-Marske, which also fell within the boundaries of my practice; but strangely, at only twenty-one years of age, Matthew had little interest in the young women of the two villages. His stay, he calculated, would be too short to acquire any but the remotest of friendships; he was far too busy with his studies to allow himself to be anything but mildly interested in the opposite sex.

Indeed, Matthew's professors had written to inform me of the brilliance of their pupil, predicting a great future for him. In the words of one of these learned gentlemen: "It is more apparent every day, from the intensity of his studies, the freshness with which he views every aspect of his work, and the hitherto untried methods which he employs in many of his tasks and experiments, that the day will come when he will be—for he surely has the potential—one of the greatest scientists in his field in the country and perhaps the whole world. Already he emulates many of the great men who, not so very long ago, were his idols, and the time draws ever nearer when he will have the capacity to exceed even the greatest of them."

And now Matthew is gone. I do not say "dead"—no, he is, as I myself may well soon be, *departed*… And yet it is my hope that I might still be able to release him from the hell which at present is his prison.

When Matthew came down to Yorkshire it was not without a purpose. He had read of how, twenty-five years ago, the German genius Horst Graumer found two completely unknown botanical specimens on the moors. This was shortly before that fatal ramble from which Graumer never returned. Since the German's disappearance—despite frequent visits to the moors by various scientific bodies—no further evidence of the Graumer Specimens had been found. Now that the original plants, at the University of Cologne, were nothing more than mummified fragments, in spite of all precautions taken to preserve them, Matthew had decided that it was time someone else explored the moors. For unless they had been faked, the *Graumer Specimens* were unique in botany, and before his disappearance

Graumer himself had described them as being "sehr sonderbare, mysteriöse Unkräuter!"—very strange and mysterious weeds...

So it was that shortly before noon on the seventh day of July Matthew set out over the moors, taking with him a rucksack, some food, and a rope. The latter was to ensure, in the event of his finding what he sought on some steep incline, that he would experience no difficulty in collecting specimens. With the fall of night he still had not returned, and although a search party was organised early the next morning no trace of him could be found. Just as Horst Graumer had disappeared a quarter of a century earlier, so now had my nephew apparently vanished from the face of the earth.

I was ready to give Matthew up for dead when, on the morning of the fourteenth, he stumbled into my study with twigs and bits of bracken sticking to the material of his rough climbing clothes. His hair was awry; he was bearded; the lower legs of his trousers were strangely slimed and discoloured, yet apart from his obvious weariness and grimy aspect he seemed perfectly sound and well nourished.

Seeing this, my first joy at having him back turned to a rage in which I demanded to know, "what the devil the young skelp meant by worrying people half to death?—And where in the name of heaven had he *been* this last week?—And did he not know that the entire countryside had been in an uproar over him?"—and so on.

Matthew apologized profusely for everything and condemned himself for his own stupidity, but when his story was told I did not have it in me to blame him for what had happened; and rightly so. It seemed that he had climbed a particularly steep knoll somewhere on the moors. Upon reaching the summit a mist had set in which prevented his exploration of the peak. Before the mist settled, however, he had been overjoyed to find a single misshapen weed that he did not recognise and which, so far as he knew, was as yet unclassified. He believed it to be similar to the much sought after *Graumer Specimens*!

Intending first to study the plant in its natural surroundings, he did not uproot it but left it as it was. He merely sat down, marked his rough position on a map he had taken with him, and waited for the mist to clear. After about an hour, by which time he was thoroughly drenched, he gave up all hope of the mist clearing before nightfall and set about making the descent.

He found that in the opaque greyness of the mist the downward route he had chosen was considerably more difficult to manoeuvre than the one by which he had climbed. Indeed, the knoll's steepness—plus the fact that he was wet and uncomfortable—caused him to slip and slither for a short distance down the wild slope. Suddenly, as his slide was coming to an end, he bumped over the edge of a narrow crack in the earth, broke through the bracken which partly covered it, and shot into space with his arms wildly failing. He fell some distance before landing on his back on a dry ledge at the bottom of the crevice.

When he somewhat dazedly had a look around, he was surprised that he had not suffered a serious injury. He had fallen some twenty feet onto a bank of sandy shingle. The place was a sort of pothole, with walls which were so sheer that in places they overhung. It was plainly impossible to climb out un-aided. At his feet was a motionless, slimy-green pool that narrowed to a mere channel at a point where it vanished under a low archway of limestone at one end of the defile.

The true horror of his situation dawned on him fully when he realized that he had lost his rucksack, and further that his rope was useless to him as he had no grappling hook. It fully appeared that unless a miracle occurred and he could somehow devise a means of getting out, he would be forced to spend the rest of his days in this dank and cheerless place; and those days would not be too many with nothing but the evil-looking water of the scummy pool as sustenance. He did have a small pocket first-aid kit that I had given to him in case of emergencies, and this he used as best he could to clean up his few bruises and abrasions.

After sitting thus occupied, recovering himself, and regaining a little of his composure, Matthew took to exploring his prison. The place had a per-ceptibly foreboding aura about it, and hanging in the air was a sickly-sweet smell so heavy it seemed almost a taste rather than an odour. All was silent except for a distant *drip, drip, drip* of water. Little light entered the hole from above, but Matthew was not too disheartened for the stone walls were cov-ered with a grey, semiluminescent moss that gave off a dim light.

He had left Eeley-on-the-Moor before noon, and he calculated that by now it must be about seven in the evening. He knew that in another hour or so I would begin to worry about him—but what could he do about it? He was virtually a prisoner, and try as he might he could think of no practical way out. Upon examining his rope he saw that it was badly frayed in two places. He cursed himself for not having checked it before setting out, then hung it over a projecting rock and swung on it to test its capacity to take his weight. The rope broke twice before he was finally left with a serviceable length of no more than twenty feet or so.

He tied one end of this remaining piece of rope to a fairly large stone but upon tossing it upwards was dismayed to find that it only reached a point a good two or three feet short of the lip of the crevice. All he could do now, he decided, was sit it out and hope that some search party would find him. He realised that no such search party would exist until early morning at the soonest, and so knew that it was pointless to try calling for help.

It did not become noticeably darker, though he knew it must fast be approaching night, and he put this down to the fact that the moss on the walls was supplementing the natural light. He knew his fancy to be correct when, a short while later, he saw twinkling through the crack above him the first stars in the night sky.

Thoroughly tired now, he sat down in the driest place he could find and fell asleep; but his sleep was troubled by nightmare visions of weird events and strange creatures. He awoke several times, stifled by the unnatural and oppressive warmth of the place, to find the echoes of his own cries of terror still ringing in the hole's foul atmosphere. Even when wide awake the next morning the dreams persisted in his memory. In them he had seemed to understand all of the horrible and strangely threatening occurrences.

In one of these dreams there had been a misty landscape of queer rock formations, unfamiliar trees, and giant ferns; plants which, to the best of Matthew's knowledge, had not existed on Earth since the dawn of time. He had been one of a crowd of loathsome ape-like beings, ugly, with flat faces and sloping foreheads. They had approached a forbidden place, a hole in the earth from which nameless vapours poured out a ghastly stench.

They had captives, these ape men, creatures like themselves—yet monstrously different—who had defied The Laws. These prisoners had lately trespassed upon this holy ground unbidden by the priests, and they had also dared to spy upon the God-things conjured in horrible rituals by those same hierophants. Because of the horror of what they saw they had practised sedition, calling for the overthrow of the priests and the expulsion of those Gods from Outside. Fearing that this call might *somewhere* be heard, the God-things had paused momentarily in their horrific pleasures to order their priests to punish the offenders—whom they would make recognisable through growing physiological differences!

And indeed those captives were different... They were slimy to the touch and seemed to exude a dreadful moisture which stank evilly. They stumbled rather than walked, apparently afflicted with some nervous disorder which caused their steps to be short and jerky.

But when in his dream Matthew had looked closer at those prisoners of the ape men, then he had seen that he was wrong. They suffered from no nervous disorder—the trouble was all physical. Their legs appeared to be joined from knee to groin by some ghastly fungoid growth, and their arms were similarly fastened to their sides. Their eyes were almost completely scaled over, and their mouths were gone, closed forever by strips of the horrid, scaly substance which was apparently growing over their whole bodies. Matthew knew somehow that this terrible leper-growth was the first phase of their punishment for what they had dared to do—and that the balance was still to be paid.

The entire unholy procession had been led by three creatures different again from the rest. Their foreheads were not so sloped, giving them a position somewhat higher on the evolutionary scale, and they were taller by a head than the others. These were the priests, and they wore the only clothing of the entire assembly: coarse, dark cloaks thrown about their shoulders.

The priests had carried flaring torches, intoning some weird chant which—while Matthew was unable to remember why—he had known in his dream to be immemorially significant. It had been in the form of an invocation to certain "Gods" of an ancient myth cycle. How he understood anything of the dream was a mystery to him; he remembered that on the few occasions when the beings talked to one another, the tongue they used was not one he should normally have been conversant with. Indeed, he said he believed it to be a language dead and vanished from the face of the Earth for some hundreds of thousands, if not millions of years.

Soon the group arrived at the malodorous pit, and at its very rim the priests stood with their torches held high over the hole while their chanting grew in volume and fervour. The evil-smelling vapours swirled up around them, occasionally enveloping them completely from the view of their followers; and then, suddenly, as the chanting reached a fever pitch, the unfortunate ones were thrust forward and one after the other were thrown bodily into that eldritch chasm. They were incapable of screaming for their mouths were scaled over, but even had that not been so they would not have screamed. No, they seemed somehow to *welcome* being thrown into the dreadful abyss.

As the bodies of the unfortunates vanished in reeking darkness, the priests slowly turned towards Matthew, approaching him with alien and horribly sly smiles upon their faces. Not knowing why he, personally, should suddenly feel so horrified, Matthew nevertheless turned to run—*but could only stumble!*—and in an instant the whole crowd was around him. The evil implication of the looks upon their faces was now all too clear, and he opened his mouth to reject their unspoken accusation, but...

...Horror upon horror—*he could barely move his jaws!*

He tried to raise his arms to protect himself but could not do so. It was as though his limbs were pinned to his body and, half knowing what he would see, he glanced down at himself. Even this simple movement seemed to be too great an effort for him, but somehow he accomplished it and saw…and saw—

He, too, was one of—*Them*!

His arms were webbed to his sides and his legs were partly joined. His skin was green and foul and he stank of an unholy, sickly-sweetness. But he was hardly given time to examine these abnormalities for the horde had already lifted him into the air and borne him to the edge of the pit!

That, mercifully, was when he awoke.

II

If my memory serves me correctly, that is the way Matthew related to me the contents of his dream in the hole. There were more dreams later, but I have told of this first one in some detail for I believe that in an inexplicable way its events are related to the rest of my story. It is my belief that in his slumbers Matthew had seen actual occurrences from the abysmal prehistory of his terrifying prison…

On his second day in the hole he waded into the pool and found it unpleasantly warm and greasy, as though composed of thick vegetable secretions rather than water. A great thirst was on him but he could not bring himself to drink that foul muck.

Finding that the pool was quite shallow, he waded to the archway and stooped beneath and beyond it. The water—if such it could be called—beyond the arch was only slightly deeper, and the living walls gave off sufficient light for him to see that the same sandy shelf continued in this secondary cave. Wet and slimy, he climbed out onto the shelf and looked about him. There were long, sharp stalactites hanging from above—for here there was no crack in the ceiling—but though these aeon-formed stone daggers were fascinating enough in themselves, it was the *other* things which primarily claimed Matthew's astounded attention.

This primeval cavern contained wonders to fill to bursting point the heart of any man of science—and especially a botanist. Protruding from the walls were plants unlike any existing upon the surface of the Earth—huge pod-like things, standing on end all around the walls with their lower roots trailing in the slimy water. Each plant seemed to be growing out of, or depending from, the wall of the cave; or perhaps they had grown up out of the water, later to fasten upon the walls in the manner of certain other climbing, clinging plants.

The things were between five and six feet long top to bottom, as green as the evil mutations in my nephew's dreams. They were also slimy and exuded a vile fluid which dripped off them into the pool. Matthew wondered if this constant dripping of vegetable secretions was the reason the pool was so odious.

Later in that secret cave, after he had recovered from his first amazement at this terrific find, he also discovered some water which was at least cleaner than that of the pool. It dripped from the tips of those dagger-like, depending rock formations, and although it had an unpleasant taste—an unwholesome acidity—it went far towards quenching his by now burning thirst. Yet he drank falteringly, as though his whole body instinctively drew back from having anything to do with that unknown hole in the earth.

But now he was filled with anger. What a find! A discovery so immense that he was "made" for life, his future assured, if he could but get out of that accursed pit. It was then that he first saw the means of his salvation. In the gravel of the shelf were many half-buried flat stones. If he could get a sufficient number of these stones to the other side of the natural archway, he could perhaps build them up to form a platform from which to throw his weighted rope over the lip of the crevice.

His difficulties were many. There was the unpleasant feel of the water (for which he had developed a morbid dread); the great weight of the large stones; the fact that he quickly exhausted the supply of readily available stones on the surface and had to dig in the sandy shingle for others.

It was when he was moving the first of these stones that he noticed, in the dim light, the intricate, runic designs cut into their surfaces. Strange cabalistic signs literally covered them, and although he had no knowledge of their meaning, still they filled him with dread. They reminded him of similar glyphs once glimpsed in the university's rare books department—in the pages of a book by von Junzt—and again he experienced that reluctance of soul encountered upon drinking the dripping water. Nonetheless, he progressed with his work until he had a platform of stones almost three feet high against the wall of his prison.

This took him halfway through his third miserable day in the hole. Though he could now almost reach the lip of the crevice with his weighted rope, he had exhausted his supply of stones and was too weak from hunger and exhaustion to dig for more. He knew that soon he would be starving and that if he was ever to complete his task and get out of the place he must have food… But what to eat?

For all he knew the plants in the inner cave may well be poisonous, but they were his only hope; and so he took his first bite from one of them. That first bite, while it made him feel sick, was nevertheless strangely satisfying. Later he was able completely to fill himself from the plant and the strength he gained from this singular food source was prodigious. After a while the sickly taste no longer made him feel ill; indeed, he began to enjoy a narcotic sense of well-being.

Just how true this was—the fact that he had deeply drugged himself—was not realised until another evil dream released him from his torpor. He had been in the hole almost seven days when his own screaming roused him from the throes of nightmare. He could fairly well gauge just how much time had passed by the heavy stubble grown on his chin.

In his new dream the priest-creatures had sealed off the sacrificial cavern with holy, inscribed stones—the very stones for which he now dug so frantically in the floor of the pit—but there had been much more than that to the dream; Matthew admitted so much but would tell me no more of that final nightmare, merely stating that it "did not bear relating".

With his new-found strength and in his frantic haste, it took him only a few hours to complete the platform. At last he was able to fling his stone-laden rope up out of the defile and, amazingly, with his very first attempt came success! The rough stone wedged, and held, and without a great deal of effort he was able to haul himself out. Elated, he scrambled down the knoll and hurried back across the moors to Eeley.

In just a few days Eeley and High-Marske got over the upset that Matthew had caused; the groups which had gathered in the village pubs to chat and wonder about his disappearance themselves dispersed. Then, after Matthew had assured police Sergeant Mellor that the pit was so out of the way as to create no menace to village children, he was able to get down to his studies again.

He had unintentionally brought back with him a portion of the plant from which he had eaten; he assured me that in his haste to escape from the pit he would never consciously have thought of it. In fact his sample was one that he had torn from the plant to eat later and which he found, upon his return, still in his pocket where he had put it. Though the fragment was rapidly deteriorating, it was still firm enough to permit him to study it.

And Matthew's studies occupied him completely for the next few days. The hybrid weed he had found atop the knoll was all but forgotten and the possibility that more such fascinating specimens existed in that area was matterless to him. For the moment all his energies were concentrated on his as yet unidentified sample.

One afternoon three or four days after his return, I was sitting in my study checking through some notes on the ailments, real or imagined, of some of my elder patients, when Matthew burst unbidden upon me from the corridor. His eyes were quite wild and he seemed somehow to have aged years. There was a look of absolute puzzlement—or shock—on his face, and his jaw hung slack in undisguised amazement.

"Uncle," he blurted, "perhaps you can help me. Goodness knows I *need* help. I just can't understand it...or don't want to. It's not natural. Natural?— why, it's *impossible*—and yet there it is..." He shook his head in defeat.

"Oh?" I said. "What's impossible, Matthew?"

For a moment he was silent, then: "Why, that plant—or *thing*! It has no right to exist. None of them has. At first I thought I must be mistaken, but then I checked and double-checked and checked again—and I know I'm right. They just can't do it!"

As patiently as I could, I asked: "Who, exactly, are 'they', and what is it that 'they' can't do?"

"The plants," he told me in an exasperated tone of voice. "They can't re-produce! Or if they can I've no idea how they do it. And that's only a part of it. In attempting to classify the things I've tried tricks that would get me locked up if any conventional botanist knew of them. Why!—I can't even say for sure that they're plants—in fact I'm almost certain that they're not. And that leads on to something else—"

He leaned forward in his chair and stared at me. "Seeing as how I've decided they're not plants, I thought perhaps they might be some obscure animal form—like those sea animals which were mistaken for plants for such a long time—I mean, anemones and the like. I've checked it all out, and...no such thing! I've got a whole library of books up there," he indi-cated with a toss of his head the upstairs room, "but nothing that's any good to me."

"So you're baffled," I said. "But surely you've made some mistake? It's obvious that whatever they are they must be one or the other, plants or an-imals. Call in a second opinion."

"Never!— Certainly not until I've done a lot more work on my own," Matthew cried. "This thing is big, fantastic. A new form of life! But you must excuse me, uncle. I have to get back to work. There's so much I've got to understand..."

Suddenly he paused, seeming uneasy; his manner became somehow, well, furtive. "I've especially got to understand that other thing—the structure of the cells, I mean. It's quite uncanny. How can it be explained? The cell-structure is almost—it's almost human!" And with that he hurried out of my room.

For a moment I laughed to myself. Everything is fantastic to the young. Matthew had made a mistake, of course, for if those things were neither animals nor plants—then what in heaven's name were they?

III

The ghastly thing started the next morning, showing first of all in small greenish patches of flaky yet slimy substance on Matthew's arms and chest. Just a few patches at first, but they refused to submit to the application of antiseptic swabs or the recently introduced fungicidal creams, and within the course of the day a loathsome green network had spread over the boy's entire frame so that I was forced to confine him to his bed.

I did all I could to reassure and comfort him, and later in the evening hung a notice on my waiting-room door informing my patients, mercifully few and with only trivial complaints, that due to alterations in my work schedule I was forced to holiday early and only very urgent calls would be answered. I added to this the address of a friend of mine in Hawthorpe, a consulting doctor whom I contacted with a similar story of altered work schedules and who willingly accepted my plan for any of my flock who might require medical attention.

All this done I attempted to fathom the horror that had overtaken my nephew, and in this I could only be doomed to failure through the completely alien nature of the thing. The only definite statement of fact I could make about it was that I knew certain of its symptoms: Matthew had hardly eaten at all since his adventure in the pit, neither had I seen him take any sort of drink, and yet he had shown no signs of hunger. I was not to know it but the metamorphosis taking place in his body was one which did not yet require to be fed. A new way of feeding was developing...

Dazedly, desperately attempting to understand this monstrous thing come so suddenly upon my house, I worked all through the night and into the next morning; but having done everything I could think of to check the vile *acceleration* of Matthew's affliction, and failing, I suggested calling in a specialist. It was the worst thing I could have done. Matthew reacted like a wild thing, screaming that there was nothing anyone could do for him and that "knowledge of those *things* in the pit must spread no further!" Plainly he believed that the disease had come back with him from the pit on the moors, that he had poisoned his system by eating of those obscene plants—and in all truth I was hardly able to dispute it.

Sobbing and shrieking, swearing that he would soon cease to be a bother to me, he made me promise not to tell anyone of the horror or bring in anyone to see him. I thought I knew his meaning about ceasing to be a bother: in all my textbooks I could find nothing like my nephew's disease; only leprosy could be said even to approximate it, and leprosy did not have its fantastic acceleration. Reluctantly I calculated that the virulence of Matthew's disease would kill him within a fortnight, and for this reason I agreed to his every request.

The next night, out for a breath of badly needed fresh air, I managed to catch Ginger, my cat. Since first Matthew returned from his prolonged ramble Ginger had refused to enter the house, preferring to howl horribly on the step outside for hours on end. I brought him in and left him in a very agitated state downstairs with a bowl of milk. The next morning—the fourth morning, I think, of the manifestation of the horror—I found Ginger's fearful, death-stiffened corpse on the dispensary floor. One of the room's small windowpanes was cracked where the unfortunate and terrified animal had tried to escape. But from what? Animals can sense things too deep for the blunted human mind to grasp—and what Ginger had sensed had frightened him to death.

Other animals, too, had noticed something strange about my house, and dogs in particular would come nowhere near the place. Even my pony, tied in a warm lean-to behind the house, had danced nervously in his stall all through those long nights…

On the same morning that I found Ginger dead, when I carefully slipped back the sheets from Matthew's sleeping form, doctor though I am and despite the fact that my experience has included every type of illness and ailment, I recoiled in terror from that which lay upon the bed. Three hours later, at about eleven in the morning, when I was satisfied that I had done everything I possibly could, I laid down my tools. I had worked with surgical swabs and scrapers, sponges and acids, and my nephew's body beneath the dressings was not a pretty sight. But at least it was clean—for the moment.

When the anesthetic wore off and Matthew awoke, though he was obviously in great pain, he managed to tell me of the new dream which had disturbed his sleep. He had seemed to be in a misty place where there was only a voice, continually repeating a phrase in an alien tongue, which as before he had somehow been able to understand. The voice had called:

"Ye shall not *associate* with them. Ye shall not *know* them or walk *among* them or *near* them..." And Matthew had been afraid for his very soul.

That afternoon we slept. Both of us were near exhaustion and it was only later in the evening, when I was disturbed by his cries, that I awoke. He was having yet another nightmare and I listened intently by his bedside in case he said something new in connection with the horror. Had I roused him then I might have saved his mind, but I am glad now that I did nothing, being satisfied to sit listening while he rambled in his sleep. It seemed to me that he was better asleep; whatever dreams he experienced, they could in no way be worse than the reality.

I was deeply shocked by the poisonous odour that drifted up from his restless form, for only a few hours earlier I had cleansed him completely of every sign of the horror. I had hoped that my extreme surgical efforts might be sufficient to halt the rapid encroachment of the dread growth, but I had been grasping at straws. That smell made it all too obvious that my hopes had been in vain. Then, as I continued watching, Matthew began to writhe and gibber dementedly.

"No, no," he gasped, "I will *not* stand like this, as though I were part of the place, with the muck dripping off me. *I will not!*" For a long moment his chest rose and fell spasmodically. Then, in a calmer voice, he continued:

"No one must learn of the pit... Sinned... Committed the ultimate abomination, and soon I must answer the call... No priests, no ceremony for me... Dead before the dinosaurs... And no one must see me... Too many inquisitive minds, curious delvers in mysteries... Spread the thing across the whole world... God knows... Tell no one... No one must know... Ultimate sin... *Heaven help me!*"

There was a long pause here, and in Matthew's sleeping attitude I could suddenly detect an air of listening. Finally he began to talk again: "But these voices! Who are they? I don't know these names. John Jamieson Hustam...Gint Rillson...Feth Bandr? And the others—what of them? Ganhfl Degrahms? Sgyss-Twell? Neblozt? Ungl? Uh'ang?"

At this point he grew even quieter. His lips drew back from his teeth and the cords of his neck stood out grotesquely. Cold sweat appeared on his brow and his low moaning became coarser, merely a cracked whisper. "That other, weak, dying voice! *Who's that? What's that?*...Whisperer—who are you? Your name sounds famil... No—no, it's not so!" Now his voice fell so low it became a mere hiss of breath:

"You...*can't*...be!"

Suddenly, with one hoarsely screamed word—or name—he sat rigidly upright, wide awake. Eyes bugging he gazed terrified, unseeing, about the room. For a moment I was at a loss to understand—but then I saw the foam gathering at the corner of his mouth and the way his eyes were beginning to roll vacantly in his poisoned, suddenly grinning face. I sat by him then, cradling him in my arms as, sobbing, he rocked back and forth, completely robbed of his sanity.

At the time I did not understand that name he screamed, but now I understand everything. Especially I know what it was that finally proved too much for my nephew's severely overtaxed mind and body. That which he had—dreamed?

Matthew did not recover, and from that moment on I had to care for him like a newborn babe; he was incapable of even the most basic rationalization. Yet in a way I believe that this was the best thing that could have happened. There was little I could do to help him, physically or mentally, and I had completely given up my brief idea of calling in a specialist. No doctor would ever have dreamed, while the chance remained of the horror being communicable, of risking passing that loathsomeness on to another human being— which was, of course, the main reason I had stopped practicing. No, I was on my own with Matthew, and all I could do was wait and see what form the advancing terror would take.

Up to this time I myself had shown no sign of having contracted the disease, and after every session with my nephew I made sure that I bathed, cleansing myself thoroughly. True, lately I had shown a loss of appetite (but surely, in retrospect, that was only to be expected?) which at the time was an additional worry for I recognised the symptom. Still, I told myself, in all probability my fears were purely psychological.

Early the following morning, while he slept, I gave Matthew a further anaesthetic and removed his dressings. By now I was almost inured to shock and the sight of that dreadful green network growing *in* the wounds—in his very flesh—only verified what I had expected. The smell from the uncovered areas was terrible, and I saw that far from being beneficial my cutting and burning had probably worsened the boy's condition. Indeed, by midday I knew that there was no hope left for him at all. His arms were webbing to his sides and his thighs already clung together; the growth was spreading so rapidly over and through him that I knew he had only a day or so left.

It is not my intention to tell the way in which the horror increased in Matthew from that time onwards. Suffice to say that I began to lace the baths I was taking with ever increasing frequency with carbolic—a little more each time—until, when I last bathed just yesterday, the percentage of acid in the water was sufficient to raise small blisters on my legs. Yet my efforts seemed worthwhile, for even after Matthew—got away—and shuffled off to the moors two days ago my body was still clean, though my appetite was nonexistent. I had hoped, indeed prayed, that this inability of mine to eat was psychological—but again all my hopes were in vain.

There, I have admitted it: yes, I too am infected! Shortly after I started to write this, yesterday evening after returning from the moors, I noticed the first discoloured, scaly spot on the back of my hand…

But in my hurry to get done with this I have jumped ahead of myself. I must go back two nights, to the evening Matthew vanished into the mist, for the worst is yet to be told.

IV

Believing that he only had a few more hours left at the most, and wanting to be near him in case he regained his sanity shortly before passing away—as has happened in less outré cases—I had been sitting by Matthew's bed. There I had dropped off to sleep, only to be roused later by the frantic tremblings and quakings from the now totally changed creature before me. By this time my nephew's only resemblance to anything human was his general outline. His eyes burned with a horrific intensity through the thin slits in the green mask which his face had become.

As I came fully awake I saw the…*Thing*—I can barely bring myself to think of it as Matthew—moving. Slowly it bent upward from the waist, trembling and straining in every part, until finally it sat upright. The awful head turned slowly in my direction, and then I heard the last words my nephew was ever to speak:

"W-water… B-bath… Get—me—to—the—b-bath…"

The thing had swung the green web which passed for the lower part of its body over the edge of the bed and somehow had managed to stand. In shuffling steps—still attired in the dressing-gown I had loaned to Matthew in compensation for quartering him in a drafty room—it made for the door. In a moment or two I recovered myself and went quickly to the aid of my…my nephew, only to discover that his mutation, whatever human attributes might have been lost, did not lack strength. Matthew's movements were only obstructed by his covering of rapidly stiffening green growth; I had merely to steady him while he grew accustomed to this new, shuffling locomotive system. Exactly how I managed I do not recall, but eventually I got the shuffler into the bath where he sat, propped up and shuddering, until I could half-fill the tub with warm water.

It was then, after running to and fro half-a-dozen times with my huge iron kettle, that I noticed something happening in the bath—something which so terrified me that I only just managed to stagger away, out of the bathroom, before I fainted dead away on the floor…

Darkness had fallen by the time I regained consciousness. Remembering what had caused me to faint, I started violently; then, feeling the stone of the floor against my cheek, I got to my feet. When I had last seen my nephew— or rather the thing which he had become—he had been *secreting* greenish droplets of some unnameable ichor into the bath. But now, except for that— liquid—the bath was empty.

Galvanized into frantic haste I followed the thing's tracks, green droplets which glistened damply on the floor, until I eventually discovered the note on my writing desk. And its message told me that the Matthew-thing was still crazed, for its contents were undeniably the ramblings of madness. Numb with shock, horror, and disbelief I deciphered the almost illegible writing upon a now odious sheet of damp, green-spattered notepaper, and made it out to read:

"Water not right… Hungry… Must go to pit… Pool… Don't try to find me… I am all right… Not diseased…

'M'"

It was after I followed those evil droplets from my desk to the back door, and found it swinging open—after I realised that the entire house could be contaminated and after I shudderingly, more closely studied the contents of the bath—that I heard the sudden scream from outside. I ran back to the door and threw it open. Staggering towards my house from the moors and moving in the direction of the village, gasping and panting, was the mist-wreathed figure of Ben Carter, the village poacher.

"Lock your doors, doctor!" he hoarsely yelled as he saw me. "There's something horrible loose on the moors—something *horrible!*" Without pausing in his stumbling run he went by my gate and gradually vanished into the mist. To an extent I was relieved; he would not be reporting the nature of what he had seen to the police. Not immediately at any rate—not with that brace of fine hares swinging round his neck. I watched Ben until the mist had completely swallowed him up and then I rapidly donned a raincoat and plunged out into the darkness.

My task was hopeless. With night already settled on the moors and a thickening mist to contend with, I stood no chance of finding him. Indeed I was fortunate in the end, over an hour later, even to find the road back to Eeley. Nonetheless I knew that with the dawn I would have to go out on the moors and try again. I could not leave him out there in that state. What if someone else were to find him?

Obviously Matthew had headed for the pit—his scrawled note had made that much at least clear—but how was I ever to find that terrible place without a clue as to its whereabouts? It was then that I remembered the map upon which Matthew said he had marked his location on the knoll. The map—of course!

I found it in his room…

I hardly slept at all that night—my dreams would not permit sleep—and early morning found me setting out over the moors. I will not describe the route I took for reasons which must be perfectly obvious. Heaven forbid it, but in the event of my final plan not working it is best that no one else knows of that place on the moors.

Eventually, in mid-morning, I found the terrible hole in the ground where all of this evil had begun. Even to my untrained eyes it was all too plain that there was something hideously wrong with the vegetation around the mouth of that pit. The plants, even those which were common and recognisable, were all strangely withered and mutated. *Sehr sonderbare, mysteriöse Unkräuter!*

I knew that if I was ever to be sure of what I had started to suspect, if I was ever to have definite proof, then I would have to climb down into the hole. All along I had foreseen this, but now the very thought of it was more than sufficient to cause me to shudder horribly... And my flesh was still creeping as I hammered my stake into the earth and made fast my rope, for even up there in the misty morning sunlight the air was tainted with an all too familiar smell.

Hurriedly now, for I feared my courage would soon desert me, I lowered myself into the hole. Climbing down into dimness, I was immediately aware of the poisonous quality of the atmosphere; but I was given little chance to dwell on the thought for soon my feet found the platform of stones which Matthew had built.

In the feeble light I could see that part of the platform had tumbled down, and close by there was a monstrously suggestive depression in the sandy shingle of the shelf. As I studied this hollow it suddenly, shockingly dawned on me that in his condition Matthew would never have been able to climb down here, even though his rope was still hanging where he had left it. The difficulties he must have faced even in the climbing of the knoll seemed insurmountable; yet I was certain that he had managed it and was even now somewhere nearby in the dimness. I was certain because of that depression in the shingle...

For while there were other marks in the sand—the signs of my nephew's previous visit—this one was plainly deeper, fresher, and *different*. It was exactly the kind of hollow one would expect a falling body to make in wet sand!... I turned my mind hurriedly away from the thought.

Matthew had described the glowing moss on the walls of the place, and sure enough it was there, but I was unwilling to explore any further in its light alone. I took out my pocket-torch and switched it on. The torch must have received a bang in my climbing for its beam was now weak and intermittent. Nor did the mist, which was thickening up above, help any; it only served to shut out the dim light filtering down from the crack.

First I shone the beam of my torch around the pallid walls and over the surface of the soupy water; then I sought out the natural archway where the pool passed out of sight. Feeling my courage ebbing again I quickly waded into the pool. The way that slime *oozed* around my legs made me tremble violently and I was vastly relieved that the foul muck did not reach the tops of my waders.

I went straight to the archway, lowering my head and bending my back to pass beyond it. There, in the dingy confines of the cave, the first things that showed in the flickering light of my torch were the hanging daggers of stone depending from the vaulted ceiling. Then, as I turned to my left, the beam passed over something else—a shape slumped against the wall.

Not daring to move I stood there, shaking feverishly, a cold sweat upon my brow. The only sound other than my pounding heart was the slow drip, drip, drip of falling droplets of God only knows what evil moisture.

The hair of my neck bristled in a fearful dread but as my fear gradually subsided I began slowly to move again, swinging my torch around to the right. This time when my beam picked out the thing against the wall I gripped my torch firmly and moved closer. It was one of the plants—but not quite as Matthew had described them. This one hung soggily from the wall of the cave and there was no firmness about it. I concluded that it was either dead or dying and saw that I must be correct when I swung my beam down the length of the thing. A great portion of it had been stripped away. I guessed that this had been the specimen from which my nephew had eaten.

Then something else caught my eye, something which very dully reflected the light from my torch. Reaching out with my free hand I touched the hard object which seemed to be imbedded in the plant about halfway up its length. Whatever it was, possibly a metallic crystal of some sort, it came away in my hand and I put it in my pocket for future reference.

More daring now, I moved further into the cave, examining more of the green pods as I came upon them, still finding them frightful in some strange way but unable to account completely for my fear. And then I stopped dead. I had almost forgotten just what I was looking for—but now I remembered…

In a dark corner one of the plant-things stood all alone with its lower roots trailing in the soupy pool. It would have been just like all the other specimens except for one shocking difference… *It was wearing the dressing-gown I had loaned to Matthew!*

And more: as I swung my torch beam in disbelief up and down the length of the thing *it blinked at me!* It blinked—thin slits opened and closed where eyes should be, and in that moment of madness, in that instant of utter insanity, as my very mind buckled—I looked into the agonised eyes of Matthew Worthy!

How to describe the rest.

Oh, I was transformed in one mind-shattering moment. My torch fell from nerveless fingers and I heard myself scream a hoarse, babbling scream of horror. I threw up my hands and staggered back, away from what I had seen, away from the brainblasting abnormality against the wall. Then I turned to flee full tilt—shrieking, splashing through the vileness of the pool— through a maze of dripping stalactites, past a host of green, insinuously oozing *things*—bumping in my haste from wall to wall, sometimes coming into contact with slimy obscenities which had no right to exist. And all the time I screamed and babbled shamelessly, even as I clawed my way up the dangling rope and hauled myself out into the daylight, even as I plummeted headlong down the steep slope heedless of life or limb, until I tripped and flew forward into merciful oblivion...

Merciful oblivion, I say, and it is the truth, for had I not knocked myself unconscious I have no doubt that I would have remained permanently mindless. What I had *seen* had been terrible enough without the other. That other which I had *heard* had been, if anything, worse. For even as the torch fell from my fingers and I screamed, other voices had screamed with me! Voices which could not be "heard" physically—for their owners were incapable of physical speech—voices I heard with my mind alone, which were utterly horrible and alien to me and full of eternal misery...

When I came to my senses I was lying at the foot of the knoll. I refrained from an immediate mental examination of what I knew now to be the horrible truth, for therein lay a return to madness. Instead I brushed myself off and hurried back as quickly as my throbbing head would allow to Eeley. My house and practice lay at the extreme edge of the village, but nonetheless I approached it from the fields and let myself in at the back door. I burnt my waders immediately, noting especially that the slime upon them blazed fiercely with a sulphurous brightness. Later, after I had scrubbed myself from head to toe, examining each limb minutely and finding no trace of the horror, I remembered the rock crystal I had put in my pocket.

In the clear daylight it was obviously not a crystal; it appeared to be more like a bracelet of some sort, and yet this fact did not properly surprise me. The soft metal links must have long since oxidized, for as I examined the rotted thing, all of it—with the exception of a small flat circle or disc—crumbled away in my hands. Even this solid, circular portion, about an inch and one half across, was mostly slimy and green. I placed it in a flask of dilute acid to clean it; by which time, of course, I knew what it was.

As I watched the acid doing its work I began, involuntarily, to tremble. My mind was a turmoil of terrible thoughts. I knew what my nephew had become, and presumably the partly eaten thing which had provided this metal clue had also once been human. Certainly it had been some sort of being from any one of many periods of time. I could not help but ask myself: in the latter stages of change or after the change was complete, *could the pit-creatures feel anything?*

Watching the seething mass in the flask I suddenly began to babble idiotically and had to battle consciously with myself to stop it. No wonder Matthew had been baffled with regard to the reproductory system of these pitiful horrors. How does a magnet cause a pin to become magnetic? Why will one rotten apple in a barrel ruin all the other fruit? Oh, yes—eating from one of the things had helped Matthew contract the change, but that was not what had started the thing. *Proximity* was sufficient! Nor was the horror truly a disease, as Matthew had tried to tell me in his awful note, but a *devolution*—a gestalt of human being and thing—both living, if such could be called life, and dependent one upon the other.

This was the sort of thing I was babbling to myself as the acid completed its work, and I shook so that I had to steady myself before I was able to draw out from the acid the flat, now shiny disc.

What was it Matthew had dreamed? "They had walked this holy ground unbidden…" Had that been sufficient in the old days—in prehistory, when the area about the pit must have been far more poisonous than it was now—to bring about the change? I think that even at the beginning Matthew must have partly guessed the truth, for had he himself not told me that he found the cell structure to be "almost human"?

Poor Matthew—that name he screamed before going mad. At last I understood it all. There it all was before me: the final, leaping horror. My own nephew, an unwilling, though perhaps not completely *unknowing* anthropophagite. A cannibal!

For the shiny thing I held in my shuddering hand was a German watch of fairly modern appearance, and on the back was an inscription in German. An inscription so simple that even I, unversed in that language, could translate it to read:

"WITH LOVE, FROM GERDA TO HORST"…

Since then it has taken long hours to pull myself together sufficiently to formulate my plan, that plan I have already mentioned and yet which even now I hardly dare think about. I had fervently hoped that I would never have to use it but now, with the spread of the poison through my body, it appears that I must…

When the ashes of my house have cooled the police will find this manuscript locked in a safe in the deep, damp cellar, but long before the flames have died down I shall have returned to the pit. I will take with me as much petrol as I can carry. My plan is simple really, and I shall know no pain. Nor will the *inhabitants* of that place know pain, not if a powerful drug may yet affect them. As the anaesthetic takes hold and while I am still able, I shall pour the petrol on the surface of that evil pool.

My statement is at an end—

—Perhaps tonight puzzled observers will wonder at the pillar of sulphurous fire rising over the moors…

DAGON'S BELL

One of Steve Jones' first choices when he was gathering tales for his 1994 Fedogan & Bremer collection, Shadows over Innsmouth—*after HPL's ill-fated seaport and its batrachian inhabitants—"Dagon's Bell" had been written all of eleven years earlier and had seen its initial printing in Paul Ganley's* Weirdbook *in 1988. Written five years before that, in those somewhat bleak years after I had done my 22-year stint and left the financial security of my job in the British Army, this story is most definitely set against HPL's Mythos backdrop. The location is my own, however (and nowhere near Innsmouth!), and so is the style of writing. I honestly believe that Lovecraft himself would have enjoyed this one.*

I: Deep Kelp

It strikes me as funny sometimes how scraps of information—fragments of seemingly dissociated fact and half-seen or -felt fancies and intuitions, bits of local legend and immemorial myth—can suddenly connect and expand until the total is far greater than the sum of the parts, like a jigsaw puzzle. Or perhaps not necessarily *funny…odd.*

Flotsam left high and dry by the tide, scurf of the rolling sea; a half-obliterated figure glimpsed on an ancient, well-rubbed coin through the glass of a museum's showcase; old-wives' tales of hauntings and hoary nights, and the ringing of some sepulchral, sunken bell at the rising of the tide; the strange speculations of sea-coal gatherers supping their ale in old North-East pubs, where the sound of the ocean's wash is never far distant beyond smoke-yellowed bull's-eye windowpanes. Items like that, apparently unconnected.

But in the end there was really much more to it than that. For these things were only the *pieces* of the puzzle; the picture, complete, was vaster far than its component parts. Indeed cosmic...

I long ago promised myself that I would never again speak or even think of David Parker and the occurrences of that night at Kettlethorpe Farm (which formed, in any case, a tale almost too grotesque for belief); but now, these years later...well, my promise seems rather redundant. On the other hand it is possible that a valuable warning lies inherent in what I have to say, for which reason, despite the unlikely circumstance that I shall be taken at all seriously, I now put pen to paper.

My name is William Trafford, which hardly matters, but I had known David Parker at school—a Secondary Modern in a colliery village by the sea—before he passed his college examinations, and I was the one who would later share with him Kettlethorpe's terrible secret.

In fact I had known David well: the son of a miner, he was never typical of his colliery contemporaries but gentle in his ways and lacking the coarseness of the locality and its guttural accents. That is not to belittle the North-Easterner in general (after all, I became one myself!) for in all truth they are the salt of the earth; but the nature of their work, and what that work has gradually made of their environment, has moulded them into a hard and clannish lot. David Parker, by his nature, was not of that clan, that is all; and neither was I at that time.

My parents were Yorkshire born and bred, only moving to Harden in County Durham when my father bought a newsagent's shop there. Hence the friendship that sprang up between us, born not so much out of straight-forward compatibility as of the fact that we both felt outsiders. A friendship which lasted for five years from a time when we were both eight years of age, and which was only renewed upon David's release from his studies in London twelve years later. That was in 1951.

Meanwhile, in the years flown between...

My father was now dead and my mother more or less confined, and I had expanded the business to two more shops in Hartlepool, both of them under steady and industrious managers, and several smaller but growing concerns much removed from the sale of magazines and newspapers in the local colliery villages. Thus my time was mainly taken up with business matters, but in the highest capacity, which hardly consisted of back-breaking work. What time remained I was pleased to spend, on those occasions when he was available, in the company of my old school friend.

And he too had done well, and would do even better. His studies had been in architecture and design, but within two short years of his return he expanded these spheres to include interior decoration and landscape gardening, setting up a profitable business of his own and building himself an enviable reputation in his fields.

And so it can be seen that the war had been kind to both of us. Too young to have been involved, we had made capital while the world was fighting; now while the world licked its wounds and rediscovered its directions, we were already on course and beginning to ride the crest. Mercenary? No, for we had been mere boys when the war started and were little more than boys when it ended.

But now, eight years later...

We were, or saw ourselves as being, very nearly sophisticates in a mainly unsophisticated society—that is to say part of a very narrow spectrum—and so once more felt drawn together. Even so, we made odd companions. At least externally, superficially. Oh, I suppose our characters, drives and ambitions were similar, but physically we were poles apart. David was dark, handsome and well-proportioned; I was sort of dumpy, sandy, pale to the point of being pallid. I was not unhealthy, but set beside David Parker I certainly looked it!

On the day in question, that is to say the day when the first unconnected fragment presented itself—a Friday in September '53, it was, just a few days before the Feast of the Exaltation, sometimes called Roodmas in those parts, and occasionally by a far older name—we met in a bar overlooking the sea on old Hartlepool's headland. On those occasions when we got together like this we would normally try to keep business out of the conversation, but there were times when it seemed to intrude almost of necessity. This was one such.

I had not noticed Jackie Foster standing at the bar upon entering, but certainly he had seen me. Foster was a foreman with a small fleet of sea-coal gathering trucks of which I was co-owner, and he should not have been there in the pub at that time but out and about his work. Possibly he considered it prudent to come over and explain his presence, just in case I *had* seen him, and he did so in a single word.

"Kelp?" David repeated, looking puzzled; so that I felt compelled to explain.

"Seaweed," I said. "Following a bad blow, it comes up on the beach in thick drifts. But—" and I looked at Foster pointedly "—I've never before known it to stop the sea-coalers."

The man shuffled uncomfortably for a moment, took off his cap and scratched his head. "Oh, once or twice ah've known it almost this bad, but before your time in the game. It slimes up the rocks an' the wheels of the lorries slip in the stuff. Bloody arful! An' stinks like death. It's lyin' feet thick on arl the beaches from here ta Sunderland!"

"Kelp," David said again, thoughtfully. "Isn't that the weed people used to gather up and cook into a soup?"

Foster wrinkled his nose. "Hungry folks'll eat just about owt, ah suppose, Mr. Parker—but they'd not eat this muck. We carl it 'deep kelp'. It's not unusual this time of year—Roodmas time or thereabouts—and generally hangs about for a week or so until the tides clear it or it rots away."

David continued to look interested and Foster continued:

"Funny stuff. Ah mean, you'll not find it in any book of seaweeds—not that ah've ever seen. As a lad ah was daft on nature an' arl. Collected birds' eggs, took spore prints of mushrooms an' toadstools, pressed leaves an' flowers in books—arl that daft stuff—but in arl the books ah read ah never did find a mention of deep kelp." He turned back to me. "Anyway, boss, there's enough of the stuff on the beach to keep the lorries off. It's not that they canna get onto the sands, but when they do they canna see the coal for weed. So ah've sent the lorries south to Seaton Carew. The beach is pretty clear down there, ah'm told. Not much coal, but better than nowt."

My friend and I had almost finished eating by then. As Foster made to leave, I suggested to David: "Let's finish our drinks, climb down the old sea wall and have a look."

"Right!" David agreed at once. "I'm curious about this stuff." Foster had heard and he turned back to us, shaking his head concernedly. "It's up to you, gents," he said, "but you won't like it. Stinks, man! *Arful!* There's kids who play on the beach arl the live-long day, but you'll not find them there now. Just the bloody weed, lyin' there an' turnin' to rot!"

II: A Wedding and a Warning

In any event, we went to see for ourselves, and if I had doubted Foster then I had wronged him. The stuff *was* awful, and it *did* stink. I had seen it before, always at this time of year, but never in such quantities. There had been a bit of a blow the night before, however, and that probably explained it. To my mind, anyway. David's mind was a fraction more inquiring.

"Deep kelp," he murmured, standing on the weed-strewn rocks, his hair blowing in a salty, stenchy breeze off the sea. "I don't see it at all."

"What don't you see?"

"Well, if this stuff comes from the deeps—I mean from really deep down—surely it would take a real upheaval to drive it onto the beaches like this. Why, there must be thousands and thousands of tons of the stuff! All the way from here to Sunderland? Twenty miles of it?"

I shrugged. "It'll clear, just like Foster said. A day or two, that's all. And he's right: with this stuff lying so thick, you can't see the streaks of coal."

"How about the coal?" he said, his mind again grasping after knowledge. "I mean, where does it come from?"

"Same place as the weed," I answered, "most of it. Come and see." I crossed to a narrow strip of sand between waves of deep kelp. There I found and picked up a pair of blocky, fist-sized lumps of ocean-rounded rock. Knocking them together, I broke off fragments. Inside, one rock showed a greyish-brown uniformity; the other was black and shiny, finely layered, pure coal.

"I wouldn't have known the difference," David admitted.

"Neither would I!" I grinned. "But the sea-coalers rarely err. They say there's an open seam way out there," I nodded toward the open sea. "Not unlikely, seeing as how this entire county is riddled with rich mines. Myself, I believe a lot of the coal simply gets washed out of the tippings, the stony debris rejected at the screens. Coal is light and easily washed ashore. The stones are heavy and roll out—downhill, as it were—into deeper water."

"In that case it seems a pity," said David. "—That the coal can't be gathered, I mean."

"Oh?"

"Why, yes. Surely, if there is an open seam in the sea, the coal would get washed ashore with the kelp. Underneath this stuff, there's probably tons of it just waiting to be shovelled up!"

I frowned and answered: "You could well be right..." But then I shrugged. "Ah, well, not to worry. It'll still be there after the weed has gone." And I winked at him. "Coal doesn't rot, you see?"

He wasn't listening but kneeling, lifting a rope of the offensive stuff in his hands. It was heavy, leprous white in the stem or body, deep dark green in the leaf. Hybrid, the flesh of the stuff was—well, fleshy—more animal than vegetable. Bladders were present everywhere, large as a man's thumbs. David popped one and gave a disgusted grunt, then came to his feet.

"God!" he exclaimed, holding his nose. And again: *"God!"*

I laughed and we picked our way back to the steps in the old sea wall.

And that was that: a fragment, an incident unconnected with anything much. An item of little real interest. One of Nature's periodic quirks, affecting nothing a great deal. Apparently…

It seemed not long after the time of the deep kelp that David got tied up with his wedding plans. I had known, of course, that he had a girl—June Anderson, a solicitor's daughter from Sunderland, which boasts the prettiest girls in all the land—for I had met her and found her utterly charming; but I had not realised that things were so advanced.

I say it did not seem a long time, and now looking back I see that the period was indeed quite short—the very next summer. Perhaps the span of time was foreshortened even more for me by the suddenness with which their plans culminated. For all was brought dramatically forward by the curious and unexpected vacancy of Kettlethorpe Farm, an extensive property on the edge of Kettlethorpe Dene.

No longer a farm proper but a forlorn relic of another age, the great stone house and its out-buildings were badly in need of repair; but in David's eyes the place had an Olde Worlde magic all its own, and with his expertise he knew that he could soon convert it into a modern home of great beauty and value. And the place was going remarkably cheap.

As to the farm's previous tenant: here something peculiar. And here too the second link in my seemingly unconnected chain of occurrences and circumstances.

Old Jason Carpenter had not been well liked in the locality, in fact not at all. Grey-bearded, taciturn, cold and reclusive—with eyes grey as the rolling North Sea and never a smile for man or beast—he had occupied Kettlethorpe Farm for close on thirty years. Never a wife, a manservant or maid, not even a neighbour had entered the place on old Jason's invitation. No one strayed onto the grounds for fear of Jason's dog and shotgun; even tradesmen were wary on those rare occasions when they must make deliveries.

But Carpenter had liked his beer and rum chaser, and twice a week would visit The Trust Hotel in Harden. There he had used to sit in the smokeroom and linger over his tipple, his dog Bones alert under the table and between his master's feet. And customers had used to fear Bones a little, but not as much as the dog feared his master.

And now Jason Carpenter was gone. Note that I do not say dead, simply gone, disappeared. There was no evidence to support any other conclusion—not at that time. it had happened like this:

Over a period of several months various tradesmen had reported Jason's absence from Kettlethorpe, and eventually, because his customary seat at The Trust had been vacant over that same period, members of the local police went to the farm and forced entry into the main building. No trace had been found of the old hermit, but the police had come away instead with certain documents—chiefly a will, of sorts—which had evidently been left pending just such a search or investigation.

In the documents the recluse had directed that in the event of his "termination of occupancy", the house, attendant buildings and grounds "be allowed to relapse into the dirt and decay from which they sprang"; but since it was later shown that he was in considerable debt, the property had been put up for sale to settle his various accounts. The house had in fact been under threat of the bailiffs.

All of this, of course, had taken some considerable time, during which a thorough search of the rambling house, its outbuildings and grounds had been made for obvious reasons. But to no avail.

Jason Carpenter was gone. He had not been known to have relatives; indeed, very little had been known of him at all; it was almost as if he had never been. And to many of the people of Harden, that made for a most satisfactory epitaph.

One other note: it would seem that his "termination of occupancy" had come about during the Roodmas time of the deep kelp…

And so to the wedding of David Parker and June Anderson, a sparkling affair held at the Catholic Church in Harden, where not even the drab, near-distant background of the colliery's chimneys and cooling towers should have been able to dampen the gaiety and excitement of the moment. And yet even here, in the steep, crowd-packed streets outside the church, a note of discord. Just one, but one too many.

For as the cheering commenced and the couple left the church to be showered with confetti and jostled to their car, I overheard as if they were spoken directly into my ear—or uttered especially for my notice—the words of a crone in shawl and pinafore, come out of her smoke-grimed miner's terraced house to shake her head and mutter:

"Aye, an' he'll take that bonnie lass to Kettlethorpe, will he? Arl the bells are ringin' now, it's true, but what about the *other* bell, eh? It's only rung once or twice arl these lang years—since old Jason had the house—but now there's word it's ringin' again, when nights are dark an' the sea has a swell to it."

I heard it as clearly as that, for I was one of the spectators. I would have been more closely linked with the celebrations but had expected to be busy, and only by the skin of my teeth managed to be there at all. But when I heard the guttural imprecation of the old lady I turned to seek her out, even caught a glimpse of her, before being engulfed by a horde of Harden urchins leaping for a handful of hurled pennies, threepenny bits and sixpences as the newlyweds' car drove off.

By which time summer thunderclouds had gathered, breaking at the command of a distant flash of lightning, and rain had begun to pelt down. Which served to put an end to the matter. The crowd rapidly dispersed and I headed for shelter.

But…I would have liked to know what the old woman had meant…

III: Ghost Story

"Haunted?" I echoed David's words.

I had bumped into him at the library in Hartlepool some three weeks after his wedding. A voracious reader, an "addict" for hard-boiled detective novels, I had been on my way in as he was coming out.

"Haunted, yes!" he repeated, his voice half-amused, half-excited. "The old farm—haunted!"

The alarm his words conjured in me was almost immediately relieved by his grin and wide-awake expression. Whatever ghosts they were at the farm, he obviously didn't fear them. Was he having a little joke at my expense? I grinned with him, saying: "Well, I shouldn't care to have been your ghosts. Not for the last thirty years, at any rate. Not with old man Carpenter about the place. That would be a classic case of the biter bit!"

"Old Jason Carpenter," he reminded me, smiling still but less brilliantly, "has disappeared, remember?"

"Oh!" I said, feeling a little foolish. "Of course he has." And I followed up quickly with: "But what do you mean, haunted?"

"Local village legend," he shrugged. "I heard it from Father Nicholls, who married us. He had it from the priest before him, and so on. Handed down for centuries, so to speak. I wouldn't have known if he hadn't stopped me and asked how we were getting on up at the farm. If we'd seen anything— you know—odd? He wouldn't have said anything more but I pressed him."

"And?"

"Well, it seems the original owners were something of a fishy bunch."

"Fishy?"

"Quite literally! I mean, they *looked* fishy. Or maybe froggy? Protuberant lips, wide-mouthed, scaly-skinned, pop-eyed—you name it. To use Father Nicholls' own expression, 'ichthyic'."

"Slow down," I told him, seeing his excitement rising up again. "First of all, what do you mean by the 'original' owners? The people who built the place?"

"Good heavens, no!" he chuckled; and then he took me by the elbow and guided me into the library and to a table. We sat. "No one knows—no one can remember—who actually built the place. If ever there were records, well, they're long lost. God, it probably dates back to Roman times! It's likely as old as the Wall itself—even older. Certainly it has been a landmark on maps for the last four hundred and fifty years. No, I mean the first *recorded* family to live there. Which was something like two and a half centuries ago."

"And they were—" I couldn't help frowning "—odd-looking, these people?"

"Right! And odd not only in their looks. That was probably just a case of regressive genes, the result of indiscriminate inbreeding. Anyway, the locals shunned them—not that there were any real 'locals' in those days, you understand. I mean, the closest villages or towns then were Hartlepool, Sunderland, Durham and Seaham Harbour. Maybe a handful of other, smaller places—I haven't checked. But this country was wild! And it stayed that way, more or less, until the modern roads were built. Then came the railways, to service the pits, and so on."

I nodded, becoming involved with David's enthusiasm, finding myself carried along by it. "And the people at the farm stayed there down the generations?"

"Not quite," he answered. "Apparently there was something of a hiatus in their tenancy around a hundred and fifty years ago; but later, about the time of the American Civil War, a family came over from Innsmouth in New England and bought the place up. They, too, had the degenerate looks of earlier tenants; might even have been an offshoot of the same family, returning to their ancestral home, as it were. They made a living farming and fishing. Fairly industrious, it would seem, but surly and clannish. Name of Waite. By then, though, the 'ghosts' were well established in local folklore. *They* came in two manifestations, apparently."

"Oh?"

He nodded. "One of them was a gigantic, wraithlike, nebulous figure rising from the mists over Kettlethorpe Dene, seen by travellers on the old coach road or by fishermen returning to Harden along the cliff-top paths. But the interesting thing is this: if you look at a map of the district, as I've done, you'll see that the farm lies in something of a depression directly between the coach road and the cliffs. Anything seen from those vantage points could conceivably be emanating from the farm itself!"

I was again beginning to find the nature of David's discourse disturbing. Or if not what he was saying, his obvious *involvement* with the concept. "You seem to have gone over all of this rather thoroughly," I remarked. "Any special reason?"

"Just my old thirst for knowledge," he grinned. "You know I'm never happy unless I'm tracking something down—and never happier than when I've finally got it cornered. And after all, I do live at the place! Anyway, about the giant mist-figure: according to the legends, it was half-fish, half-man!"

"A merman?"

"Yes. And now—" he triumphantly took out a folded sheet of rubbing parchment and opened it out onto the table—"*Ta-rah!* And what do you make of that?"

The impression on the paper was perhaps nine inches square; a charcoal rubbing taken from a brass of some sort, I correctly imagined. It showed a mainly anthropomorphic male figure seated upon a rock-carved chair or throne, his lower half obscured by draperies of weed bearing striking resemblance to the deep kelp. The eyes of the figure were large and somewhat protuberant; his forehead sloped; his skin had the overlapping scales of a fish, and the fingers of his one visible hand where it grasped a short trident were webbed: The background was vague, reminding me of nothing so much as cyclopean submarine ruins.

"Neptune," I said. "Or at any rate, a merman. Where did you get it?"

"I rubbed it up myself," he said, carefully folding the sheet and replacing it in his pocket. "It's from a plate on a lintel over a door in one of the outbuildings at Kettlethorpe." And then for the first time he frowned. "Fishy people and a fishy symbol…"

He stared at me strangely for a moment and I felt a sudden chill in my bones—until his grin came back and he added: "And an entirely fishy story, eh?"

We left the library and I walked with him to his car. "And what's your real interest in all of this?" I asked. "I mean, I don't remember you as much of a folklorist?"

His look this time was curious, almost evasive. "You just won't believe that it's only this old inquiring mind of mine, will you?" But then his grin came back, bright and infectious as ever.

He got into his car, wound down the window and poked his head out. "Will we be seeing you soon? Isn't it time you paid us a visit?"

"Is that an invitation?"

He started up the car. "Of course—any time."

"Then I'll make it soon," I promised.

"Sooner!" he said.

Then I remembered something he had said. "David, you mentioned two manifestations of this—this ghostliness. What was the other one?"

"Eh?" He frowned at me, winding up his window. Then he stopped winding. "Oh, that. The bell, you mean…"

"Bell?" I echoed him, the skin of my neck suddenly tingling. "What bell?"

"A ghost bell!" he yelled as he pulled away from the kerb. "What else? It tolls underground or under the sea, usually when there's a mist or a swell on the ocean. I keep listening for it, but—"

"No luck?" I asked automatically, hearing my own voice almost as that of a stranger.

"Not yet."

And as he grinned one last time and waved a farewell, pulling away down the street, against all commonsense and logic I found myself remembering the old woman's words outside the church: "What about the *other* bell, eh?"

What about the other bell, indeed…

IV: "Miasma"

Half-way back to Harden it dawned on me that I had not chosen a book for myself. My mind was still full of David Parker's discoveries; about which, where he had displayed that curious excitement, I still experienced only a niggling disquiet.

But back at Harden, where my home stands on a hill at the southern extreme of the village, I remembered where once before I had seen something like the figure on David's rubbing. And sure enough it was there in my antique, illustrated two-volume Family Bible; pages I had not looked into for many a year, which had become merely ornamental on my bookshelves.

The item I refer to was simply one of the many small illustrations in Judges XIII: a drawing of a piscine deity on a Philistine coin or medallion. Dagon, whose temple Samson toppled at Gaza.

Dagon…

With my memory awakened, it suddenly came to me where I had seen one other representation of this same god. Sunderland has a fine museum and my father had often taken me there when I was small. Amongst the museum's collection of coins and medals I had seen...

"Dagon?" The curator answered my telephone inquiry with interest. "No, I'm afraid we have very little of the Philistines; no coins that I know of. Possibly it was a little later than that. Can I call you back?"

"Please do, and I'm sorry to be taking up your time like this."

"Not at all, a pleasure. That's what we're here for."

And ten minutes later he was back. "As I suspected, Mr. Trafford. We do have that coin you remembered, but it's Phoenician, not Philistine. The Phoenicians adopted Dagon from the Philistines and called him Oannes. That's a pattern that repeats all through history. The Romans in particular were great thieves of other people's gods. Sometimes they adopted them openly, as with Zeus becoming Jupiter, but at other times—where the deity was especially dark or ominous, as in Summanus—they were rather more covert in their worship. Great cultists, the Romans. You'd be surprised at how many secret societies and cults came down the ages from sources such as these. But...there I go again...lecturing!"

"Not at all," I assured him, "that's all very interesting. And thank you very much for your time."

"And is that it? There's no other way in which I can assist?"

"No, that's it. Thank you again."

And indeed that seemed to be that...

I went to see them a fortnight later. Old Jason Carpenter had not had a telephone, and David was still in the process of having one installed, which meant that I must literally drop in on them.

Kettlethorpe lies to the north of Harden, between the modern coast road and the sea, and the view of the dene as the track dipped down from the road and wound toward the old farm was breathtaking. Under a blue sky, with seagulls wheeling and crying over a distant, fresh-ploughed field, and the hedgerows thick with honeysuckle and the droning of bees, and sweet smells of decay from the streams and hazelnut-shaded pools, the scene was very nearly idyllic. A far cry from midnight tales of ghouls and ghosties!

Then to the farm's stone outer wall—almost a fortification, reminiscent of some forbidding feudal structure—which encompassed all of the buildings including the main house. Iron gates were open, bearing the legend "Kettlethorpe" in stark letters of iron. Inside...things already were changing.

The wall surrounded something like three and a half to four acres of ground, being the actual core of the property. I had seen several rotting "Private Property" and "Trespassers Will be Prosecuted" notices along the road, defining Kettlethorpe's exterior boundaries, but the area bordered by the wall was the very heart of the place.

In layout: there was a sort of geometrical regularity to the spacing and positioning of the buildings. They formed a horseshoe, with the main house at its apex; the open mouth of the horseshoe faced the sea, unseen, something like a mile away beyond a rise which boasted a dense-grown stand of oaks. All of the buildings were of local stone, easily recognisable through its tough, flinty-grey texture. I am no geologist and so could not give that stone a name, but I knew that in years past it had been blasted from local quarries or cut from outcrops. To my knowledge, however, the closest of these sources was a good many miles away; the actual building of Kettlethorpe must therefore have been a Herculean task.

As this thought crossed my mind, and remembering the words of the curator of Sunderland's museum, I had to smile. Perhaps not Herculean but something later than the Greeks. Except that I couldn't recall a specific Roman strong-man!

And approaching the house, where I pulled up before the stone columns of its portico, I believed I could see where David had got his idea of the age of the place. Under the heat of the sun the house was redolent of the centuries; its walls massive, structurally Romanesque. The roof especially, low-peaked and broad, giving an impression of strength and endurance.

What with its outer wall and horseshoe design, the place might well be some strange old Roman temple. A temple, yes, but wavery for all its massiveness, shimmering as smoke and heat from a small bonfire in what had been a garden drifted lazily across my field of vision. A temple—ah!—but to what strange old god?

And no need to ponder the source of *that* thought, for certainly the business of David's antiquarian research was still in my head; and while I had no intention of bringing that subject up, still I wondered how far he had progressed. Or perhaps by now he had discovered sufficient of Kettlethorpe to satisfy his curiosity. Perhaps, but I doubted it. No, he would follow the very devil to hell, that one, in pursuit of knowledge.

"Hello, there!" He slapped me on the back, causing me to start as I got out of my old Morris and closed its door. I started...reeled...

...He had come out of the shadows of the porch so quickly... I had not seen him... My eyes...the heat and the glaring sun and the drone of bees...

"Bill!" David's voice came to me from a million miles away, full of concern. "What on earth…?"

"I've come over queer," I heard myself say, leaning on my car as the world rocked about me.

"Queer? Man, you're pale as death! It's the bloody sun! Too hot by far. And the smoke from the fire. And I'll bet you've been driving with your windows up. Here, let's get you into the house."

Hanging on to his broad shoulder, I was happy to let him lead me staggering indoors. "The hot sun," he mumbled again, half to me, half to himself. "And the honeysuckle. Almost a miasma. Nauseating, until you get used to it. June has suffered in exactly the same way."

V: The Enclosure

"Miasma?" I let myself fall into a cool, shady window seat.

He nodded, swimming into focus as I quickly recovered from my attack of—of whatever it had been. "Yes, a mist of pollen, invisible, borne on thermals in the air, sweet and cloying. Enough to choke a horse!"

"Is that what it was? God!—I thought I was going to faint."

"I know what you mean. June has been like it for a week. Conks out completely at high noon. Even inside it's too close for her liking. She gets listless. She's upstairs now, stretched out flat!"

As if the very mention of her name were a summons, June's voice came down to us: "David, is that Bill? I'll be down at once."

"Don't trouble yourself on my account," I called out, my voice still a little shaky. "And certainly not if you don't feel too well."

"I'm fine!" her voice insisted. "I was just a little tired, that's all."

I was myself again, gratefully accepting a scotch and soda, swilling a parched dryness from my mouth and throat.

"There," said David, seeming to read my thoughts. "You look more your old self now."

"First time that ever happened to me," I told him. "I suppose your 'miasma' theory must be correct. Anyway, I'll be up on my feet again in a minute." As I spoke I let my eyes wander about the interior of what would be the house's main living-room.

The room was large, for the main part oak-panelled, almost stripped of its old furniture and looking extremely austere. I recalled the bonfire, its pale flames licking at the upthrusting, worm-eaten leg of a chair…

One wall was of the original hard stone, polished by the years, creating an effect normally thought desirable in modern homes but perfectly natural here and in no way contrived. All in all a charming room. Ages-blackened beams bowed almost imperceptibly toward the centre where they crossed the low ceiling wall to wall.

"Built to last," said David. "Three hundred years old at least, those beams, but the basic structure is—" he shrugged "—I'm not sure, not yet. This is one of five lower rooms, all about the same size. I've cleared most of them out now, burnt up most of the old furniture; but there were one or two pieces worth renovation. Most of the stuff I've saved is in what used to be old man Carpenter's study. And the place is—will be—beautiful. When I'm through with it. Gloomy at the moment, yes, but that's because of the windows. I'm afraid most of these old small-panes will have to go. The place needs opening up."

"Opening up, yes," I repeated him, sensing a vague irritation or tension in him, a sort of urgency.

"Here," he said, "are you feeling all right now? I'd like you to see the plate I took that rubbing from."

"The Dagon plate," I said at once, biting my tongue a moment too late.

He looked at me, stared at me, and slowly smiled. "So you looked it up, did you? Dagon, yes—or Neptune, as the Romans called him. Come on, I'll show you." And as we left the house he yelled back over his shoulder: "June—we're just going over to the enclosure. Back soon."

"Enclosure?" I followed him toward the mouth of the horseshoe of buildings. "I thought you said the brass was on a lintel?"

"So it is, over a doorway—but the building has no roof and so I call it an enclosure. See?" and he pointed. The mouth of the horseshoe was formed of a pair of small, rough stone buildings set perhaps twenty-five yards apart, which were identical in design but for the one main discrepancy David had mentioned—namely that the one on the left had no roof.

"Perhaps it fell in?" I suggested as we approached the structure.

David shook his head. "No," he said, "there never was a roof. Look at the tops of the walls. They're flush. No gaps to show where roof support beams might have been positioned. If you make a comparison with the other building you'll see what I mean. Anyway, whatever its original purpose, old man Carpenter filled it with junk: bags of rusty old nails, worn-out tools, that sort of thing. Oh, yes and he kept his firewood here, under a tarpaulin."

I glanced inside the place, leaning against the wall and poking my head in through the vacant doorway. The wall stood in its own shadow and was cold to my touch. Beams of sunlight, glancing in over the top of the west wall, filled the place with dust motes that drifted like swarms of aimless microbes in the strangely musty air. There was a mixed smell of rust and rot, of some small dead thing, and of...the sea? The last could only be a passing fancy, no sooner imagined than forgotten.

I shaded my eyes against the dusty sunbeams. Rotted sacks spilled nails and bolts upon a stone-flagged floor; farming implements red with rust were heaped like metal skeletons against one wall; at the back, heavy blocks of wood stuck out from beneath a mould-spotted tarpaulin. A dead rat or squirrel close to my feet seethed with maggots.

I blinked in the hazy light, shuddered—not so much at the sight of the small corpse as at a sudden chill of the psyche—and hastily withdrew my head.

"There you are," said David, his matter-of-fact tone bringing me back down to earth. "The brass."

Above our heads, central in the stone lintel, a square plate bore the original of David's rubbing. I gave it a glance; an almost involuntary reaction to David's invitation that I look, and at once looked away. He frowned, seemed disappointed. "You don't find it interesting?"

"I find it...disturbing," I answered at length. "Can we go back to the house? I'm sure June will be up and about by now."

He shrugged, leading the way as we retraced our steps along sun-splashed, weed-grown paths between scrubby fruit trees and dusty, cobwebbed shrubbery. "I thought you'd be taken by it," he said. And, "How do you mean, 'disturbing'?"

I shook my head, had no answer for him. "Maybe it's just me," I finally said. "I don't feel at my best today. I'm not up to it, that's all."

"Not up to what?" he asked sharply, then shrugged again before I could answer. "Suit yourself." But after that he quickly became distant and a little surly. He wasn't normally a moody man, but I knew him well enough to realise that I had touched upon some previously unsuspected, exposed nerve; and so I determined not to prolong my visit.

I did stay long enough to talk to June, however, though what I saw of her was hardly reassuring. She looked pinched, her face lined and pale, showing none of the rosiness one might expect in a newlywed, or in any healthy young woman in summertime. Her eyes were red-rimmed; their natural blue seeming very much watered-down; her skin looked dry, deprived of moisture; even her hair, glossy-black and bouncy on those previous occasions when we had met, seemed lacklustre now and disinterested.

It could be, of course, simply the fact that I had caught her at a bad time. Her father had died recently, as I later discovered, and of course that must still be affecting her. Also, she must have been working very hard, alongside David, trying to get the old place put to rights. Or again it could be David's summer "miasma"—an allergy, perhaps.

Perhaps...

But why any of these things—David's preoccupation, his near-obsession (or mine?) with occurrences and relics of the distant past; the old myths and legends of the region, of hauntings and misty phantoms and such; and June's queer malaise—why any of these things should concern me beyond the bounds of common friendship I did not know, could not say. I only knew that I felt as if somewhere a great wheel had started to roll, and that my friend and his wife lay directly in its path, not even knowing that it bore down upon them...

VI: Dagon's Bell

Summer rolled by in warm lazy waves; autumn saw the trees shamelessly, mindlessly stripping themselves naked (one would think they'd keep their leaves to warm them through the winter); my businesses presented periodic problems enough to keep my nose to the grindstone, and so there was little spare time in which to ponder the strangeness of the last twelve months. I saw David in the village now and then, usually at a distance; saw June, too, but much less frequently. More often than not he seemed haggard—or if not haggard, hagridden, nervous, agitated, *hurried*—and she was...well, spectral. Pale and willow-slim, and red-eyed (I suspected) behind dark spectacles. Married life? Or perhaps some other problem? None of my business.

Then came the time of the deep kelp once more, which was when David made it my business.

And here I must ask the reader to bear with me. The following part of the story will seem hastily written, too thoughtlessly prepared and put together. But this is how I remember it: blurred and unreal, and patterned with mismatched dialogue. It *happened* quickly; I see no reason to spin it out...

David's knock was urgent on a night when the sky was black with falling rain and the wind whipped the trees to a frenzy; and yet he stood there in shirt-sleeves, shivering, gaunt in aspect and almost vacant in expression. It took several brandies and a thorough rub-down with a warm towel to bring him to a semblance of his old self, by which time he seemed more ashamed of his behaviour than eager to explain it. But I was not letting him off that lightly. The time had come, I decided, to have the thing out with him; get it out in the open, whatever it was, and see what could be done about it while there was yet time.

"Time?" He finally turned his gaze upon me from beneath his mop of tousled hair, a towel over his shoulders while his shirt steamed before my open fire. "*Is* there yet time? Damned if I know…" He shook his head.

"Well then, *tell* me," I said, exasperated. "Or at least try. Start somewhere. You must have come to me for something. Is it you and June? Was your getting married a mistake? Or is it just the place, the old farm?"

"Oh, come on, Bill!" he snorted. "You know well enough what it is. Something of it, anyway. You experienced it yourself. Just the place?" The corners of his mouth turned down, his expression souring. "Oh, yes, it's the place, all right. What the place was, what it might be even now…"

"Go on," I prompted him; and he launched into the following:

"I came to ask you to come back with me. I don't want to spend another night alone there."

"Alone? But isn't June there?"

He looked at me for a moment and finally managed a ghastly grin. "She is and she isn't," he said. "Oh, yes, yes, she's there—but still I'm alone. Not her fault, poor love. It's that bloody awful place!"

"Tell me about it," I urged.

He sighed, bit his lip. And after a moment: "I think," he began, "—I think it was a temple. And I don't think the Romans had it first. You know, of course, that they've found Phoenician symbols on some of the stones at Stonehenge? Well, and what else did the ancients bring with them to old England, eh? What did we worship in those prehistoric times? The earth-mother, the sun, the rain—the sea? We're an island, Bill. The sea was everywhere around us! And it was bountiful. It still is, but not like it was in those days. What more natural than to worship the sea—and what the sea brought?"

"Its bounty?" I said.

"That, yes, and something else. Cthulhu, Pischa, the Kraken, Dagon, Oannes, Neptune. Call him—it—what you will. But it was worshipped at Kettlethorpe, and it still remembers. Yes, and I think it comes, in certain seasons, to seek the worship it once knew and perhaps still…still…"

"Yes?"

He looked quickly away. "I've made…discoveries."

I waited.

"I've found things out, yes, yes—and—" His eyes flared up for a moment in the firelight, then dulled.

"And?"

"Damn it!" He turned on me and the towel fell from his shoulders. Quickly he snatched it up and covered himself—but not before I had seen how thin mere months had made him. "Damn it!" he mumbled again, less vehemently now. "Must you repeat everything I say? God, I do enough of that myself! I go over everything—over and over and over…"

I sat in silence, waiting. He would tell it in his own time.

And eventually he continued. "I've made discoveries, and I've heard…things." He looked from the fire to me, peered at me, ran trembling fingers through his hair. And did I detect streaks of grey in that once jet mop? "I've heard the bell!"

"Then it's time you got out of there!" I said at once. "Time you got June out, too."

"I know, I *know!*" he answered, his expression tortured. He gripped my arm. "But I'm not finished yet. I don't know it all, not yet. It lures me, Bill. I have to know…"

"Know what?" It was my turn to show my agitation. "What do you need to know, you fool? Isn't it enough that the place is evil? You know *that* much. And yet you stay on there. Get out, that's my advice. Get out now!"

"No!" His denial was emphatic. "I'm not finished. There has to be an end to it. The place must be cleansed." He stared again into the fire.

"So you do admit it's evil?"

"Of course it is. Yes, I know it is. But leave, get out? I can't, and June—"

"Yes?"

"She *won't!*" He gave a muffled sob and turned watery, searching eyes full upon me. "The place is like…like a magnet! It has a *genius loci.* It's a focal point for God-only-knows-what forces. Evil? Oh, yes! An evil come down all the centuries. But I bought the place and I shall cleanse it—end it forever, whatever it is."

"Look," I tried reasoning with him, "let's go back, now, the two of us. Let's get June out of there and bring her back here for the night. How did you get here anyway? Surely not on foot, not on a night like this?"

"No, no," he shook his head. "Car broke down halfway up the hill. Rain must have got under the bonnet. I'll pick it up tomorrow." He stood up, looked suddenly afraid, wild-eyed. "I've been away too long. Bill, will you run me back? June's there—alone! She was sleeping when I left. I can fill you in on the details while you drive…"

VII: Manifestation

I made him take another brandy, threw a coat over his shoulders, bustled him out to my car. Moments later we were rolling down into Harden and he was telling me all that had happened between times. As best I remember, this is what he said:

"Since that day you visited us I've been hard at work. Real work, I mean. Not the other thing, not delving—not all of the time, anyway. I got the grounds inside the walls tidied up, even tried a little preliminary landscaping. And the house: the old windows out, new ones in. Plenty of light. But still the place was musty. As the summer turned I began burning old Carpenter's wood, drying out the house, ridding it of the odour of centuries—a smell that was always thicker at night. And fresh paint, too, lots of it. Mainly white, all bright and new. June picked up a lot; you must have noticed how down she was? Yes, well, she seemed to be on the mend. I thought I had the—the 'miasma' on the run. *Hah!*" He gave a bitter snort. "A 'summer miasma', I called it. Blind, blind!"

"Go on," I urged him, driving carefully through the wet streets.

"Eventually, to give myself room to sort out the furniture and so on, I got round to chucking the old shelves and books out of Carpenter's study. That would have been okay, but...I looked into some of those books. That was an error. I should have simply burned the lot, along with the wormy old chairs and shreds of carpet. And yet, in a way, I'm glad I didn't." I could feel David's fevered eyes burning on me in the car's dark interior, fixed upon me as he spoke.

"The *knowledge* in those books, Bill. The dark secrets, the damnable mysteries. You know, if anyone does, what a fool I am for a mystery. I was hooked; work ceased; I had to know! But those books and manuscripts: the *Unter-Zee Kulten* and *Hydrophinnae*. Doorfen's treatise on submarine civilizations and the *Johansen Narrative* of 1925. A great sheaf of notes purporting to be from American government files for 1928, when federal agents 'raided' Innsmouth, a decaying, horror-haunted town on the coast of New England; and other scraps and fragments from all the world's mythologies, all of them concerned with the worship of a great god of the sea."

"Innsmouth?" My ears pricked up. I had heard that name mentioned once before. "But isn't that the place—?"

"—The place which spawned that family, the Waites, who came over and settled at Kettlethorpe about the time of the American Civil War? That's right," he nodded an affirmative, stared out into the rain-black night. "And old Carpenter who had the house for thirty years, he came from Innsmouth, too!"

"He was of the same people?"

"No, not him. The very opposite. He was at the farm for the same reason I am—now. Oh, he was strange, reclusive—who wouldn't be? I've read his diaries and I understand. Not everything, for even in his writing he held back, didn't explain too much. Why should he? His diaries were for him, aids to memory. They weren't meant for others to understand, but I fathomed a lot of it. The rest was in those government files.

"Innsmouth prospered in the time of the clipper ships and the old trade routes. The captains and men of some of those old ships brought back wives from Polynesia—and also their strange rites of worship, their gods. There was queer blood in those native women, and it spread rapidly. As the years passed the entire town became infected. Whole families grew up tainted. They were less than human, amphibian, creatures more of the sea than the land. Merfolk, yes! Tritons, who worshipped Dagon in the deeps: 'Deep Ones', as old Carpenter called them. Then came the federal raid of '28. But it came too late for old Carpenter.

"He had a store in Innsmouth, but well away from the secret places—away from the boarded-up streets and houses and churches where the worst of them had their dens and held their meetings and kept their rites. His wife was long dead of some wasting disease, but his daughter was alive and schooling in Arkham. Shortly before the raid she came home, little more than a girl. And she became—I don't know—lured. It's a word that sticks in my mind. A very real word, to me.

"Anyway, the Deep Ones took her, gave her to something they called out of the sea. She disappeared. Maybe she was dead, maybe something worse. They'd have killed Carpenter then, because he'd learned too much about them and wanted revenge, but the government raid put an end to any personal reprisals or vendettas. Put an end to Innsmouth, too. Why, they just about wrecked the town! Vast areas of complete demolition. They even depth-charged a reef a mile out in the sea…

"Well, after things quieted down Carpenter stayed on a while in Innsmouth, what was left of it. He was settling his affairs, I suppose, and maybe ensuring that the evil was at an end. Which must have been how he learned that it wasn't at an end but spreading like some awful blight. And because he suspected the survivors of the raid might seek haven in old strongholds abroad, finally he came to Kettlethorpe."

"Here?" David's story was beginning to make connections, was starting to add up. "Why would he come here?"

"Why? Haven't you been listening? He'd found something out about Kettlethorpe, and he came to make sure the Innsmouth horror couldn't spread here. Or perhaps he knew it was already here, waiting, like a cancer ready to shoot out its tentacles. Perhaps he came to stop it spreading further. Well, he's managed that these last thirty years, but now—"

"Yes?"

"Now he's gone, and I'm the owner of the place. Yes, and I have to see to it that whatever he was doing gets finished!"

"But what *was* he doing?" I asked. "And at what expense? Gone, you said. Yes, old Carpenter's gone. But gone where? What will all of this cost you, David? And more important by far, what will it cost June?"

My words had finally stirred something in him, something he had kept suppressed, too frightened of it to look more closely. I could tell by the way he started, sat bolt upright beside me. "June? But—"

"But nothing, man! Look at yourself. Better still, take a good look at your wife. You're going down the drain, both of you. It's something that started the day you took that farm. I'm sure you're right about the place, about old Carpenter, all that stuff you've dredged up—but now you've got to forget it. Sell Kettlethorpe, that's my advice—or better still, raze it to the ground! But whatever you do—"

"Look!" He started again and gripped my arm in a suddenly claw-hard hand.

I looked, applied my brakes, brought the car skidding to a halt in the rain-puddled track. We had turned off the main road by then, where the track winds down to the farm. The rain had let up and the air had gone still as a shroud. Shroudlike, too, the silky mist that lay silently upon the near-distant dene and lapped a foot deep about the old farm's stony walls. The scene was weird under a watery moon—but weirder by far the morbid *manifestation* which was even now rising up like a wraith over the farm.

A shape, yes—billowing up, composed of mist, writhing huge over the ancient buildings. The shape of some monstrous merman—the ages-evil shape of Dagon himself!

I should have shaken David off and driven on at once, of course I should, down to the farm and whatever waited there; but the sight of that figure mushrooming and firming in the dank night air was paralysing. And sitting there in the car, with the engine slowly ticking over, we shuddered as one as we heard, quite distinctly, the first muffled gonging of some damned and discordant bell. A tolling whose notes might on another occasion be sad and sorrowful, which now were filled with a menace out of the aeons.

"The bell!" David's gasp galvanised me into action.

"I hear it," I said, throwing the car into gear and racing down that last quarter-mile stretch to the farm. It seemed that time was frozen in those moments, but then we were through the iron gates and slewing to a halt in front of the porch. The house was bright with lights, but June—

While David tore desperately through the rooms of the house, searching upstairs and down, crying her name, I could only stand by the car and tremblingly listen to the tolling of the bell; its dull, sepulchral summons seeming to me to issue from below, from the very earth beneath my feet. And as I listened so I watched that writhing figure of mist shrink down into itself, seeming to glare from bulging eyes of mist one final ray of hatred in my direction, before spiralling down and disappearing—into the shell of that roofless building at the mouth of the horseshoe!

David, awry and babbling as he staggered from the house, saw it too. "There!" he pointed at the square, mist-wreathed building. "That's where it is. And that's where she'll be. I didn't know she knew…she must have been watching me. Bill—" he clutched at my arm "—are you with me?—Say you are, for God's sake!" And I could only nod my head.

Hearts racing, we made for that now ghastly edifice of reeking mist—only to recoil a moment later from a figure that reeled out from beneath the lintel with the Dagon plate to fall swooning into David's arms. June, of course—but how could it be? How could this be June?

Not the June I had known, no, but some other, some revenant of that June…

VIII: "That Place Below…"

She was gaunt, hair coarse as string, skin dry and stretched over features quite literally, shockingly altered into something…different. Strangely, David was not nearly so horrified by what he could see of her by the thin light of the moon; far more so after we had taken her back to the house. For quite apart from what were to me undeniable alterations in her looks in general—about which, as yet, he had made no comment—it then became apparent that his wife had been savaged and brutalised in the worst possible manner.

I remember, as I drove them to the emergency hospital in Hartlepool, listening to David as he cradled her in his arms in the back of the car. She was not conscious, and David barely so (certainly he was oblivious to what he babbled and sobbed over her during that nightmare journey) but my mind was working overtime as I listened to his crooning, utterly distraught voice:

"She must have watched me, poor darling, must have seen me going to that place. At first I went for the firewood—I burned up all of old Jason's wood—but then, beneath the splinters and bits of bark, I found the mill-stone over the slab. The old boy had put that stone there to keep the slab down. And it had done its job, by God! Must have weighed all of two hundred and forty pounds. Impossible to shift from those slimy, narrow steps below. But I used a lever to move it, yes—and I lifted the slab and went down. Down those ancient steps—down, down, down. A maze, down there. The earth itself, honeycombed!....

"...What were they for, those burrows? What purpose were they supposed to fulfill? And *who* dug them? I didn't know, but I kept it from her anyway—or thought I had. I couldn't say why, not then, but some instinct warned me not to tell her about...about that place below. I swear to God I meant to close it up forever, choke the mouth of that—that pit! with concrete. And I'd have done it, I swear it, once I'd explored those tunnels to the full. But that millstone, June, that great heavy stone. How did you shift it? *Or were you helped?*

"I've been down there only two or three times on my own, and I never went very far. Always there was that feeling that I wasn't alone, that things moved in the darker burrows and watched me where I crept. And that sluggish stream, bubbling blindly through airless fissures to the sea. That stream which rises and falls with the tides. And the kelp all bloated and slimy. Oh, my God! My God!"...

...And so on. But by the time we reached the hospital David had himself more or less under control again. Moreover, he had dragged from me a promise that I would let him—indeed help him—do things his own way. He had a plan which seemed both simple and faultless, one which must conclusively write *finis* on the entire affair. That was to say *if* his fears for Kettlethorpe and the conjectural region he termed "that place below" were soundly based.

As to why I so readily went along with him—why I allowed him to brush aside unspoken any protests or objections I might have entertained—quite simply, I had seen that mist-formed shape with my own eyes, and with my own ears had heard the tolling of that buried and blasphemous bell. And for all that the thing seemed fantastic, the conviction was now mine that the farm was a seat of horror and evil as great and maybe greater than any other these British Isles had ever known...

✤ ✤ ✤

We stayed at the hospital through the night, gave identical, falsified statements to the police (an unimaginative tale of a marauder; seen fleeing under cover of the mist towards the dene), and in between sat together in a waiting area drinking coffee and quietly conversing. Quietly now, yes, for David was exhausted both physically and mentally; and much more so after he had attended that examination of his wife made imperative by her condition and by our statements.

As for June: mercifully she stayed in her traumatic state of deepest shock all through the night and well into the morning. Finally, around 10:00 a.m. we were informed that her condition, while still unstable, was no longer critical; and then, since it was very obvious that we could do nothing more, I drove David home with me to Harden.

I bedded him down in my guest-room, by which time all I wanted to do was get to my own bed for an hour or two; but about 4.00 p.m. I was awakened from uneasy dreams to find him on the telephone, his voice stridently urgent. As I went to him he put the phone down, turned to me haggard and red-eyed, his face dark with stubble. "She's stabilised," he, said, and: "Thank God for that! But she hasn't come out of shock—not completely. It's too deep-seated. At least that's what they told me. They say she could be like it for weeks…maybe longer."

"What will you do?" I asked him. "You're welcome to stay here, of course, and—"

"Stay here?" he cut me short. "Yes, I'd like that—afterwards."

I nodded, biting my lip. "I see. You intend to go through with it. Very well—but there's still time to tell the police, you know. You could still let them deal with it."

He uttered a harsh, barking laugh. "Can you really imagine me telling all of this to your average son-of-the-sod Hartlepool bobby? Why, even if I showed them that…the place below; what could they do about it? And should I tell them about my plan, too? What!—mention dynamite to the law, the local authorities? Oh, yes, I can just see that! Even if they didn't put me in a straight jacket it would still take them an age to get round to doing anything. And meanwhile, if there is something down there under the farm—and Bill, we know there is—what's to stop it or them from moving on to fresh pastures?"

When I had no answer, he continued in a more controlled, quieter tone. "Do you know what old Carpenter was doing? I'll tell you: he was going down there in the right seasons, when he heard the bell ringing—going down below with his shotgun and blasting all hell out of what he found in those

283

foul black tunnels! Paying them back for what they did to him and his in Innsmouth. A madman who didn't know what he wrote in those diaries of his? No, for we've *seen* it, Bill, you and I. And we've heard it—heard Dagon's bell ringing in the night, summoning that ancient evil up from the sea.

"Why, that was the old man's sole reason for living there: so that he could take his revenge! Taciturn? A recluse? I'll say he was! He lived to kill—*to kill them*! Tritons, Deep Ones, amphibian abortions born out of a timeless evil, inhuman lust and black, alien nightmare. Well, now I'll finish what he started, only I'll do it a damn sight faster! It's my way or nothing." He gazed at me, his eyes steady now and piercing, totally sane, strong as I had rarely seen him. "You'll come?"

"First," I said. "there's something you must tell me. About June. She—her looks—I mean…"

"I know what you mean." His voice contained a tremor, however tightly controlled. "It's what makes the whole thing real for me. It's proof positive, as if that were needed now, of all I've suspected and discovered of the place. I told you she wouldn't leave the farm, didn't I? But did you know it was her idea to buy Kettlethorpe in the first place?"

"You mean she was…lured?"

"Oh, yes, that's exactly what I mean—but by what? By her blood, Bill! She didn't know, was completely innocent. Not so her forebears. Her great-grandfather came from America, New England. That's as far as I care to track it down, and no need now to take it any further. But you must see why I personally have to square it all away?"

I could only nod.

"And you will help?"

"I must be mad," I answered, nodding again, "—or at best an idiot—but it seems I've already committed myself. Yes, I'll come."

"Now?"

"Today? At this hour? That *would* be madness! Before you know it, it'll be dark, and—"

"Dark, yes!" he broke in on me. "But what odds? It's always dark down there, Bill. We'll need electric torches, the more the better. I have a couple at the farm. How about you?"

"I've a good heavy-duty torch in the car," I told him. "Batteries, too."

"Good! And your shotguns—we'll need them, I think. But we're not after pheasant this time, Bill."

"Where will you get the dynamite?" I asked, perhaps hoping that this was something which, in his fervour, he had overlooked.

He grinned—not his old grin but a twisted, vicious thing and said: "I've already got it. Had it ever since I found the slab two weeks ago and first went down there. My gangers use it on big landscaping jobs. Blasting out large boulders and tree stumps saves a lot of time and effort. Saves money, too. There's enough dynamite at the farm to demolish half of Harden!"

David had me, and he knew it. "It's now, Bill, now!" he said. And after a moment's silence he shrugged. "But—if you haven't the spit for it—"

"I said I'd come," I told him, "and so I will. You're not the only one who loves a mystery, even one as terrifying as this. Now that I know such a place exists, of course I want to see it. I'm not easy about it, no, but…"

He nodded. "Then this is your last chance, for you can be sure it won't be there for you to see tomorrow!"

IX: Descent Into Madness

Within the hour we were ready. Torches, shotguns, dynamite and fuzewire—everything we would need—all was in our hands. And as we made our way from the house at Kettlethorpe along the garden paths to the roofless enclosure, already the mists were rising and beginning to creep. And I admit here and now that if David had offered me the chance again, to back out and leave him to go it alone, I believe I might well have done so.

As it was, we entered under the lintel with the plate, found the slab as David had described it, and commenced to lever it up from its seatings.

As we worked my friend nodded his head towards a very old and massive millstone lying nearby. "That's what Jason Carpenter used to seal it. And do you believe June could have shifted that on her own? Never! She was helped—must have been helped from below!"

At that moment the slab moved, lifted, was awkward for a moment but at our insistence slid gratingly aside. I don't know what I expected, but the blast of foul, damp air that rushed up from below took me completely by surprise. It blew full into my face, jetting up like some noxious, invisible geyser, a pressured stench of time and ocean, darkness and damp, and alien things. And I knew it at once: that tainted odour I had first detected in the summer, which David had naively termed "a miasma".

Was this the source, then, of that misty phantom seen on dark nights, that bloating spectre formed of fog and the rushing reek of inner earth? Patently it was, but that hardly explained the shape the thing had assumed…

✤ ✤ ✤

In a little while the expansion and egress of pent-up gases subsided and became more a flow of cold, salty air. Other odours were there, certainly, but however alien and disgusting they no longer seemed quite so unbearable.

Slung over our shoulders we carried part-filled knapsacks which threw us a little off balance. "Careful," David warned, descending ahead of me, "it's steep and slippery as hell!" Which was no exaggeration.

The way was narrow, spiralling, almost perpendicular, a stairwell through solid rock which might have been cut by some huge and eccentric drill. Its steps were narrow in the tread, deep in the rise, and slimy with nitre and a film of moisture clammy as sweat. And our powerful torches cutting the way through darkness deep as night, and the walls winding down, down, ever down.

I do not know the depth to which we descended; there was an interminable sameness about that corkscrew of stone which seemed to defy measurement. But I recall something of the characters carved almost ceremoniously into its walls. Undeniably Roman, some of them, but I was equally sure that these were the most recent! The rest, having a weird, almost glyphic angularity and coarseness—a barbaric simplicity of style—must surely have predated any Roman incursion into Britain.

And so down to the floor of that place, where David paused to deposit several sticks of dynamite in a dark niche. Quickly he fitted a fuze, and while he worked so he spoke to me in a whisper which echoed sibilantly away and came rustling back in decreasing sussurations. "A long fuze for this one. We'll light it on our way out. And at least five more like this before we're done. I hope it's enough. God, I don't even know the extent of the place! I've been this far before and farther, but you can imagine what it's like to be down here on your own…"

Indeed I could imagine it, and shuddered at the thought.

While David worked I stood guard, shotgun under my arm, cocked, pointing it down a black tunnel that wound away to God-knows-where. The walls of this horizontal shaft were curved inward at the top to form its ceiling, which was so low that when we commenced to follow it we were obliged to stoop. Quite obviously the tunnel was no mere work of nature; no, for it was far too regular for that, and everywhere could be seen the marks of sharp tools used to chip out the stone. One other fact which registered was this: that the walls were of the same stone from which Kettlethorpe Farm— in what original form?—must in some dim uncertain time predating all memory, myth and legend have been constructed.

And as I followed my friend, so in some dim recess of my mind I made note of these things, none of which lessened in the slightest degree the terrific weight of apprehension resting almost tangibly upon me. But follow him I did, and in a little while he was showing me fresh marks on the walls, scratches he had made on previous visits to enable him to retrace his steps.

"Necessary," he whispered, "for just along here the tunnels begin to branch, become a maze. Really—a maze! Be a terrible thing to get lost down here…"

My imagination needed no urging, and after that I followed more closely still upon his heels, scratching marks of my own as we went. And sure enough, within a distance of perhaps fifty paces more, it began to become apparent that David had in no way exaggerated with regard to the labyrinthine nature of the place. There were side tunnels, few at first but rapidly increasing in number, which entered into our shaft from both sides and all manner of angles; and shortly after this we came to a sort of gallery wherein many of these lesser passages met.

The gallery was in fact a cavern of large dimensions with a domed ceiling perhaps thirty feet high. Its walls were literally honeycombed with tunnels entering from all directions, some of which descended steeply to regions deeper and darker still. Here, too, I heard for the first time the sluggish gurgle of unseen waters, of which David informed: "That's a stream. You'll see it shortly."

He laid another explosive charge out of sight in a crevice, then indicated that I should once more follow him. We took the tunnel with the highest ceiling, which after another seventy-five to one hundred yards opened out again onto a ledge that ran above a slow-moving, blackly gleaming rivulet. The water gurgled against our direction of travel, and its surface was some twenty feet lower than the ledge; this despite the fact that the trough through which it coursed was green and black with slime and incrustations almost fully up to the ledge itself. David explained the apparent ambiguity.

"Tidal," he said. "The tide's just turned. It's coming in now. I've seen it fifteen feet deeper than this, but that won't be for several hours yet." He gripped my arm, causing me to start. "And look! Look at the kelp…"

Carried on the surface of the as yet sluggish stream, great ropes of weed writhed and churned, bladders glistening in the light from our torches. "David," my voice wavered, "I think—"

"Come on," he said, leading off once more. "I know what you think—but we're not going back. Not yet." Then he paused and turned to me, his eyes burning in the darkness. "Or you can go back on your own, if you wish…?"

"David," I hissed, "that's a rotten thing to—"

"My *God*, man!" he stopped me. "D'you think you're the only one who's afraid?"

However paradoxically, his words buoyed me up a little, following which we moved quickly on and soon came to a second gallery. Just before reaching it the stream turned away, so that only its stench and distant gurgle stayed with us. And once more David laid charges, his actions hurried now, nervous, as if in addition to his admitted fear he had picked up something of my own barely subdued panic.

"This is as far as I've been," he told me, his words coming in a sort of rapid gasping or panting. "Beyond here is fresh territory. By my reckoning we're now well over a quarter-mile from the entrance." He flashed the beam of his torch around the walls, causing the shadows of centuries-formed stalactites to flicker and jump. "There, the big tunnel. We'll take that one."

And now, every three or four paces, or wherever a side tunnel opened into ours, we were both scoring the walls to mark a fresh and foolproof trail. Now, too, my nerves really began to get the better of me. I found myself starting at every move my friend made; I kept pausing to listen, my heartbeat shuddering in the utter stillness of that nighted place. Or was it still? Did I hear something just then? The echo of a splash and the soft *flop, flop* of furtive footsteps in the dark?

It must be pictured:

We were in a vast subterrene warren. A place hollowed out centuries ago by…by whom? By what? And what revenants lurked here still, down here in these terrible caverns of putrid rock and festering, sewage-like streams?

Slap, slap, slap…

And that time I definitely had heard something. "David—" my voice was thin as a reedy wind. "For God's sake—"

"*Shh!*" he warned, his cautionary hiss barely audible. "I heard it too, and they might have heard us! Let me just get the rest of this dynamite planted— one final big batch, it'll have to be—and then we'll get out of here." He used his torch to search the walls but could find no secret place to house the explosives. "Round this next bend," he said. "I'll find a niche there. Don't want the stuff to be found before it's done its job."

We rounded the bend, and ahead—

—A glow of rotten, phosphorescent light, a luminescence almost sufficient to make our torches redundant. We saw, and we began to understand.

The roofless building up above—the enclosure that was merely the entrance. This place here, far underground, was the actual place of worship, the subterranean temple to Dagon. We knew it as soon as we saw the great nitre-crusted bell hanging from the centre of the ceiling—the bell and the rusted iron chain which served as its rope, hanging down until its last link dangled inches above the surface and centre of a black and sullenly rippling lake of scum and rank weed…

For all that horror might follow on our very heels, still we found ourselves pulled up short by the sight of that fantastic final gallery. It was easily a hundred feet wall to wall, roughly circular, domed over and shelved around, almost an amphitheatre in the shape of its base, and obviously a natural, geological formation. Stalactites hung down from above, as in the previous gallery, and stalagmitic stumps broke the weed-pool's surface here and there, showing that at some distant time in our planet's past the cave had stood well above sea level.

As to the source of the pool itself: this could only be the sea. The deep kelp alone was sufficient evidence of that. And to justify and make conclusive this observation, the pool was fed by a broad expanse of water which disappeared under the ledge beneath the far wall, which my sense of direction told me lay towards the sea. The small ripples or wavelets we had noted disturbing the pool's surface could only be the product of an influx of water from this source, doubtless the flow of the incoming tide.

Then there was the light: that same glow of putrescence or organic decomposition seen in certain fungi, an unhealthy illumination which lent the cave an almost submarine aspect. So that even without the clean light of our electric torches, still the great bell in the ceiling would have remained plainly visible.

But that bell…who could say where it came from? Not I. Not David. Certainly this was that bell whose sepulchral tolling had penetrated even to the surface, but as to its origin…

In that peculiar way of his, David, as if reading my thoughts, confirmed: "Well, it'll not ring again—not after this lot goes off!" And I saw that he had placed his knapsack full of dynamite out of sight beneath a low, shallow ledge in the wall and was even now uncoiling a generous length of fuze wire. Finishing the task, he glanced at me once, struck a match and set sputtering fire to the end of the wire, pushing it, too, out of sight.

"There," he grunted, "and now we can get—" But here he paused, and I knew why.

The echo of a voice—a *croak?*—had come to us from somewhere not too far distant. And even as our ears strained to detect other than the slow gurgle of weed-choked waters, so there echoed again that damnably soft and furtive *slap, slap, slap* of nameless feet against slimy stone…

X: Deep Ones!

At that panic gripped both of us anew, was magnified as the water of the pool gurgled more loudly yet and ripples showed which could *not* be ascribed solely to an influx from the sea. Perhaps at this very moment something other than brine and weed was moving toward us along that murky and mysterious watercourse.

My limbs were trembling, and David was in no better condition as, throwing caution to the wind, we commenced scramblingly to retrace our steps, following those fresh marks where we had scratched them upon the walls of the maze. And behind us the hidden fuze slowly sputtering its way to that massive charge of dynamite; and approaching the great pool, some entirely conjectural thing whose every purpose we were sure must be utterly alien and hostile. While ahead…who could say?

But one thing was certain: our presence down here had finally stirred something up—maybe many somethings—and now their noises came to us even above our breathless panting, the hammering of our hearts and the clattering sounds of our flight down those black tunnels of inner earth. Their *noises*, yes, for no man of the sane upper world of blue skies and clean air could ever have named those echoing, glutinous bursts of sporadic croaking and clotted, inquiring gurgles and grunts as speech; and no one could mistake the slithering, slapping, *flopping* sounds of their pursuit for anything remotely human. Or perhaps they were remotely human, but so sunken into hybrid degeneracy as to seem totally alien to all human expectations. And all of this without ever having seen these Deep Ones—"Tritons", as David had named them—or at least, not yet!

But as we arrived at the central gallery and paused for breath, and as David struck a second match to light the fuze of the charge previously laid there, that so far merciful omission commenced to resolve itself in a manner I shall never forget to my dying day.

It started with the senses-shattering gonging of the great bell, whose echoes were deafening in those hellish tunnels, and it ended…but I go ahead of myself.

Simultaneous with the ringing of the bell, a renewed chorus of croaking and grunting came to us from somewhere dangerously close at hand; so that

David at once grabbed my arm and half-dragged me into a small side tunnel leading off at an angle from the gallery. This move had been occasioned not alone by the fact that the sounds we had heard were coming closer, but also that they issued from the very burrow by which we must make our escape! But as the madly capricious gods of fate would have it, our momentary haven proved no less terrifying in its way than the vulnerable position we had been obliged to quit.

The hole into which we had fled was no tunnel at all but an "L"-shaped cave which, when we rounded its single corner, laid naked to our eyes a hideous secret. We recoiled instinctively from a discovery grisly as it was unexpected, and I silently prayed that God—if indeed there was any good, sane God—would give me strength not to break down utterly in my extreme of horror.

In there, crumpled where he had finally been overcome, lay the ragged and torn remains of old Jason Carpenter. It could only be him; the similarly broken body of Bones, his dog, lay across his feet. And all about him on the floor of the cave, spent shotgun cartridges; and clasped in his half-rotted, half-mummied hand, that weapon which in the end had not saved him.

But he had fought—how he had fought! Jason, and his dog, too…

Theirs were not the only corpses left to wither and decay in that tomb of a cave. No, for heaped to one side was a pile of quasi-human—*debris*—almost beyond my powers of description. Suffice to say that I will not even attempt a description, but merely confirm that these were indeed the very monstrosities of David's tale of crumbling Innsmouth. And if in death the things were loathsome, in life they would yet prove to be worse by far. That was still to come…

And so, with our torches reluctantly but necessarily switched off, we crouched there in the fetid darkness amidst corpses of man, dog and nightmares, and we waited. And always we were full of that awful awareness of slowly burning fuzes, of time rapidly running out. But at last the tolling of the bell ceased and its echoes died away, and the sounds of the Deep Ones decreased as they made off in a body towards the source of the summoning, and finally we made our move.

Switching on our torches we ran crouching from the cave into the gallery—and came face to face with utmost terror! A lone member of that flopping, frog-voiced horde had been posted here and now stood central in the gallery, turning startled, bulging batrachian eyes upon us as we emerged from our hiding place.

A moment later and this squat obscenity this—part-man, part-fish, part-frog creature—threw up webbed hands before its terrible face; screamed a hissing, croaking cry of rage and possibly agony, and finally hurled itself at us...

...Came frenziedly lurching, flopping and floundering, headlong into a double-barrelled barrage from the weapon I held in fingers which kept on uselessly squeezing the trigger long after the face and chest of the monster had flown into bloody tatters and its body was lifted and hurled away from us across the chamber.

Then David was yelling in my ear, tugging at me, dragging me after him, and...and all of the rest is a chaos, a madness, a nightmare of flight and fear.

I seem to recall loading my shotgun—several times, I think—and I have vague memories of discharging it a like number of times; and I believe that David, too, used his weapon, probably more successfully. As for our targets: it would have been difficult to miss them. There were clutching claws, and eyes bulging with hatred and lust; there was foul, alien breath in our faces, slime and blood and bespattered bodies obstructing our way where they fell; and always a swelling uproar of croaking and flopping and slithering as that place below became filled with the spawn of primal oceans.

Then...the Titan blast that set the rock walls to trembling, whose reverberations had no sooner subsided when a yet more ominous rumbling began... Dust and stony debris rained down from the tunnel ceilings, and a side tunnel actually collapsed into ruin as we fled past its mouth...but finally we arrived at the foot of those upward-winding stone steps in the flue-like shaft which was our exit.

Here my memory grows more distinct, too vivid if anything—as if sight of our salvation sharpened fear-numbed senses—and I see David lighting the final fuze as I stand by him, firing and reloading, firing and reloading. The sharp smell of sulphur and gunpowder in a haze of dust and flickering torch beams, and the darkness erupting anew in shambling shapes of loathsome fright. The shotgun hot in my hands, jamming at the last, refusing to break open.

Then David taking my place and firing point-blank into a mass of mewling horror, and his voice shrill and hysterical, ordering me to climb, climb and get out of that hellish place. From above I look down and see him dragged under, disappearing beneath a clawing, throbbing mass of bestiality; and their frog-eyes avidly turning upwards to follow my flight...fangs gleaming in grinning, wide-slit mouths...an instant's pause before they come squelching and squalling up the steps behind me!

And at last...at last I emerge into moonlight and mist. And with a strength born of madness I hurl the slab into place and weight it with the millstone. For David is gone now and no need to ponder over his fate. It was quick, I saw it with my own eyes, but at least he has done what he set out to do. I know this now, as I feel from far below that shuddering concussion as the dynamite finishes its work.

Following which I stumble from the roofless building and collapse on a path between stunted fruit trees and unnaturally glossy borders of mist-damp shrubbery. And lying there I know the sensation of being shaken, of feeling the earth trembling beneath me, and of a crashing of masonry torn from foundations eaten by the ages.

And at the very end, sinking into a merciful unconsciousness, at last I am rewarded by a sight which will allow me, with the dawn, to come awake a sane, whole man. That sight which is simply this: a great drifting mass of mist, dissipating as it coils away over the dene, melting down from the shape of a rage-tormented merman to a thin and formless fog.

For I know that while Dagon himself lives on—as he has "lived" since time immemorial—the seat of his worship which Kettlethorpe has been for centuries is at last no more...

That is my story, the story of Kettlethorpe Farm, which with the dawn lay in broken ruins. Not a building remained whole or standing as I left the place, and what has become of it since I cannot say for I never returned and I have never inquired. Official records will show, of course, that there was "a considerable amount of pit subsidence" that night, sinkings and shiftings of the earth with which colliery folk the world over are all too familiar; and despite the fact that there was no storm as such at sea, still a large area of the ocean-fringing cliffs were seen to have sunken down and fallen onto the sands or into the sullen water.

What more is there to say? There was very little deep kelp that year, and in the years since the stuff has seemed to suffer a steady decline. This is hearsay, however, for I have moved inland and will never return to any region from which I might unwittingly spy the sea or hear its wash.

As for June: she died some eight months later giving premature birth to a child. In the interim her looks had turned even more strange, ichthyic, but she was never aware of it for she had become a happy little girl whose mind would never be whole again. Her doctors said that this was just as well, and for this I give thanks.

As well, too, they said, that her child died with her...

THE THING FROM THE
BLASTED HEATH

*If I had to choose a favourite story by a favourite author, it
would be somewhere between Jack Vance's Dying Earth fantasies
and HPL's horror stories: an especially difficult choice. If we were to
restrict the subject matter to horror, however, then I know which
way I would have to vote: I would have to settle for H.P. Lovecraft,
whose story would be (please forgive my English spelling) "The
Colour Out of Space"; which in a way, in connection with this current volume, is something of a paradox because "Colour" isn't a
Mythos story! You won't find a single mention of Cthulhu in it, or
any other god or demon of the Mythos pantheon, nor any of the
standard titles of those volumes of dark lore we're so used to, nor
anything else to connect it to the Cthulhu Mythos, except perhaps
its New England location. The paradox I mentioned is that in my
first year of writing—in September 1967, to be exact—I was so
steeped in Mythos lore that I had written "The Thing From the
Blasted Heath" as an homage to HPL, and to the Mythos. It's a
peripheral Mythos tale, to be sure, but Mythos for all that, and it
saw print in hardcovers, in* The Caller of the Black, *my first
Arkham House collection, in 1971.*

That which I once boasted of as being the finest
collection of morbid and macabre curiosities outside of
the British Museum is no more—and *still* I am unable to sleep. When night's
furtive shadow steals over the moors I lock and bolt my door to peer fearfully through my window at that spot in the garden which glows faintly,
with its own inexplicable light, and about which the freshly grown grass is
yellow and withered. Though I constantly put down seeds and crumbs no

bird ever ventures into my garden, and without even the bees to visit them my fruit trees are barren and dying. No more will Old Cartwright come to my house of an evening to chat in the drowsy firelight or to share with me his home-pressed wines; for Old Cartwright is dead.

I have written of it to my friend in New England, he who sent me the shrub from the blasted heath, warning him never to venture again where once he went for me lest he share a similar fate.

From the moment I first read of the blasted heath I knew I could never rest until I had something of it in my collection. I found myself a pen-friend in New England, developed a strong friendship with him and then, when by various means I had made him beholden to me, I sent him to do my bidding at the blasted heath. The area is a reservoir now, in a valley west of witch-haunted Arkham, but before men flooded that grey desolation the heath lay like a great diseased sore in the woods and fields. It had not always been so. Before the coming of the fine grey dust the place had been a fertile valley, with orchards and wildlife in plenty—but that was all before the strange meteorite. Disease had followed the meteorite and after that had come the dust. Many and varied are the weird tales to come filtering out of that area, and fiction or superstition though they may or may not be the fact remains that men will not drink the water of that reservoir. It is tainted by a poison unknown to science which brings madness, delirium and a lingering, crumbling death. The entire valley has been closed off with barbed-wire fences and warning notices stand thick around its perimeter.

Nonetheless, my friend climbed those fences and ventured deep into the haunted heart of the place, to the very water's edge, where he dug in the rotting earth before leaving with my prize. Within twenty-four hours the thing was on its way to me, and after seeing it I could readily understand his haste in getting rid of it. I could not even give the thing a name. I doubt if anyone could have named that shrub for it was the child of strange radiation, not of this world, and therefore unknown to man. Its leaves were awful, hybrid things—thick, flaccid and white like a sick child's hands—and its slender trunk and branches were terribly twisted and strangely veined. It was in such a poor state when I planted it in my garden that I did not think it would live. Unfortunately I was wrong; it soon began its luxuriant growth and Old Cartwright often used to warily prod it with his cane when he came visiting.

"What was you burnin' t'other night?" he asked me one morning in the garden. "I seen t'glow from me winder. Looked like you was burnin' old films or summat! Funny, silver lookin' flames they was."

I was puzzled by his remarks. "Burning? Why, nothing! Where did you see this fire, Harry?"

"'Ere in t'garden, or so I tho't! P'raps it were just t'glow from your fire reflected in yon winder." He nodded towards the house and spat expertly at the shrub. "Seemed to be just about there where yon thing is." He moved a pace closer to the shrub and prodded it with his cane. "Gettin' right fat, aint 'e?" Then he turned and looked at me curiously. "Can't rightly say as I like yon."

"It's just a plant, Harry, like any other," I answered. Then, on afterthought: "Well, perhaps not *quite* like any other. It looks ugly, I'll admit—but it's perfectly harmless. Surprises me you don't like it! You don't seem to mind my Death-Masks or the other things I've got."

"'Armless, *they* be," he said. "Interestin' toys and nowt else—but you wouldn't catch me plantin' yon in *my* garden!" He grinned at me in that way of his which meant 'I-know-something-you-don't-know', and said: "Anyhow, can you answer me this, Mr. Bell? What kind o' bush is it what t'birds don't settle on, eh?" He glanced sharply at the plant and then at me. "Never seen a sparrer on it yet, I aint…" He spat again. "Not as I blames 'em, mind you. I shouldn't fancy sittin' on *that* thing myself. Just look at them leaves what never seem to move in t'wind; and that lepry-white colour of the trunk and branches. Why! Yon looks more like a queer, leafy octopus than a shrub."

At the time I thought very little of our conversation. Old Cartwright was always full of strange fancies and had said more or less the same things about my conches when he first saw them. Yet a few weeks later, when I noticed the first *really* odd thing about the tree from the heath, I thought of his words again.

Oh, yes! It was a tree by then. It had nearly trebled its size since I planted it and was almost three feet tall. It had put out lots of new, greyly-mottled branches and because its trunk and lower branches had thickened, the weirdly knotted dark veins stood out clearly against the drowned-flesh texture of the tree's limbs. It was that day that I had to stop Old Cartwright from pestering it. I had thought he was going just a bit heavy with his cane, for after all, the tree *was* the show-piece of my collection and I did not want it damaged.

"It's you, aint it, what glows at night?" he had asked of the thing, prodding away. "It's you what shines like them yeller toadstools do! I come over 'ere last night, Mr. Bell, but you was already in bed. Tho't I seen a fire in your garden again, but it weren't a fire—'twas 'im!" He prodded the tree harder, actually shaking it. "What kind o' tree is it?" he asked, "what t'birds don't sit on and what glows at night, eh?" That was when I got angry and told him to leave the tree alone.

He could be petulant at times, Old Harry, and off he went in a huff in the direction of his cottage. I walked back towards the house and then, thinking I had been perhaps a bit too gruff with the old boy, I turned to call him back for a drink. Before I could open my mouth to shout I noticed the tree. *As God is my witness the thing was straining after Old Cartwright like a leashed dog strains after a cat. Its white leaves were all stretched out straight like horrid hands, pointing in his direction, and the trunk had literally bent towards his retreating figure....*

He was right. That night I stayed up purposely and saw it for myself. The tree *did* glow in the night, with a strange, silvery St. Elmo's Fire of its own. It was then that I decided to get rid of it, and what I found in the garden the next morning really clinched the matter.

I do not think that at the time the glowing really bothered me. As Old Harry himself had remarked, certain toadstools are luminous in the dark and I knew that the same thing holds true of one or two species of moss. Even higher life-forms—for instance many fishes of the great deeps—are known to carry their own peculiar lighting systems, and plankton lies luminous even upon the ocean's surface. No, I was sure that the glowing was not important; but that which I found in the morning was something else! For none of the aforementioned life-forms are capable of doing that which I was ready to believe the tree had somehow done that night.

I noticed the thing's horrid new luxuriance the moment I stepped into the garden. It looked altogether...*stronger*, and the leaves and veins seemed somehow to be of a darker tint than before. I was so taken up by the change in the plant that I did not see the cat until I almost stepped on it. The body was lying in the grass at the foot of the tree and when I turned it over with my boot I was surprised that it was not stiff. The animal was obviously dead, being merely skin and bone, and...

I kneeled to examine the small, furry corpse—and felt the hackles suddenly rise at the back of my neck! *The body of the cat was not stiff—because there was nothing to stiffen!*

There were only bones inside that unnatural carcass; and looking closer I saw that the small mouth, nostrils and the anal exit were terribly mutilated. Of course, a car could have gone over the poor creature's body and forced its innards (I shuddered) outwards; but then who would have thrown the body into my garden?

And then I noticed something else: there were funny little molehills all about the foot of the tree! Now, I asked myself, since when are moles flesh-eaters? Or had they perhaps been attracted by the smell of the corpse? Funny, because I was damned if *I* could smell it! No, this was a freshly dead cat.

I had studied the tree before, of course, but now I gave it a really thorough going over. I suppose, in the back of my mind, that I was thinking of my *Dionaea Muscipulas*—my Venus-Flytraps—but for the life of me I could in no way match the two species. The leaves of *this* tree were not sticky, as I knew the leaves of some flesh-eaters to be, and their edges were not spiked or hinged. Nor did the plant seem to have the necessary *drainage* apparatus to do that which I feared had been done. There were no spines or thorns on the thing at all, and so far as I could tell there was nothing physically poisonous about it.

What then had *happened* to the cat? My own cat, a good companion of many years, had died of old age long before I ever heard of the blasted heath. I had always intended to get another. Now I was glad I had not done so. I did not know how this animal had died but one thing I was sure of—I could no longer abide the blasphemy from the heath in my garden. Collection or not, it had to go.

That same day I walked into Marske and put through a telephone call to a botanist friend in London. It was he who had sold me my fly-traps. I told him all about my tree and after I had assured him I was not "pulling his leg" he said he would come up over the weekend to have a look at it. He told me that if the specimen was anything like my description he would be only too pleased to have it and would see that I did not lose on the deal.

That was on Thursday, and I went home from the village happy in the belief that by Sunday I would be rid of the thing from the blasted heath and the birds would be singing in my garden once again. I could not have even dreamt it then, but things were to happen before Sunday which would make it impossible for me ever to be happy again, or for that matter, ever again to have a good night's sleep.

That evening I developed an awful headache. I had a good double brandy and went to bed earlier than usual. The last thing to catch my attention before I dozed off was the silvery glow in the garden. It was so plain out there that I was surprised I had not noticed it before Old Harry Cartwright brought it to my attention.

My awakening was totally inexplicable. I found myself stretched flat on my face on the garden path just outside my front door. My headache had worsened until the pounding inside my skull was like a trip hammer.

"What in hell…?" I said aloud as I looked dazedly about. I had obviously tripped over the draught-strip on the doorstep; *but how had I come to be there in the first place?*

From my prone position I looked down the garden toward the tree. The clatter of my fall onto the gravel of the path must have disturbed the thing. It was straining in my direction with the same horrible eagerness it had displayed towards Old Cartwright. I got painfully to my feet and, as I turned to go into the house, saw that the tree was already swaying *away* from me to point up the road in the direction of Old Cartwright's place.

"What's bothering the thing now?" I wondered, going inside and locking the door again. I sat on my bed and tried to work it all out. Thank God for the draught-strip! I had been threatening all summer to remove it because hardly a day went by that I did not trip over it. "Just as well I didn't," I muttered to myself, unknowingly understating the fact. My meaning was simply that if people had seen me walking down the country road in the middle of the night dressed only in my pyjama bottoms—well, it just did not bear thinking about. The Marske villagers probably already thought me a bit queer because of my collection—Old Harry was a real gossip at times.

The night was perfectly calm and hardly a breeze disturbed the warm air. It was when this stillness was broken that I awoke once more. I had heard the iron gate to the garden slam shut. Thoroughly disgruntled by the night's disturbances I leapt out of bed and threw open the window. Old Cartwright was in the garden beside the tree. His eyes were wide open and staring at the thing, which was leaning toward him in that horribly familiar fashion.

Though I was surprised that the old boy was out there I was doubly astonished to note that he was attired only in his nightshirt. Could it be that he also was walking in his sleep? It seemed so. I opened my mouth to call out to him—but even as I did so I saw something which caused the breath to whoosh out of my lungs as my body constricted in a sudden agony of horror.

Something was happening to the ground around the plant's base! My first thought was molehills sprouting up about the trunk of the freak from the heath and around Old Harry's feet.

But the things coming up out of those little mounds of soil were not moles! Roots!

My mind went numb with dreadful terror, a gibbering evil gripped my brain as I stumbled from the window to reel away across the room. I tried to cry out, to scream, but my throat seemed completely paralysed. The weirdness of the tree's mobility and the queer nocturnal gropings of its roots aside—*I had finally recognised in Old Cartwright's actions an exact replica of my own earlier that night!*

I lurched drunkenly down the hall to the door and unlocked it with fumbling, dead fingers. I tottered out into the night knowing that something monstrously unnatural was happening, aware that but for pure good fortune I might have been in the old man's place. As the night air hit me I regained control and ran down the garden yelling to the old man to get away—to get well away from the tree, the glowing horror…

But I was too late!

His naked feet stuck out from under the bright monster's branches—branches which were all folded downwards, covering his body. Then, as I went down on my knees in shock and disbelief, I saw that which twisted my mind and blasted my nerves into these useless knots that they have been ever since.

I had had the right idea about the tree—but I had looked at the problem in the wrong way! The thing was a freak, a mutation caused by radiations from another world. It had no parallel on Earth; and I, like a fool, had tried to compare it with the fly-traps. True, the thing from the blasted heath *did* draw its nourishment from living things, *but the manner of its feeding was nonetheless the same as for most other soil-sprouted plants—it fed through its roots*!

Those slender roots, hidden from above by the way in which the branches had folded down, were all sharply thorned—and for each thorn there was a tiny sucker. Even as I watched, hypnotised, those vile roots were pulsing down into Cartwright's open mouth…until his lips began to split under the strain of their loathsome contents!

I began to scream as I saw the veins in the trunk and branches start their scarlet pulsing, and, as the entire plant commenced throbbing with a pale, pinkish suffusion, I passed into a merciful oblivion. *For Old Cartwright's entire body was jerking and twitching with a nauseating internal action which was not its own—and all the time his dead eyes stared and stared…*

There is not much more to tell. When I recovered consciousness I was still half insane. In a gibbering delirium I staggered to the woodshed and returned with the axe. Moaning in morbid loathing I cut the tree—once, twice—deeply across the trunk, and in a fit of uncontrollable twitching I watched the horror literally *bleed* to death!

The end had to be seen to be believed. Slowly the evil roots withdrew from Cartwright's body, shuddering and sluggishly pulling back underground, releasing their grisly internal hold on his bloodless form. The branches and leaves writhed and twined in a morbid dance of death; the horrible veins—*real* veins—pulsed to a standstill and the whole tree started to slope sideways as a terrible disintegration took hold on it. The unnatural glow surrounding the thing dimmed as it began visibly to rot where it stood. The smell of utter corruption which soon started to exude from the compost the hell-plant was rapidly becoming forced me to back away, dragging Old Cartwright's corpse after me.

I was brought up short by the garden fence and that was where I stayed, shivering and staring at the rapidly blackening mass in the garden.

When at last the glow had died away completely and all that remained of the tree was an odorous, sticky, reddish-black puddle, I noticed that the first light of dawn was already brightening the sky. It was then that I formed my plan. I had had more than my fill of horror—all I wanted to do was forget—and I knew the authorities would never believe my story; not that I intended trying to tell it.

I made a bonfire over the stinking spot where the plant had been, and as the first cock crowed in the distance I set fire to the pile of leaves and sticks and stood there until there was only a blackened patch on the grass to show that the horror from the heath had ever stood there. Then I dressed and walked into Marske to the police station.

No one could quite understand the absence of Old Cartwright's blood or the damage to his mouth and the other—internal—injuries which the post-mortem later showed; but it was undeniable that he had been "queer" for a long time and lately had been heard to talk openly about things that "glowed at night" and trees with hands instead of leaves. Everyone had known, it appeared, that he would end up "in a funny way".

After I made my statement to the police—about how I had found Old Cartwright's body at dawn, in my garden—I put through another call to London and told my botanist friend that the tree had been destroyed in a garden fire. He said that it was unfortunate but did not really matter. He had to catch an evening plane to South America anyway and would be away for many months.

He asked me to see if I could get another specimen in the meantime.

But that is not quite the end of the story. All that I have related happened last summer. It is already spring. The birds have still not returned to my garden and though each night I take a sleeping pill before locking my door I cannot rest.

I thought that in ridding myself of the remainder of my collection I might also kill the memory of that which once stood in my garden. I was wrong.

It makes no difference that I have given away my conches from the islands of Polynesia and have shattered into fragments the skull I dug from beneath the ground where once stood a Roman ruin. Letting my *Dionaea Muscipulas* die from lack of their singular nourishment has not helped me at all! My devil-drums and death-masks from Africa now rest beneath glass in Wharby Museum along with the sacrificial gown from Mua-Aphos. My collection of ten nightmare paintings by Pickman, Chandler Davies and Clark Ashton Smith now belong to an avid American collector, to whom I have also sold my complete set of Poe's works. I have melted down my Iceland meteorite and parted forever with the horribly inscribed silver figurine from India. The silvery fragments of unknown crystal from dead G'harne rest untended in their box and I have sold in auction all my books of Earth's elder madness.

Yes, that which I once boasted of as being the finest collection of morbid and macabre curiosities outside of the British Museum is no more; yet still I am unable to sleep. There is something—some fear that keeps me awake—which has caused me of late to chain myself to the bed when I lie down.

You see, I know that my doctor's assurance that it is "all in my mind" is at fault, and I know that if ever I wake up in the garden again it will mean permanent insanity—or worse!

For the spot where the spring grass is twisted and yellow continues to glow feebly at night. Only a week ago I decided to clear the very soil from that area but as soon as I drove my spade into the ground I was sure I saw something black and wriggly—*like a looped off root*—squirm quickly down out of sight! Perhaps it is my imagination but I have also noticed, in the dead of night, that the floorboards sometimes creak beneath my room—and then, of course, there is that *other* thing.

I get the most dreadful headaches.

DYLATH-LEEN

In my first couple of months as a recruiter—in March 1969, to be precise—I wrote my first Dreamlands story, "after" HPL of course. While "Dylath-Leen" would later go into my Titus Crow/De Marigny Mythos novel The Clock of Dreams *as a chapter in its own right, at the time of writing it was my first attempt at this sort of story. As such it was mainly unconnected to later Dreamlands stories that would feature David Hero (called "Hero of Dreams") and his fellow adventurer Eldin ("the Wanderer"), which wouldn't be written until the late 1970s–early '80s. Anyway, after reading the story in my Arkham collection* The Caller of The Black, *L. Sprague de Camp particularly liked it and wrote to ask if he might include it in a fantasy collection he was planning. Well, that never happened, but in any case it was nice to know that this fine author had enjoyed it. And it's my hope that you will too.*

> *"If aught of evil ever befalls the people of Dylath-Leen, through their traffick with certain traders of ill repute, then it will not be my fault."*
> —Randolph Carter

I

Three times only have I visited the basalt-towered, myriad-wharved city of Dylath-Leen; three curious visits which spanned I fancy almost a century of that city's existence. Now I pray that I have seen it for the last time; for though Dylath-Leen exists only in dream, beyond the ghoul-guarded gateways of slumber, when I think back on my visits there—remembering my waking studies and those tales heard in my youth of dreams and how they affect the waking world—then I shudder in strange dread.

I went there first in my late teens, filled with a longing—engendered by continuous study of such works as *The Arabian Nights* and Gelder's *Atlantis Found*—for wondrous places of antique legend and fable and centuried cities of ages past; nor was my longing disappointed.

I first saw the city from afar, wandering in along the river Skai with a caravan of merchants from distant places, and at sight of the tall black towers which form the city's ramparts I felt a strange fascination for the place. Later, lost in awe and wonder, I took leave of my merchant friends to walk Dylath-Leen's ancient streets and alleys, to visit the wharfside sea-taverns and chat with seamen from every land on Earth—and with a few from more distant places. I never once pondered my ability to chatter in their many tongues, for often things are simpler in dream, nor did I wonder at the ease with which I fitted myself into the alien yet surprisingly friendly scene; after all, I was attired in robes of dream's styling, and my looks were not unlike those of many of dream's peoples. I was a little taller than average, true, but overall Dylath-Leen's diverse folks might well have passed for those of any town of the waking world, and vice versa.

Yet there were in the city others, strange traders from across the Southern Sea, whose appearance and *odour* filled me with a dread loathing so that I could not abide to stay near where they were for long. Of these traders and their origin I questioned the tavern-keepers, to be told that I was not the first from the waking world whose instinct found in those traders traces of hinted evil and deeds not to be mentioned. Another had warned long ago that they were fiends not to be trusted, whose only desire was to spread horror and evil throughout all the lands of dream. Certain of the taverners even remembered that dreamer's name; Randolph Carter, he had called himself, and had been known to be a personal friend of that great lord of sky-floating Serannian and of the rose-crystal Palace of the Seventy Delights at Celephais, King Kuranes, once a dreamer of no mean repute himself. But when I heard Carter's name mentioned I was quietened, for an amateur at dreaming such as myself could not dare aspire to walk even in the shadow of one such as he. Why! Carter was rumoured to have been even to Kadath in the Cold Waste, to confront Nyarlathotep the Crawling Chaos, and more—he had returned from that place unscathed! How many could boast of that?

Yet loath though I was to have anything to do with those traders, I found myself one morning in the towering tavern of Potan-Lith, in a high bar-room the windows of which looked out over the Bay of Wharves, waiting for the galley I had heard was coming to the city with a cargo of rubies from an unknown shore. I wanted to discover just what it was of them which so repelled me, and the best way to do this, I thought, would be to observe them from a safe distance and location at which I, myself, might go unobserved. I did not wish to bring myself to the notice of those queerly frightening people of unguessed origin. Potan-Lith's tavern with its ninety-nine steps served my purpose admirably. I could see the whole of the wharf-side spread beneath me in the morning light; the nets of the fishermen drying, with smells of rope and deep ocean floating up to my window; the smaller craft of private tradesmen rolling gently at anchor, sails lowered and hatches laid back to let the sun dry out their musty holds; the thagweed merchants unloading their strongly scented, dream-within-dream-engendering opiates garnered in exotic Eastern parts; and, eventually appearing on the horizon, the sails of the black galley for which I so vigilantly waited. There were other traders of the sane race already in the city, to be sure, but how could one get close to them without attracting unwanted attention? My plan of observation was best, I was certain, but I did not know just what it was I wished to observe—nor why…

It was not long before the black galley loomed against the entrance to the bay. It slipped into the harbour past the great basalt lighthouse and a strange stench driven by the South Wind came with it. As with the coming of all such craft and their weird masters, uneasiness rippled all along the waterfront as the silent ship closed with its chosen wharf and its three banks of briskly moving oars stilled and slipped in through their oarlocks to the unseen and equally silent rowers within. I watched eagerly then, waiting for the galley's master and crew to come ashore, but only five persons—if persons they truly were—chose to leave that enigmatic craft. This was the best look at such traders I had so far managed, and what I saw did not please me at all.

I have intimated my doubts with regard to the humanity of those…men? Let me explain why. Firstly their mouths were far too wide. Indeed, I thought that one of them glanced up at my window as he left the ship, smiling a smile which only just fell within the boundaries of that word's limitations, and it was horrible to see just how wide his evil mouth was. Now what would any eater of normal foods want with a mouth of such abnormal proportions? And for that matter, why did the owners of such mouths wear such queerly moulded turbans? Or was it simply the way in which the turbans were worn? For they were humped up in two points over the foreheads of the wearers in what seemed especially bad taste. And as for their shoes: well, those shoes were certainly the most peculiar footwear I had ever seen—in or out of dreams—being short, blunt-toed and flat, as though the feet within were not feet at all! I thoughtfully finished off my mug of muth-dew and wedge of bread and cheese, turning from the window to leave the tavern of Potan-Lith.

My heart seemed to leap into my mouth. There in the low entrance stood that same merchant who had so evilly smiled up at my window! His turbaned head turned to follow my every move as I sidled out past him and flew down the ninety-nine steps to the wharf below. An awful fear pursued me as I ran through the alleys and streets, making my feet fly faster on the basalt flags of the wider pavements, until I reached the well known, green-cobbled court-yard wherein I had my room. But even there I could not get the face of that strangely turbaned, wide-mouthed trader from beyond the Southern Sea out of my mind—nor his smell from my nostrils—so I paid my landlord his due, moving out there and then to head for that side of Dylath-Leen which faces away from the sea and which is clean with the scents of window-box flowers and baking bread, where the men of the sea-taverns but rarely venture.

There, in the district called S'eemla, I found myself lodging with a family of basalt quarriers. I was accorded my own garret room with a wide window, a bed and mattress of fegg-down; and soon it was as though I had been born into the family, or might have seemed so had I been able to imagine myself a brother to comely Litha.

Within the month I was firmly settled in, and from then on I made it my business to carry on Randolph Carter's word of warning, putting in my word against the turbaned traders at every opportunity. My task was made no easier by the fact that I had nothing concrete to hold against them. There was only the feeling, already shared by many of the folk of Dylath-Leen, that trade between the city and the black galleys could bring to fruition nothing of any good.

Eventually my knowledge of the traders grew to include such evidences as to make me more certain than ever of their evil nature. Why should those black galleys come in to harbour, discharge their four or five traders, and then simply lie there at anchor, emitting their foul odours, showing never a sign of their silent crews? That there were crews seems needless to state; with three great banks of oars to each ship there must have been many rowers! But what man could say just who or what such rowers were? Too, the grocers and butchers of the city grumbled over the apparent frugality of those singularly shy crews, for the only things the traders bought with their great and small rubies were gold and stout Pargian slaves. This traffic had gone on for years, I was told, and in that time many a fat black man had vanished, never to be seen again, up the gangplanks into those mysterious galleys to be transported to lands across uncharted seas—if, indeed, such lands were their destination! And where did the queer traders get their rubies, the like of which were to be found in no known mine in all Earth's dreamland? Yet those rubies came cheaply enough, too cheaply in fact, so that every home in Dylath-Leen sported them, some large enough to be used as paperweights in the homes of the richer merchants. Myself, I found those gems strangely loathsome, seeing in them only the reflections of the traders who brought them from across nameless oceans.

So it was that in the district called S'eemla my interest in the ruby-traders waxed to its full, paled, waned and finally withered—but never died completely. My new interest, however, in dark-eyed Litha, Bo-Kareth's daughter, grew with each passing day, and my nights were filled with dreams within dreams of Litha and her ways, so that only occasionally were my slumbers invaded by the unpleasantly turbaned, wide-mouthed traders from unknown parts.

One evening, after a trip out to Ti-Penth, a village not far from Dylath-Leen where we had enjoyed the annual Festival of Plenty, as Litha and I walked back, hand in hand, through the irrigated green valley called Tanta towards our black towered city, she told me of her love and we sank together to the darkling sward. That night, when the city's myriad twinkling lights had all blinked out and the bats chittered thick without my window, Litha crept into my garret room and only the narg-oil lamp on the wall could tell of the wonders we knew with each other.

In the morning, rising rapidly in joy from my dreams within dreams, I broke through too many layers of that flimsy stuff which constitutes the world of the subconscious, to waken with a cry of agony in the house of my parents at Norden on the North-East coast. Thereafter I cried myself to sleep for a year before finally I managed to convince myself that my dark-eyed Litha existed only in dreams.

II

I was thirty years old before I saw Dylath-Leen again. I arrived in the evening, when the city was all but in darkness, but I recognised immediately the feel of those basalt flagstones beneath my feet, and, while the last of the myriad lights flickered out in the towers and the last tavern closed, my heart leaped as I turned my suddenly light feet towards the house of Bo-Kareth. But something did not seem right, and a horror grew rapidly upon me as I saw in the streets thickening crowds of carousing, nastily chattering, strangely turbaned people not quite so much men as monsters. And many of them had had their turbans disarrayed in their sporting so that protuberances glimpsed previously only in books of witchcraft and the like and in certain biblical paintings showed clearly through! Once I was stopped and pawed vilely by a group of them who conferred in low, menacing tones. I tore myself free and fled for they were, indeed, those same evil traders of yore, and I was horrified that they should be there in my City of Black Towers in such great numbers!

I must have seen hundreds of those vile—creatures—as I hurried through the city's thoroughfares; yet somehow I contrived to arrive at the house of Bo-Kareth without further pause or hindrance, and there I hammered at his oaken door until a light flickered behind the round panes of blue glass in the upper sections of that entrance. It was Bo-Kareth himself who eventually came to answer my banging, and he came wide-eyed in a fear I could well understand. Relief showed visibly in his whole aspect when he saw that only a man stood upon his step. Although he seemed amazingly *aged*—so aged, in fact, I was taken aback, for I did not then know of the differences in time between the worlds of dream and waking—he recognised me at once, whispering my name:

"Grant! Grant Enderby...my friend...my *old* friend...! Come in, come in..."

"Bo-Kareth," I burst out, "Bo, I—"

"Shhh!" He pressed a finger to his lips, eyes widening even further than before, leaning out to glance up and down the street before pulling me in and quickly closing and bolting the door behind me. "Quietly, Grant, quietly— this is a city of silence now, where *they* alone carouse and make their own hellish brand of merry—and they may soon be abroad and about their business."

"*They?*" I questioned, instinctively knowing the answer.

"Those you once tried to warn us of—the turbaned traders!"

"I thought as much," I answered, "and they're already abroad, I've seen them—but what *business* is this you speak of?"

Then Bo-Kareth told me a tale that filled my heart with horror and determined me never to rest until I had at least attempted to right a great wrong.

It had started a number of years earlier, according to my host—(I made no attempt to pin-point a date; how could I when Bo-Kareth had apparently aged thirty years to my twelve?)—and had involved the bringing to the city of a ruby so gigantic that it had to be seen to be believed. This great gem had been a gift, an assurance of the traders' regard for Dylath-Leen's peoples, and as such had been set on a pedestal in the city's main square. But only a few nights later the horror had started to make itself noticeable. The keeper of a tavern near the square, peering from his windows after locking the doors for the night, had noticed a strange, deep, reddish glow from the giant gem's heart; a glow which seemed to pulse with an alien life all its own, and when the tavern-keeper told the next day of what he had seen an amazing thing came to light. All the other galley-brought rubies in the city—the smaller gems set in rings, amulets and instruments, and those larger, less ornamental, almost rude stones owned purely for the sake of ownership by certain of the city's richer gentlemen—had *all* glowed through the night to a lesser degree, as if in response to the greater activity of their bulky brother. And with that unearthly glowing of the gems had come a strange partial paralysis, making all the people of the city other than the turbaned traders themselves slumbrous and weak, incapable and unwanting of any festivity and barely able to go about their normal duties and businesses. As the days passed and the power of the great ruby and its less regal relatives waxed, so also did the strange drowsiness upon Dylath-Leen's folks; and it was only then, too late, that the plot was seen and its purpose recognised.

For a long time there had been a shortage of the fat black slaves of Parg. They had been taken from the city by the traders faster than they came in, until only a handful remained; and that handful, on hearing one day of a black galley soon due to dock, had fled their master and left the city to seek less suspicious bondage. That had been shortly before the horned traders brought the great jewel to Dylath-Leen, and since that time, as the leering, gem-induced lethargy had increased until its effects were felt in daylight almost as much as they were at night—so had the number of strangely shod traders grown until the docks were full of their great black galleys. Then inexplicable *absences* began to be noticed; a taverner here and a quarrier there, a merchant from Ulthar and a thagweed curer and a silversmith's son; and soon any retaining sufficient will-power sold up their businesses, homes and houses and left Dylath-Leen for Ti-Penth, Ulthar and Nir. I was glad to learn that Litha and her brothers had thus departed, though it made me strangely sad to hear that when lithe Litha went she took with her a handsome husband and two laughing children.

She was old enough now, her father told me, to be mistaken for my mother; but she still retained her great beauty.

By this time the hour of midnight was well passed and all about the house tiny red points of light had begun to glow in an eerie, slumber-engendering coruscation. As Bo-Kareth, talked his monologue interrupted now with many a yawn and shake of his head, I tracked down the sources of those weird points of radiance and found them to be rubies. It was as Bo-Kareth had described it, rubies!—ten tiny gems set in the base of an ornamental goblet; many more of the small red stones enhancing the looks of hanging silver and gold plates; fire-flashing splinters of precious crystal embedded in the spines of certain of my host's leather-bound books of prayer and dream-lore—and when his mumbling had died away completely I turned from my investigations to find the old man asleep in his chair, lost in distressing dreams which pulled his grey face into an expression of muted terror.

I had to see the great gem. I make no excuse for such a rash and head-strong decision (one does things in dreams which one would never consider for a moment in the waking world), but I knew I could make no proper plans nor rest easy in my mind until I had seen that great ruby for myself.

I left the house by the back door, locking it behind me and pocketing the key. I knew Bo-Kareth had a duplicate key and besides, I might later need to be into the house without delay. The layout of the city was well known to me and thus it was not difficult for me to find my way through labyrinthine back streets to the main square. That square was away from the district of S'eemla, far nearer to the docks, and the closer I drew to the waterfront the more careful I crept. Why!—the whole area was alive with the alien and evil traders! The wonder is that I was not spotted in the first few minutes; and when I saw what those hellish creatures were up to, thus confirming beyond a shadow of a doubt Bo-Kareth's worst fears, the possibility that I might yet be observed—and the consequences such an unfortunate discovery would bring—caused me to creep even more carefully. Each street corner became a focal point for terror, where lurking, unseen presences caused me to glance over my shoulder or jump at the slightest flutter of bat-wings or scurry of mouse-feet. And then, almost before I knew it, I came upon the square.

I came at the run, my feet flying frantically, for I knew now for sure what the horned ones did at night and a fancy had grown quickly on me that something followed in the dark; so that when I suddenly burst from that darkness into a blaze of red firelight I was taken completely by surprise. I literally keeled over backwards as I contrived to halt my flight of fear before it plunged me into the four turbaned terrors standing at the base of the dais of the jewel. My feet skidded as I pivoted on my heels and my fingers scrabbled madly at the round cobbles of the square as I fell. In truth it could scarce be called a real fall—I was no sooner down than up—but in that split second or so as I fought to bring my careening body under control those guardians of the great stone were after me. Glancing fearfully back I saw them darting rat-like in my wake.

My exit from that square can only properly be described as panic-stricken, but brief though my visit had been I had seen more than enough to strenghthen that first resolve of mine to do something about the loathsome and insidious invasion of the traders. Backtracking, bounding through the night streets I went, with the houses and taverns towering blackly on both sides, seeing in my mind's eye that horrible haunting picture which I had but glimpsed in the main square. There had been the four guards with great knives fastened in their belts, the dais with pyramid steps to its flat summit, four hugely flaring torches in blackly forged metal holders, and, atop the basalt altar itself, a great reddish mass pulsing with inner life, its myriad facets catching and reflecting the fire of the torches in a mixture with its own evil radiance. The hypnotic horror—the malignant monster—the great ruby!

Then the vision changed as I heard close behind me a weird, ululant cry—a definite *alert*—which carried and echoed in Dylath-Leen's canyon alleys. In rampant revulsion I pictured myself linked by an iron anklet to the long chain of mute, unprotesting people which I had seen only minutes earlier being led in the direction of the docks and the black galleys, and this monstrous mental image drove my feet to a frenzied activity that sent me speeding headlong down the dark passages between the city's basalt walls. But fast and furious though my flight was it soon became apparent that my pursuers were gaining on me. A faint padding came to my ears as I ran, causing me to accelerate, forcing my feet to pump even faster. The effort was useless—if anything, *worse* than useless—for I soon tired and had to slow up. Twice I stumbled and the second time, as I struggled to rise, the fumbling of slimy fingers at my feet lent them wings and shot me out in front again. It became as one of those nightmares (which indeed it was), where you run and run through vast vats of subconscious molasses, totally unable to increase the distance between yourself and your ethereal pursuer; the only difference being, dream or none, that I knew for a certainty I was running for my life!

It was a few moments later, when an added horror had just about brought me to the verge of giving up hope, that I found an unexpected but welcome reprieve. Slipping and stumbling, panting for air, I had been brought up short by a mad fancy that the soft padding of alien feet now came from the very direction in which I was heading, from somewhere in *front* of me! And as those sounds of demon footfalls came closer, closing in on me, I flattened myself to the basalt wall, spreading my arms and groping desperately with my hands at the bare, rough stone; and there, beneath my unbelieving fingers—*an opening!*—a narrow crack or entry, completely hidden in jet shadows, between two of the street's bleak bindings. I squeezed myself in, trying to get my breathing under control, fighting a lunatic urge to cry out in my terror. It was pitch black, the blackness of the pit, and a hideous thought suddenly came to me. What if this tunnel of darkness—this possible doorway to sanity—what if it were closed, a dead end? Then, as if in answer to my silent, frantic prayers, even as I heard the first squawk of amazed frustration from somewhere behind me, I squirmed from the other end of the division to emerge in a street mercifully void of the evil aliens.

My flight had carried me in a direction well away from Bo-Kareth's house; but in any case, now that my worst fears were realized and the alarm raised, it would have been completely idiotic to think of hiding anywhere in the city. I had to get away, to Ulthar or Nir, as far as possible—and as fast as possible—until I could try to find a way to rid Dylath-Leen of its inhuman curse.

Less than an hour later, with the city behind me, I was in an uninhabited desert area heading in a direction which I hoped would eventually bring me to Ulthar. It was cool beneath that full, cloud-floating moon, yet a long while passed before the fever of my panic-flight left me. When it did I was almost sorry, for soon I found myself shivering as the sweat of my body turned icy chill, and I wrapped my cloak more tightly about me for I knew it must grow still colder before the dawn. I was not particularly worried about food and water, there are many water-holes and oases between Dylath-Leen and Ulthar; no, my main cause for concern lay in orientation. I did not want to end up wandering in one of the many great parched deserts! My sense of direction in open country had never been very good.

Before long great clouds came drifting in from a direction I took to be the South, obscuring the moon until only the stars in the sky ahead gave any light by which to travel. Then, it seemed, the dune-cast shadows grew blacker and longer and an eerie sensation of not being alone waxed in me. I found myself casting sharp, nervous glances over my shoulder and shuddering to an extent not entirely warranted by the chill of the night. There came fixed in my mind an awful suspicion which I had to resolve one way or the other.

I hid behind a dune and waited, peering back the way I had come. Soon I saw a darting shadow moving swiftly over the sand, following my trail—and that shadow was endowed with twin points at its top and chuckled obscenely as it came. My hair stood on end as I saw the creature stop to study the ground, then lift its wide-mouthed face to the night sky. I heard again that weird, ululant cry of alert and I waited no longer.

In a passion of fear even greater than that I had known in the streets of Dylath-Leen I fled—racing like a madman over the night sands, gibbering and mumbling in my flight, scrambling and often falling head over heels down the sides of the steeper sandhills—until my head struck something hard in the shadow of a dune and I passed into the even deeper darkness of lower unconsciousness.

This time I was far from sorry when I leapt screaming awake at my home in Norden; and in the sanity of the waking world I recognised the fact that all those horrors of dream and the night had existed only in my slumbers; so that in a few days my second visit to Dylath-Leen was all but forgotten. The mind soon forgets that which it cannot bear to remember.

III

I was forty-three when next—when last—I saw Dylath-Leen. Not that my dream took me straight to the basalt city; rather I found myself first on the outskirts of Ulthar, the City of Cats! Ulthar is well named, for in that city an ancient law decrees that no man may kill a cat, and the streets crowd with many a variety of soft-furred feline. I stooped to pet a fat tom lazily sunning himself in the street, and an ancient shopkeeper seated outside his store beneath a great shade called out to me in a friendly, quavering voice:

"It is good, stranger—it is good when a stranger pets the cats of Ulthar! Have you journeyed far?"

"Far," I affirmed, "from the waking world—but even there I stop to play when I see a cat. Tell me, Sir—can you direct me to the house of Litha, daughter of Bo-Kareth of Dylath-Leen?'

"Indeed, I know her well," he nodded his old head, "'for she is one of the few in Ulthar with as many years to count as I. She lives with her husband and family not far from here. Until some years ago her father—who was ancient beyond belief, second only in years to Atal, climber of Hatheg-Kla and priest and patriarch of Ulthar's Temple of the Elder Ones—also lived at his daughter's house. He came out of Dylath-Leen mazed and mumbling, and did not live long here in Ulthar. Now no man goes to Dylath-Leen."

But the old man had soured at the thought of Dylath-Leen and did not wish to talk any longer. I took his directions and started off with mixed feelings along the street he had indicated; but only half-way up that street I cut off down a dusty alley and made for the Temple of the Elder Ones instead. It could do no good to see Litha now. What use to wake old memories?—if indeed she were capable of remembering anything of those Elysian days of her youth—and it was not as though she might help me solve my problem—that same problem of thirteen waking years ago: how to avenge the outraged peoples of Dylath-Leen; and how to rescue those of them—if any such existed—still enslaved. For there was still a feeling of yearning in me for the black-towered city and its peoples of yore. I remembered the friends I had known and my many walks through the high-walled streets and along the farm lanes of the outskirts. Yet even in Elysian S'eemla the knowledge that certain offensive black galleys moored in the docks had somehow always sufficed to dull my appetite for living, had even impaired the happiness I had known with dark-eyed Litha, in the garret of Bo-Kareth's house, with the bats of night clustered thick and chittering beneath the sill without my window.

As quickly as the vision of Litha the girl came I put it out of my mind, striding out more purposefully for the Temple of the Elder Ones. If any man could help me in my bid for vengeance against the turbaned traders Atal, the Priest of the Temple, was that man. Atal had even climbed the forbidden peak, Hatheg-Kla, in the stony desert, and had come down again alive and sane! It was rumoured that in the temple he had keep of many incredible volumes of sorcery. His great knowledge of the darker mysteries was, in fact, my main reason for seeking his aid. I could hardly hope to engage the forces of the hell-traders with physical means alone.

It was then, as I left the little green cottages and neatly fenced farms and shady shops of the suburbs behind me, as I pressed more truly into the city proper, that I received a shock so powerful my soul almost withered within me.

I had allowed myself to become interested in the old peaked roofs, the overhanging upper storeys, numberless chimney-pots and narrow, old cobbled streets of the city, so that my attention had been diverted from the path my feet followed, causing me to bump rudely into someone coming out of the narrow door of a shop. Of a sudden the air was foul with shuddersome, well-remembered odours of hideous connection, and my hackles rose as I backed quickly away from the strangely turbaned, squat figure I had chanced into. The slightly tilted eyes regarded me curiously and a wicked smile played around the too wide mouth.

One of *Them*! Here in Ulthar?

I mumbled incoherent apologies, slipped past the still evilly grinning figure, and ran all the rest of the way to the Temple of the Elder Ones. If there had been any suggestion of half-heartedness to my intentions earlier there was certainly none now! It seemed obvious to me the course events were taking. First it had been Dylath-Leen, now an attempt at Ulthar—where next? Nowhere, if I had anything to say of it.

The Temple of the Elder Ones stands round and towering, of ivied stone, atop Ulthar's highest hill; and there, in the Room of Ancient Records, I found the patriarch I sought—Atal of Hatheg-Kla; Atal the Ancient. He sat, in flowing black and gold robes, at a centuried wooden bench, fading eyes studiously lost in the yellowed pages of a great aeon-worn book, its metal hasps dully agleam in a stray beam of sunlight striking in from the single high window.

He looked up, starting as if in shock as I entered the musty room with its myriad book-shelves. Then he pushed his book away and spoke:

"The Priest of the Temple greets you, stranger. You *are* a stranger, are you not?"

"I have seen Ulthar before," I answered, "but, yes, I am a stranger here in the Temple of the Elder Ones. I come from the waking world, Atal, to seek your help…"

"You—you *surprised* me. You are not the first from the waking world to ask my aid. I thought at first sight that I knew you of old. How are you named and in what manner might I serve you?"

"My name is Grant Enderby, Atal, and the help I ask is not for myself. I come in the hope that you might be able to help me rid Dylath-Leen of a certain contagion; but since coming to Ulthar today I have learned that even here the sores are spreading. Are there not even now in Ulthar strange traders from no clearly named land? Is it not so?"

"It is so," he nodded his venerable head. "Say on."

"Then you should know that they are those same traders who brought Dylath-Leen to slavery—an evil, hypnotic slavery—and I fancy that they mean to use the same black arts here in Ulthar to a like end. Do they trade rubies the like of which are found in no known mine in the whole of dreamland?"

Again he nodded: "They do; but say no more—I am already aware. At this very moment I search for a means by which the trouble may be put to an end. But I work only on rumours, and I am unable to leave the temple to verify those rumours. My duties are all important, and in any case, these bones are too old to wander far. Truly, Dylath-Leen did suffer an evil fate; but think not that her peoples had no warning! Why, even a century ago the city's reputation was bad, through the presence of those very traders you have mentioned! Another dreamer before you saw the doom in store for the city, speaking against those traders vehemently and often; but his words were soon forgotten by all who heard them and people went their old ways as of yore. No man may help him who will not help himself! But it is the presence of those traders here in Ulthar which has driven me to this search of mine. I cannot allow the same doom to strike here—whatever that doom may be— yet it is difficult to see what may be done. No man of this town will venture anywhere near Dylath-Leen. It is said that the streets of that city have known no human feet for more than twenty years, nor can any man say with any certainty where the city's peoples have gone."

"I can say!" I answered. "Not *where*, exactly; but *how* at least! Enslaved, I said, and told no lie. I had it first from Bo-Kareth, late of Dylath-Leen, who told me that when those traders had taken all the fat black slaves of Parg in exchange for those evil stones of theirs, they brought to the city the biggest ruby ever seen—a boulder of a gem—leaving it on a pedestal in the main square as a false token of esteem. It was the evil influence of this great jewel that bewitched the people of Dylath-Leen, bemusing them to such a degree that in the end they, too, became slaves to be led away to the black galleys of the traders. And now, apparently, those traders have...*used up*...all the peoples of that ill-omened city and are starting their monstrous game here! And Bo-Kareth's story was true in every detail, for with my own eyes—"

"A great ruby...hmmm!" Atal musingly cut me off, stroking his face and frowning in concentration. "That puts a different complexion on it—yes, I believe that in the *Fourth Book*...there may be a mention! Shall we see?"

I nodded my eager agreement and at Atal's direction lifted down from a corner shelf the largest and weightiest tome I had ever seen. Each single page—pages of no material I had ever known before—glowed with burning letters which stood out with fire-fly definition in the dimness of the room. I could make nothing of the unique ciphers within that book, but Atal seemed thoroughly familiar with each alien character, translating easily, mumbling to himself in barely discernable tones, until suddenly he stopped. He lurched shakily to his feet then, slamming the priceless volume shut, horror burning in his ancient eyes.

"So!" he exclaimed, hissing out the word, "It is *that*! The Fly-the-Light from Yuggoth on the Rim, a vampyre in the worst meaning of the word; and we must make sure that it is never brought to Ulthar!" He paused, visibly taking hold of himself before he could continue:

"Let me tell you...

318

"Long ago, before dreams, in the primal mist of the pre-dawn Beginning of All, the great ruby was brought from distant Yuggoth on the Rim by the Old Ones. Within that jewel, prisoned by light and the magic of the Old Ones, lurks a basic avatar of the prime evil, a thing hideous as the pit itself! Understand, Grant Enderby, it is not the stone that induces the hypnotic weariness of which you have spoken, but the thing *within* the stone, the evil influence of the Fly-the-Light from dark Yuggoth on the Rim! Few men know the history of that huge jewel, and I do not consider myself fortunate to be one of the few.

"It is told that it was discovered after coming down in an avalanche from the heights of forbidden Hatheg-Kla—which I can believe for I know much of that mountain—discovered and carried away by the Black Princess, Yath-Lhi of Tyrhhia. And when her caravan reached her silver-spired city it was found that all Yath-Lhi's men at arms, her slaves, even the Black Princess herself, were as zombies, altered and mazed. It is not remembered now where Tyrhhia once stood, but many believe the centuried desert sands to cover even its tallest spire, and that the remains of its habitants lie putrid within their buried houses.

"But the ruby was not buried with Tyrhhia, more's the pity, and rumour has it that it was next discovered in a golden galley on the Southern Sea twixt Dylath-Leen and the isle of Oriab. A strange ocean is the Southern Sea, and especially between Oriab and Dylath-Leen; for there, many fathoms deep, lies a basalt city with a temple and monolithic altar. And sailors are loath to pass over that submarine city, fearing the great storms which legend has it strike suddenly; even when there is no breath of wind to stir the sails! However, there the great jewel was found, aboard a great golden galley, and the crew of that galley were very beautiful even though they were not men, and all were long dead but not corrupt! Only one sailor, mad and babbling, was later rescued from the sea off Oriab to gibber pitifully the tale of the golden galley, but of his fellow crew-mates nothing more is known. It is interesting to note that it is further writ how only certain peoples—they who are horned and who dance to the evil drone of pipes and rattle of crotala in mysterious Leng—are unaffected by the stone's proximity!" Atal looked at me knowingly. "And I can see you have already noticed how strangely our traders wear their turbans.

"But I digress. Again the jewel survived whatever fate overtook the poor seamen who rescued it from the golden galley, and it was later worshipped by the enormous dholes in the Vale of Pnath, until three leathery night-gaunts flew off with it over the Peaks of Throk and down into those places of subterrene horror of which certain dim myths hint most terribly. For that underworld is said to be a place litten only by pale death-fires, a place reeking of ghoulish exhalations and filled with the primal mists which swirl in the pits at Earth's core. Who may say what form the inhabitants of such a place might take?"

At this point Atal's eyes cleared of their far-away look and turned from the dark places of his tale to the present and to me. He placed his rheumy hands on my shoulders, peering at me earnestly: "Well, so says legend and the *Fourth Book of D'harsis*; and now, you say, the great ruby is come again into the known places of Earth's dreamland. Now hear you, Grant Enderby, I know what must be done—but how may I ask any man to take such risks? For my plan involves not only the risk of destruction to the mortal body— but the possible eternal damnation of the immortal soul!"

"I have pledged myself," I told him, "to avenge the peoples of Dylath-Leen. My pledge still stands, for though Dylath-Leen is lost, yet are there other towns and cities in dreams which I would dream again—but not to see them corrupted by horned horrors that trade in fever-cursed rubies! Atal—tell me what I must do."

Atal then got to it, and there was much for him to do. I could not help him with the greater part of his work, tasks involving the translation into language I could understand of certain tracts from the *Fourth Book of D'harsis*, for, even though many things are simpler in dream, those passages were not meant to be read by any man—neither awake nor sleeping—who did not understand their importance.

Slowly but surely the hours passed and Atal laboured as I watched, putting down letter after letter in the creation of pronounceable syllables from the seemingly impossible mumbo-jumbo of the great book from which he drew. I began to recognise certain symbols I had seen in allegedly "forbidden" tomes in the waking world, and even began to mumble the first of them aloud— *"Tetragrammaton Thabaite Sabaoth Tethiktos"*—until Atal silenced me by jerking to his feet and favouring me with a gaze of pure horror.

"It is almost night," he remonstrated, striking a flint to a wax candle, his hands shaking more than even his extreme age might reasonably explain, "and outside the shadows are lengthening. Would you call *That* forth without first having protection? For make no mistake, distance is no matter to this invocation, and if we wished we could call out the Fly-the-Light even from here. But first you must cast a spell over Dylath-Leen, to contain the thing when you release it from the ruby; for certainly unless it is contained it will ravish the whole of dreamland; and you, the caller, The Utterer of The Words, would be one of the first to die—horribly!"

I gulped my apologies and sat silently from then on, listening attentively to Atal's instructions even as my eyes followed his scratching pen. "You must go to Dylath-Leen," he told me, "taking with you the two incantations I now prepare. One of them, which you will keep at your left, is to build the Wall of Naach-Tith about the city. To work this spell you must journey around Dylath-Leen, returning to your starting point and crossing it, chanting the words as you go. This means, of course, that you will need to cross the bay; and I suggest that you do this by boat, for there are things in the night sea that do not take kindly to swimmers. When you have crossed your starting point the wall will be builded. Then you may use the other chant, spoken only once, to shatter the great gem. You should carry the second chant at your right. This way you will not confuse the two—a mistake which would prove disastrous! I have used inks which shine in the dark; there will be no difficulty in reading the chants: So, having done all I have told you your revenge will be complete and you will have served all the lands of dream greatly. No creature or thing will ever be able to enter Dylath-Leen again, nor leave the place, and the Fly-the-Light will be loosed amongst the horned ones. One warning though, Grant Enderby—*do not watch the results of your work*! It will be as was never meant for the eyes of men!"

IV

I came through the desert towards Dylath-Leen at dusk, when the desert grasses made spiky silhouettes atop the dunes and the last kites circled high, their shrill cries telling of night's stealthy approach. Night was indeed coming, striding across dreamland in lengthening shadows which befriended and hid me as I tethered my yak and made for the western point of the bay. I would start there; making my way from shadow to shadow, with the wall-building chant of Naach-Tith on my lips, to the opposite side of the bay; and then I would see about crossing the water back to my starting point.

I was glad that the moon was thinly horned, glad the desert was not more brightly illumined, for I could not be sure that there were no sentries out from the unquiet city. Whatever joys Dylath-Leen may once have held for me, now the place was unquiet. No normal lights shone in its streets and squares, but, as night came more quickly, there soon sprang up many thousands of tiny points of evil red, and in one certain area a great morbidly red blotch glowed in strange reminiscence of Jupiter's huge eye-like spot, glimpsed often in my youth through a friend's telescope. Empty though the city now was of all normal life, that poisoned jewel in the main square still filled the town with its loathsomeness, a terror ignored by the abnormal traders as the statues of past heroes are ignored in saner places.

Half way round the city's perimeter there came to my ears the strains of music—if such evilly soul-disturbing sounds warrant placing in any such category—and leaping fires sprang up in Dylath-Leen's outer streets, so that I could see and shudder at the horned figures that leapt and cavorted round those ritual hell-fires, observing the way their squat bodies jerked and shook to the jarring cacophony of bone-dry crotala and strangled flutes. I could neither bear to hear nor watch, so I passed quickly on, chanting breathlessly to myself and feeling about me a weird magic building up to a thrill of unseen energies in the night air.

I was more than three-quarters towards the eastern side of the bay when I heard behind me a distant sound that stiffened the short hairs on the back of my neck and brought a chill sweat to my brow. It was the terrified cry of my yak, and following that single shrill scream of animal fear there came another sound—one which caused me to quicken my pace almost to a run as I emerged from the dunes to the washed pebbles of the shore—the horrid, ululant cry of alarm of the horned ones!

Stranded on the beach was a small one-man craft as used of old by the octopus fishers of Dylath-Leen. Frail and unsafe though it looked, beggars cannot be choosers, and thus thinking I leapt within its tar-planked shell and found the round-bladed paddle. Still chanting those mad words of Atal's deciphering I paddled strongly for the black outline of the far side of the bay, and ungainly though my craft had at first looked it fairly cleft the dark water as I drove furiously at the paddle. By now there were squattish outlines on the shore behind me, dancing in anger at my escape to the sea, and I wondered if the horned ones had a means of communication with which more orthodox creatures—such as men!—were unfamiliar. If so, then perhaps I would find monstrous welcomers awaiting my beaching on the western point!

Half-way across the bay things happened to make me forget the problem of what might wait for me on landing. I felt a tug at my paddle from the oily water and a dark mass rose up out of the depths before my boat. I screamed then, as the thin moonlight lit on the sharp teeth of that unknown swimmer, and lashed out with my paddle as it came alongside, taking a deep breath when it turned away and submerged. I continued then with my frenzied paddling and chanting until the western point loomed out of the dark and the shallow keel of my boat bit sand. As I leapt overboard into the night-chill water I imagined soggy gropings at my legs and ploughed in an agony of terror for the pebbles of the beach—

—And in that same instant, as I touched dry land, there loped out of the dark from the direction of the city the squat forms of a dozen or so of those foul, horned creatures whose brothers dwell in nighted Leng! Before they could reach me, even as their poisonous paws stretched out for me, I raced across my starting point and there came a clap of magical thunder that flung me down face first into the sand. I leapt up again, to my feet, and there within arm's length, clawing at an unseen barrier—the Wall of Naach-Tith— were those thwarted horned ones of elder dreams. Hateful their looks and murderous their strangled intent as they clawed with vile purpose at thin air, held back by the invisible spell of Naach-Tith's barrier.

Without pause I snatched out the second of those papers given me by Atal and commenced the invocation of the Fly-the-Light, the spell to draw forth the horror from the ruby! As the first of those weird syllables passed my lips the horned ones fell back, unbelievable terror twisting their already awful features…

"*Tetragrammaton Thabaite Sabaoth Tethiktos*—:" and as I chanted on, by the dim light of that thin-horned moon, the snarls of those creatures at bay turned to pleading mewls and gibbers as they began to grovel at the base of the Wall of Naach-Tith; and eventually I spoke the last word and there came a silence which was as that quiet that rules at the core of the moon.

Then, out of the silence, a low and distant rumble was born; growing rapidly in volume to a roar, to a blast of sound, to an ear-splitting shriek as of a billion banshees—and from the heart of Dylath-Leen a cold wind blew, extinguishing in an instant the hellfires of the horned ones; and all the tiny red points of light went out in a second; and there came a loud, sharp crack, as of a great crystal disintegrating—and soon thereafter I heard the first of the screams.

I remembered Atal's warning "not to watch", but found myself unable to turn away. I was rooted to the spot, and as the screams from the dark city rose in horrid intensity I could but stare into the darkness with bulging eyes, straining to pick out some detail of what occurred there in the midnight streets. Then, as the grovellers at the wall broke and scattered, *It* came; rushing from out the bowels of the terrified town, bringing with it a wind that bowled over the fleeing creatures beyond the invisible wall as though they had no weight at all; and I saw it!

Blind and yet all-seeing—without legs and yet running like flood water— the poisonous mouths in the bubbling mass—the Fly-the-Light beyond the wall. Great God! The sight of the creature was mind-blasting! And what it *did* to those now pitiful things from Leng!

Thus it was and is.

Three times only have I visited the basalt-towered, myriad-wharved city of Dylath-Leen, and now I pray that I have seen that city for the last tine. For who can say but that should there be a next time I might find myself as I did once before within that city's walls—perhaps even within the Wall of Naach-Tith! For the road twixt the waking world and the world of dream knows no barrier other than that of sleep—and even now I grow drowsy. Yet dare I sleep? I fear that one night I shall awaken to the beams of a thin and haunted moon, within basalt-towered Dylath-Leen, and that the thing from the great ruby shall find me there, trapped within a prison of my own making...

THE MIRROR OF NITOCRIS

Another tale from The Caller of the Black, *"Mirror" was written in mid-1968 while I was still in Berlin. August Derleth wrote me to say, "There's some very good writing here…" which did my ego no end of good! (His comments weren't always so kind.) "Mirror" is a one-of-a-kind story, in that it's the only one of my short tales that stars Titus Crow's sidekick, Henri-Laurent de Marigny, as the principal character and narrator. But Henri did go on, of course, to further adventures with Crow in his battle against "The Burrowers Beneath", also against Ithaqua the Wind-Walker, "In the Moons of Borea"; even against Cthulhu himself, in "Elysia" the home of the Elder Gods.*

Hail, The Queen!
Bricked up alive,
Never more to curse her hive;
Walled-up 'neath the pyramid,
    Where the sand
    Her secret hid.
    Buried with her glass
    That she,
At the midnight hour might see
Shapes from other spheres called;
    Alone with them,
    Entombed, appalled
    —To death!

                    —Justin Geoffrey

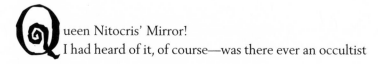

Queen Nitocris' Mirror!
I had heard of it, of course—was there ever an occultist

who had not?—I had even read of it, in Geoffrey's raving *People of the Mono-lith,* and knew that it was whispered of in certain dark circles where my presence is abhorred. I knew Alhazred had hinted of its powers in the forbidden *Necronomicon,* and that certain desert tribesmen still make a heathen sign which dates back untold centuries when questioned too closely regarding the legends of its origin.

So how was it that some fool auctioneer could stand up there and declare that this was Nitocris' Mirror? How *dare* he?

Yet the glass was from the collection of Bannister Brown-Farley—the explorer-hunter-archaeologist who, before his recent disappearance, was a recognised connoisseur of rare and obscure *objets d'art*—and its appearance was quite as outré as the appearance of an object with its alleged history ought to be. Moreover, was this not the self-same auctioneer, fool or otherwise, who had sold me Baron Kant's silver pistol only a year or two before? Not, mind you, that there was a single shred of evidence that the pistol, or the singular ammunition that came with it, had ever really belonged to the witch-hunting Baron; the ornately inscribed "K" on the weapon's butt might stand for anything!

But of course, I made my bid for the mirror and for Bannister Brown-Farley's diary, and got them both. "Sold to Mr., er, it is Mr. de Marigny, isn't it, sir? Thought so!—sold to Mr. Henri-Laurent de Marigny, for…" For an abominable sum.

As I hurried home to the grey stone house which has been my home ever since my father sent me out of America, I could not help but wonder at the romantic fool in me which prompts me all too often to spend my pennies on such pretty tomfooleries as these. Obviously an inherited idiosyncrasy which, along with my love of dark mysteries and obscure and antique wonders, was undoubtedly sealed into my personality as a permanent stamp of my world-famous father, the great New Orleans mystic Etienne-Laurent de Marigny.

Yet if the mirror really *was* once the possession of that awful sovereign— why! What a wonderful addition to my collection. I would hang the thing between my bookshelves, in company with Geoffrey, Poe, d'Erlette, and Prinn. For of course the legends and myths I had heard and read of it were purely legends and myths, and nothing more; heaven forbid!

With my ever-increasing knowledge of night's stranger mysteries I should have known better.

At home I sat for a long time, simply admiring the thing where it hung on my wall, studying the polished bronze frame with its beautifully moulded serpents and demons, ghouls and afreets; a page straight out of *The Arabian Nights.* And its surface was so perfect that even the late sunlight, striking through my windows, reflected no glare but a pure beam of light which lit my study in a dream-engendering effulgence.

Nitocris' Mirror!

Nitocris. Now *there* was a woman—or a monster—whichever way one chooses to think of her. A sixth-dynasty Queen who ruled her terror-stricken subjects with a will of supernatural iron from her seat at Gizeh—who once invited all her enemies to a feast in a temple below the Nile, and drowned them by opening the watergates—whose mirror allowed her glimpses of the netherpits where puffed Shoggoths and creatures of the Dark Spheres carouse and sport in murderous lust and depravity.

Just suppose this was the real thing, the abhorred glass which they placed in her tomb before sealing her up alive; where could Brown-Farley have got hold of it?

Before I knew it, it was nine, and the light had grown so poor that the mirror was no more than a dull golden glow across the room in the shadow of the wall. I put on my study light, in order to read Brown-Farley's diary, and immediately—on picking up that small, flat book, which seemed to fall open automatically at a well-turned page—I became engrossed in the story which began to unfold. It appeared that the writer had been a niggardly man, for the pages were too closely written, in a crabbed hand, from margin to margin and top to bottom, with barely an eighth of an inch between lines. Or perhaps he had written these pages in haste, begrudging the seconds wasted in turning them and therefore determined to turn as few as possible?

The very first word to catch my eye was—*Nitocris*!

The diary told of how Brown-Farley had heard it put about that a certain old Arab had been caught selling items of fabulous antiquity in the markets of Cairo. The man had been gaoled for refusing to tell the authorities whence the treasures had come. Yet every night in his cell he had called such evil things down on the heads of his gaolers that eventually, in fear, they let him go. And he had blessed them in the name of Nitocris! Yet Abu Ben Reis was not one of those tribesmen who swore by her name—or against it! He was not a Gizeh man, nor even one of Cairo's swarthy sons. His home tribe was a band of rovers wandering far to the east, beyond the great desert. Where, then, had he come into contact with Nitocris' name? Who had taught him her foul blessing—or where had he read of it? For through some kink of fate and breeding Abu Ben Reis had an uncommon knack with tongues and languages other than his own.

Just as thirty-five years earlier the inexplicable possessions of one Mohammad Hamad had attracted archaeologists of the calibre of Herbert LE.

Winlock to the eventual discovery of the tomb of Thutmosis III's wives, so now did Abu Ben Reis's hinted knowledge of ancient burial grounds—and in particular the grave of the Queen of elder horror—suffice to send Brown-Farley to Cairo to seek his fortune.

Apparently he had not gone unadvised; the diary was full of bits and pieces of lore and legend in connection with the ancient Queen. Brown-Farley had faithfully copied from Wardle's *Notes on Nitocris* and in particular the paragraph on her "Magical Mirror":

> ...handed down to their priests by the hideous gods of inner-Earth before the earliest civilisations of the Nile came into existence—a "gateway" to unknown spheres and worlds of hellish horror in the shape of a mirror. Worshipped, it was; by the pre-Imer Nyahites in Ptathlia at the dawn of Man's domination of the Earth, and eventually enshrined by Nephren-Ka in a black crypt on the banks of the Shibeli. Side by side it lay with the Shining Trapezohedron, and who can say what things might have been reflected in its depths? Even the Haunter of the Dark may have bubbled and blasphemed before it! Stolen, it remained hidden, unseen for centuries, in the bat-shrouded labyrinths of Kith, before finally falling into Nitocris' foul clutches. Numerous the enemies she locked away, the mirror as sole company, full knowing that by the next morning the death-cell would be empty save for the sinister, polished glass on the wall. Numerous the vilely chuckled hints she gave of the features of those who leered at midnight from out the bronze-barriered gate. But not even Nitocris herself was safe from the horrors locked in the mirror, and at the midnight hour she was wise enough to gaze but fleetingly upon it...

The midnight hour! Why! It was ten already. Normally I would have been preparing for bed by this time; yet here I was, so involved now with the diary that I did not give my bed a second thought. Better, perhaps, if I had...

I read on. Brown-Farley had eventually found Abu Ben Leis and had plied him with liquor and opium until finally he managed to do that which the proper authorities had found impossible. The old Arab gave up his secret—though the book hinted that this knowledge had not been all that easy to extract—and the next morning Brown-Farley had taken a little-used camel-track into the wastes beyond those pyramids wherein lay Nitocris' *first* burial place.

But from here on there were great gaps in the writing—whole pages having been torn out or obliterated with thick, black strokes, as though the writer had realised that too much was revealed by what he had written—and there were rambling, incoherent paragraphs on the mysteries of death and the lands beyond the grave. Had I not known the explorer to have been such a fanatical antiquarian (his auctioned collection had been unbelievably varied) and were I not aware that he had delved, prior to his search for Nitocris' second tomb, into many eldritch places and outré settings, I might have believed the writer mad from the contents of the diary's last pages. Even in this knowledge I half believed him mad anyway.

Obviously he had found the last resting place of Nitocris—the scribbled hints and suggestions were all too plain—but it seemed there had been nothing left worth removing. Abu Ben Leis had long since plundered all but the fabled mirror, and it was after Brown-Farley had taken that last item from the ghoul-haunted tomb that the first of his real troubles began. From what I could make out from the now-garbled narrative, he had begun to develop a morbid fixation about the mirror, so that by night he kept it constantly draped.

But it was no good; before I could continue my perusal of the diary I had to get down my copy of Feery's *Notes on the Necronomicon*. There was something tickling me, there at the back of my mind, a memory, something I should know, something which Alhazred had known and written about. As I took down Feery's book from my shelves I came face to face with the mirror. The light in my study was bright and the night was quite warm—with that oppressive heaviness of air which is ever the prelude to violent thunderstorms—yet I shuddered strangely as I saw my face reflected in that glass. Just for a moment it had seemed to leer at me.

I shrugged off the feeling of dread which immediately sprang up in my innermost self and started to look up the section concerning the mirror. A great clock chimed out the hour of eleven somewhere in the night and distant lightning lit up the sky to the west beyond the windows of my room. One hour to midnight.

Still, my study *is* the most disconcerting place. What with those eldritch books on my shelves, their aged leather and ivory spines dully agleam with the reflection of my study light; and the *thing* I use as a paperweight, which has no parallel in any sane or ordered universe; and now with the mirror and diary, I was rapidly developing an attack of the fidgets unlike any I had ever known before. It was a shock for me to realise that I was just a little uneasy.

I thumbed through Feery's often fanciful reconstruction of the *Necronomicon* until I found the relevant passage. The odds were that Feery had not altered this section at all, except, perhaps, to somewhat modernise the "mad" Arab's old-world phraseology. Certainly it read like genuine Alhazred. Yes, there it was. And there, yet again, was that recurring hint of happenings at midnight:

> ...*for while the Surface of the Glass is still—even as the Crystal Pool of Yith-Shesh, even as the Lake of Hali when the Swimmers are not at the Frothing—and while its Gates are locked in all the Hours of Day; yet, at the Witching Hour, One who knows—even One who guesses— may see in it all the Shades and Shapes of Night and the Pit, wearing the Visage of Those who saw before. And though the Glass may lie forgotten for ever its Power may not die, and it should be known:*

> *That is not dead which can for ever lie;*
> *And with strange aeons even death may die...*

For many moments I pondered that weird passage and the even weirder couplet which terminated it, and the minutes ticked by in a solemn silence hitherto outside my experience at The Aspens.

It was the distant chime of the half-hour which roused me from my reverie to continue my reading of Brown-Farley's diary. I purposely put my face away from the mirror and leaned back in my chair, thoughtfully scanning the pages. But there were only one or two pages left to read, and as best I can remember the remainder of that disjointed narrative rambled on in this manner:

> 10th. The nightmares on the *London*—all the way out from Alexandria to Liverpool—Christ knows I wish I'd flown. Not a single night's sleep. Appears the so-called "legends" are not so fanciful as they seemed. Either that or my nerves are going! Possibly it's just the echo of a guilty conscience. If that old fool Abu hadn't been so damned close-mouthed—if he'd been satisfied with the opium and brandy instead of demanding money—and for what, I ask? There was no need for all that rough stuff. And his poxy waffle about "only wanting to protect me". Rubbish! The old beggar'd long since cleaned the place out except for the mirror... That damned mirror! Have to get a grip on myself. What state must my nerves be in that I need to cover the thing up at night? Perhaps I've read too much from the *Necronomicon*! I wouldn't be the first fool to fall for that blasted book's

hocus-pocus. Alhazred must have been as mad as Nitocris herself. Yet I suppose it's possible that it's all just imagination; there are drugs that can give the same effects, I'm sure. Could it be that the mirror has a hidden mechanism somewhere which releases some toxic powder or other at intervals? But what kind of mechanism would still be working so perfectly after the centuries that glass must have seen? And why always at midnight? Damned funny! And those *dreams*! There is one sure way to settle it, of course. I'll give it a few more days and if things get no better, well—we'll have to wait and see.

13th. That's it, then. Tonight we'll have it out in the open. I mean, what good's a bloody psychiatrist who insists I'm perfectly well when I know I'm ill? That mirror's behind it all! "Face your problems," the fool said, "and if you do they cease to bother you." That's what I'll do, then, tonight.

13th. Night. There, I've sat myself down and it's eleven already. I'll wait 'til the stroke of midnight and then I'll take the cover off the glass and we'll see what we'll see. God! That a man like me should twitch like this! Who'd believe that only a few months ago I was steady as a rock? And all for a bloody mirror. I'll just have a smoke and a glass. That's better. Twenty minutes to go; good—soon be over now—p'raps tonight I'll get a bit of sleep for a change! The way the place goes suddenly quiet, as though the whole house were *waiting* for something to happen. I'm damned glad I sent Johnson home. It'd be no good to let him see me looking like this. What a God-awful state to get oneself into! Five minutes to go. I'm tempted to take the cover off the mirror right now! There—midnight! Now we'll have it!

And that was all there was!

I read it through again, slowly, wondering what there was in it which so alarmed me. And what a coincidence, I thought, reading that last line for the second time; for even as I did so the distant clock, muffled somewhere by the city's mists, chimed out the hour of twelve.

I thank God, now, that he sent that far-off chime to my ears. I am sure it could only have been an act of Providence which caused me to glance round upon hearing it. For that still glass—that mirror which is quiet as the crystal pool of Yith-Shesh all the hours of day—*was still no longer*!

A *thing*, a bubbling blasphemous shape from lunacy's most hellish nightmare, was squeezing its flabby pulp out through the frame of the mirror into my room—*and it wore a face where no face ever should have been.*

I do not recall moving—opening my desk drawer and snatching out that which lay within—yet it seems I must have done so. I remember only the deafening blasts of sound from the bucking, silver-plated revolver in my clammy hand; and above the rattle of sudden thunder, the whine of flying fragments and the shivering of glass as the hell-forged bronze frame buckled and leapt from the wall.

I remember too, picking up the strangely *twisted* silver bullets from my Boukhara rug. And then I must have fainted.

The next morning I dropped the shattered fragments of the mirror's glass overboard from the rail of the Thames Ferry and I melted down the frame to a solid blob and buried it deep in my garden. I burned the diary and scattered its ashes to the wind. Finally, I saw my doctor and had him prescribe a sleeping-draught for me. I knew I was going to need it.

I have said the thing had a face.

Indeed, atop the glistening, bubbling mass of that hell-dweller's bulk there *was* a face. A composite face of which the two halves did not agree! *For one of them was the immaculately cruel visage of an ancient Queen of Egypt and the other was easily recognisable—from photographs I had seen in the newspapers—as the now anguished and lunatic features of a certain lately vanished explorer!*

THE SECOND WISH

*I wrote this story in 1976 for Arkham House's Ramsey Camp-
bell-edited* New Tales of the Cthulhu Mythos *(1980). Not only
a homage to Lovecraft (you will find several allusions to HPL's stories in this one) but also to Robert E. Howard of Conan fame, "The
Second Wish" is a fully fledged Mythos tale with just about every
Mythos prop. But it's also one of my personal favourites. Most recently it was reprinted in my hardcover collection,* Beneath the
Moors & Darker Places, *TOR Books, 2002.*

The scene was awesomely bleak: mountains gauntly grey
and black towered away to the east, forming an uneven
backdrop for a valley of hardy grasses, sparse bushes, and leaning trees. In
one corner of the valley, beneath foothills, a scattering of shingle-roofed
houses, with the very occasional tiled roof showing through, was enclosed
and protected in the Old European fashion by a heavy stone wall.

A mile or so from the village—if the huddle of time-worn houses could
properly be termed a village—leaning on a low rotting fence that guarded the
rutted road from a steep and rocky decline, the tourists gazed at the oppressive bleakness all about and felt oddly uncomfortable inside their heavy
coats. Behind them their hired car—a black Russian model as gloomy as the
surrounding countryside, exuding all the friendliness of an expectant
hearse—stood patiently waiting for them.

He was comparatively young, of medium build, dark-haired, unremark-
ably good-looking, reasonably intelligent, and decidedly idle. His early adult
years had been spent avoiding any sort of real industry, a prospect which a
timely and quite substantial inheritance had fortunately made redundant before it could force itself upon him. Even so, a decade of living at a rate far in
excess of even his ample inheritance had rapidly reduced him to an almost

penniless, unevenly cultured, high-ranking rake. He had never quite lowered himself to the level of a gigolo, however, and his womanizing had been quite deliberate, serving an end other than mere fleshly lust.

They had been ten very good years by his reckoning and not at all wasted, during which his expensive lifestyle had placed him in intimate contact with the cream of society; but while yet surrounded by affluence and glitter he had not been unaware of his own steadily dwindling resources. Thus, towards the end, he had set himself to the task of ensuring that his tenuous standing in society would not suffer with the disappearance of his so carelessly distributed funds; hence his philandering. In this he was not as subtle as he might have been, with the result that the field had narrowed down commensurately with his assets, until at last he had been left with Julia.

She was a widow in her middle forties but still fairly trim, rather prominently featured, too heavily made-up, not a little calculating, and very well-to-do. She did not love her consort—indeed she had never been in love—but he was often amusing and always thoughtful. Possibly his chief interest lay in her money, but that thought did not really bother her. Many of the younger, unattached men she had known had been after her money. At least Harry was not foppish, and she believed that in his way he did truly care for her.

Not once had he given her reason to believe otherwise. She had only twenty good years left and she knew it; money could only buy so much youth...Harry would look after her in her final years and she would turn a blind eye on those little indiscretions which must surely come—provided he did not become too indiscreet. He had asked her to marry him and she would comply as soon as they returned to London. Whatever else he lacked he made up for in bed. He was an extremely virile man and she had rarely been so well satisfied...

Now here they were together, touring Hungary, getting "far away from it all".

"Well, is this remote enough for you?" he asked, his arm around her waist.

"Umm," she answered. "Deliciously barren, isn't it?"

"Oh, it's all of that. Peace and quiet for a few days—it was a good idea of yours, Julia, to drive out here. We'll feel all the more like living it up when we reach Budapest."

"Are you so eager, then, to get back to the bright lights?" she asked. He detected a measure of peevishness in her voice.

"Not at all, darling. The setting might as well be Siberia for all I'm concerned about locale. As long as we're together. But a girl of your breeding and style can hardly—"

"Oh, come off it, Harry! You can't wait to get to Budapest, can you?"

He shrugged, smiled resignedly, thought: *You niggly old bitch!* and said, "You read me like a book, darling—but Budapest is just a wee bit closer to London, and London is that much closer to us getting married, and—"

"But you have me anyway," she again petulantly cut him off. "What's so important about being married?"

"It's your friends, Julia," he answered with a sigh. "Surely you know that?" He took her arm and steered her towards the car. "They see me as some sort of cuckoo in the nest, kicking them all out of your affections. Yes, and it's the money, too."

"The money?" she looked at him sharply as he opened the car door for her. "What money?"

"The money I haven't got!" He grinned ruefully, relaxing now that he could legitimately speak his mind, if not the truth. "I mean, they're all certain it's your money I'm after, as if I was some damned gigolo. It's hardly flattering to either one of us. And I'd hate to think they might convince you that's all it is with me. But once we're married I won't give a damn what they say or think. They'll just have to accept me, that's all."

Reassured by what she took to be pure naïveté, she smiled at him and pulled up the collar of her coat. Then the smile fell from her face, and though it was not really cold she shuddered violently as he started the engine.

"A chill, darling?" He forced concern into his voice.

"Umm, a bit of one," she answered, snuggling up to him. "And a headache too. I've had it ever since we stopped over at—oh, what's the name of the place? Where we went up over the scree to look at that strange monolith?"

"Stregoicavar," he answered her. "The 'Witch-Town'. And that pillar-thing was the Black Stone. A curious piece of rock that, eh? Sticking up out of the ground like a great black fang! But Hungary is full of such things: myths and legends and odd relics of forgotten times. Perhaps we shouldn't have gone to look at it. The villagers shun it…"

"Mumbo jumbo," she answered. "No, I think I shall simply put the blame on *this* place. It's bloody depressing, really, isn't it?"

He tut-tutted good humouredly and said: "My God!—the whims of a woman, indeed!"

She snuggled closer and laughed in his ear. "Oh, well, that's what makes us so mysterious, Harry. Our changeability. But seriously, I think maybe you're right. It is a bit late in the year for wandering about the Hungarian countryside. We'll stay the night at the inn as planned, then cut short and go on tomorrow into Budapest. It's a drive of two hours at the most. A week at Zjhack's place, where we'll be looked after like royalty, and then on to London. How does that sound?"

"Wonderful!" He took one hand from the wheel to hug her. "And we'll be married by the end of October."

The inn at Szolyhaza had been recommended for its comforts and original Hungarian cuisine by an innkeeper in Kecskemét. Harry had suspected that both proprietors were related, particularly when he first laid eyes on Szolyhaza. That had been on the previous evening as they drove in over the hills.

Business in the tiny village could hardly be said to be booming. Even in the middle of the season, gone now along with the summer, Szolyhaza would be well off the map and out of reach of the ordinary tourist. It had been too late in the day to change their minds, however, and so they had booked into the solitary inn, the largest building in the village, an ancient stone edifice of at least five and a half centuries.

And then the surprise. For the proprietor, Herr Debrec, spoke near-perfect English; their room was light and airy with large windows and a balcony (Julia was delighted at the absence of a television set and the inevitable "Kultur" programs); and later, when they came down for a late-evening meal, the food was indeed wonderful!

There was something Harry had wanted to ask Herr Debrec that first evening, but sheer enjoyment of the atmosphere in the little dining-room— the candlelight, the friendly clinking of glasses coming through to them from the bar, the warm fire burning bright in an old brick hearth, not to mention the food itself and the warm red local wine—had driven it from his mind. Now, as he parked the car in the tiny courtyard, it came back to him. Julia had returned it to mind with her headache and the talk of ill-rumoured Stregoicavar and the Black Stone on the hillside.

It had to do with a church—at least Harry suspected it was or had been a church, though it might just as easily have been a castle or ancient watchtower—sighted on the other side of the hills beyond gaunt autumn woods. He had seen it limned almost as a silhouette against the hills as they had covered the last few miles to Szolyhaza from Kecskemét. There had been little enough time to study the distant building before the road veered and the car climbed up through a shallow pass, but nevertheless Harry had been left with a feeling of—well, almost of déjà vu—or perhaps presentiment. The picture of sombre ruins had brooded obscurely in his mind's eye until Herr Debrec's excellent meal and luxurious bed, welcome after many hours of driving on the poor country roads, had shut the vision out.

Over the midday meal, when Herr Debrec entered the dining room to replenish their glasses, Harry mentioned the old ruined church, saying he intended to drive out after lunch and have a closer look at it.

"That place, mein Herr? No, I should not advise it."

"Oh?" Julia looked up from her meal. "It's dangerous, is it?"

"Dangerous?"

"In poor repair—on the point of collapsing on someone?"

"No, no. Not that I am aware of, but—" he shrugged half-apologetically.

"Yes, go on," Harry prompted him.

Debrec shrugged again, his short fat body seeming to wobble uncertainly. He slicked back his prematurely greying hair and tried to smile. "It is…very old, that place. Much older than my inn. It has seen many bad times, and perhaps something of those times still—how do you say it?—yes, 'adheres' to it."

"It's haunted?" Julia suddenly clapped her hands, causing Harry to start.

"No, not that—but then again—" the Hungarian shook his head, fumbling with the lapels of his jacket. He was obviously finding the conversation very uncomfortable.

"But you must explain yourself, Herr Debrec," Harry demanded. "You've got us completely fascinated."

"There is…a dweller," the man finally answered. "An old man—a holy man, some say, but I don't believe it—who looks after…things."

"A caretaker, you mean?" Julia asked.

"A keeper, madam, yes. He terms himself a 'monk', I think, the last of his sect. I have my doubts."

"Doubts?" Harry repeated, becoming exasperated. "But what about?"

"Herr, I cannot explain," Debrec fluttered his hands. "But still I advise you, do not go there. It is not a good place."

"Now wait a min—" Harry began, but Debrec cut him off.

"If you insist on going, then at least be warned: do not touch…anything. Now I have many duties. Please to excuse me." He hurried from the room.

Left alone they gazed silently at each other for a moment. Then Harry cocked an eyebrow and said: "Well?"

"Well, we have nothing else to do this afternoon, have we?" she asked.

"No, but—oh, I don't know," he faltered, frowning. "I'm half inclined to heed his warning."

"But why? Don't tell me you're superstitious, Harry?"

"No, not at all. It's just that—oh, I have this feeling, that's all."

She looked astounded. "Why, Harry, I really don't know which one of you is trying hardest to have me on: you or Debrec!" She tightened her mouth and nodded determinedly. "That settles it then. We *will* go and have a look at the ruins, and damnation to all these old wives' tales!"

Suddenly he laughed. "You know, Julia, there might just be some truth in what you say—about someone having us on, I mean. It's just struck me: you know this old monk Debrec was going on about? Well, I wouldn't be surprised if it turned out to be his uncle or something! All these hints of spooky goings-on could be just some sort of put-on, a con game, a tourist trap. And here we've fallen right into it! I'll give you odds it costs us five pounds a head just to get inside the place!" And at that they both burst out laughing.

The sky was overcast and it had started to rain when they drove away from the inn. By the time they reached the track that led off from the road and through the grey woods in the direction of the ruined church, a ground mist was curling up from the earth in white drifting tendrils.

"How's this for sinister?" Harry asked, and Julia shivered again and snuggled closer to him. "Oh?" he said, glancing at her and smiling. "Are you sorry we came after all, then?"

"No, but it is eerie driving through this mist. It's like floating on milk!...Look, there's our ruined church directly ahead."

The woods had thinned out and now high walls rose up before them, walls broken in places and tumbled into heaps of rough moss-grown masonry. Within these walls, in grounds of perhaps half an acre, the gaunt shell of a great Gothic structure reared up like the tombstone of some primordial giant. Harry drove the car through open iron gates long since rusted solid with their massive hinges. He pulled up before a huge wooden door in that part of the building which still supported its lead-covered roof.

They left the car to rest on huge slick centuried cobbles, where the mist cast languorous tentacles about their ankles. Low over distant peaks the sun struggled bravely, trying to break through drifting layers of cloud.

Harry climbed the high stone steps to the great door and stood uncertainly before it. Julia followed him and said. with a shiver in her voice: "Still think it's a tourist trap?"

"Uh? Oh! No, I suppose not. But I'm interested anyway. There's something about this place. A feeling almost of—"

"As if you'd been here before?"

"Yes, exactly! You feel it too?"

"No," she answered, in fine contrary fashion. "I just find it very drab. And I think my headache is coming back."

For a moment or two they were silent, staring at the huge door.

"Well," Harry finally offered, "nothing ventured, nothing gained." He lifted the massive iron knocker, shaped like the top half of a dog's muzzle, and let it fall heavily against the grinning metal teeth of the lower jaw. The clang of the knocker was loud in the misty stillness.

"Door creaks open," Julia intoned, "revealing Bela Lugosi in a black high-collared cloak. In a sepulchral voice he says: 'Good evening…'" For all her apparent levity, half of the words trembled from her mouth.

Wondering how, at her age, she could act so stupidly girlish, Harry came close then to telling her to shut up. Instead he forced a grin, reflecting that it had always been one of her failings to wax witty at the wrong time. Perhaps she sensed his momentary annoyance, however, for she frowned and drew back from him fractionally. He opened his mouth to explain himself but started violently instead as, quite silently, the great door swung smoothly inward.

The opening of the door seemed almost to pull them in, as if a vacuum had been created…the sucking rush of an express train through a station. And as they stumbled forward they saw in the gloom, the shrunken, flame-eyed ancient framed against a dim, musty-smelling background of shadows and lofty ceilings.

The first thing they really noticed of him when their eyes grew accustomed to the dimness was his filthy appearance. Dirt seemed ingrained in him! His coat, a black full-length affair with threadbare sleeves, was buttoned up to his neck where the ends of a grey tattered scarf protruded. Thin grimy wrists stood out from the coat's sleeves, blue veins showing through the dirt. A few sparse wisps of yellowish hair, thick with dandruff and probably worse, lay limp on the pale bulbous dome of his head. He could have been no more than sixty-two inches in height, but the fire that burned behind yellow eyes, and the vicious hook of a nose that followed their movements like the beak of some bird of prey, seemed to give the old man more than his share of strength, easily compensating for his lack of stature.

"I...that is, we..." Harry began.

"Ah!—*English*! You are English, yes? Or perhaps American?" His heavily accented voice, clotted and guttural, sounded like the gurgling of a black subterranean stream. Julia thought that his throat must be full of phlegm, as she clutched at Harry's arm.

"Tourists, eh?" the ancient continued. "Come to see old Möhrsen's books? Or perhaps you don't know why you've come?" He clasped his hands tightly together, threw back his head, and gave a short coughing laugh.

"Why, we...that is..." Harry stumbled again, feeling foolish, wondering just why they *had* come.

"Please enter," said the old man, standing aside and ushering them deeper, irresistibly in. "It is the books, of course it is. They all come to see Möhrsen's books sooner or later. And of course there is the view from the tower. And the catacombs..."

"It was the ruins," Harry finally found his voice. "We saw the old building from the road, and—"

"Picturesque, eh. The ruins in the trees... Ah!—but there are other things here. You will see."

"Actually," Julia choked it out, fighting with a sudden attack of nausea engendered by the noisome aspect of their host, "we don't have much time..."

The old man caught at their elbows, yellow eyes flashing in the gloomy interior. "Time? No time?" His hideous voice grew intense in a moment. "True, how true. Time is running out for all of us!"

It seemed then that a draught, coming from nowhere, caught at the great door and eased it shut. As the gloom deepened Julia held all the more tightly to Harry's arm, but the shrunken custodian of the place had turned his back to guide them on with an almost peremptory: "Follow me."

And follow him they did.

Drawn silently along in his wake, like seabirds following an ocean liner through the night, they climbed stone steps, entered a wide corridor with an arched ceiling, finally arrived at a room with a padlocked door. Möhrsen unlocked the door, turned, bowed, and ushered them through.

"My library," he told them, "my beautiful books."

With the opening of the door light had flooded the corridor, a beam broad as the opening in which musty motes were caught, drifting, eddying about in the disturbed air. The large room—bare except for a solitary chair, a table, and tier upon tier of volume-weighted shelves arrayed against the walls—had a massive window composed of many tiny panes. Outside the sun had finally won its battle with the clouds; it shone wanly afar, above the distant mountains, its autumn beam somehow penetrating the layers of grime on the small panes.

"Dust!" cried the ancient. "The dust of decades—of decay! I cannot keep it down." He turned to them. "But see, you must sign."

"Sign?" Harry questioned. "Oh, I see. A visitors' book."

"Indeed, for how else might I remember those who visit me here? See, look at all the names…"

The old man had taken a leather-bound volume from the table. It was not a thick book, and as Möhrsen turned the parchment leaves they could see that each page bore a number of signatures, each signature being dated. Not one entry was less than ten years old. Harry turned back the pages to the first entry and stared at it. The ink had faded with the centuries so that he could not easily make out the ornately flourished signature. The date, on the other hand, was still quite clear: "Frühling, 1611."

"An old book indeed," he commented, "but recently, it seems, visitors have been scarce…" Though he made no mention of it, frankly he could see little point in his signing such a book.

"Sign nevertheless," the old man gurgled, almost as if he could read Harry's mind. "Yes, you must, and the madam too." Harry reluctantly took out a pen; and Möhrsen watched intently as they scribbled their signatures.

"Ah, good, good!" he chortled, rubbing his hands together. "There we have it—two more visitors, two more names. It makes an old man happy, sometimes, to remember his visitors… And sometimes it makes him sad."

"Oh?" Julia said, interested despite herself. "Why sad?"

"Because I know that many of them who visited me here are no more, of course!" He blinked great yellow eyes at them.

"But look here, look here," he continued, pointing a grimy sharp-nailed finger at a signature. "This one: 'Justin Geoffrey, 12 June, 1926'. A young American poet, he was. A man of great promise. Alas, he gazed too long upon the Black Stone!"

"The Black Stone?" Harry frowned. "But—"

"And here, two years earlier: 'Charles Dexter Ward'—another American, come to see my books. And here, an Englishman this time, one of your own countrymen, 'John Kingsley Brown'." He let the pages flip through filthy fingers. "And here another, but much more recently. See: 'Hamilton Tharpe, November, 1959'. Ah, I remember Mr. Tharpe well! We shared many a rare discussion here in this very room. He aspired to the priesthood, but—" He sighed. "Yes, seekers after knowledge all, but many of them ill-fated, I fear…"

"You mentioned the Black Stone," Julia said. "I wondered—?"

"Hmm? Oh, nothing. An old legend, nothing more. It is believed to be very bad luck to gaze upon the stone."

"Yes," Harry nodded. "We were told much the same thing in Stregoicavar."

"Ah!" Möhrsen immediately cried, snapping shut the book of names, causing his visitors to jump. "So you, too, have seen the Black Stone?" He returned the volume to the table, then regarded them again, nodding curiously. Teeth yellow as his eyes showed as he betrayed a sly, suggestive smile.

"Now see here—" Harry began, irrational alarm and irritation building in him, welling inside.

Möhrsen's attitude, however, changed on the instant. "A myth, a superstition, a fairy story!" he cried, holding out his hands in the manner of a conjurer who has nothing up his sleeve. "After all, what is a stone but a stone?"

"We'll have to be going," Julia said in a faint voice. Harry noticed how she leaned on him, how her hand trembled as she clutched his arm.

"Yes," he told their wretched host, "I'm afraid we really must go."

"But you have not seen the beautiful books!" Möhrsen protested. "Look, look—" Down from a shelf he pulled a pair of massive antique tomes and opened them on the table. They were full of incredible, dazzling, illuminated texts; and despite themselves, their feelings of strange revulsion, Harry and Julia handled the ancient works and admired their great beauty.

"And this book, and this." Möhrsen piled literary treasures before them. "See, are they not beautiful? And now you are glad you came, yes?"

"Why, yes, I suppose we are," Harry grudgingly replied.

"Good, good! I will be one moment—some refreshment—please look at the books. Enjoy them…" And Möhrsen was gone, shuffling quickly out of the door and away into the gloom.

"These books," Julia said as soon as they were alone. "They must be worth a small fortune!"

"And there are thousands of them," Harry answered, his voice awed and not a little envious. "But what do you think of the old boy?"

"He—frightens me," she shuddered. "And the way he smells!"

"Ssh!" He held a finger to his lips. "He'll hear you. Where's he gone, anyway?"

"He said something about refreshment. I certainly hope he doesn't think I'll eat anything he's prepared!"

"Look here!" Harry called. He had moved over to a bookshelf near the window and was fingering the spines of a particularly musty-looking row of books. "Do you know, I believe I recognise some of these titles? My father was always interested in the occult, and I can remember—"

"The occult?" Julia echoed, cutting him off, her voice nervous again. He had not noticed it before, but she was starting to look her age. It always happened when her nerves became frazzled, and then all the makeup in the world could not remove the stress lines.

"The occult, yes," he replied. "You know, the 'Mystic Arts', the 'Supernatural', and what have you. But what a collection! There are books here in Old German, in Latin, Dutch—and listen to some of the titles:

"*De Lapide Philosophico...De Vermis Mysteriis...Othuum Omnicia...Liber Ivonis...Necronomicon.*" He gave a low whistle, then: "I wonder what the British Museum would offer for this lot? They must be near priceless!"

"They *are* priceless!" came a guttural gloating cry from the open door. Möhrsen entered, bearing a tray with a crystal decanter and three large crystal glasses. "But please, I ask you not to touch them. They are the pride of my whole library."

The old man put the tray upon an uncluttered corner of the table, unstoppered the decanter, and poured liberal amounts of wine. Harry came to the table, lifted his glass, and touched it to his lips. The wine was deep, red, sweet. For a second he frowned, then his eyes opened in genuine appreciation. "Excellent!" he declared.

"The best," Möhrsen agreed, "and almost one hundred years old. I have only six more bottles of this vintage. I keep them in the catacombs. When you are ready you shall see the catacombs, if you so desire. Ah, but there is something down there that you will find most interesting, compared to which my books are dull, uninteresting things."

"I don't really think that I care to see your—" Julia began, but Möhrsen quickly interrupted.

"A few seconds only," he pleaded, "which you will remember for the rest of your lives. Let me fill your glasses."

The wine had warmed her, calming her treacherous nerves. She could see that Harry, despite his initial reservations, was now eager to accompany Möhrsen to the catacombs.

"We have a little time," Harry urged. "Perhaps—?"

"Of course," the old man gurgled, "time is not so short, eh?" He threw back his own drink and noisily smacked his lips, then shepherded his guests out of the room, mumbling as he did so: "Come, come—this way—only a moment—no more than that."

And yet again they followed him, this time because there seemed little else to do; deeper into the gloom of the high-ceilinged corridor, to a place where Möhrsen took candles from a recess in the wall and lit them; then on down two, three flights of stone steps into a nitrous vault deep beneath the ruins; and from there a dozen or so paces to the subterranean room in which, reclining upon a couch of faded silk cushions, Möhrsen's revelation awaited them.

The room itself was dry as dust, but the air passing gently through held the merest promise of moisture, and perhaps this rare combination had helped preserve the object on the couch. There she lay—central in her curtain-veiled cave, behind a circle of worn, vaguely patterned stone tablets, reminiscent of a miniature Stonehenge—a centuried mummy-parchment figure, arms crossed over her abdomen, remote in repose. And yet somehow…unquiet.

At her feet lay a leaden casket, a box with a hinged lid, closed, curiously like a small coffin. A design on the lid, obscure in the poor light, seemed to depict some mythic creature, half toad, half-dog. Short tentacles or feelers fringed the thing's mouth. Harry traced the dusty raised outline of this chimaera with a forefinger.

"It is said she had a pet—a companion creature—which slept beside her in that casket," said Möhrsen, again anticipating Harry's question.

Curiosity overcame Julia's natural aversion. "Who is…who *was* she?"

"The last true Priestess of the Cult," Möhrsen answered. "She died over four hundred years ago."

"The Turks?" Harry asked.

"The Turks, yes. But if it had not been them…who can say? The cult always had its opponents."

"The cult? Don't you mean the order?" Harry looked puzzled. "I've heard that you're—ah—a man of God. And if this place was once a church—"

"A man of God?" Möhrsen laughed low in his throat. "No, not of your God, my friend. And this was not a church but a temple. And not an order, a cult. I am its priest, one of the last, but one day there may be more. It is a cult which can never die." His voice, quiet now, nevertheless echoed like a warning, intensified by the acoustics of the cave.

"I think," said Julia, her own voice weak once more, "that we should leave now, Harry."

"Yes, yes," said Möhrsen, "the air down here, it does not agree with you. By all means leave—but first there is the legend."

"Legend?" Harry repeated him. "Surely not another legend?"

"It is said," Möhrsen quickly continued, "that if one holds her hand and makes a wish…"

"*No!*" Julia cried, shrinking away from the mummy. "I couldn't touch that!"

"Please, please," said Möhrsen, holding out his arms to her, "do not be afraid. It is only a myth, nothing more."

Julia stumbled away from him into Harry's arms. He held her for a moment until she had regained control of herself, then turned to the old man. "All right, how do I go about it? Let me hold her hand and make a wish—but then we *must* be on our way. I mean, you've been very hospitable, but—"

"I understand," Möhrsen answered. "This is not the place for a gentle, sensitive lady. But did you say that you wished to take the hand of the priestess?"

"Yes," Harry answered, thinking to himself: "if that's the only way to get to hell out of here!"

Julia stepped uncertainly, shudderingly back against the curtained wall as Harry approached the couch. Möhrsen directed him to kneel; he did so, taking a leathery claw in his hand. The elbow joint of the mummy moved with surprising ease as he lifted the hand from her withered abdomen. It felt not at all dry but quite cool and firm. In his mind's eye Harry tried to look back through the centuries. He wondered who the girl had really been, what she had been like. "I wish," he said to himself, "that I could know you as you were…"

Simultaneous with the unspoken thought, as if engendered of it, Julia's bubbling shriek of terror shattered the silence of the vault, setting Harry's hair on end and causing him to leap back away from the mummy. Furthermore, it had seemed that at the instant of Julia's scream, a tingle as of an electrical charge had travelled along his arm into his body.

Now Harry could see what had happened. As he had taken the mummy's withered claw in his hand, so Julia had been driven to clutch at the curtains for support. Those curtains had not been properly hung but merely draped over the stone surface of the cave's walls; Julia had brought them rustling down. Her scream had originated in being suddenly confronted by the hideous bas-reliefs which completely covered the walls, figures and shapes that seemed to leap and cavort in the flickering light of Möhrsen's candles.

Now Julia sobbed and threw herself once more into Harry's arms, clinging to him as he gazed in astonishment and revulsion at the monstrous carvings. The central theme of these was an octopodal creature of vast proportions—winged, tentacled, and dragonlike, and yet with a vaguely anthropomorphic outline—and around it danced all the demons of hell. Worse than this main horror itself, however, was what its attendant minions were doing to the tiny but undeniably human figures which also littered the walls.

And there, too, as if directing the nightmare activities of a group of these small, horned horrors, was a girl—with a leering dog-toad abortion that cavorted gleefully about her feet!

Hieronymus Bosch himself could scarcely have conceived such a scene of utterly depraved torture and degradation, and horror finally burst into livid rage in Harry as he turned on the exultant keeper of this nighted crypt. "A temple, you said, you old devil! A temple to what?—to that obscenity?"

"To Him, yes!" Möhrsen exulted, thrusting his hook-nose closer to the rock-cut carvings and holding up the candles the better to illuminate them. "To Cthulhu of the tentacled face, and to all his lesser brethren."

Without another word, more angry than he could ever remember being, Harry reached out and bunched up the front of the old man's coat in his clenched fist. He shook Möhrsen like a bundle of moth-eaten rags, cursing and threatening him in a manner which later he could scarcely recall.

"God!" he finally shouted. "It's a damn shame the Turks didn't raze this whole nest of evil right down to the ground! You…you can lead the way out of here right now, at once, or I swear I'll break your neck where you stand!"

"If I drop the candles," Möhrsen answered, his voice like black gas bubbles breaking the surface of a swamp, "we will be in complete darkness!"

"No, please!" Julia cried. "Just take us out of here…"

"If you value your dirty skin," Harry added, "you'll keep a good grip on those candles!"

Möhrsen's eyes blazed sulphurous yellow in the candlelight and he leered hideously. Harry turned him about, gripped the back of his grimy neck, and thrust him ahead, out of the blasphemous temple. With Julia stumbling in the rear, they made their way to a flight of steps that led up into daylight, emerging some twenty-five yards from the main entrance.

They came out through tangled cobwebs into low decaying vines and shrubbery that almost hid their exit. Julia gave one long shudder, as if shaking off a nightmare, and then hastened to the car. Not once did she look back.

Harry released Möhrsen who stood glaring at him, shielding his yellow eyes against the weak light. They confronted each other in this fashion for a few moments, until Harry turned his back on the little man to follow Julia to the car. It was then that Möhrsen whispered:

"Do not forget: I did not force you to do anything. I did not make you touch anything. You came here of your own free will."

When Harry turned to throw a few final harsh words at him, the old man was already disappearing down into the bowels of the ruins.

In the car as they drove along the track through the sparsely clad trees to the road, Julia was very quiet. At last she said: "That was quite horrible. I didn't know such people existed."

"Nor did I," Harry answered.

"I feel filthy," she continued. "I need a bath. What on earth did that creature want with us?"

"I haven't the faintest idea. I think he must be insane."

"Harry, let's not go straight back to the inn. Just drive around for a while." She rolled down her window, breathing deeply of the fresh air that flooded in before lying back in the seat and closing her eyes. He looked at her, thinking: "God!—but you're certainly showing your age now, my sweet"…but he couldn't really blame her.

There were two or three tiny villages within a few miles of Szolyhaza, centres of peasant life compared to which Szolyhaza was a veritable capital. These were mainly farming communities, some of which were quite picturesque. Nightfall was still several hours away and the rain had moved on, leaving a freshness in the air and a beautiful warm glow over the hills, so that they felt inclined to park the car by the roadside and enjoy a drink at a tiny *Gasthaus*.

Sitting there by a wide window that overlooked the street, while Julia composed herself and recovered from her ordeal, Harry noticed several posters on the wall of the building opposite. He had seen similar posters in Szolyhaza, and his knowledge of the language was just sufficient for him to realise that the event in question—whatever that might be—was taking place tonight. He determined, out of sheer curiosity, to question Herr Debrec about it when they returned to the inn. After all, there could hardly be very much of importance happening in an area so out-of-the-way. It had already been decided that nothing should be said about their visit to the ruins, the exceedingly unpleasant hour spent in the doubtful company of Herr Möhrsen.

Twilight was settling over the village when they got back. Julia, complaining of a splitting headache, bathed and went straight to her bed. Harry, on the other hand, felt strangely restless, full of physical and mental energy.

When Julia asked him to fetch her a glass of water and a sleeping pill, he dissolved two pills, thus ensuring that she would remain undisturbed for the night. When she was asleep he tidied himself up and went down to the bar.

After a few drinks he buttonholed Herr Debrec and questioned him about the posters; what was happening tonight? Debrec told him that this was to be the first of three nights of celebration. It was the local shooting carnival, the equivalent of the German *Schützenfest*, when prizes would be presented to the district's best rifle shots.

There would be sideshows and thrilling rides on machines specially brought in from the cities—members of the various shooting teams would be dressed all in hunter's green—beer and wine would flow like water and there would be good things to eat—oh, and all the usual trappings of a festival. This evening's main attraction was to be a masked ball, held in a great barn on the outskirts of a neighbouring village. It would be the beginning of many a fine romance. If the Herr wished to attend the festivities, Debrec could give him directions…?

Harry declined the offer and ordered another drink. It was odd the effect the brandy was having on him tonight: he was not giddy—it took a fair amount to do that—but there seemed to be a peculiar *excitement* in him. He felt much the same as when, in the old days, he'd pursued gay young debutantes in the Swiss resorts or on the Riviera.

Half an hour and two drinks later he checked that Julia was fast asleep, obtained directions to the *Schützenfest*, told Herr Debrec that his wife was on no account to be disturbed, and drove away from the inn in fairly high spirits. The odds, he knew, were all against him, but it would be good fun and there could be no possible comeback; after all, they were leaving for Budapest in the morning, and what the eye didn't see the heart wouldn't grieve over. He began to wish that his command of the language went a little further than "good evening" and "another brandy, please". Still, there had been plenty of times in the past when language hadn't mattered at all, when talking would have been a positive hindrance.

In no time at all he reached his destination, and at first glance he was disappointed. Set in the fields beside a hamlet, the site of the festivities was noisy and garishly lit, in many ways reminiscent of the country fairgrounds of England. All very well for teenage couples, but rather gauche for a civilized, sophisticated adult. Nevertheless, that peculiar tingling with which Harry's every fibre seemed imbued had not lessened, seemed indeed heightened by the whirling machines and gaudy, gypsyish caravans and sideshows; and so he parked the car and threaded his way through the swiftly gathering crowd.

Hung with bunting and festooned with balloons like giant ethereal multi-hued grapes, the great barn stood open to the night. Inside, a costumed band tuned up while masked singles and couples in handsome attire gathered, preparing to dance and flirt the night away. Framed for a moment in the huge open door, frozen by the camera of his mind, Harry saw among the crowd the figure of a girl—a figure of truly animal magnetism—dressed almost incongruously in peasant's costume.

For a second masked eyes met his own and fixed upon them across a space of only a few yards, and then she was gone. But the angle of her neck as she had looked at him, the dark unblinking eyes behind her mask, the fleeting, knowing smile on her lips before she turned away—all of these things had spoken volumes.

That weird feeling, the tingling that Harry felt, suddenly suffused his whole being. His head reeled and his mouth went dry; he had consciously to fight the excitement rising from within; following which he headed dizzily for the nearest wine tent, gratefully to slake his thirst. Then, bolstered by the wine, heart beating fractionally faster than usual, he entered the cavernous barn and casually cast about for the girl whose image still adorned his mind's eye.

But his assumed air of casual interest quickly dissipated as his eyes swept the vast barn without sighting their target, until he was about to step forward and go among the tables in pursuit of his quarry. At that point a hand touched his arm, a heady perfume reached him, and a voice said: "There is an empty table on the balcony. Would you like to sit?"

Her voice was not at all cultured, but her English was very good; and while certainly there was an element of peasant in her, well, there was much more than that. Deciding to savour her sensuous good looks later when they were seated, he barely glanced at her but took her hand and proceeded across the floor of the barn. They climbed wooden stairs to an open balcony set with tables and cane chairs. On the way he spoke to a waiter and ordered a bottle of wine, a plate of dainties.

They sat at their tiny table overlooking the dance floor, toying with their glasses and pretending to be interested in completely irrelevant matters. He spoke of London, of skiing in Switzerland, the beach at Cannes. She mentioned the mountains, the markets of Budapest, the bloody history of the country, particularly of this region. He was offhand about his jet-setting, not becoming ostentatious; she picked her words carefully, rarely erring in pronunciation. He took in little of what she said and guessed that she wasn't hearing him. But their eyes—at first rather fleetingly—soon became locked; their hands seemed to meet almost involuntarily atop the table.

Beneath the table Harry stretched out a leg towards hers, felt something cold and hairy arching against his calf as might a cat. A cat, yes, it must be one of the local cats, fresh in from mousing in the evening fields. He edged the thing to one side with his foot...but she was already on her feet, smiling, holding out a hand to him.

They danced, and he discovered gypsy in her, and strangeness, and magic. She bought him a red mask and positioned it over his face with fingers that were cool and sure. The wine began to go down that much faster...

It came almost as a surprise to Harry to find himself in the car, in the front passenger seat, with the girl driving beside him. They were just pulling away from the bright lights of the *Schützenfest*, but he did not remember leaving the great barn. He felt more than a little drunk—with pleasure as much as with wine.

"What's your name?" he asked, not finding it remarkable that he did not already know. Only the sound of the question seemed strange to him, as if a stranger had spoken the words.

"Cassilda," she replied.

"A nice name," he told her awkwardly. "Unusual."

"I was named after a distant...relative."

After a pause he asked: "Where are we going, Cassilda?"

"Is it important?"

"I'm afraid we can't go to Szolyhaza—" he began to explain.

She shrugged, "My...home, then."

"Is it far?"

"Not far, but—"

"But?"

She slowed the car, brought it to a halt. She was a shadowy silhouette beside him, her perfume washing him in warm waves. "On second thoughts, perhaps I had better take you straight back to your hotel—and leave you there."

"No, I wouldn't hear of it," he spoke quickly, seeing his hopes for the night crumbling about him, sobered by the thought that she could so very easily slip out of his life. The early hours of the morning would be time enough for slipping away—and *he* would be doing it, not the girl. "You'd have to walk home, for one thing, for I'm afraid I couldn't let you take the car..." To himself he added: And I know that taxis aren't to be found locally.

"Listen," he continued when she made no reply, "you just drive yourself home. I'll take the car from there back to my hotel."

"But you do not seem steady enough to drive."

"Then perhaps you'll make me a cup of coffee?" It was a terribly juvenile gambit, but he was gratified to see her smiling behind her mask.

Then, just as quickly as the smile had come, it fell away to be replaced by a frown he could sense rather than detect in the dim glow of the dashboard lights. "But you must not see where I live."

"Why on earth not?"

"It is not...a rich dwelling."

"I don't care much for palaces."

"I don't want you to be able to find your way back to me afterward. This can be for one night only..."

Now this, Harry thought to himself, is more like it! He felt his throat going dry again. "Cassilda, it can't possibly be for more than one night," he gruffly answered. "Tomorrow I leave for Budapest."

"Then surely it is better that—"

"Blindfold me!"

"What?"

"Then I won't be able to see where you live. If you blindfold me I'll see nothing except...your room." He reached across and slipped his hand inside her silk blouse, caressing a breast.

She reached over and stroked his neck, then pulled gently away. She nodded knowingly in the darkness: "Yes, perhaps we had better blindfold you, if you insist upon handling everything that takes your fancy!"

She tucked a black silk handkerchief gently down behind his mask, enveloping him in darkness. Exposed and compromised as she did this, she made no immediate effort to extricate herself as he fondled her breasts through the silk of her blouse. Finally, breathing the words into his face, she asked:

"Can you not wait?"

"It's not easy."

"Then I shall make it easier." She took his hands away from her body, sat back in her seat, slipped the car into gear and pulled away. Harry sat in total darkness, hot and flushed and full of lust.

"We are there," she announced, rousing him from some peculiar torpor. He was aware only of silence and darkness. He felt just a trifle queasy and told himself that it must be the effect of being driven blindfolded over poor roads. Had he been asleep? What a fool he was making of himself!

"No," she said as he groped for the door handle. "Let's just sit here for a moment or two. Open a bottle, I'm thirsty."

"Bottle? Oh, yes!" Harry suddenly remembered the two bottles of wine they had brought with them from the *Schützenfest*. He reached into the back seat and found one of them. "But we have no glasses. And why should we drink here when it would be so much more comfortable inside?"

She laughed briefly. "Harry, I'm a little nervous…"

Of course! French courage!—or was it Dutch? What odds? If a sip or two would help her get into the right frame of mind, why not? Silently he blessed the manufacturers of screw-top bottles and twisted the cap free. She took the wine from him, and he heard the swishing of liquid. Her perfume seemed so much stronger, heady as the scent of poppies. And yet beneath it he sensed…something tainted?

She returned the bottle to him and he lifted it to parched lips, taking a long deep draught. His head immediately swam, and he felt a joyous urge to break into wild laughter. Instead, discovering himself the victim of so strange a compulsion, he gave a little grunt of surprise.

When he passed the bottle back to her, he let his hand fall to her breast once more—and gasped at the touch of naked flesh, round and swelling! She had opened her blouse to him—or she had removed it altogether! With trembling fingers he reached for his mask and the handkerchief tucked behind it.

"No!" she said, and he heard the slither of silk. "There, I'm covered again. Here, finish the bottle and then get out of the car. I'll lead you…"

"Cassilda," he slurred her name. "Let's stop this little game now and—"

"You may not take off the blindfold until we are in my room, when we both stand naked." He was startled by the sudden coarseness of her voice—the lust he could now plainly detect—and he was also fired by it. He jerked violently when she took hold of him with a slender hand, working her fingers expertly, briefly, causing him to gabble some inarticulate inanity.

Momentarily paralysed with nerve-tingling pleasure and shock, when finally he thought to reach for her she was gone. He heard the whisper of her dress and the click of the car door as she closed it behind her.

Opening his own door he almost fell out, but her hand on his shoulder steadied him. "The other bottle," she reminded him.

Clumsily he found the wine, then stumbled as he turned from the car. She took his free hand, whispering: "Ssh! Quiet!" and gave a low guttural giggle.

Blind, he stumbled after her across a hard, faintly familiar surface. Something brushed against his leg, cold, furry and damp. The fronds of a bushy plant, he suspected.

"Lower your head," she commanded. "Carefully down the steps. This way. Almost there…"

"Cassilda," he said, holding tightly to her hand. "I'm dizzy."

"The wine!" she laughed.

"Wait, wait!" he cried, dragging her to a halt. "My head's swimming." He put out the hand that held the bottle, found a solid surface, pressed his knuckles against it and steadied himself. He leaned against a wall of sorts, dry and flaky to his touch, and gradually the dizziness passed.

This is no good, he told himself: I'll be of no damn use to her unless I can control myself! To her he said, "Potent stuff, your local wine."

"Only a few more steps," she whispered.

She moved closer and again there came the sound of sliding silk, of garments falling. He put his arm around her, felt the flesh of her body against the back of his hand. The weight of the bottle slowly pulled down his arm. Smooth firm buttocks—totally unlike Julia's, which sagged a little—did not flinch at the passing of fingers made impotent by the bottle they held.

"God!" he whispered, throat choked with lust. "I wish I could hold on to you for the rest of my life…"

She laughed, her voice hoarse as his own, and stepped away, pulling him after her. "But that's your second wish," she said.

Second wish… Second wish? He stumbled and almost fell, was caught and held upright, felt fingers busy at his jacket, the buttons of his shirt. Not at all cold, he shivered, and deep inside a tiny voice began to shout at him, growing louder by the moment, shrieking terrifying messages into his inner ear.

His second wish!

Naked he stood, suddenly alert, the alcohol turning to water in his system, the unbelievable looming real and immense and immediate as his four sound senses compensated for voluntary blindness.

"There," she said. "And now you may remove your blindfold!"

Ah, but her perfume no longer masked the charnel musk beneath; her girl's voice was gone, replaced by the dried-up whisper of centuries-shrivelled lips; the hand he held was—

Harry leapt high and wide, trying to shake off the thing that held his hand in a leathery grip, shrieking his denial in a black vault that echoed his cries like lunatic laughter. He leapt and cavorted, coming into momentary contact with the wall, tracing with his burning, supersensitive flesh the tentacled monstrosity that gloated there in bas-relief, feeling its dread embrace!

And bounding from the wall he tripped and sprawled, clawing at the casket which, in his mind's eye, he saw where he had last seen it at the foot of her couch. *Except that now the lid lay open!*

Something at once furry and slimy-damp arched against his naked leg—and again he leapt frenziedly in darkness, gibbering now as his mind teetered over vertiginous chasms.

Finally, dislodged by his threshing about, his blindfold—the red mask and black silk handkerchief he no longer dared remove of his own accord—slipped from his face… And then his strength became as that of ten men, became such that nothing natural or supernatural could ever have held him there in that nighted cave beneath black ruins.

Herr Ludovic Debrec heard the roaring of the car's engine long before the beam of its headlights swept down the black deserted road outside the inn. The vehicle rocked wildly and its tyres howled as it turned an impossibly tight corner to slam to a halt in the inn's tiny courtyard.

Debrec was tired, cleaning up after the day's work, preparing for the morning ahead. His handful of guests were all abed, all except the English Herr. This must be him now, but why the tearing rush? Peering through his kitchen window, Debrec recognised the car—then his weary eyes widened and he gasped out loud. But what in the name of all that…? The Herr was naked!

The Hungarian landlord had the door open wide for Harry almost before he could begin hammering upon it—was bowled to one side as the frantic, gasping, bulge-eyed figure rushed in and up the stairs—but he had seen enough, and he crossed himself as Harry disappeared into the inn's upper darkness.

"Mein Gott!" he croaked, crossing himself again, and yet again. "The Herr has been in *that* place!"

Despite her pills, Julia had not slept well. Now, emerging from unremembered, uneasy dreams, temples throbbing in the grip of a terrific headache, she pondered the problem of her awakening. A glance at the luminous dial of her wristwatch told her that the time was ten after two in the morning.

Now what had startled her awake? The slamming of a door somewhere? Someone sobbing? Someone crying out to her for help? She seemed to remember all of these things.

She patted the bed beside her with a lethargic gesture. Harry was not there. She briefly considered this, also the fact that his side of the bed seemed undisturbed. Then something moved palely in the darkness at the foot of the bed.

Julia sucked in air, reached out and quickly snapped on the bedside lamp. Harry lay naked, silently writhing on the floor, face down, his hands beneath him.

"Harry!" she cried, getting out of bed and going to him. With a bit of a struggle she turned him on to his side, and he immediately rolled over on his back.

She gave a little shriek and jerked instinctively away from him, revulsion twisting her features. Harry's eyes were screwed shut now, his lips straining back from his teeth in unendurable agony. His hands held something to his heaving chest, something black and crumbly. Even as Julia watched, horrified, his eyes wrenched open and his face went slack. Then Harry's hands fell away from his chest; in one of them, the disintegrating black thing seemed burned into the flesh of his palm and fingers. It was unmistakably a small mummified hand!

Julia began to crawl backwards away from him across the floor; as she did so something came from behind, moving sinuously where it brushed against her. Seeing it, she scuttled faster, her mouth working silently as she came up against the wall of the room.

The—creature—went to Harry, snatched the shrivelled hand from him, turned away…then, as if on an afterthought, turned back. It arched against him for a moment, and, with the short feelers around its mouth writhing greedily, quickly sank its sharp teeth into the flesh of his leg. In the next instant the thing was gone, but Julia didn't see where it went.

Unable to tear her eyes away from Harry, she saw the veins in his leg where he had been bitten turn a deep, dark blue and stand out, throbbing beneath his marble skin. Carried by the now sluggish pulsing of his blood, the creature's venom spread through him. But…poison? No, it was much more, much worse, than poison. For as the writhing veins came bursting through his skin, Harry began to melt. It went on for some little time, until what was left was the merest travesty of a man: a sticky, tarry thing of molten flesh and smoking black bones.

Then, ignoring the insistent hammering now sounding at the door, Julia drew breath into her starving lungs—drew breath until she thought her chest must burst—and finally expelled it all in one vast eternal scream…

THE HYMN

One of my most recent stories, "The Hymn" was written in July/August 2003, specifically for a new "pulp", H. P. Lovecraft's Magazine of Horror. So here we are as I write this, two years or more later, and the No. 3 issue—allegedly a "Lumley issue"—still hasn't appeared. History repeats! Presumably it will have appeared, at least by the time you read "The Hymn" in this current collection.*

*I received my copies 1st November 2006.

There were six of us—eight, if I include the two men in the cell. Not a cell as in a prison, more a large partitioned room or apartment—or rather a closed, controlled environment with all the necessary life-support systems; also a fail-safe which could be brought into play to cancel the said life-supports in the unlikely event that such action became imperative.

The cell's walls, floors and ceilings were of welded five-inch thick carbon steel plates, buttressed on the outside; the inlet and outlet conduits, as few as possible, had bores of no more than two inches; the entire structure— its adjuncts and supporting complex—was subterranean in a mountainous region, thus making use of a nuclear shelter left over from a war that had never come to pass. There had been lesser wars, certainly, but not the BIG ONE that we had all been afraid of back in the early '60s.

Actually, it was during the aftermath of one of those so-called "lesser" wars (as if there ever was any such thing) that the events leading to my current position as director and coordinator of T.M.I. or "The Mythos Investigation" had taken place—but to speak of that now would be to jump the gun as it were, and anyway it will come up later, wherefore it better serves my purpose to proceed with my description of the subterrene facility, also to explain something of my fellow observers, and then to let the principal participants in the experiment, our human guinea pigs in the cell, tell the story in their own words.

So, there was myself: a Foundation Member (I'm afraid I can say no more on that subject), also one other Foundation Member, an elderly colleague; there were two men from military intelligence, both high-ranking, inferior only to the highest governmental authorities; there was a female psychiatric specialist, and finally a technician, a man who—having been responsible for the design and construction of the cell, its adjuncts and surroundings—was completely familiar with its workings. He knew how to run the place, and just as importantly how to shut it down. As for myself and my elderly colleague: we were there by virtue of our alleged expertise in certain matters of grotesque myth and legend.

With regard to the names and physical descriptions of the team: I deem these particulars unnecessary; at this late date I see no reason to compromise anyone. And details of the precise location of our sub-sierran venue are likewise out of the question, since I have no doubt it remains a much guarded secret to this day.

And so back to the cell:

The cell had no windows…it wasn't required that the men inside should be able to look out. That would be a distraction, and they certainly wouldn't want to see us looking in. We were, of course, "looking in", though not through windows as such; for even one-way viewports would not have allowed total visual access. But recessed into the interior walls, ceilings and various fittings were tiny closed-circuit cameras each with an exterior screen. Audio was similarly available, indeed absolutely necessary.

The cell was equipped with small bedrooms, bathrooms, cooking facilities, and a large refrigerator containing enough food and drink for several weeks. Lighting was of course artificial; it could be switched off in the bedrooms, so that our subjects might sleep. But even there we were not to be excluded: bedroom cameras could be switched to infrared. It was of the utmost importance that we should be able to see them—and perhaps even listen to them—when they slept.

As to their names: while I am certain that their real names may be found in Foundation archives, where I have no doubt they are kept secure, I shall nevertheless provide them with pseudonyms…. Letters such as this one may not be as safe as Foundation records. They were Jason and James. On the other hand, I will give them at least something of physical descriptions, if only to enhance the reader's mental picture of them during the discoursive passages to follow.

They were of a height, perhaps five-nine or ten; also of an age, say thirty-two, with Jason the elder by five or six months. Jason was a redhead, outspoken, careless in both dress and attitude, often flippant but never insulting. Lanky and jaunty if a little lopsided in his gait, he had green eyes, a long straight nose and gaunt cheeks. James was quite Jason's opposite. Admitting to a sedentary lifestyle, he had wisps of thinning, prematurely grey hair on a bulbous skull, sharp, permanently narrow and penetrating blue eyes, a small mouth and receding chin, all set on a burly, powerful if under-utilized frame. In short, and if in the near future he did not take up some form of exercise, he could expect to go to seed. Also, where Jason was invariably plain speaking James frequently tended to more elaborate prose, perhaps to affect a semblance of personal mystery, an esoteric éclat or occult ambiance.

And why not? Since by his own admittance James was "psychically endowed", for which reason he'd become one of our guinea pigs of course. As for Jason: at first he had seemed bewildered by the whole thing. But he had been unemployed, and we had made him an irresistible offer.

Their induction had come following various checks and controls. First: they were just two out of two and a half thousand applicants who answered our ad in national broadsheets. Second: after discarding the sad, mistaken, lying, wannabe, and lunatic two thousand four hundred, the finalists had undergone an exhaustive series of parapsychological tests, which further narrowed the field. Both James and Jason had passed with flying colours, once again to the latter's apparent astonishment. Third: during Zener Card testing at a government establishment, they had been brought into close proximity with an "alien artefact"; this had been caused to occur while they slept in a dormitory unaware of what was happening and under close, covert observation. Both of them had experienced troubling dreams, indeed nightmares.

(Additional to my description of the cell: the "alien artefact" mentioned in the preceeding paragraph was fixed centrally in a strengthened glass sphere upon a marble pedestal in the living area, where its influence if any would be unavoidable by the two men.)

Oh, and one other factor conducive to their recruitment: they were both readers of other-worldly romances, with a penchant for the macabre; and so they were acquainted with the speculative fiction facet of matters which the Foundation had been attempting to fathom for several decades. In short, their minds would not be closed to themes, theories, and suggestions which narrower, more orthodox intellects might find unacceptable and immediately refute: they were "familiar" with notions of parallel dimensions, UFOs, alien encounters, and et cetera.

Enough: I have set the scene as clearly as possible within certain limits. So now let James and Jason speak for themselves.

One last point. While the following conversations are accurate (as covertly recorded by myself) I've excised and replaced certain names and references as a further security measure. For as elsewhere stated correspondence such as this—intended only for the eyes of my former Foundation colleagues—may not be as safe as their archive records.

NOTE: for easy recognition, all such altered sections will be parenthesized...

Jason, yawning: "What time do you have?"

James, showing great disinterest: "Does it really matter? After all, we're not going anywhere."

Jason: "I like to be regular in my habits and I'm feeling a bit hungry, so I suspect it's time to eat."

James: "You could regulate your habits by wearing a watch—but since I know you'll only ask again, and since I'm already bored by this meaningless conversation...it's six-forty. And before you ask, that's p.m."

Jason, grinning: "Thank you. Most gracious of you. And it seems I was right: time to eat."

James: "I'm not hungry."

Jason: "Then don't eat. Me, I'm frying up mushrooms with a few slices of liver and bacon."

James, suddenly restless: "Then perhaps I will eat, after all."

Jason, going to the fridge: "I'll be sure to set out equal, fresh portions for you...unless you want me to cook them for you?"

James, sighing: "Would that be such an inconvenience?"

Jason: "No more than glancing at your watch occasionally, no."

James, changing the subject, staring fixedly at the artefact in its glass sphere, where its pedestal rose through the centre of the circular table at which he was seated: "Did you dream last night?"

Jason, frowning, and squirting a mist of olive oil into a frying pan: "Three nights, three dreams, yes."

James: "The same dream?"

Jason, perhaps slightly troubled: "The very same: But very vague... More a set of sensations than a dream proper. Nothing clearly visual, nothing spoken out loud. Mental whispers, or—I don't know—instinctive knowledge? Well, if you know what I mean."

James: "Interesting. And of course I know what you mean! Do you think you're more sensitive to this stuff than I am? I have been living with the knowledge of the truth of all this for…for longer than I care to think. Oh, yes. And I was dreaming my dreams long before they sat me in front of this thing." He indicated the artefact, enlarged and distorted by the glass of its globe.

Jason, with perhaps a hint of amusement or gentle sarcasm in his voice: "You have always known you were, er, psychic?"

James: "My parapsychological or ESP skills are different from yours—each to his own mentality—but yes, I have always known. I feel things from afar, and in my dreams they are made manifest. Even though I am not given to understand everything, still I see what is *now*…unlike you who sees what will be."

Jason, nodding, turning slivers of liver and bacon slices in his pan: "Or so I've lately discovered—but I didn't know, not for sure. Or maybe I did, but tried to avoid it—because it worried me."

James, with a snort: "Being able to see the future worried you? You were too dim to find a use for a skill like that? You scored 78 per cent on the Zener test, yet you were too poor to afford a wristwatch? And if you were 'trying to avoid it', why on earth did you answer the ad in the first place?"

Jason: "*Because* I was too poor to afford a wristwatch—or anything else for that matter! We weren't all born with silver spoons in our mouths, you know! Anyway, why do I annoy you? Is there that about me which reminds you of something intolerably nasty that you stepped in at one time or another? Or could it be some kind of jealousy, because my skills are apparent while yours are—let's face it—more or less, er, obscure?"

James, straightening up, narrowing his eyes more yet: "My skills may be obscure, as you put it, but our sponsors saw fit to choose me no less than you. In fact, I have always been…chosen. From the very first moment I read of (Cxxxxxx) and the others of the pantheon I knew that they were real; and that one day—when my stars were in the ascendant—I would communicate with them."

Jason, not quite sneering, but with a cynical twist to his mouth: "Why can't you say what you mean?"

James, sharply: "I beg your pardon?"

Jason: "Don't you mean, 'when the stars are right'?"

James, with a cold sidelong glance at Jason: "Interpret my words as you will—and (Axxxxxxx's) if you dare! But he wasn't such a madman, that old Arab. Or if he was, it was what he half knew but could not fathom that made him that way." And, after a brief pause: "Doesn't it concern you that you could be a millionaire instead of a pauper?"

Jason, returning to the table with two plates of sizzling food: "Are you talking about gambling again? How I could have beaten the bookies, cleaned up at roulette, broken the bank at Monte Carlo? But you know what they say about practice, how it makes perfect?... Maybe I didn't want to perfect what I might have suspected I could do. Perhaps I didn't want to see things—certain things—any clearer. It could even be that some of the futures I had seen were too clear by half."

The pair, lapsing into silence while they eat. But after a while James asking: "What is it you saw that frightened you so? Myself, I have no fear with regard to the Mythos. I might possibly fear my own imaginings, which are not real, but I cannot fear what *is* real—and imminent! What is real exists, and what exists will find ways to impinge and may not be avoided. Wherefore what use to fear it?"

Jason, around his last mouthful of food: "But exactly! *Que sera, sera!* Ah, but would you really want to know the day, hour, and minute of your own death? And can't you see how knowing it you would try to avoid it?—to no avail. *Que sera, sera!*"

James, his eyes fully open, staring now: "You saw your own death?"

Jason, thoughtfully: "Not my death, no—but my brother's, and my mother's. Enough to put me off."

James: "Interesting. Can you tell me about it?"

Jason: "Not now. Some other time, maybe. But now I'm tired. A glass of white wine might help me sleep...hopefully not to dream."

James: "But that is why we are here! Surely you've divined that much?"

Jason: "Of course. But still I get paid, whether I dream or not. And I prefer not."

To which there is no answer...

Jason tosses, turns, and sweats in his sleep. He cries out, but feebly, on several occasions. The wine has not helped.

James is similarly affected. But he isn't so much nightmaring as experiencing; which is to say that while Jason is trying to escape from whatever pursues or threatens, James accepts it. His claim that he does not fear the Mythos (the effects wrought by the artefact) appear to be borne out. Our psychiatric specialist is at least of that opinion: that unlike Jason, James has been having—or perhaps receiving?—dreams such as this for a long time, even as long as he claims, and has become inured.

But he is voluble.

He speaks of a (Shining Txxxxxxxxxxxx): an odd geometrical figure, and of a "prehistoric city, Mnar"—*not* the ruins in the Deer Park at Benares. He spouts of "the outer spheres" and "star-spawn", and "the lenses of light", before his subconscious ramblings become unintelligible gibberings—a mush and a mumble, defying reproduction by normal human vocal chords, and proving equally difficult to represent, even as writing. Then, after a period of lying perfectly still in an attitude of rapt attention, as if he were listening to something or someone, he states quite clearly, "I shall be your vessel, your gate, your embodiment. And through you I shall visit the farthest places: that roiling lake where the puffed (Sxxxxxxxx) spawn, the spiralling Towers of (Txxxxxxx), the dark light-years twirling like leaves blown in a storm. But...this 'great harvest' of which you speak. Pray tell me, what shall we harvest?"

And then a gasp, a cry choked off, his body snapping into a weird rigidity and only very slowly relaxing, and his breathing steadying as his face slackens and he falls more deeply asleep, as if soothed by some unseen hypnotist's persuasions...

The night passes. The pair sleep late, and when they rise they avoid each other...James very deliberately, Jason because he can't be bothered with the surliness of the other's moods.

Jason cooks breakfast for himself; James doesn't eat until well into the afternoon when he makes a small cheese sandwich, then sits eating it, scowling at the artefact. And finally:

James: "I believe I heard you call out in the night?"

Jason: "Unlike the outer shell of this place, the partitions between our rooms are thin as cardboard! You could hear a mouse fart on the other side. As for my outcry: well, my dream was a particularly bad one."

James: "Which doubtless accounts for your mood."

Jason: "Oh?"

James: "Your silence."

Jason: "Listen who's talking! We were here for forty-eight hours before you so much as grunted!"

James: "As I recall, you complained to me about the lack of a TV. You asked why not. I did not grunt. I pointed out that as well as the absence of a TV there was no radio and indeed nothing that might interfere with our seclusion, concentration, the immanence of ulterior forces. And incidentally, I don't dislike you. You accused me of disliking you, but that is not so. It is simply that I am remote from you...my thoughts are rarely mundane. And when I am disturbed—when my thoughts are interrupted—then naturally it becomes an inconvenience, an annoyance. So you see it isn't the case that I dislike you, rather that I despise idle prattle. Not dislike but disinclination, disinterest."

Jason, sighing, shaking his head: "You don't seem to realise just how insulting such remarks are. Now I'm not normally a surly fellow, but I can certainly feel myself sliding that way. Today *you* were the one who commenced 'prattling', and I suspect you're not yet done!"

James: "Because while *you* fail to excite my interest, your dreams are quite another matter. On several occasions I am sure I heard you cry out. This was before I myself fell asleep. Were you dreaming of your brother? Or perhaps your mother? I believe I heard you call a name. But I was only half awake and so can't be sure."

Jason: "Is this important to you? I can't see why. And what with your lack of interest in me—the fact that my presence is 'an inconvenience' and even 'an annoyance'—I don't see why I should trouble myself to talk to you at all, not a single word! And certainly not about my poor dead mother or brother."

James: "But the fact is you were prescient in the matter of their deaths. Could it be that your dreams represent guilt? You foresaw their deaths and could do nothing about it...*que sera, sera*. And now they come back to haunt you. As to why this is of interest to me: I see the NOW while failing to understand where it is going, while you see what is to be without knowing how to avoid it. I seek to probe deeper, while you turn away from your talent."

Jason, shrugging: "So? Is there a lesson to be learned from these supposed facts? What is your conclusion?"

James, a trifle reluctantly: "That...perhaps we ought to work together? After all, that presumably is why they saw fit to lodge us as a pair."

Jason: "Possibly, but it's a shame they couldn't have found me a female guinea pig partner. That way I wouldn't be spending quite so much time dreaming."

James, raising an eyebrow: "Sex? I have no time for it and never will have. It is an animal activity. Out beyond the stars...their procreation is different. More a melding, a substitution, a flowing together, and an explosive multiplication."

Jason, singing: "...It's the name of the game, and each generation..."

James, apparently aghast: "You would do well not to mock!"

Jason: "Oh, really? I shouldn't mock? When what you've just said sounded like you were describing a clan of alien amoebas?"

James, apparently in disgust: "Pshaw!"

✤ ✤ ✤

Later:

Jason, sitting at the table staring at the artefact, then bursting abruptly into speech: "My brother—and especially my mother—bring me warnings. Yes, I'm oneiromantic, but my precognition isn't so much advanced knowledge of what to do or to avoid doing but, as you might have it, knowledge of the direction in which my current position or standing is leading me. In other words, their warnings are useless by reason of the fact that the outcome cannot be avoided. They can warn of my going to hell, but they can't offer me a fire-proof parachute!"

James: "*Que...*"

Jason, cutting the other off: "Yes, yes! Of course! What will be will be."

James, nodding sagely: "So then, the dead go on; at least their thoughts: they are not dead who can forever lie. Having undergone their change—knowing more of Being by experiencing Not Being—they attempt to communicate their knowledge, their warnings, to the living loved ones they left behind. In which case I suspect—no, I affirm—that we have this in common with the gods of outer spheres. They too go on forever. Except they don't die but are truly immortal! In my dreams I've seen them; their myriad shapes seeping down from the stars!"

Jason: "I only know of me and mine, which are real things. As for alien beings 'seeping' down from the stars: the nearest star—other than Sol—is four and a half light-years away. That is one hell of a seep! I am convinced it's all a fiction. Think about it. A certain star is a billion light years away. Even at the speed of light your alien 'gods' will take a billion years to get here. And if they are only 'seeping'...?"

James, with a shrug: "As for it being a fiction, our hosts don't seem to think so, else why are we here? And as for 'seeping': a poetic turn of phrase. The Old Gentleman might just as well have used 'filtering', which is another slow process."

Jason: "Yes, he used 'seeping'; but he meant it like poison in a wound, like pus from an open sore. And remember: the gods of his pantheon were evil. Is that what you crave, the destruction of everything we consider good?"

James, sneeringly: "*Hah!* Good, bad, love, hate—emotions in general—*They* are beyond, above all that! And anyway, you miss what should be obvious: that they are timeless."

Jason, grunting, and the corners of his mouth turning down: "Timeless—sleeping but not dead—oh yeah, sure."

James, dreamily, ignoring Jason's obvious sarcasm: "Immortal they journey, wandering between the stars, pausing now and then, but only long enough to...to *harvest* their worlds."

Jason: "Immortal? They will be here until the end? Doesn't that imply that they were here at the beginning? How, immortal? Though I'll grant you they would need to be to 'seep' down from the stars!"

James: "Exactly! And that is the point you missed. For when you speak of the speed of light you should not forget that time stands still at such a speed! It is the secret of their immortality: that during their journey *they do not age!*"

Jason does not answer immediately; when he does, it is only to frown and ask: "Do you think that perhaps we're confused? Do *you* feel confused? Our conversations, our arguments, seem to go in circles. And personally my mind never felt so cluttered! But...maybe I've asked you that before? Or did you ask me?"

James, ignoring the other's question and indicating with a nod of his head and a pointed finger the artefact in its glass globe: "There it is: a 'lens of light', or so I believe. But do you know where they found it, these people who are using us in an attempt to prove its properties?"

Jason, blinking rapidly, as if to clear his head of confusing thoughts: "No, do you?"

James: "Absolutely! Before I volunteered my person for this experiment, I had them volunteer their sources, their whys and wherefors. Are you interested?"

Jason: "I shall try to be."

James: "It was five years ago, in Iraq, after the war that deposed Saddam the Dictator."

Jason: "Ah, yes! Saddam Hussein and his alleged, er, weapons of mass destruction? I remember."

James: "The American forces stopped a truck on its way to Syria. They found a large amount of gold, a million dollars in hundred dollar bills, and certain items of immense antiquity—including an old book or scroll written in an ancient, indecipherable script. The book contained a map of the desert—with a certain area marked out in the shape of a five-pointed star. It transpired that the book's ancient text was the language of a sunken city or continent lost in Pacific deeps."

Jason: "By any chance, (R'xxxx)? Where (Cxxxxxx) lies dreaming?"

James, nodding: "The same—or so I suspect—though for some reason no one has deigned to confirm my suspicion in that regard. But, learning of the book's existence, a certain esoteric organisation took steps to obtain it. Among our hosts are members of that organisation....Do you want to know more?"

Jason: "All very interesting. And by all means carry on."

James: "As you wish. The five-pointed star symbol is well known; indeed its powers, if any, have long been prone to argument among certain savants—"

Jason: "Savants?"

James: "Authorities, such as you and I."

Jason: "But I don't consider myself an 'authority,' merely a reader of weird and macabre fiction."

James, scornfully: "Not to mention someone who catches the occasional glimpse of the future! But let me proceed:

"The map indicated or superimposed this pentagram on a portion of the Iraqi desert. And the most important thing is this, that the desert has not changed in a million years, not to any significant degree. Anyway, the esoteric organisation of which I speak sent their agents to investigate, ostensibly to search out elusive weapons of mass destruction said to be hidden somewhere in those great wastelands. But in fact they had predetermined to locate the points of the star symbol—and from these to determine its geometric centre.

"This was not nearly as difficult as it might at first have seemed. The locals offered up information; they said that there were five 'holy men' who occupied the selfsame locations out in the desert. And each of the five—drug-addicted Dervishes, as it transpired, and completely bereft of reason as perceived in our Western society—was discovered to be in possession of a star-stone! Alas, they were also in possession of Russian small arms, which they did not hesitate to turn on the investigators. Enter the military, who dealt with these five 'terrorists' with despatch...or so I assume since the star-stones were confiscated or 'commandeered.'

"Now we move to the geometric centre: a dried-up well, into which our investigators descend, and down below discover a vast natural cavern, once a waterway—but how many millennia ago?—whose walls are carved with myriad foreign or alien sigils. And upon a marble pedestal at the approximate centre—"

Jason, pointing at the artefact in its glass bubble: "That thing."

James: "Indeed!"

Jason: "I see. And the star-stones kept it secure, turning aside its malign influence. Correct?"

James, shaking his head: "This is not how I perceive it...though I can see how such confusion in the Mythos arose originally. No, I believe that upon a time the cavern housed a Being. As for 'malign': I fail to see anything malign in this. What I do see is that there are travellers out there among the stars; not gods, not evil aliens, in no way a threat, but scientists! Different, certainly—our superiors in as many fields as you care to number, and in others that you can't even imagine, you may be sure—but 'kept secure', yes, I can agree with that."

Jason: "Secure against what?"

James: "Secure against being disturbed! It is a marker, and perhaps even a Gateway, for those who wander the star spaces."

Jason, whose sneer no longer carries conviction: "Sure, and who perform their wandering, seeping, or filtering at the speed of light, eh? As for these five Arab madmen, these zealots: why were they so protective of the star-stones, or rather, this so-called 'lens of light'? Why would they lay down their lives for it? Were they protecting it as some kind of holy relic, or were they in fact protecting us, humankind, *from* it?"

James: "Bah! Your thoughts are mired in fear! You're a pronounced xenophobe!"

Jason: "Possibly, and on a cosmic scale at that! But in the light of my precognizance, ask yourself this: what do you suppose I am most afraid of?"

James: "Of the (Gxxxx Oxx Oxxx), the Outer Ones, of course. Of the thought of *Them* in the spaces between the spaces we know—in the stellar voids—riding the gravitic waves of exploding stars! Of their superiority!"

Jason: "Wrong! But you've mentioned two things that do concern me. One: you spoke of Them harvesting their worlds—"

James, starting, blinking, obviously taken aback: "Eh? Did I? A harvest? Yes, indeed, I seem to recall saying something of the sort. I may even have dreamed something of it. But now…I can't seem to remember what it was about."

Jason: "There are beads of sweat on your brow. Are you now feeling confused?"

James, wiping his forehead: "Quite right. It's suddenly hot in here. Whoever controls the temperature is not doing his job. But confused? I'm…not sure." Then, after a moment's thought: "And two?"

Jason: "Two?"

James: "The second thing I said that concerns you. What was it?"

Jason: "Ah yes! You called the lens a 'Gateway'. And if so, well, wouldn't that be something to fear?"

James, throwing his arms wide: "For *thought*! A Gateway that allows my thoughts to reach out to *Them*…and theirs to reach me—to reach us, if you would only help me, assist me in opening up our minds to them!"

Jason, thoughtfully: "I think we've both been somewhat confused ever since being put in this place. I certainly have not been thinking clearly, and you've blown hot and cold—contradicted yourself—on several occasions. But if what you say is right: that the lens is a Gateway for mental communication…well, perhaps that would explain it."

James, snapping his fingers: "And there you have it! Their thoughts are incompatible with ours, or at best only marginally readable. Can we explain ourselves to sea snakes or gibbons? No of course not! Likewise their purpose—their messages—come unclear, distorted, and misunderstood by us."

Jason: "You admit it, then? That we are being influenced by that thing in the globe?"

James: "Is there any need to admit what was obvious to me from the start? It is why we are here; to enable our observers to discover to what degree we are influenced. For after all, we are the guinea pigs—the ones with enhanced psychic senses—whereas they are merely…observers."

NOTE: In this James was only partly right. I was not lacking in certain psychic sensitivities myself; not as intense as James's or Jason's, true, but certainly I had experienced and was still experiencing something of the lens's peculiar influence, a sort of mental confusion—as had the Dervishes in the Iraqi desert, to the extent that prolonged exposure was probably responsible for their madness. It was not our intention, however, to allow so grave a deterioration in our subjects; the experiment could be brought to a close at any time. No, our main interest lay in whatever other properties the lens might or might not possess.

James, continuing: "So then, shall we work together rather than continue to constantly needle each other?"

Jason: "If I have needled it was only or mainly in riposte. And I think I'll sleep on the idea of working together. Perhaps someone will advise me in that regard."

James: "Your…relatives?"

Jason: "Perhaps. My mother was clairvoyant, and my brother…was my twin. We were all three in a traffic accident. I saw it coming but could do nothing about it. In the moment of their deaths…maybe something transferred to me. It strikes me as possible that they had seen it coming, too. As to why that may be relevant to our current situation: I have been experiencing similar feelings of imminence."

James: "You are worried that you're going to die?"

Jason: "I feel…a sense of transference, metamorphosis—as if I were about to take flight!"

James, nodding: "Light-headedness. I can feel it, too—the pressure of my thoughts."

Jason: "Ah yes, thoughts! Which reminds me of something you said earlier. On that same subject, tell me if you will how you intend to exchange thoughts with alien Beings who could be billions of light years away? That is, assuming the speed of light to be the ultimate reach of material things."

James: "But you have supplied the answer to your own question! Thought is *not* material. It may take time and myriad small electrical impulses to cogitate, but once a thought is set free it exists everywhere. The lens amplifies thoughts, directs them and makes them accessible. But a thought in itself, in its immanence, is as far ranging as the entire universe!"

Jason: "Accessible, but not understandable?"

James, nodding: "Hence the confusion, our confusion. We are less than successful at comprehending the incomprehensible, the mental emanations of minds that think in a great many more dimensions than our pitiful three."

Jason, tiredly now: "Well anyway, let's sleep on it…"

But of course the observers must sleep too. We were taking the watch in shifts; that night it was the turn of our psychiatric specialist and myself. The technician slept as best possible on a couch in a room adjacent. It was not the best of times for my mental processes; I was feeling the strain; indeed, the thought had crossed my mind that despite the strength and thickness of the cell's walls I, too, was in close proximity to the lens.

The lens:

Three inches across, a scalloped, faceted disc of what appeared to be smoky quartz. Its constituent elements had not been analysed for fear of damaging its as yet unknown properties. It seemed inactive; had never shown any kind of activity; might as well have been some not especially elegant paperweight.

I asked my companion of the night watch for her thoughts on the subject.

"The lens?" She brought the object in its glass bubble into focus on one of the screens. "I find it…disturbing."

"Its looks, shape, opacity?"

"Its presence."

She meant its proximity, of course. "Do you feel in any way…confused?"

She smiled. "Tiredness, that's all. Leading to a perfectly natural lack of concentration." Which confirmed what I had suspected…

James, his eyes hollow, red-rimmed: "Well, we've slept on it—myself, badly. And frankly, I have had enough of this so-called experiment. I suggest we put our minds to it, see or experience what we see or experience, and however it goes we call it a day and demand to be out of here. As far as I am concerned they can keep their money. I know what I know, and that must suffice."

Jason, cooking breakfast, his voice far-distant: "I dreamed of dinosaurs; herds of them, thousands of them, stampeding."

James, with a start, his sore eyes blinking rapidly: "Why, so did I!" And then, recovering himself and rather more calmly, "What do you suppose it means?"

Jason, having apparently failed to hear, or having ignored James' question: "I also dreamed of my mother and brother. They didn't say anything and looked sad, but in any case I knew what they were thinking: that I wouldn't be joining them."

James: "That you are not going to die? A good omen, eh?"

Jason, shaking his head: "No, just that I won't be joining them. I also heard a song or a chant…no, it was more properly a hymn or song of—I don't know—thanksgiving? Possibly." And giving himself a shake. "Breakfast is up. We might as well enjoy it." Then, as they commence eating: "We always assumed it was a meteorite or comet that took out the dinosaurs, right?"

James: "So?"

Jason: "What if it was *Them?*"

James, nodding: "I know what you mean, but it just doesn't fit the picture. You're talking about prehistory. Who was there here to call them down from the stars? Man's earliest ancestors hadn't as yet crawled up out of the oceans, let alone come down from the trees!"'

Jason, bringing the food—eggs and bacon—seating himself close to James and handing him a plate; then absentmindedly, or even fatalistically picking at his own food: "What if *They* were already here? Or maybe they just happened to be passing by, and saw how rich it was—the planet, I mean. Personally, I believe that one of them was here, alone in a crazily angled city maybe something like (R'xxxx). And he/she/it called through a lens to its friends in the stars. And the closest of them came—"

James: "—To the harvest? Is that what you are saying? But even if I thought you could be right, still it might have taken them millions of years to get here."

Jason: "But the dinosaurs were here for millions of years—for a whole lot longer than we've been here, anyway."

James: "And that cavern out in the Iraqi desert? You think it's all that remains of that prehistoric city? Forget it! That cave is recent by comparison. A million, or perhaps two million years old, but no more than that."

Jason: "I agree. No, I think who or whatever was there in the Iraqi cavern got called away long ago, perhaps to a harvesting somewhere out in the stars. But he had seen the beginnings of Homo sapiens, and he left the lens for us to find. Maybe old (Axxxx) was something of a dreamer—maybe he was gifted, that old Arab—like us, but he got it wrong. Maybe the stars don't 'come right' until some intelligence finds them *and takes them away*! Because they aren't stars in the sky after all but starstones buried deep in the earth! Too many maybes, I agree, but maybe, just maybe..."

James, scathingly: "And maybe, just maybe, you want to give in, quit right now—right?"

Jason: "Quit? On the contrary. I think we should go ahead, speak to them through the lens. Why? Because we can't avoid the unavoidable. And I know you'll do it anyway, because you're ignorant, arrogant and pig-headed. And what the hell... *Que sera, sera!*" He shrugs, again fatalistically.

James, tight-lipped: "Putting insults such as that aside—if only because contact will probably be easier with your help—when do you propose we do it? Tonight?"

Jason, shrugging: "Tonight, tomorrow night, next Friday...what difference does it make down here? Why not right now?"

James, turning to stare at the lens in its glass globe, the lens that Jason has been staring at from the moment he sat down at the table: "Right now? Are you sure?"

Jason, putting his plate aside: "It's all...all very confusing, isn't it?"

James: "Do you feel you're being lured?"

Jason: "Lured? Let me think about that." And a brief moment later: "Yes, I believe I can feel that thing tugging at me. But mainly I just feel as I think you feel—that come what may we have to know. Or we have to know come what *will*."

James, also pushing his plate of untouched food aside, and resting his chin in his cupped hands: "Very well then, let's do it..."

NOTE: Following our night shift—myself and our good lady psychiatrist—we could by now have been asleep; but something had kept us at our stations, where we had been joined by our Military companions and my Foundation colleague. Our technician was drowsing in a room close by, but such were my feelings of—of what? Uncertainty, confusion, imminence—of interference with my thinking, that I had known I would be unable to sleep. Which was probably also true of my night's companion.

I have mentioned my own somewhat shallow extrasensory perceptions; but now through the medium of this ESP I "perceived" a current that was almost electric, a faint tingle in my scalp. And I was aware that on my viewscreen the forms of the two men in the cell had taken on a kind of rigidity. Their eyes—and their sensitive minds, obviously—were now rapt upon the lens in its bowl atop the pedestal.

And that was when I fought back against my own feelings of almost hypnotic lethargy to send one of our Military number to wake the technician…

Jason, his eyes wide open, staring; his mouth agape; his voice little more than a whisper: "I can hear them singing. The same song or hymn I heard in my dream. It's dark, yet somehow joyful…a strange dark joy."

James, excitedly, but at the same time oddly dull or vacant of volume: "Then rejoice in the contact! Out there in the stars, they have heard us!"

Jason: "In the stars, or between the spaces we know? Is the lens a telepathic transmitter, or is it in fact a true Gateway? What if *They*…what if they're extra-dimensional?"

James, a bubble of foam forming at the corner of his mouth: "How far away is an extra-dimension? 'Beyond' the universe?"

Jason, twitching, his knuckles turning white on the table's rim: "But what…what if…what if it's parallel?"

James, beginning to shudder violently: "I hear the singing, too! And although it's alien, I believe there are parts that I recognise or at least understand."

Jason, his body jerking, threatening to topple his chair: "Their thoughts are merging with ours; either that or they are translating them for us, making them recognisable. And the lens…it *is* a Gateway. And they're using it! They're coming!"

James, dead white, foaming at the mouth, his eyes bulging, entire body vibrating: "I think…I think we should stop now. I think we should…think we have to withdraw. I sense chaos. And the lens: it's glowing, blazing, opening! *Ah! Ahhh! Ahhhh!"*

⊕ ⊕ ⊕

NOTE: It is difficult to describe what we saw happening on our screens from this point on. But I shall try.

The lens in its globe was shimmering, emitting lances and arcs of bright white light that came through the glass to dart around the cell like living things, like snakes of fire. These dozen or so streamers or coruscations were certainly sentient; they appeared to be searching, or perhaps surveying, the immediate vicinity, but in something less than five or six seconds they converged into two main beams that struck unerringly home at the heads of our subjects. It happened that fast, literally with lightning speed, and "confused" as we four observers were (our technician and the Military man I had sent to awaken him were only now returning) there was nothing we could do to stop it. And on our screens—

—The pair appeared to be melting! Their faces were showing extraordinary agony; they glowed until their eyes and gaping mouths were black sockets in bright, luminous silhouettes; their shaking seemed to be tearing them apart, so that glowing bits were drifting from them like fiery snowflakes…and yet they were singing!

Over and above a high-pitched, alien keening—a blast of noise I can only describe as a battle of unknown elements, the sound of waves breaking on some cosmic shore—came the words of that song driven into their shattered minds and out through their mouths, that "hymn" translated from its original form by who or whatever they had contacted. And in my own mind I *heard* or *sensed* something of that original form—that hideous cacophony that human vocal chords could never hope to duplicate—and I knew its relevance!

"Stop it!" I cried then, to anyone who was listening—*if* anyone was listening. "Shut the thing down!"

My companions were reeling—shocked, numbed, made useless, by what they, too, were receiving from the lens, that now fully open portal. But as for the *physical* intruders, those shafts of alien light or sentient fire: they were only the vanguard. For what was coming through now was more properly the stuff of our most terrifying nightmares.

They moved too quickly, too strangely, to be viewed in any kind of clear detail. But in colour they were a pulsing yellow-veined or marbled purple and black, and in shape reminiscent of spiders, scorpions, octopi or dragons…all these things from moment to moment, and others utterly indescribable. Yet I knew that even these were only a squad of advance troops.

James and Jason: they were beginning to slump into themselves, like slowly collapsing columns or candles of intense white light; but even so, quite beyond pain as we understand it, they *continued* to sing their joyful song.

"Shut the damn thing down!" I yelled again, this time right in the ear of our technician, who was looking at his instrument panel as if he had never seen it in his life before! His confusion was apparent from his gaping mouth and bulging, stupefied eyes. While in the cell a nightmarish metamorphosis was taking place.

What was it James had said that time, of alien procreation? Something about, "A melding, a substitution, a flowing together and explosive multiplication"? Well, what was happening in the cell may not have been procreation—unless it was by assimilation and duplication—but it was certainly everything else he had spoken of. The scuttling insect-octopus-dragons were invading the radiance of our disintegrating guinea-pig subjects only to emerge in a stream of yet more fantastic shapes and figures; and as James and Jason melted to nothingness, so the star-spawn multiplied in number, bursting forth from those—consumed?—human remnants to come nosing, thrusting at the tiny cameras.

They bloated large on our screens; they *knew* we were looking at them, scrabbled to send hairy, spiked and multi-jointed legs right through the audio and visual systems—*through the screens themselves*—into our control room! While in the cell the globe containing the lens shivered to shards and something huge, black, bloated and baneful began to squeeze through from some Other Place, some other space, into ours.

One of our military men was leaning forward, his hands supporting him on the ledge in front of his screen, hypnotised by what he could see but scarcely believe was taking place in the cell. A vibrating black spider-leg eighteen inches long stabbed through the screen into his mouth and out the back of his skull—and he jerked like a puppet as he hung there suspended on it.

I cried out—a gurgled shriek, something quite inarticulate—and aimed a blow at the back of our technician, catching him between the shoulder blades. Driven forward, he flailed his arms; his hand came down on one of the controls…sheer luck!

Five pipes or shafts, pneumatic conduits descending at different angles to locations buried in the steel walls, hummed and pulsed. And from up above five star-stones hurtled under pressure down these channels to form the points of a pentagram surrounding the cell. With which it was over.

The alien insect things shrivelled to nothing; the cell exploded with such force that the walls were actually scarred and even buckled in several places; the gonging reverberations were such that my eardrums burst and I lost consciousness. But I was fortunate, for the others with me lost a lot more than that…

From then until now I have kept mainly silent, and from time to time I've mimicked the conditions of my four surviving colleagues, which has meant spending time in various institutions. But I did not want anyone questioning me too deeply; I did not want to become any kind of guinea pig in my own right; I had no more interest in any facet of the Mythos Investigation.

You see, I know why I was the sole survivor—the only one to live through it with his person and sanity intact—for I, too, had heard their singing; *They* saw me as a possible future vessel, or as a radio signal, or a lighthouse to guide them in to harbour. Which is why it is only now, as my cancer kills me and I have mere days to live, that I'm able to report the occurrences of that time as they happened.

As for the lens Gateway: it was vaporised in the blast, of course. I can only hope no other device of that sort exists in our world. The star-stones were likewise destroyed; I hope and pray others have been discovered, or that you, my once colleagues in The Foundations are at least seeking them out.

And meanwhile:

I have come to believe in God and would even be a regular churchgoer…except I cannot bring myself to attend services in the harvest time. There is a certain hymn they'd be sure to sing, and I know I couldn't abide it. Even now I find it difficult to think about it, and even harder to write the words of the song down. But since this is probably the best way to make you understand:

> Waiting for the harvest, and the time of reaping,
> We shall come rejoicing, bringing in the sheaves.
> Bringing in the sheaves, bringing in the sheaves,
> We shall come rejoicing, bringing in the sheaves.

Sometimes I dream of great lizards—dinosaurs stampeding in terror through tree-fern forests—and then I wonder about all the other mass extinctions our planet has known. But—

—I long ago retired to Dublin, Ireland, where I discovered that while white wine doesn't help a lot with my sleeplessness, Guinness does the trick every time.

SYNCHRONICITY OR SOMETHING

Back in the 1980s, a young man called Carl Ford published a multiple award-winning Cthulhu Mythos RPG (role-playing game) fan magazine called Dagon. *Toward the end of that decade Carl contacted me and commissioned a Mythos story with an RPG theme which he intended to publish in the same format as his magazine. The story I eventually sent to him was "Synchronicity or Something". It contains quite a few in-jokes—the somewhat skewed names of a small handful of contemporary horror writers, for example (not to mention that of a certain young publisher)—and like that, but it is also quite nasty. And with an ending that is suitably Cthulhu Mythosian, "Synchronicity" saw light of day as an excellently presented "Dagon Press Production", in 1989.*

Jim Slater sat glowering, nursing his pint, plainly annoyed. His drinking companion, Andrew Paynter, was a bit put off, especially since he'd just asked Slater to be his best man.

It was a Friday night and both men had just finished divorce cases; which is to say, they'd gathered sufficient evidence of adultery to satisfy any court of law in the land that their respective clients should be granted divorces, and compensation to boot. Tomorrow they would go into the office, put their reports in order and check their pigeonholes, then with a bit of luck take the rest of the weekend off. They worked for a detective agency specializing in the usual dirt-digging, with no excuse except "somebody has to do it".

"So…what's eating you?" said Paynter. He was young, not yet thirty, lean and handsome in a colourless sort of way. After spending five years in the Intelligence Corps and two more in shiny boots on the Metropolitan beat, he'd finally taken his chances on private-eyeing. It was shitty work but it paid the bills, and so far it had been something of a not-so-private eye-opener. Infidelity-wise, the world was abustle! As for Phillip Marlow-type cases: forget it.

"Nothing's wrong with *me*," Slater answered. He was Paynter's senior by maybe ten years, himself divorced for three of them, and wore his cynicism like armour. A big man, there was a touch of the early Robert Mitchum about him, the same sleepy eyes and deep, dull voice. But he looked so much the part that usually people didn't think he could be what he was. A nice fellow when he was one hundred percent sober, but as often as not he was eighty percent proof. He had taken the younger man under his wing when Paynter joined the agency, and Paynter hadn't forgotten it.

"Are you saying there's something wrong with me?" Paynter grinned. "Or is it just the world in general?"

"Since you've asked," Slater answered, "it's you. See, I thought you had a brain in your head. I mean, how long have you been with us? A year…longer? How many days—or more properly nights—spent traipsing around checking out all the illicit screwing? Taking your sly little compromising pictures, listening to sobbing wives or husbands telling you their worst fears or suspicions, discovering them to be right and in the process finding out that the 'innocent' party is also balling or being balled? Son, it's a cesspool!"

"Our job? Tell me something new."

"The world, for Christ's sake! There isn't a bird out there, married or single, who can't be pulled at the right time, in the right place, for the right reason, and there isn't a bloke who isn't trying to pull one. Sometimes I think it's not the act itself, just that it's a *guilty* act! You know? Stolen apples taste the sweetest? Well, maybe they do—until they cramp your stomach. But they do it *because* it's forbidden. Some of them, anyway. And others just because it's there."

"Like climbing a mountain?"

"Smart bastard! I'm *serious*. Every timid little fink you see is a potential stud, and every sweet, innocent little thing is probably getting it six nights a week. And the married ones are the worst."

Paynter shrugged. "That's life, Jim. But apart from work, what's it got to do with me?"

"Everything. Now you tell me you're getting married, to Judy Dexter, the boss's daughter—and that you want *me* to be your best man!"

Paynter's smile slipped a little. "I'm not following you," he said, hoping he wasn't.

Slater finished his beer, ordered two more. "Yes you are," he said. "You just turned sour, so I know you are. Listen, *I* was married! Did you know that?"

Paynter knew. Three years ago she'd gone off with the milkman or a door-to-door insurance salesman or something. He'd heard it mentioned in the office, but never when Slater was around. Jim was too big and too volatile to take chances with. Apparently it had broken him up for a long time: the fact that while he was out nooky-snooping, some jerk had been doing it with *his* wife. Hence the creeping alcohol dependency, the cynicism, and now this bitter anti-connubial harangue. If Jim Slater didn't straighten up, he'd soon become a marinaded misogynist. Or, if tonight was typical, he was one already.

"You know?" Slater said again, insistently, his words beginning to slur a little. "I said I had a *wife*!" He used the last word like it was poison.

"There are good ones and bad ones, Jim," Paynter answered, wishing he could change the subject. "You had a mother and a father, too, but did they split up?" He knew he'd made a mistake as soon as he said it.

Slater eyed him across the table. "Actually, yes," he said. "But good and bad? I suppose there are. At least I used to think so." He looked away, peered into his beer, seemed to find it fascinating. At length he took a swig, said: "Tell me, what's the most expensive thing you'll ever buy in your life?"

"Eh?" (Maybe the subject had decided to change itself.) "A house, I suppose."

"You suppose wrong," said Slater. "But it's a good try. Let me tell you: you buy a house to cage a bird. Before the bird, digs are good enough, or a grotty old bachelor flat. But when she comes along it has to be a house, for the kids. So…point made. Try again. The most expensive thing you'll ever buy?"

Paynter's sense of humour was rapidly evaporating. "A car?"

"A car? *Hah*! No imagination. But again, it's an example of how the mind works. Why do young guys buy cars, eh? To pull the birds. And why do birds like guys with flash cars? 'Cos they're handy for how's-your-father. Anyway, you're wrong again."

"So what *is* the most expensive thing I'll ever buy?"

Slater scowled. "Your bloody marriage certificate, ding-dong!"

Paynter had to admit the wit of it, however misplaced, mordant. "Jim," he said, "Judy and me are different. I mean, are you really worrying about us?" He smiled, sadly shaking his head, trying to convince Slater how wrong he was. "We're…different," he said again.

Slater couldn't be swayed. "See, I've worked for Dexter for a long time," he said. "His little girl Judy's been around ever since she was oh, fifteen? You think you're the only young, good-looking filth-ferret in the business?"

Paynter was still smiling, but it was frozen on his face now, totally humourless. "I think you've said enough, Jim," he said.

"Eh?" It was the other's turn to display his surprise. "You think I've said—? Well if *that's* what you think, then I haven't said nearly enough!"

"Enough for me, anyway," said Paynter. He stood up, almost sent their beers flying, headed for the door. Snatching his overcoat from a peg, he knew Slater was right behind him. The bartender called good night after them, but neither one answered him. And then they stood outside on the pavement like strangers, buttoning their coats, silent in the dark and the drizzle. Slater radiated misery, Paynter anger, and each was physically aware of the other's aura.

After a while Paynter said, "Forget it." He looked this way and that, uncomfortably.

"Yeah, yeah," Slater mumbled. As close as he would get to an apology. "Hey, my car's round the corner. I'll drop you off."

"No, it's...are you sure?"

"Sure. You can't walk in this. It's only fit for fish. Soaks through everything—even a soak like me!" Another apology.

Paynter softened. "You'll be OK to drive?"

Slater managed a smile, however wry. "When I've had a few is the only time I *am* safe to drive!" They ran through layers of mist and rain to find his car. When they pulled up in front of Paynter's place fifteen minutes later, and as the younger man was getting out of the car, Slater said: "Andrew, if I turn this best man thing down, you won't think too badly of me?"

"I guess not. No one knows I was going to ask you, anyway, so no one can get upset."

"It's just that—"

"It's OK, Jim. I know..."

❖ ❖ ❖

The next morning Paynter "overheard" a conversation where Slater and Dexter talked in the latter's office. In fact the entire office overheard it, for Dexter was angry and Slater surly. "Jim," Dexter's voice was hot, exasperated, "I just don't know what gets into you. You called this woman...*names*!"

"She deserved every one of them," Slater answered, his voice rumbling as always.

"What? But that wasn't for you to decide, Jim. We're lucky that this one will probably end up settled out of court, because if it went *through* a court we'd be the losers. Oh, not the case—our reputation. Now look, Jim, it's taken me too many years to build this thing up to have some woman-hating gumshoe tear it down."

"I called the girl a slut," Slater's voice was a little louder now, "and she is. A young slut eating up boyfriends like the world was running out of men. Which wouldn't be quite so bad if she weren't already married—to a rich idiot! I watched her for a fortnight and even *I* didn't believe it! I was afraid I might catch something just following her!"

"But you're not the judge and jury!" Dexter's voice was louder, too. "And you're far too experienced a detective to just let them catch you watching them. I say you *let* yourself be seen! It was a deliberate provocation. That man lost two teeth! If he wasn't so badly compromised you'd be explaining all of this to a judge right now—and this agency would be hiding under whatever cover it could find!"

"The guy went for me!" Slater pretended astonishment, but Paynter knew from his voice that it was an act. "Was I supposed to just stand there and let him take me to pieces?"

"You nearly hospitalised him! Look, I've had it with you, Jim. No more arguing on this one—or the last one—or the one before that. Get this through your skull: these people aren't Big Criminals, they're just people who cheat on their husbands or wives."

"Right. They fuck fraudulently." Slater wasn't cowed.

"Whatever they do, they're our bread and butter. If you want to beat them up and toss them in a dungeon for their sins, then maybe you should emigrate to South Africa, get yourself fixed up with a sjambok and…and what the hell! Something like that, anyway. But you certainly don't belong here!"

"I'm sacked?" Slater's voice was calmer now, almost resigned.

And after a pause: "No," said Dexter, sourly. "Not sacked, just warned. And Jim, this time it's the last warning."

"Is that it? Are you finished?"

"Yes."

People scattered in the main office, began filing things away where they didn't need filing, opening envelopes, picking their fingernails. Someone started whistling tunelessly, and Paynter went back to checking a perfectly good report. Dexter's door opened and Slater stood there looking out, his head cocked on one side. He saw the exaggerated bustle and smiled humourlessly. Over his shoulder came Dexter's voice, still angry: "Look in your pigeonhole, Jim. It's for next weekend. Worth big money. It *might* keep you off the bottle and get you out of my hair for a while all in one go!" Dexter had intended the entire office to hear every word, and Slater knew it.

He slammed the door behind him…

Two hours later when Paynter left the office, Slater was waiting for him. "A quick one?"

"Drink or word?"

"Both, now that you mention it."

They went to their local, ordered beers. Paynter had things to do; without his saying anything, the half-pint he ordered underlined the fact that he wasn't staying.

"What, have I got leprosy or something?" Jim Slater scowled.

"It's the weekend," Paynter reminded him. "What's left of it. Me, I want to enjoy it. I thought you wanted to talk? You didn't say anything about a booze-up."

Slater took a long Manilla envelope out of his pocket, slapped it down on the bar. "What do you make of this?"

Paynter took up the envelope, shook out a letter, a couple of photographs, several cuttings from foreign newspapers and typed translations of the same. "The job Dexter gave you? For next weekend?"

Slater was impatient. "Yes, but what do you *think* about it?"

Paynter sighed. "You expect me to read all of this?"

"Hey, let's not pull any punches here!" Slater put on a hurt look. "I mean, wow! Here's this total stranger asking for a whole ten minutes of your time!"

Paynter nodded, and quietly, resignedly said, "OK." And he started to read the contents of the envelope. At first it didn't make much sense, but then it began to sink in. "Well," he eventually commented, "at least it's not a sneak-and-peek job!"

"It's not any sort of job that I can see!" Slater snorted. "It's a kid's job, a get-paid-for-nothing job, something you'd give to a keen, bright-eyed, oh-gee-this-is-my-first-assignment-snot!"

"Money for old rope," Paynter shrugged. "And you're on twenty five per cent of the take. And the cheque is a big one! So what are you making all the fuss about? Hey, if you don't want this, give it to me!"

Slater scowled but made no immediate reply. After a little while he said, "Did you get the gist of it?"

Paynter was reading through it again. "Eh?" he briefly looked up, continued his reading. "Yes, I think so. A nutter, obviously. *Phew!* Somebody is a real fruitcake!"

Slater nodded. "Quite apart from the fact that it's what Dexter said it was—namely, a way of getting me the hell out of it for a while—it's weird, too. I mean, it isn't that I don't know how to go about it, but while I'm doing it I'll feel about as balmy as the old girl who's paying for it!"

Paynter had to agree that it was weird, but the cheque that accompanied it was *very* real. He frowned. "I'm trying to work it out."

"Here." Slater slid him a sheet of A-4. "This is how I broke it down." Paynter peered at the beer-stained, minutely scrawled page:

(1) Role-Playing Game Conventions: Milan, Berne, Rheims.

(2) Signora Minatelli's son, Antonio, eighteen years old, attends a weekend convention in Milano (Milan, Italy) and comes home with some story that the German Guest of Honour, Hans Guttmeier, disappeared from his room on the Saturday evening (17 or 18 July). Antonio is disgusted; Guttmeier had a big game the next day against an Italian challenge team for his world title. The Italian fans reckon he chickened out and did a moonlight flit back to Germany.

(3) Antonio, who can't get enough of this gaming stuff, attends the Berne (Switzerland) convention two weeks later. Signora Minatelli expects him home late Sunday night or in the early hours of Monday. But he doesn't show. Finally she telephones the hotel in Berne; they tell her his bill is unpaid and his car is still in the hotel car park—but no sign of Antonio.

(4) Meanwhile, news has broken that Hans Guttmeier didn't make it back home to Frankfurt. And now it becomes clear that when he disappeared from the hotel in Milan he left all his gear in his room—including his Deutsche Marks and return rail ticket! Spurred on by interested parties, (top of the list being S. Minatelli) German, Italian and Swiss police get together on the job but there doesn't appear to be any connection. So a couple of young blokes disappear in foreign parts—so what? It happens all the time. Tourists, especially in France and Italy, go missing regular as clockwork. Routine police work, that's all; and the investigations grind slowly on...

(5) S. Minatelli—a real Italian Momma who loves her son dearly—gets in touch with the Surete about an upcoming French convention in Rheims, all set for the end of the third week in August. She has it all figured out: a wandering lunatic is doing the rounds of the gaming conventions, killing off attendees. Nice theory, but there are big holes in it. Like, no bodies? Anyway, the Surete thank her for the tip and assure her they'll do what they can—which, as it turns out, amounts to nothing. No one goes missing from the convention in Rheims. But...S. Minatelli isn't satisfied, and still her

son hasn't shown up. She gets a list of attendees at the French con., tracks them down, discovers that several were hippy-types of no fixed abode. So one or more of them could have gone missing after all…

(6) By now, though, S. Minatelli has come up with a second theory: her son has perhaps fallen in love with a young lady of similar bent ("bent" seeming very appropriate) with whom he is now doing the round of the cons. Apparently he'd mentioned in passing this girl he met at the Milan bash. Having remembered this much, Tony's mother simply ignores the fact that his name isn't on the Rheims list, and the coincidence of Hans Guttmeier's disappearance. In short, she's now clutching at straws.

(7) She contacts Interpol, the CID, Scotland Yard—you name it— and passes on all information, cuttings connected with the disappearances, photographs of her son, etc., etc. Will someone please look for him at the con coming up in London in mid-September? Which is to say, next weekend. We can only imagine what Interpol, CID, Scotland Yard think of all this; but…they say OK, they'll have someone drop in at regular intervals over the weekend and case the crowd for Antonio Minatelli.

(8) She still isn't satisfied: she contacts a PI—Dexter, of course— and he gives the job to me…

"Questions," said Paynter, returning the notes to Slater. "What is a role-playing game?"

"The players act out roles under the guidance of an umpire. Where there are decisions to be made or alternate routes which may be taken a dice-throw decides what's what. Or maybe it's left to the umpire, the 'games-master', to decide. See, there are lots of alternatives. Obviously, experience counts. You have to know the theory of the game: the books the game is based on, the skills you require to win, the scenario." Slater studied Paynter's blank expression. "Are you getting any of this?"

Paynter nodded. "I think so. It's something like war-gaming, right?"

"Sure. In *Star Trek* scenarios it usually *is* war-gaming—but set in space. But I can't be too dogmatic about it because I'm a little out of my depth myself."

Paynter thought about it for a moment. "Of course, remove the background picture and you're left with simple missing persons cases—or a missing persons case, if we're just talking about your job: Antonio Minatelli."

"You can't ignore the background," said Slater. "You know that. The background *is* the case." He grinned. "You know, I'd passed this place downtown a thousand times and thought I'd never noticed it until I got this brief. Then I at once remembered it. Powers of observation! After I left the office this morning I went down to this specialist dealer and picked up some stuff."

He produced a much larger envelope from his briefcase, tipped out its contents. "These kids publish their own magazines, worship their own idols, live in their own weird worlds—from what I can see. Look at these titles, will you? *Vaults and Vampires*, and...*Cerebellum*? And what about *Judge Druid*, and all this other stuff? Everything from the Dark Ages to James Bond! This one," he indicated a slim pamphlet with a horror comics cover, "is an amateur magazine: a 'fanzine'. But get the title, will you? They go for strange, strange titles!"

"Dugong?"

Slater shrugged. "A sea beast. Like an overstuffed walrus. Old-time sailors thought they were mermaids. But a sea creature, anyway. You see, *Dugong*'s for the aficionados of, er, this guy." He slapped down a garish magazine on the top of the bar. "See, all the things that live in the sea worship the Great Sea God, pictured there."

Paynter looked at the magazine's cover. A sentient, leprous squid-thing seemed to look back at him, leering out from under an almost unpronounceable title. *"The Call of—?"*

They both squinted at the magazine, pulled faces.

"Er, Cuth-lu?" Paynter ventured again.

"Your guess is as good as mine," Slater shrugged. "Hell, the guy in the shop *whistled* it at me!"

"Eh?"

Slater nodded. "Future shock," he said, shrugging. "Maybe I'm getting too old to keep up anymore. But when I bought this stuff, the guy checked the titles, got to this one and said: 'Oh, yeah, *The Call of Tootle-tootle?*' I'm not kidding! Here's another: *The Shoggoth Pit!* Dedicated to this same Tootle-tootle. Do you believe this stuff? Hey, have I lost you?"

"Only slightly," said Paynter, sarcasm dripping.

"Snap!" said Slater. "But I'll keep at it. At least I'll earn my twenty-five percent."

Paynter laughed. "You're a strange one, Jim. Fifteen minutes ago you were complaining about this job. But to tell the truth, I actually think you're looking forward to it!"

Slater's expression changed on the instant. "I was complaining about being got shot of," he growled. "Like a kid sent to bed early without his supper."

"Not just a kid," Paynter corrected him. "A bad kid! And anyway, that was just part of it. Your main beef was that this was a job for a snotnose, that it was demeaning to send a supersnoop like you out on this sort of job."

"And you don't think it is, eh?" Slater raised an eyebrow.

"Like I said: if you don't want it, give it to me."

"Yeah," said Slater, finishing his pint. "Snow job."

"Nothing of the sort," Paynter insisted. "And just suppose you do find out what happened to Antonio Minatelli, eh? Or better still if you find the kid himself! Wouldn't that be something: to walk into Dexter's office with the goods, and shove them right up his nose?"

Slater considered that and grinned. "It gets me away from the sleaze-beat, anyway," and his face at once turned sour again. "Monday I have another divorce to process, and Thursday I'm to 'talk' to a guy about a little sexual harassment he's been engaging in. Jesus!"

"Just remember to keep your paws off him," Paynter warned. And then, to change the subject, "But think: Saturday you go up to the Smoke, all expenses paid, for some fun and frolics with the weird set! Great!"

Slater scowled. "Are you sure you're not just taking the Old Peculiar?"

"No way!" Paynter denied. "And to prove it, I'll have another half with you. It's your round anyway…"

The following week came and went. The other investigators in the office seemed to have their hands full, but Paynter was pretty much at loose ends. When he wasn't gophering for Dexter he did a little reading, stuff connected with Slater's upcoming weekend jaunt to London. Not that London was anything special—the offices of DPI (Dexter's Private Investigations) were in Croydon, and the Smoke was just up the road but it was a different sort of job. And Paynter was glad that Jim Slater had pulled it.

On the other hand, Slater hadn't asked him to research anything for him; he probably wouldn't appreciate it if he knew; but again, it was sufficiently removed from the actual case that Paynter had gone ahead anyway. And his conscience was clear: the fact was that he would like to help Slater out if he could, but unobtrusively, so as not to put his back up.

Slater had been in the office Monday, mumbling something about a court appearance Tuesday, had disappeared midday and didn't show up again until Wednesday when he looked in his pigeonhole and found nothing.

Thursday he successfully "warned off" a blackmailer (a loathsome creature who had demanded sex for silence) with a threat, turned the thing over to the police, and delivered his report to Dexter who seemed well satisfied. Friday, payday, and Slater was in again and his nose looked less puffy; less blooming, so that Paynter guessed he'd been keeping clear of the booze.

That lunchtime, however, they did have a beer and a sandwich together. "Been doing some reading," Paynter opened, having decided that his interest wouldn't be misconstrued.

"Wonderful!" said Slater, in that dull, booming Bob Mitchum way of his. "Never knew you had it in you. It'll be 'riting and 'rithmatic next."

"No," Paynter grinned, "I mean seriously. In connection with your missing person."

"Eh?" Slater was at once suspicious.

Paynter held up a hand. "Not *on* the job—just background stuff. You did say that background was all-important. Stuff on H. P. Lovecraft, the Mythos Circle writers. Stuff about Cthulhu…"

"Old Tootle-tootle?"

"Do it how you like," said Paynter. "Cthulhu's good enough for me."

"Cthul who?"

"Also some Charles Fort stuff," Paynter ignored him. "Really weird."

"And Von Daniken?" Slater raised a natural-born sceptic's eyebrow. "UFO's? How about Lobsam Rampa and Rambling Sid Rumbold?"

"I said I'm being serious," Paynter insisted.

Slater nodded. "I can see you are. And how about me? Have I been wasting my time or something?"

"You've been reading the same stuff?" Paynter was surprised. "I mean, I only started because I found it interesting, and because—" He paused.

"Because you wanted to help? Because you thought people had been down on me and you were my friend? Well, thanks for the fact that you're my friend, but no thanks for the sympathy. We all get what we ask for in life. As for your research: I skimmed all that stuff you mentioned, but when I discovered that Lovecraft himself derided it…anyway, I got the overall picture. And that's what I wanted: to discover what it is about this stuff that switches the kids on. So why did they like Dracula or Frankenstein? Same story: when you're young you need something that grips the imagination. A pity they have to grow up. As soon as the sap starts rising, to hell with the imagination! That's when they start looking to get the other bits gripped! So much for the background, but the job itself is more basic. I've looked at things like recent Interpol missing persons lists, tried to come up with possible motives, doublechecked lists of attendees at the various conventions, made or tried to make a couple of connections—"

"Connections?"

"Sure," said Slater. "Like—how these disappearances are connected. Or are they entirely coincidental? And where does the common factor of RPG Conventions come into it? And if there really is a crazed kidnapper or murderer on the loose, well...obviously he or she connects in both Milan and Berne. So I might find his or her name on both of those lists. See what I mean? A jigsaw isn't a picture until all the bits connect up. The bits are there, it's putting them together that gives the thing perspective."

"And do like names appear on both lists?" Paynter was fascinated.

Slater nodded. "You know some of them do. Hans Guttmeier for one. He was scheduled to appear in Berne after the Milan con. Strike Guttmeier, for of course he's a victim. Likewise, obviously, Antonio Minatelli. But then there's a couple of others..."

Paynter leaned closer. "Oh?"

"Like Cindy Patterson, yes. She's a young American, a publisher who produces the games and associated products. She controls a lot of rights, and she's heavily into spreading her empire abroad. A shrewd young lady. She's also the moving force behind the conventions, helps coordinate them. That's why they fall so conveniently, with gaps of a couple of weeks in between, so that she and a couple of guys from her outfit can hop from one to the next without overlapping. Also to enable her to spend a week or so in each location, promoting her stuff. The Americans are big on advertising, you know? And it seems this RPG thing is rapidly becoming big business."

"And you think these Americans are connected, right?"

Slater pursed his lips, slowly shook his head. "If they are, I really can't see how. What? They should run around killing off their future livelihood?"

"A spot of judicial culling?"

Slater frowned. "Where's the motive? These were fans. They weren't rival publishers, weren't exerting pressures. Guttmeier was a top player, he was good advertising! And Minatelli was nuts on Moribund's stuff."

"Moribund?"

"The name of Cindy Patterson's publishing house. So no motive there— or if there is, it's not yet apparent. And anyway, you can strike the Americans because they missed the Berne convention. There were problems back in the US of A, apparently, that needed sorting out. They only just got back in time for Rheims."

"How do you know all of this?" Paynter ordered more drinks. "I mean, who's your informant? You obviously didn't speak to anyone who might be involved, for you'd tip their hand. So who gave you all of this stuff?"

Slater grinned, said: "Elementary, my dear Andrew. If you want to know the state of the church's rafters, don't ask the bellringer, ask the deathwatch beetle! The people on the inside. So who to speak to on the inside? Someone who wasn't at any of the foreign conventions. Karl P. Ferd, is who."

"Who?"

"Ferd, the editor and publisher of *Dugong*. The entire scene is an open book to him. You know, *Dugong* is one of as many as eighty fanzines—in this country alone! Anyway, Karl seems a genuine young guy, and he knows just about everyone in or on the fringe of the game—or games. Fans and pros alike. I've talked to him and I like him, so much in fact that I felt something of a shit laying my scam on him. I told him I was doing some research for someone who's doing a book on the whole gaming thing. It would mean a lot of publicity for *Dugong* and a couple of the better amateur 'zines."

Paynter nodded. "So you're building up a stack of background information here," he said, "but as yet nothing solid on the case itself. And yet I sense you're onto something. Something you haven't told me?"

Slater grinned, nodded. "Ferd tells me there's a certain nut name of Kevin Blacker who's a kind of gamer's guru. He's full of shit about the Tootle-tootle Mythos, attends all the cons—can't play worth a bent penny but talks a good fight—and talks, and talks, and talks. And apparently he's a true believer."

"A what?"

"He thinks it's all real. Or at least, that's how he makes it sound. The Mythos is real! Cthul—who do you say it?—is real, existing between the spaces we know, waiting to take over the world again, and—"

"Hold it!" Paynter cut in. "Surely Cthulhu's dreaming in his house in R'-lyeh?"

"OK, his minions, then," Slater shrugged. "The rest of the gang. They're ex-directory, sort of, but they keep in touch. And when the stars are right and the cult is big enough—"

"What cult?" Paynter was trying hard, but Slater could move fast when he wanted to.

Slater sighed. "The Cthulhu cult, obviously! Like I said, this ding-dong Blacker thinks the stories—the original Lovecraft, Smith, Howard and etc. you name it, stories—were based on the real thing. Facts which only a handful of people were privy to. The guy's crazy! So says Karl P. Ferd."

Paynter was thoughtful. "Crazy enough to kidnap people, or at least make them disappear—maybe even kill them? And the motive?"

Slater inclined his head, opened his slitted eyes wide and said: *"Ah!"*

"Was he on the convention lists?" Paynter pressed. "Did he attend?"

"No to the first; yes, probably, to the second. See, Ferd says he doesn't operate like that. He's a guru, likes to appear mysteriously and vanish the same way. He just shows up, stays a couple of hours or maybe a day, expounds to his followers and anyone else credulous enough to listen, then moves on. So while it's unlikely he'd appear on the official lists, it's just as unlikely that he'd miss a con. He goes to all of them! He was in Milan, I've learned that much. And I'm betting he was at Berne and Rheims, too."

"You didn't mention the motive." Paynter wanted to pin Slater down. *"Ah!* isn't a motive."

"Guttmeier is or was the world champion player. He knew the stories, books and rules backwards. Gaming-wise, he went where angels fear to tread because he had the measure of Old Tentacle-face and the rest of the starspawn. But Blacker says it's not just a game. Maybe this is his way of proving a point, eh? He's convinced himself, so now he has to convince the others. Don't mess with Tootle-tootle, 'cos he'll get you! Same goes for Tony Minatelli: he's crazy keen on the game and one day could be a challenge. Blacker can't stand people who look like they might steal his glory. He *has* to be the centre of Cthulhoid attention, and—"

"Cthul*hoid?*"

"Pertaining to Cthulhu. See, even I can say it now! Anyway, you get my point."

"So...it seems you have a lead." Paynter seemed disappointed.

"Oh, hey!" Slater said, with exaggerated gaity. "Oh, joy, let's all be happy-happy! Jimbo has a lead!" He stopped mincing about on his barstool and turned his half-shuttered eyes on Paynter again. "So what's eating you?"

"Well, actually," Paynter began—and broke off. "Hell, I suppose it did sound like that, didn't it?"

"It's OK," Slater nodded. He smiled with one side of his mouth. "I get the feeling I've popped your bubble. So what was your theory?"

"Theory?" Paynter snorted. "My trouble, you mean! See, I've had a—well, a sort of sneaking admiration for the Adamskis, the Rampas, Von Danikens and Charles Forts of this world. And it's a bit disappointing to be put down. To be put *right,* I mean. When I was a kid I read Westerns. Loved the J. T. Edson things. They were so...*authentic!* Then I discovered Edson was an over-weight postman from Melton Mowbray, Leicestershire. A nice man, but hardly Zane Grey. And *never* John Wayne! I feel the same about these other guys. It would just be sort of nice if something like this turned out to be true once in a while, you know? So this last week I tossed logic out of the window and went for the esoteric instead. And I thought I'd found something— one thing, anyway—that was kind of scary. Except it now seems silly."

"Are you telling me you wish there really was a Cthulhu and Co? That *has* to be scary! OK, I know what you mean. So say on, I'm all ears. What did you think you'd found?"

"Oh, there's no 'think' about it. It's there, all right—except I suppose it has to be a coincidence. Do you know what ley lines are?"

"Ley lines? Oh, yeah. Imaginary lines on the surface of the earth that connect up points of pre-historic or religious interest. Like churches or other places of worship, or maybe the sites of primitive rituals."

"Rituals of sacrifice?"

Slater squinted at Paynter. "What's on your mind?"

Paynter shrugged. "A coincidence, that's all. But if you line up Milan, Berne, Rheims and London—"

"A ley line?"

"That's right. Not quite accurate, but close enough."

"Well, you really did toss logic out the window, didn't you? What if those places had formed a circle, or a triangle? Coincidence, that's all."

"Synchronicity," said Paynter. "Or something..."

"Never heard of it." The other shook his head.

Now Paynter shook *his* head. "Wrong word anyway," he said. "It means events happening in different places at the same time, apparently connected but purely coincidental. Something like that anyway. But what we have here are predictable events occurring at a predictable time and place."

"Too deep for me," said Slater. "And wrong in any case. These disappearances were only 'predictable' in hindsight! If you know that they happen at conventions. I don't go with that. It's like saying: 'how queer, last week Saturday followed Friday followed Thursday followed...' See what I mean? It's not queer at all, because that's the way things are."

"Charles Fort and his fishers from outside," said Paynter. "Adams Adamski and his UFO."

"Cranks," said Slater.

"The time-scale fits, too."

"Oh?"

"If you look at those places again on a map, and measure the distance between...it's weird, that's all."

"Well, go on." Slater nudged his elbow. "Don't keep me in suspenders."

"Just suppose," said Paynter, "that every now and then a sort of door opens between worlds, between universes. A gap in...hell I don't know! In what we call space. A fissure into—or out of—the spaces *between* the spaces we know."

Slater sighed. "Well, you did warn me. You did say that this was peculiar stuff. So you think maybe Tootle-tootle's crowd are fishing through the fissure, eh?"

The faraway look left Paynter's face and he grinned sheepishly. "Maybe I should see a shrink, right?"

"Tell me about this time-scale you mentioned," Slater urged.

Paynter continued to look sheepish. "If there was a crack in space-time," he continued, "a door to another dimension...I mean if the two surfaces of ours and some other universe were slowly sliding together and causing a fissure—"

"Hold it!" said Slater. "Milan: mid-July. Berne: end of July. Rheims: third weekend in August. London: mid-September. Distances?"

Paynter shrugged. "Calculate approximately ten miles every day and it all fits in. Dates and places, the lot."

For a moment Slater frowned, but then he shook his head and grinned. "You see what we have here?" he said. "Listen, we have an invisible steam-driven spaceship flying at ten mpd (that's miles per *day*) across Europe, crewed by awesome creatures from the dawn of time, fishing through a fissure."

Paynter scratched his chin. "Yes," he said. "Sorry."

Slater stood up. "You've had too much to drink. And I don't intend to, because tomorrow I have a date with a bunch of even weirder characters. I'm grateful for your thoughts on all of this, but me?—I reckon I'll stick with Kevin Blacker. For now, anyway."

"I'll finish my beer," said Paynter, staying where he was. He watched Slater walk away from the bar, turn at the door and wave. And he thought: *Synchronicity, or something. Now what the hell is the word?* And he answered himself: *Coincidence! That's the word. Just coincidence—you ding-dong!*

Slater didn't wait until Saturday but went up to London that night. He booked into a local hotel and checked the registration book. This was nothing more than habit, but it produced results. Cindy Patterson's name was in there, along with Hank Merne's and Darrell le Sant. Slater guessed they'd be her two from Moribund. "A convention?" he innocently inquired of the receptionist.

"Something of the sort," she answered. "At the Horticultural Society Hall. Greycoat Street. We have a half-dozen of them staying here. They'll probably be in the bar later."

"Oh?" he said. "A quiet lot?"

She sniffed. "A funny lot! We've had 'em before. But they're no trouble."

He dumped his case in his room, left the hotel and inclined his face into the fine, drifting rain, heading for Greycoat Street. At the Hall: there was no missing or mistaking the gamers. They were setting up, getting organised, fixing up their tables and props. Some were dealers, with their stuff in boxes piled under their tables, not yet displayed; others were players, moving through the crowd looking for their friends; very few of them would be more than twenty-two or twenty-three years old. It was a pretty much male-dominated scene, but there were some girls there: girl-friends most of them, but also one or two players, Slater guessed.

Slater hung his overcoat over his arm, stood to one side and smoked a cigarette. He knew he stuck out like a sore thumb, and that it was a big disadvantage, but the fact was that even if he wasn't "an old guy" still he couldn't have pictured himself as part of this crowd. Even if he were young again, you wouldn't find him here.

A good many of the youths were just that: pimply, gawky, gangling, uncoordinated and mainly out-of-work youths. Respectable, most of them, Slater supposed, by their looks, anyway. Not criminal types, he'd stake it all on that. But who could go on looks anymore? The young man with the dark, brooding eyes and the black, waxed, pointy beard, for instance: he was probably respectable. And the two overweight guys who could be brothers, like a pair of mobile haystacks, hairy, ungainly and unwashed, but probably respectable. In their way. And there were rich kids, too, all smartly if casually dressed, fairly well-groomed, poised and polite, with plums in their mouths and their pockets full of money. A crowd that cross-sectioned the spectrum, this one. And the games seemed innocuous enough.

But…of course there were the freaks, too. Not physical freaks, RPG freaks. Like that bunch there with the green-dyed faces and Spock ears: Trekkies, obviously. And the little tubby guy with the rubber mouth-mask fringed with bouncing, writhing tentacles. Old Tootle-tootle himself. The latter, meeting friends, invariably greeted them with: "N'gah, R'lyeh, Cthulhu *fhtagn!*" Terrific…

And how about the one with the gold and silver balloons clustered about his head? He wore a T-shirt printed with "Yog loves Lavinny", and behind the balloons a rubber mask festooned with boils and quivering, protruding pustules. Slater thought: *but I'll bet your Mum loves you.*

"Mr. Slater?" Someone touched his elbow. The voice was quiet, almost shy. But it was quietly confident, too. Slater looked down a little from his seventy four inches at a slight, unassuming, bright-eyed specimen who couldn't be more than twenty or twenty-one. He wore middle-length hair and an inquiring half-smile. "I'm Karl Ferd. Er, I suppose you are Mr. Slater?"

"Right first time," said Slater, offering his hand. "I won't ask how you picked me out of this lot!"

Ferd grinned, glanced all about. "Good crowd, innit?"

"Is it? Look, er, Karl: you'd better treat me as an ignoramus. I'm here on assignment, remember? I'm gathering information and atmosphere on behalf of someone else. This is all very strange to me. In fact, it's strange period! So you're the expert and I'm the novice. Which means that if I just seem to stand here and let you rattle on, don't think I've been struck dumb or something. It's just that I'll be trying hard to follow what you're saying, OK?"

"Sure," said the other, still scanning the crowd. He was beginning to look a little disappointed.

"Something wrong?"

"Er, no. I'd hoped to see a few more foreigners, that's all. I was hoping there'd be a lot of 'em this time—to buy up the latest *Dugong* and take it home with them, spread the word abroad. So far there are a couple of Krauts—er, Germans. And a few Frenchies."

"Frogs?"

Ferd grinned again. "They're all right," he said. "Thing is, if Guttmeier had won in Milan, he might have showed up. That would have been interesting."

Slater played dumb. "Guttmeier?"

"Hans Guttmeier, yeah. It seems he quit before play started—in Milan, I mean—and just walked out. They say he chickened out, but I can't see it. He knew his stuff."

"Oh," Slater nodded. "He was some sort of champion, right?"

"World's finest player!" said Ferd.

"So you get the French and the Germans attending these, er, conventions. Any others? What about the Swiss, or the Italians?"

Ferd shrugged. "Not a lot. Frogs and Belgiques, mainly. Oh, and some of the pro publishers. The Green Goblin people from over here, and occasionally one of the American outfits. Cindy Patterson was in earlier, from Moribund. I mean, she *is* Moribund!" He grinned. "If you know what I mean. She said they'd have a couple of drinks and make an early night of it, be back tomorrow morning in time to see things get under way."

Slater nodded. "I'm in a hotel just up the road. This Cindy Patterson and her American friends are staying there too. They're probably in the bar right now. In fact there are quite a few gamers staying there. Fancy a pint?"

"Sure, why not? Nothing much is going to happen here until tomorrow."

They went back to Slater's hotel. In the bar were maybe two dozen people, and Ferd nudged Slater's elbow, directing his glance to a corner table. "Cindy Patterson," he whispered. "With Hank Merne and Darrell Le Sant. Big names!"

Slater looked. Cindy Patterson was in her early thirties, small and chubby, looking like lumpy putty and wearing glasses so thick they gave her an owlish expression. There was a plate of sandwiches on her table, and she had a tomato seed stuck in her teeth. Her companions were debating something or other while she listened, adding very little to their conversation. Hank Merne was of the same shape, size and constitution as Cindy, and Darrell le Sant was thin as a beanpole with his fair hair cropped a half-inch all over. But sinister? Forget it.

But then the door opened and in came the enigmatic pointy-beard with a bunch of friends. One of them was a Spock whose green was starting to run, and another was still wearing his "Yog loves Lavinny" T-shirt, though mercifully he'd dumped his balloons and diseased mask. The others seemed entirely normal, but very bright-eyed and excited.

"Oh-oh!" said Ferd, warningly. "The mobile mouth there is Kevin 'Cthulhu lives' Blacker, the gaseous guru. He's full of it. Gives us a bad name, that one."

Slater's interest climbed a notch. he asked: "What's his speciality?"

"Same as mine," said Ferd, sourly. "The Mythos. But where I'm a fan publisher, he's a prophet of doom! That's his story, anyway. Hang around a bit and you'll see what I mean."

Blacker had spotted Ferd standing at the bar. He saw his friends into their seats at a central table, then briefly came over. He was only young, maybe twenty two, but his voice was straight from his boots. Also there was a sweet, unmistakable odour about him, so that Slater guessed he smoked the occasional funny cigarette. Blacker ordered drinks for the people at his table, turned to Ferd. He didn't seem to notice Slater.

"Hello there, Karl," he grunted. "Still publishing your blasphemous crap, I see." He slapped a copy of the latest *Dugong* down on the bar, prodded it with a pointed fingernail. His voice sank even lower as he said: "Don't you know that this stuff is an open invitation? Can't you see that you're inviting them in?"

"Course I can, Kev'," Ferd sneered. "But I don't recall inviting you. Do you mind? I'm enjoying a pint—or I was!"

Blacker scowled, shook his head in a half-angry, half-frustrated, pitying way, and returned to this group. Slater said: "If he's so down on the Mythos, how come he associates with the Yog-loves-Lavinny, guy?"

"Trying to save them," Ferd growled.

Slater's interest went up another notch. "Are they in danger? Save them from what?"

"From themselves. A one-man Salvation Army. Danger? Yeah—they might drown in all that garbage he talks! See, there he goes, oiling his larynx."

Blacker downed a pint of Guinness in one long pull, wiped his mouth and ordered another. And then he was off and running:

"They were here before us," he said, his voice rising over all the other bar sounds, "they're here now, and they'll be here after they've cleared us off. The old cults are dead, gone, except in a handful of lonely, dark places. But the *new* cults are here in bright, shiny disguises—yes, and the new *cultists* are also disguised! The difference is this: that they don't *know* they're cultists! Who am I talking about?" His voice was rising as he gathered impetus. "I'm talking about you," he prodded T-shirt in the chest. "And you," he snarled at the Spock character. "And especially you!" He pointed across the room directly at the Americans around their corner table. "Moribund? *God*, how right you are! You and your acolytes, like…him!" And this time the accusing finger was aimed at Ferd.

Slater watched and listened, soaking it all up. He had a feeling that this was it, that he'd found what he was looking for. Blacker was plainly off his trolley, but still there was something darkly fascinating about him. He was like a young, slim Aleister Crowley—a sort of unholy roller—or would be if he wasn't on the other side. As he talked the bar lights flickered, dimmed a little, at which his dark eyes brightened to scintillant pin-points. "Can't you *feel them* in the very air?" he raved. "Can't you almost smell them? Their energies are all about you, energies which you yourselves *attract*, and their emissaries watch you with false human eyes. You hear their massed voices in the convention halls, and you fail to recognise them. Your players call their names and you invoke them with your gibberish—and yet ye know not what ye do!"

While all of this was going on, several changes had occurred. For one, Cindy Patterson and her two had left their drinks and departed. Obviously they'd encountered Blacker before or knew his reputation—or they simply didn't like the look or sound of him. Slater couldn't blame them. But there'd also been a new arrival. In the old days, ten years and more ago—before Slater got married, and long before the experience had turned him right off women—this would have been just his style.

She wore black trousers with a white jacket, a lightly frilled shirt whose cuffs showed fluffily around her wrists, a card saying PRESS under her left-hand breast pocket, (which Slater thought a bit daring, especially in a place packed with peculiar or at least curious people) and a tiny pager in the pocket itself, with its aerial extended and sticking up level with the top of her head. Her black high-heels made her about five-ten; her black hair was very shiny and bounced on her shoulders; dark eyes in a creamy face lost the rest of her features in the shadows they seemed to cast. Slater was aware of a small nose and a red Cupid's bow mouth, but the eyes were the main attraction.

She found a chair at Blacker's table, didn't wait to be invited but simply sat herself down, making quick shorthand notes in a pad while Blacker continued to spout. The fans where they made room for her were very much impressed; they seemed torn between listening to him and ogling her, and it looked like she was going to win hands down.

"*Phew!*" said Karl Ferd in Slater's ear.

"Damn right," said Slater. But to himself: *yeah, go right ahead, young Karl. Mess with that one and see where it gets you. She's broken more hearts than you've had warm pints.* But at the same time he knew that if he were ten years younger, he'd very likely be considering messing with it himself.

Blacker had meanwhile noticed her. He would have to be dead not to. Stopped in his tracks, he blinked at her and said, "Eh?"

A policeman came in out of the rain. He wore an issue cape, spiked helmet, whistle chain, the lot. A Bobby off the beat. Things grew quieter as he went to the bar and leaned on it, speaking to the bartender in lowered tones. He showed him a photograph, waited while he scanned it. Slater was all ears.

"Nope," said the barman, wiping a glass. "Eyetie, innit? Bad lot, is he?"

"Missing," said the Bobby.

Slater had managed to get an inverted glance at the picture: Antonio Minatelli. Good grief! This was someone's idea of how to unobtrusively check out the convention! They hadn't even bothered to send a plainclothesman. That was how likely *they* thought it was that Minatelli was going to turn up here. As the policeman left, Blacker started up again. And having noted that the new girl—woman—at his table was a reporter, now he really got his teeth into it:

"Alhazred, crazy? It's you people who think he wasn't real who are crazy! Oh, that may not have been his name, but he was real, all right. A prophet, a doomsayer: 'repent ye sinners, for the end is nigh!' Lovecraft himself was another, only not so outspoken. He cloaked his realities in fiction. His stories were *warnings!* If you can't see it you're blind. Blinded by your own cleverness. But Alhazred, Lovecraft—oh, and plenty of others—yes, and me, too, we…"

The lights flickered again, went very dim, and Blacker pointed at the wavering bulbs here and there around the room. "They *know*, do you see? They hear me speak the truth and they *fear* it! They fear discovery, for the stars are not yet right! But I *have* discovered them, and so can you, if only—"

The lights went out.

Behind the bar a shadowy figure said, "Shit!" and went scrambling for the fuse box. Midnight shapes groped and collided in the darkness. Someone said: "*Ohhh!*" And someone else—Slater figured it must be the Yog-loves-Lavinny—shrilled: "Ia, R'lyeh! Cthulhu *fhtagn!*"

Slater didn't know why, but for some peculiar reason that last made his skin crawl. It had sounded so fluent, very weird and alien. The midnight shapes continued to slither and grope in the darkness, and Slater (again for some reason he couldn't pin down) pictured them closing in on Blacker. "Jesus!" he whispered to himself. His imagination was in full flight. He pictured alien things with huge, shiny hooks, thrusting them through Blacker's flesh, at the same time gagging him, dragging him choking and dripping blood through a hole in the darkness into an even darker dark…

Then the lights came back on. Like a camera, Slater froze the film—the scene—on his mind's eye. Blacker wasn't there. The reporter-lady stood over his empty seat, her eyes huge and astonished. But Blacker definitely wasn't there. *Jesus!*

Slater had almost forgotten Ferd standing beside him. But now Ferd said, "A fuse." That simple statement saved Slater from what might have caused him a lot of acute embarrassment. For at that moment:

"Did you see *that?*" came Blacker's hoarse cry of triumph and terror from the doorway to the toilets. He stuck his head out, glanced all about the room. He was pale now, and trembling. "*They* have their ways—but they don't get me that easily! They're near, I tell you. No—they're *here!*" He made for the exit, rushed out into the night and the rain.

"A real nutter," Karl Ferd commented, neatly threading his way through customers at the bar, heading after Blacker. "But he's got style." And over his shoulder to Slater: "I'll be right back."

Slater started to follow on, then changed his mind. He settled back against the bar, felt his excitement ebb away. He took a deep breath and wondered if maybe he was getting a bit old for this sort of stuff…

The reporter-lady had spotted Slater at the bar. He caught her glance, the silent appraisal, and thought: she's thinking, *he's not much but he's the best this place has to offer. At least he's a guaranteed free drink. Maybe even two.* "Hi," he rumbled as she came over.

"Are you here for the convention?" she asked.

"In a way. I'm looking for someone, that's all. But no, I don't play games."

"Don't you?" She cocked her head a little on one side. "That's a pity."

Ah, well—that's the preliminaries over and done. "Would you like a drink?"

"Why not? May I have a gin and tonic?"

Slater ordered. Ten minutes patter and she'll drift away. "And you?" he said. "An article on the convention?"

"That's part of it." She pressed up against him to let people squeeze by. "Sort of two birds with one stone, really."

"Oh?"

She sipped her drink, grinned at him. "You show me yours and I'll show you mine," she said.

Slater did his Robert Mitchum double-take. "Hussy!"

"You know what I mean," she grinned. And she was at once serious again. "I'm looking for Antonio Minatelli."

Why not? Slater thought. *I'm looking for him; the police are looking for him; why shouldn't she be?* "I've a feeling he won't show."

"You're Old Bill!" she accused.

He shook his head. "No, just an interested party. What difference does it make?"

"What, him not showing or you being…whatever you are? Never mind. It makes no difference."

"Good," said Slater.

"Minatelli was top of my list, but…when one story dies on you, you look for another. I'll rearrange my priorities, that's all."

Slater ordered more drinks. He'd had two beers, three brandies, nothing to eat. If he was going to carry on drinking he really ought to eat. "What are your priorities?" he inquired.

"The next in line after Minatelli just ran out on me," she answered, ruefully. "The one with the beard and the mouth."

"Kevin Blacker? If he's not careful he'll frighten himself to death! I believe he really does believe. The guy's a nut. I mean, it's one thing to 'believe' in Hilda Ogden, but Cthulhu's something else."

"Hlu-hlu," she said, without smiling.

He shrugged. "Suit yourself."

"I'm Belinda Laine," she introduced herself, glanced at her watch. "And I just went off-duty."

It was 10:15. "Slater," he answered. "Jim Slater, and I'm hungry."

The bar was filling up; people jostled; Karl Ferd came twining through the crush. "The next on my list," said Belinda Laine, as Ferd joined them. Ferd looked at Slater with eyes that said, *you don't waste any time, do you?*

Slater said: "Do you two know each other?"

"Er, no." Ferd appeared a little shy. "I'm Karl Ferd."

"I know," she said. "You're *Dugong*, right? Britain's answer to Bob Prout's *Shoggoth Pit?*"

Ferd tried not to preen. "*Dugong* is OK," he shrugged.

"You're too modest, Karl," she said. "But you've done some deep stuff lately: like the tongue-in-cheek issue where every article offered 'proof' that the whole Mythos thing is real. The only 'name' that was missing from your contents page was Kevin Blacker."

Again Ferd's shrug, and his sour grin. "That's 'cos it was tongue-in-cheek!"

"But *very* well done," she complimented him. "A lot of your readers— close to a thousand of them?—might get the idea that you believe in this stuff, too. I mean, you present some damning 'evidence'."

"I got some clever writers, that's all."

Her serious look slowly evaporated, and she smiled. Which was worth seeing. Slater had been thinking: *she knows her stuff. She's talking to him on his own level. She's researched this better than I have!* "I'm hungry," he said again. "Do you want to eat, you two?"

"Not me," Ferd answered. "I'm off home. I've a pal down at the Hall who has offered me a lift."

"Before you go," said Slater, "tell me: why did you go running after Blacker like that?"

"I wanted to check if he'd be around tomorrow to mess up the games," Ferd answered at once. "He makes people uncomfortable."

"And will he be around?" Belinda Laine was interested.

Ferd shook his head. "No. He says he's delivered his warning and now it's up to us. He's on his way back home to Oxford."

She seemed disappointed. "But you'll be here, right?"

"Oh, sure."

"Maybe we'll get a few minutes to talk in private."

Down, boy! Slater thought, seeing Ferd's eager expression. "Great!" the young man answered. "Long as you like." He turned to Slater, said: "Cheers, then."

"Cheers." They watched him leave.

"Where will we eat?" She smiled.

They took a taxi to a steak house and had a small meal. She hardly touched her food. Slater got through his, and through a bottle of house white which tasted dreadful. She had a gin and tonic but only drank half of it. While she toyed with her food and drink, he asked, "How did you get onto this? What's your angle?"

"Not fair," she answered. "You already know about me. Ace reporter and all that. Assignment: check out the games convention, look for missing kids; get some sort of a story, anyway. Possibilities. Why are so many young people so deeply into this thing? What's the attraction? Etc, etc. You know all that, but I only know your name. "

True, he thought. "I'm a PI," he said, breaking Rule Number One. "Tony Minatelli's Mum wants her son back. But I don't think she'll ever see him again. Young guys don't run off and leave their cars behind. He's a goner. Oh, and you did say you were looking for missing kids. Plural. My opinion: Hans Guttmeier's a goner, too."

She opened her eyes wide. "You're well informed," she said. "How about Jean Daniel de Marigny?"

"Eh?"

"Young Frenchman." She stared hard at Slater. "Disappeared in Rheims."

I'm well informed! he thought. "Maybe we should team up," he suggested. "Also, you're in the wrong business. Give the newspaper job the elbow, Belinda, and open up a detective agency! You're well ahead of me."

She laughed, then went serious again. "Are you a believer, Jim?"

"Only in Santa Claus. You mean this 'they're here, walking among us' business? Naw! Oh, *someone* is walking among us, all right: a crazy man, a psycho. Maybe Kevin Blacker. But aliens? Elder Gods? Invaders from the spaces between the spaces?"

She sat back.

"Now Andrew Paynter," he went on, "—a pal of mine back at the agency in Croydon—he's just gullible enough to make something big of all this."

"He is?"

The wine was getting to Slater. "Universes sliding together," he mumbled. "Fishers through fissures. Him and Kevin Blacker could have a really heavy session together." He looked at the empty bottle and her eyes followed his.

"Will the bar be open back at your hotel?"

He shrugged. "Dunno—but I've a half-bottle of Martell in my room."

"Strictly business," she said, but she was smiling.

"Of course," said Slater, thinking: *you stupid bastard!* Meaning himself, naturally.

In the taxi she snuggled up to him, said: "What if it was all real? I mean, why would they be taking out these people? Guttmeier, Minatelli, de Marigny…"

"Guttmeier was the world's No. 1. Maybe it was more than just a game to him. Maybe he'd seen through the curtain. Minatelli? Perhaps he knew or guessed something. I don't know. But it isn't real. If it were…surely there'd be bigger targets? Like this Moribund outfit."

"No." She snuggled closer. "Moribund only produces the games—they're in it for the dollars. They don't believe. They're Blacker's unconscious cultists. And they're doing a great job, spreading the word—but without believing a word of it."

"*If* it were real," Slater mused, aware of her beside him, "Blacker would have to go. He'd be high on their list."

He felt her nod in the darkness of the back seat. "Maybe Karl Ferd, too."

"I like Karl," he said, "and so I'm glad it's not real. On the other hand I'm also glad you are."

"That's nice," she said.

He was silent for a moment, then asked: "Why Karl Ferd? He's no true believer."

"No, but he's a deep one. I mean, not a Deep One, but inquisitive, questioning, investigative."

"Everybody's trying to get into the act," said Slater. And after a moment: "But you know, I think I'll stick with this one. There's more to it than meets the eye. It warrants a little in-depth scrutiny."

"And you're good at that, right?"

"Once I get my teeth into something, yes."

It had stopped raining when they got back to the hotel. They went up to Slater's room where he produced his bottle. "If that's what it takes," she said, "go ahead. It's unflattering, but flattery isn't what I need right now."

Suddenly nervous as a kid, Slater drank while she showered. Over her splashing, the telephone rang. The receptionist put Andrew Paynter on the line. "Hello, Jim? I've been trying to get you all night."

"Make it short," Slater slurred. "What's up?"

"It's nothing, really," Paynter said. And now he sounded uncomfortable. "See, I just found out that Judy reads weird fiction. She's a horror-freak!"

"Ho-hum," Slater yawned. "Believe me, you've got more shocks than that coming."

"No, listen—this is interesting. She mentioned how she'd like us to go up to a convention in Birmingham next week. The British Fantasy Society or some such outfit. All her favourite authors will be there. People like Curly Grant and J. Caspar Ramble—and Edward J. Waggler, the guy who did the Blaine series. So I'm thinking of taking her."

"What you're thinking of is a dirty weekend," said Slater.

"Will you *listen* to me?" Paynter insisted. "There's more."

Slater sighed. "I'm listening," he said.

"See," said Paynter uneasily, "there'll be a whole bunch of Mythos writers up there; and I just happened to be checking out a road route, and—"

"Birmingham sits right on your ley line, right?"

"That's right! And the time-scale is right, too!"

"Ho-hum," said Slater again. He began to sing: "They're coming to take me away, ha-ha..."

"Well *I* think it's interesting," said Paynter. "You...you—oh, *bollocks!*" The phone went click and started to beep. Slater grinned and replaced it in its cradle.

"Huffy bastard!" he said. And then he sat very still for five minutes and listened to Belinda Laine splashing...

When she came out from the shower she was naked as newborn and scrubbed just as pink. Slater looked at her and discovered he'd forgotten how long it had been. The sight of her drew the alcohol like tweezers draw a bee sting; in a moment he was half sober again. Removing his clothes with fingers that weren't quite his own—or which at least behaved like they were someone else's, and someone stupid at that—he wondered: Christ, how long *has* it been?!

"You're a hard one to get close to," she said, drawing him stumbling into the bedroom. "I couldn't tell if you wanted me or not. And I'm *still* not sure!"

But a cool one? Even stretching him out on the bed, she leaned over to adjust the position of her pager on the bedside table. Bloody "ace reporter"!

After that...obviously it wasn't love, wasn't even lust—it was need! Like a good meal after fasting for a week, or a drink after hiking across the Gobi Desert, or fresh air after an eight-hour stakeout in a smoky motel room with no air-conditioning. And it felt good! And while they were doing it he had to admit (if only to himself, and then grudgingly) that it was a sight better than risking wanker's cramp in a tepid bath of scummy water.

But that was while they were doing it. Immediately after—when the weight was off and the sugar was melting from his brain, when he'd stopped groaning and could unclench his teeth, unscrew his eyes and look her in her lovely face—in short, when he could start thinking again...

...It was the same as it had always been. It was nothing. Or if anything, it was disgust. With himself, but even more so with her. So that he thought: *Lord, as close up as this she isn't even good-looking!* And instead of the sugar she'd sprinkled there for a little while, now the acid was back in his brain, putting words in his mouth he knew he shouldn't say to a dog let alone someone he'd just emptied himself into:

"For an ace reporter," he heard himself say, "You make a bloody good hooker!" But having said it, instead of biting his tongue, it was as if the words themselves bred more acid. Acid that burned away his perceptions until they warped right out of shape and started lying to him and feeding him wrong information. Suddenly she didn't even feel like a woman any more, and her face was like so much rubber and downright ugly!

"A what?" she said, apparently stunned, but not yet outraged. She seemed more surprised than shocked. Maybe that in itself should have told him something, but he was too far gone now—too angry with himself that he'd succumbed. She was WOMAN, and they were all the same. "A tart! A piece! A slimy bloody *hooker!*"

"*Ah!*" she said, with a lot of emphasis; and she smiled at him with her suddenly mobile, swiftly metamorphosing face. Her left arm held him tightly and her legs wound about him. Her left hand grew three-inch claws sharp as needles that sank all the way into his back. One of them pierced his spine expertly to paralyse him, so that his scream came out a shrill, gasping whistle. "*No,*" she said, in a voice which flowed like her unbelievable features, "not a hooker—just a hook!"

He shook on her, jerking like he was ready to come again, vibrating in agony—the agony of *knowing,* and in knowing there was nothing he could do about it. Her right arm uncoiled from his back and lifted the pager from the bedside table, and something sharp and shiny pressed its button.

There came a crackle of static, and something else that might have been speech, might even have been a question. But not in any language of Earth. She answered it in the same—tongue?—and sank a second needle into Slater's spinal column to still his twitching and calm him down a little.

Before the darkness came, he realised he knew beyond any reasonable doubt that she'd been speaking through the fissure, and also that he knew what she'd said.

"OK," she'd said. "You can reel us in now…"

THE BLACK RECALLED

It was my intention originally to use "Caller" and "The Black Recalled" as a diptych, with the first to open the book and the second, its sequel, to close it. But then I decided that the end should in fact be THE END...I know you'll get my meaning when you reach "the end" of this volume's final story. Anyway, this Titus Crow story (wherein paradoxically our occultist hero is never actually seen!)was commissioned by Bob Weinberg for the Book of the World Fantasy Convention, 1983. Paul Ganley later got me to write a Titus Crow "origin" story, "Lord of the Worms", and I went one better by following that up with an even earlier "origin" short story entitled "Inception". Now, that last was not a Mythos tale, but it was done for a special reason: so that Paul could put the entire thing together in a book called—no prizes for guessing it—The Compleat Crow, which wasn't in fact complete because of the Crow novels (six of them!) that were still out there somewhere! But at least we'd covered the short stories and novellas. Anyway, Paul published all the novels, too, so that was that all squared up.

"**D**o you remember Gedney?" Geoffrey Arnold asked of his companion Ben Gifford, as they stood on the weed-grown gravel drive before a shattered, tumbled pile of masonry whose outlines roughly suggested a once-imposing, sprawling dwelling. A cold November wind blew about the two men, tugging at their overcoats, and an equally chilly moon was just beginning to rise over the near-distant London skyline.

"Remember him?" Gifford answered after a moment. "How could I forget him? Isn't that why we chose to meet here tonight—to remember him? Well, I certainly do—I remember fearing him mightily! But not as much as

I feared this chap," and he nodded his head toward the nettle- and weed-sprouting ruin.

"Titus Crow?" said Arnold. "Yes, well, we've all had reason to fear him in our time—but more so after Gedney. Actually, it was Crow who kept me underground all those years, keeping a low profile, as it were. When I picked up the reins from Gedney—became 'chairman' of the society, so to speak, 'donned the Robes of Office'—it seemed prudent to be even more careful. Let's face it, we hadn't really been aware that such as Crow existed. But at the same time it has to be admitted that old Gedney really stuck his neck out. And Crow…well, he was probably one of the world's finest headsmen!"

"Our mutual enemy," Gifford nodded, "and yet here we pay him homage!" He turned down the corners of his mouth and still somehow summoned a sardonic grin. "Or is it that we've come to make sure he is in fact dead, eh?"

"Dead?" Arnold answered, and shrugged. "I suppose he is—but they never did find his body. Neither his nor de Marigny's."

"Oh, I think it's safe to say he's dead," Gifford nodded. "Anyway, he's eight years gone, disappeared, and that's good enough for me. *They* took him, and when *they* take you…well, you stay taken."

"They? The CCD, you mean? The Cthulhu Cycle Deities? Well, that's what we've all suspected, but—"

"Fact!" Gifford cut him short. "Crow was one of their worst enemies, too, you know…"

Arnold shuddered—entirely from the chill night air—and buttoned the top button of his coat just under his chin. Gifford took out and lighted a cigarette, the flame of his lighter flickeringly illuminating his own and Arnold's faces where they stood in what had once been the garden of Blowne House, residence of the white wizard, Titus Crow.

Arnold was small, thin-faced, his pale skin paper-thin and his ears large and flat to his head. He seemed made of candle wax, but his eyes were bright with an unearthly mischief, a malicious evil. Gifford was huge—bigger than Arnold remembered him from eight years earlier—tall and overweight; his heavy jowls were pock-marked in a face lined, roughened and made coarse by a life of unnatural excesses.

"Let's walk," the smaller man finally said. "Let's see, one last time, if we can't somehow resolve our differences, come to an agreement. I mean, when all's said and done, we do both serve the same Master." They turned away from the ruined house, whose stone chimney stack, alone intact, poked at the sky like a skeleton finger. Beyond the garden, both lost in their own thoughts, they followed a path across the heath.

Arnold's mind had returned again to that morning eight years ago when, greatly daring, he had come to Leonard's-Walk Heath and passed himself off as a friend and colleague of Crow, actually assisting the police in their search of the ruins. For on the previous night Blowne House had suffered a ferocious assault—a "localised freak storm" of unprecedented fury—which had quite literally torn the place to pieces. Of Titus Crow and his friend Henri-Laurent de Marigny, no slightest trace; but of the occultist's books and papers, remains aplenty! And these were the main reason Geoffrey Arnold was there, the magnet which had lured him to Blowne House. He had managed to steal certain documents and secrete them away with him; later he had discovered among them Crow's notes on The Black, that manifestation of Yibb-Tstll which years earlier Crow had turned back upon Arnold's onetime coven-master, James D. Gedney, to destroy him.

Yibb-Tstll, yes...

Ben Gifford's mind also centred upon that dark, undimensioned god of lightless infinities—his mind and more than his mind—and he too remembered James Gedney and the man's use and misuse of black magic and powers born of alien universes. Powers which had rebounded in the end.

In those days Gifford and Arnold had been senior members of Gedney's cult or coven. And they had prospered under the man's tutelage and had shared his ill-gotten gains as avidly as they had partaken of his dark rites and demoniac practices. For Gedney had been no mere dabbler; his studies had taken him to all the world's strange places, from which he rarely returned empty-handed. All the lore of elder earth lay in books, Gedney had claimed, and certainly his occult library had been second to none. But his power sprang from the way in which he *understood* and *used* those books.

It was as if, in James Gedney, a power had been born to penetrate even the blackest veils of myth and mysticism; an ability to take the merest fragments of time-lost lore and weave them into working spells and enchantments; a masterly erudition in matters of linguistics and cryptography, which would unlock for him even the most carefully hidden charm or secret of the old mages, those wizards and necromancers long passed into dust, whose legacy lay in Gedney's decades-assembled library.

And uppermost in Gedney's itinerary of research and study had been the pantheon of Cthulhu and the star-spawned Old Ones, lords and masters of this Earth in its prime, before the advent of mere man and before the dinosaurs themselves. For in those ages before memory Cthulhu and his spawn had come down from strange stars to a largely inchoate, semi-plastic Earth and built their cities here, and they had been the greatest magicians of all!

Their "magic," according to Gedney, had been simply the inconceivable science of alien abysses, the knowledge of dark dimensions beyond the powers of men even to perceive; and yet something of their weird science had found its way down all the eons.

That would seem, on the surface, purely impossible; but Gedney had an answer for that, too. The CCD were not dead, he had claimed. Men must not forget Alhazred's conjectural couplet:

> "That is not dead which can forever lie,
> And with strange aeons even death may die."

—and The Atht's much less cryptic fragment:

> "Where weirdly angled ramparts loom,
> Gaunt sentinels whose shadows gloom
> Upon an undead hell-beast's tomb—
> And gods and mortals fear to tread;
> Where gateways to forbidden spheres
> And times are closed, but monstrous fears
> Await the passing of strange years—
> When that will wake which is not dead...

—in which the reference was surely to Cthulhu himself, dreaming but undead in his house in R'lyeh, ocean-buried in vast and pressured vaults of the mighty Pacific. Something had happened in those eon-hidden prehistoric times, some *intervention* perhaps of Nature, perhaps of alien races more powerful yet, whose result had been a suppression or sundering of the CCD; and they had either fled or been "banished" into exile from a world already budding with life of its own.

The regions in which the "gods" of the cycle had interred themselves or had been "prisoned" (they could never really die) had been varied as the forms they themselves had taken. Cthulhu was locked in sunken R'lyeh; Hastur in the star-distant deeps of Hali; Ithaqua the Wind-Walker confined to icy Arctic wastes where, in five-year cycles, to this very day he is still known to make monstrous incursions; and so on.

Yet others of the cycle had been dealt with more harshly: the Tind'losi Hounds now dwelled beyond Time's darkest angles, locked *out* from the three sane dimensions; and Yog-Sothoth had been encapsulated in a place bordering all time and space but impinging into neither facet of the continuum—except should some foolhardy wizard call him out! And Yibb-Tstll, too—he also had his place…

But if these gods or demons of the conjectural Cthulhu Mythology were largely inaccessible to men, certain manifestations of them were not. Masters of telepathy, the CCD had long discovered the vulnerable minds of men and insinuated themselves into the dreams of men. On occasion such dreamers would be "rewarded", granted powers over lesser mortals or even elevated to the priesthood of the CCD. In ancient times, even as now, they would become great wizards and warlocks. And James Gedney had been one such, who had collected all the works of wizards gone before and learned them, or as much of them as he might. Titus Crow had been another, but where Gedney's magic had been black, Crow's had been white.

Looking back now, Gifford could see that it had been inevitable that the two must clash. Clash they had, and Darkness had lost to Light. And for a little while the world had been a cleaner place…

"Do you remember how it all came to a head?" Gifford asked. "Crow and Gedney, I mean?"

The moon was fully up now, its disk silvering distant spires, turning the path to a night-white ribbon winding its way across the heath. And the path itself had grown narrower, warning that perhaps the two had chosen the wrong route, which might well peter out into tangles of gorse and briar. But they made no effort to turn back.

"I remember," said Arnold. "Gedney had discovered a way to call an avatar of Yibb-Tstll up from hell. 'The Black', he called it: putrid black blood of Yibb-Tstll, which would settle upon the victim like black snow, thicker and thicker, suffocating, destroying—and leaving not only a lifeless but a *soulless* shell behind. For the demon was a soul-eater, a wampir of psyche, of id!" He shuddered, and this time not alone from the chill of the night air. And his eyes were hooded where they gloomed for a moment upon the other's dark silhouette where it strolled beside him. And in his mind he repeated certain strange words or sounds, a conjuration, ensuring that he had the rune right.

"Your memory serves you well," said Gifford. "He'd found a way to call The Black, all right—and he'd used it. I saw Symonds die that way, and I knew there had been others before him. People who'd crossed Gedney; and of course The Black was a perfect murder weapon."

Arnold nodded in the moonlight. "Yes, it was…" And to himself: …*And will be again!*

"Do you recall the actual machinery of the thing?" Gifford asked.

413

Careful—something warned Arnold—*careful!* He shrugged. "Something of it. Not much."

"Oh, come now!" Gifford chided. "Eight years as leader of your coven, and far more powerful now than Gedney ever was, and you'd tell me you never bothered to look into the thing? Hah!" And to himself: *Ah, no, friend Arnold. You'll have to do better than that. Squirm, my treacherous little worm, squirm!*

"Something of it!" Arnold snapped. "It involves a card, inscribed with Ptetholite runes. That was the lure, the scent by which The Black would track its victim, Gedney's sacrifice. The card was passed to the victim, and then…then…"

"Then Gedney would say the words of the invocation," Gifford finished it for him. "And The Black would come, appearing out of nowhere, black snowflakes settling on the sacrifice, smothering, drowning, sucking out life and soul!"

Arnold nodded. "Yes," he said. "Yes…"

They had come to the end of the path, a bank that descended to a broad, moonlit expanse of water rippled by the light wind. "Hah!" Gifford grunted. "A lake! Well, we'll just have to retrace our steps, that's all. A waste of time—but still, it allowed us a little privacy and gave us the chance to talk. A lot has happened, after all, since I went off to America to start a coven there, and you stayed here to carry on."

They turned back. "A lot, yes," Arnold agreed. "And as you say, I am far more powerful now than ever Gedney was. But what of you? I've heard that you, too, have had your successes."

"Oh, you know well enough that I've prospered," Gifford answered. "My coven is strong—stronger, I suspect, than yours. But then again, I am its leader." He quickly held up a hand to ward off protests. "That was not said to slight you, Arnold. But facts speak for themselves. It wasn't idle chance that took me abroad. I went because of what I knew I'd find there. Oh, we divided Gedney's knowledge, you and I—his books—but I knew of others. And more than mere books. There are survivals even now in old New England, Arnold, if a man knows where to seek them out. Cults and covens beyond even my belief when I first went there. And all of them integrated now—under me! Loosely as yet, it's true, but time will change all that."

"And you'd integrate us, too, eh?" the smaller man half-snarled, rounding on his companion. "And you even had the nerve to come here and tell me it to my face! Well, your American influence can't help you here in England, Gifford. You were a fool to come alone!"

"Alone?" the other's voice was dangerously low. "I am *never* alone. And you are the fool, my friend, not I."

In their arguing the two had strayed from the path. They stumbled on a while in rough, damp turf and through glossy-leaved shrubbery—until once more the stack of an old chimney loomed naked against the moon. And now that they had their bearings once more, both men reached a simultaneous decision—that it must end here and now.

"Here," said Arnold, "right here is where Gedney died. He gave Crow one of his cards, called The Black, and loosed it upon the man."

"Oh, Crow had set up certain protections about his house," Gifford continued the tale, "but they were useless against this. In the end he had to resort to a little devilishness of his own."

"Aye, a clever man, Crow," said Arnold. "He knew what was writ on Geph's broken columns. The Ptetholites had known and used Yibb-Tstll's black blood, and they'd furnished the clue, too."

"Indeed," Gifford mocked, "and now it appears you know far more than you pretended, eh?" And in a low tone he chanted:

> *"Let him who calls The Black*
> *Be aware of the danger—*
> *His victim may be protected*
> *By the spell of running water,*
> *And turn the called-up darkness*
> *Against the very caller…"*

Arnold listened, smiled grimly and nodded. "I looked into it later," he informed. "Crow kept records of all of his cases, you know? An amazing man. When he found himself under attack he heeded a certain passage from the *Necronomicon*. This passage:

> "'…from the space which is not space, into any time when the Words are spoken, can the holder of the Knowledge summon The Black, blood of Yibb-Tstll, that which liveth apart from him and eateth souls, that which smothers and is called Drowner. Only in water can one escape the drowning; that which is in water drowneth not…'"

"It was easy," Arnold continued, "—for a man with nerves of steel! While yet The Black settled on him in an ever thickening layer, he simply stepped into his shower and turned on the water!"

Backing away from Arnold, Gifford opened his mouth and bayed like a great hound. "Oh, yes!" he laughed. "*Yes!* Can't you just picture it? The great James Gedney cheated like that! And how he must have fought to get into the shower with Crow, eh? For of course Crow must have given him his card back, turning The Black 'against the very caller...' And Crow fighting him off, keeping him out of the streaming water until The Black finished its work and carried Gedney's soul back to Yibb-Tstll in his place. Ah!—what an *irony!*"

Arnold too had backed away, and now the modern magicians faced each other across the rubble of Blowne House.

"But no running water here tonight, my friend." Arnold's grin was ferocious, his face a white mask in the moonlight.

"What?" Gifford's huge body quaked with awful mirth. "A threat? You wouldn't dare!"

"Wouldn't I? Your left-hand coat pocket, Gifford—that's where it is!"

And as Gifford drew out the rune-inscribed card, so Arnold commenced to gabble out loud that nightmarish invocation to summon Yibb-Tstll's poisoned blood from a space beyond all known spaces. That demented, droning, cacophonous explosion of sounds so well rehearsed, whose effect as its final crescendo reverberated on the heath's chill night air immediately began to make itself apparent—but in no wise as Arnold had anticipated!

"Fool, I named you," Gifford taunted across the rubble of Blowne House, "and great fool you are! Did you think I would ignore a power strong enough to snuff out a man like Gedney?" As he spoke his voice grew louder and even deeper, at the last resembling nothing so much as a deep bass croaking. And weird energies were at work, drawing mist from the earth to smoke upward in spiralling wreaths, so that the tumbled remains of the house between the two men now resembled the scene of a recent explosion.

Arnold backed away more yet, turned to run, tripped over moss-grown bricks and fell. He scrambled to his feet, looked back—and froze!

Gifford was still baying his awful laughter, but he had thrown off his overcoat and was even now tearing his jacket and shirt free and tossing them to the reeking earth. Beneath those garments—

—*The gross body of the man was black!*

Not a Negroid black, not even the jet of ink or deepest ebony or purest onyx. Black as the spaces between the farthest stars—black as the black blood of Yibb-Tstll himself!

"Oh, yes, Arnold," Gifford boomed, his feet in writhing mist while his upper torso commenced to quiver, a slithering blot on normal space. "Oh, yes! Did you think I'd be satisfied merely to skim the surface of a mystery? I had to go deeper! Control The Black? Man, I *am* The Black! Yibb-Tstll's priest on Earth—his High-Priest, Arnold! No longer born of the dark spaces, of alien dimensions, but of me! I am the host body! And you dare call The Black? So be it..." And he tore in pieces the rune-written card and pointed at the other across the smoking ruins.

It seemed then that darkness peeled from Gifford, that his upper body erupted in myriad fragments of night which hovered for a moment like a swarm of midnight bees—then split into two streams which moved in concert *around* the outlines of the ruins.

Geoffrey Arnold saw this and had time, even in his extreme of utter terror, to wonder at it. But time only for that. In the next moment, converging, those great pythons of alien matter reared up, swept upon him and layered him like lacquer where he stood and screamed. Quickly he turned black as the stuff thickened on him, and his shrill screams were soon shut off as the horror closed over his face.

Then he danced—a terrible dance of agony—and finally fell, a bloated blot, to the mist-tortured earth. For long seconds he jerked, writhed and twisted, and at last lay still.

Benjamin Gifford had watched all of this, and yet for all that he was a devotee of evil had gained little pleasure from it. Wizard and necromancer though he was, still he knew that there were far greater sources of evil. And for Great Evil there is always Great Good. The balance is ever maintained.

Now Gifford stopped laughing, his mouth slowly closing, the short hairs rising at the back of his neck. He sniffed like a hound at some suspicious odour; he sensed that things were far from right; he questioned what had happened—or rather, the *way* it had happened—and he grew afraid. His body, naked now and slenderer far than when The Black shrouded him, shivered in the spiralling mists.

Those mists, for example: he had thought them part of Arnold's conjuring, a curious side-effect. But no, for Arnold was finished and still the reeking, strangely twisting mists poured upward from the ruins of the old house. The ruins of Titus Crow's old house...

And why had The Black chosen to split and deflect *around* that smoking perimeter of ruin? Unless—

"No!" Gifford croaked, the dark iron vanished now from his voice. "No, that can't be!" It could *not* be...could it?

No slightest vestige of life remained in Arnold now. The Black lifted *en masse* from his body where it lay contorted in death's rigors, lifted like a jagged hole torn in normal space and paused, hovering at the edge of the ruins of Blowne House. And slowly that cloud of living evil formed into two serpents, and slowly they retraced their paths around the ruins.

Menacing they were, in their slow, *sentient* approach. And at last Gifford thought he knew why. Crow was long gone but the protections he had placed about Blowne House remained even now, would stay here until time itself was extinct and all magics—black and white—gone forever. The place was a focal point for good, *genius loci* for all the great benevolent powers which through all the ages men have called God! And those powers had not waned with Crow's passing but had fastened upon this place and waxed ever stronger.

To have called The Black here, now, in this place was a blasphemy, and the caller had paid in full. But to have *brought* The Black here—to have worn it like a mantle, to have been Yibb-Tstll's priest—that were greater blasphemy far. This place was sacrosanct, and it would remain that way.

"*No!*" Gifford croaked one last time, an instant before The Black fell upon him. Priest no more, he was borne under…

When the mists ceased their strange spiralling the ruins of Blowne House lay as before, silvered under a cleansing moon. Except that now there were corpses in the night. Pitiful shapes crumpled under the moon, where morning would find them chill as the earth where they lay.

But the earth would have a soul…

THE SORCERER'S DREAM

If you read my introductory note to "The Black Recalled", then here in respect of publishing data we have a similar situation. "The Sorcerer's Dream" is a Primal Land story, the first of which ("The House of Cthulhu",) had been the lead story in Stuart Schiff's Whispers' initial issue back in 1973. So, "The Sorcerer's Dream" being the intended fade-out tale in some future Primal Lands volume, it seemed only right I should sell it to Schiff who had published the first one. Er, are we okay so far? Anyway, he did indeed buy and publish it in "Whispers No. 13/14" (a double issue) in October 1979. But let me reiterate: when I wrote "Dream" in February 1976, I never intended it to be the last Primal Lands story, only that it would be the final tale in the foreseen and/or hoped for, above mentioned, eventual, Primal Lands volume…(Phew!) Which is exactly how it worked out: I would write several Primal Lands tales in the following years, which eventually my good friend and publisher W. Paul Ganley (wouldn't you just know it would be him?) would join up into one of Weirdbook Press's fastest-selling titles. Namely, The House of Cthulhu & Others. *And exactly as I had foreseen it, "Dream" was the last story in the book—just as it is here, at the very end…*

As translated by Thelred Gustau, from Teh Atht's Legends of the Olden Runes

I, Teh Atht, have dreamed a dream; and now, before dawn's light may steal it from my old mind—while yet Gleeth the blind God of the Moon rides the skies over Klühn and the stars of night peep and leer hideously—I write it down in the pages of my rune-book, wherein all the olden runes are

419

as legends unfolded. For I have pondered the great mysteries of time and space, have solved certain of the riddles of the Ancients themselves, and all such knowledge is writ in my rune-book for the fathoming of sorcerers as yet unborn.

As to why I dreamed this dream, plumbing the Great Abyss of future time to the very END itself, where only the gaunt black Tomb of the Universe gapes wide and empty, my reasons were many. They were born in mummy-dust sifting down to me through the centuries; in the writings of mages ancient when the world was still young; in cipherless hieroglyphs graven in the stone of Geph's broken columns; aye, and in the vilest nightmares of shrieking madmen, whose visions had driven them mad. And such as these reasons were they drew me as the morning sun draws up the ocean mists on Theem'hdra's bright strand, for I cannot suffer a mystery to go undiscovered.

The mystery was this: that oft and again over the years I had heard whispers of a monstrous alien God who seeped down from the stars when the world was an inchoate infant—whose name, Cthulhu, was clouded with timeless legends and obscured in half-forgotten myths and nameless lore—and such whispers as I had heard troubled me greatly…

Concerning this Cthulhu a colleague in olden Chlangi, the warlock Nathor Tarqu, had been to the temple of the Elder Ones in Ulthar in the land of Earth's dreams to consult the Pnakotic Manuscript; and following that visit to Ulthar he had practised exceedingly strange magicks before vanishing forever from the known world of men. Since that time Chlangi has become a fallen city, and close by in the Desert of Sheb the Lamia Orbiquita has builded her castle, so that now all men fear the region and call Chlangi the Shunned City.

I, too, have been to Ulthar, and I count it a blessing that on waking I could not recall what I read in the Pnakotic Manuscript—only such awful names as were writ therein, such as Cthulhu, Tsathoggua, and Ubbo-Sathla. And there was also mention of one Ghatanothoa, a son of Cthulhu to whom a dark temple even now towers in Theem'hdra, in a place that I shall not name. For I know the place is doomed, that there is a curse upon the temple and its priests, and that when they are no more their names shall be stricken from all records…

Even so, and for all this, I would never have entertained so long and unhealthy an interest in loathly Lord Cthulhu had I not myself heard His call in uneasy slumbers; that call which turns men's minds, beckoning them on to vile worship and viler deeds. Such dreams visited themselves upon me after I had spoken with Zar-thule, a barbarian reaver—or rather, with the fumbling mushroom *thing* that had once been a reaver—locked away in Klühn's deepest dungeon to rot and gibber hideously of unearthly horrors. For Zar-thule had thought to rob the House of Cthulhu on Arlyeh the forbidden isle, as a result of which Arlyeh had gone down under the waves in a great storm…but not before Zar-thule gazed upon Cthulhu, whose treasures were garnets of green slime, red rubies of blood and moonstones of malignancy and madness!

And when dreams such as those conjured by Zar-Thule's story came to sour the sweet embrace of Shoosh, Goddess of the Still Slumbers, I would rise from my couch and tremble, and pace the crystal floors of my rooms above the Bay of Klühn. For I was sorely troubled by this mystery; even I, Teh Atht, whose peer in the occult arts exists not in Theem'hdra, troubled most sorely.

So I went up into the Mount of the Ancients where I smoked the Zhaweed and sought the advice of my wizard ancestor Mylakhrion of Tharamoon—dead eleven hundred years—who told me to look to the ORIGIN and the AFTERMATH, the BEGINNING and the END, that I might know. And that same night, in my secret vault, I sipped a rare and bitter distillation of mandrake and descended again into deepest dreams, even into dreams long dead and forgotten before ever human dreamers existed. Thus in my search for the ORIGIN I dreamed myself into the dim and fabulous past.

And I saw that the Earth was hot and in places molten, and Gleeth was not yet born to sail the volcanic clouds of pre-dawn nights. Then, drawn by a force beyond my ken, I went out into the empty spaces of the primal void, where I saw, winging down through the vasty dark, shapes of uttermost lunacy. And first among them all was Cthulhu of the tentacled face, and among His followers came Yogg-Sothoth, Tsathoggua, and many others which were like unto Cthulhu but less than Him; and lo!—Cthulhu spoke the Name of Azathoth, whereupon stars blazed forth as He passed and all space gloried in His coming.

Down through the outer immensities they winged, alighting upon the steaming Earth and building great cities of a rare architecture, wherein singular angles confused the eye and mind until towers were as precipices and solid walls gateways! And there they dwelt for aeons, in their awful cities under leaden skies and strange stars. Aye, and they were mighty sorcerers,

Cthulhu and His spawn, who plotted great evil against Others who were once their brethren. For they had not come to Earth of their own will but had fled from Elder Gods whose codes they had abused most terribly.

And such were their thaumaturgies in the great grey cities that those Elder Gods felt tremors in the very stuff of Existence itself, and they came in haste and great anger to set seals on the houses of Cthulhu, wherein He and many of His kin were prisoned for their sins. But others of these great old sorcerers, such as Yogg-Sothoth and Yibb-Tstll, fled again into the stars, where they were followed by the Elder Gods who prisoned them wherever they were found. Then, when all was done, the great and just Gods of Eld returned whence they had come; and aeon upon aeon passed and the stars revolved through strange configurations, moving inexorably toward a time when Cthulhu would be set free...

So it was that I saw the ORIGIN whereof my ancestor Mylakhrion of Tharamoon had advised me, and awakening in my secret vault I shuddered and marvelled that this Loathly Lord Cthulhu had come down all the ages unaltered. For I knew that indeed He lived still in His city sunken under the sea, and I was mazed by His immortality. Then it came to me to dwell at length upon the latter; on Cthulhu's immortality, and to wonder if He was truly immortal... And of this also had Mylakhrion advised, saying; "Look to the ORIGIN and the AFTERMATH, the BEGINNING and the END."

Thus it was that last night I sipped again of mandrake fluid and went out in a dream to seek the END. And indeed I found it...

There at the end of time all was night, where all the universe was a great empty tomb and nothing stirred. And I stood upon a dead sea bottom and looked up to where Gleeth had once graced the skies; old Gleeth, long sundered now and drifted down to Earth as dust. And I turned my saddened eyes down again to gaze upon a gaunt, solitary spire of rock that rose and twisted and towered up from the bottom of the dusty ocean.

And because curiosity was ever the curse of sorcerers, it came to me to wonder why, since this was the END, time itself continued to exist. And it further came to me that time existed only because space, time's brother, had *not quite* ended, life was *not quite* extinct. With this thought, as if born of the thought itself, there came a mighty rumbling and the ground trembled and shook. All the world shuddered and the dead sea bottom split open in many places, creating chasms from which there at once rose up the awful spawn of Cthulhu!

And lo!—I knew now that indeed Cthulhu was immortal, for in Earth's final death spasm He was reborn! The great twisted spire of rock—all that was left of Arlyeh, Cthulhu's house—shattered and fell in ruins, laying open to my staggering gaze His sepulchre. And shortly thereafter, preceded by a nameless stench, He squeezed Himself out from the awful tomb into the gloom of the dead universe.

Then, when they saw Cthulhu, all of them that were risen up from their immemorial prisons rushed and flopped and floundered to His feet, making obeisance to Him. And He blinked great evil octopus eyes and gazed all about in wonderment, for His final sleep had endured for aeon upon aeon, and he had not known that the universe was now totally dead and time itself at an end.

And Cthulhu's anger was great! He cast His mind out into the void and gazed upon cinders that had been stars; He looked for light and warmth in the farthest corners of the universe and found only darkness and decay; He searched for life in the great seas of space and found only the tombs at time's end. And His anger waxed *awesome!*

Then He threw back His tentacled head and bellowed out the Name of Azathoth in a voice that sent all of the lesser Beings at His feet scurrying back to their chasm sepulchres, and lo!...nothing happened! The sands of time were run out, and even the greatest Magicks had lost their potency.

And so Cthulhu raged and stormed and blasphemed as only He might until, at the height of His anger, *suddenly He knew me!*

Dreaming as I was and far, far removed from my own age, nevertheless He sensed me and in an instant turned upon me, face tentacles writhing and reaching out for my dreaming spirit. And then, to my eternal damnation, before I fled shrieking back down the corridors of time to leap awake drenched in a chill perspiration in my secret vault, I gazed deep into the demon eyes of Cthulhu.

Now it is dawn and I am almost done with the writing of this, and soon I will lay down my rune-book and set myself certain tasks for the days ahead. First I will see to it that the crystal dome of my workshop tower is covered with black lacquer, for I fear I can no longer bear to look out upon the stars... Where once they twinkled afar in chill but friendly fashion, now I know that they leer down in celestial horror as they move inexorably toward Cthulhu's next awakening. For surely He will rise up many times before that final awakening at the very END.

Aye, and if I had thought to escape the Lord of Arlyeh when I fled from him in my dream, then I was mistaken. Cthulhu was, He is, and He will always be; and I know now that this is the essence of that great mystery which so long perplexed me. For Cthulhu is a Master of Dreams, and now He knows me. And He will follow me through my slumbers all the days of my life, and evermore I shall hear His call...Even unto THE END.